Chapter One

Sylvia Wright parked the car as far off the road as the snowbanks would allow. Walking around to the trunk, she lifted out the snowshoes, pulled up the hood of her coat, and wrapped the woollen scarf around her neck, covering her chin and mouth. The snowflakes were large and quickly accumulating. She should probably have stayed in Moncton or at least waited awhile at the Irving station before turning onto this deserted road.

Beach Daze, Sea You Later, and *Seas the Day* were three of the signs posted on the closed-up cottages hunkered down for another winter. The small yellow building she'd parked in front of had shutters pulled snugly over the windows. She imagined the people closing up their little piece of paradise and driving away, hoping it would weather the gusts and storms of winter. *Luna Sea,* read the oval sign swinging from a post at the end of the drive. Had they forgotten to unhook the chain and store the sign away? Or had it been left on the post to speak to her about this mission she was on?

Fourteen seaside acres, old structure in need of some renovation. Privacy, natural beauty, and wooded splendour. It was a small ad in a real-estate supplement she'd almost thrown into the recycling bin but had taken the time to look through. The small ad on page seven had no photo and no attention-grabbing features, but it had caught her attention. She had ripped the page out, circled the small ad, and stuck it up on the bulletin board in her office—the office she seldom entered and hadn't actually sat in to write for over a year.

Her schedule was still fairly packed with engagements, and it had been under the guise of coming to one that this plan evolved. She'd participated in the pre-event interviews and media coverage leading up to today's literary festival event at the Moncton library. But on a call to one of the organizers last night, she'd offered a last-minute apology, briefly referencing a family emergency. The fact she had responsibility for the care of her elderly grandmother and Sophie of course was public knowledge, and there had been times when Sylvia had to use the demands of both as reasons for cancelling engagements. But lately, more and more, she found herself fabricating emergencies.

She had known for weeks that she would call Nancy Price the night before and apologize profusely. She knew as she packed the author copies of her six novels and her bookmarks and printed off her well-prepared reading list and preamble. She'd known when she replied to her publisher's email regarding her accommodations and travel arrangements. She had known when she read the bookseller's email regarding the number of books they would have available for sale. She'd known when she proofread the introduction she'd been sent for clarification. None of it was necessary.

This trip to New Brunswick had been a ploy right from the moment she received the email from her publisher asking her to participate.

Sylvia walked over and unhooked the chains fastening the oval sign to its post. Perhaps the owners would think they'd put it away and would search for it when they reopened the cottage; perhaps they would remember leaving it on the post and conclude the high winds coming off the Northumberland Strait had whipped it off and flung it to goodness knows where. But next spring, when the owners returned to their little haven by the sea, they would not guess it had been taken and stowed in the trunk of a rental car by a woman who happened along on a snowy afternoon in January; a woman who believed her escape might be the desolate property she'd come to see, just metres away.

Sylvia always carried memories of the New Brunswick seaside with her, even though she'd lived in Toronto for more than thirty years. Wrong coastline, but the same rugged beauty and remoteness that she'd known growing up on White Head Island with Nan and Papa. Had the words *privacy, natural beauty, and wooded splendour* been enough to motivate her to where she now found herself? She hadn't told anyone she was coming. As far as Kent knew, she was staying at the Hotel Beausejour for two nights, attending the literary event, and then flying back home Friday morning.

Sylvia looked around before shutting the trunk and bending down to put on the snowshoes. She had contacted the real estate agent and he'd sent her Google map directions to the property but made no offer to meet her there. He had in fact spent more time talking up the qualities of several other properties in the area, dismissing her interest in the listing she was inquiring about.

"That property would scare a person off this time of the year. I've only been there the one time to leave a sign, which I expect has long since blown away. The landscape is pretty rugged and there is no power on site. The building has been empty for quite some time. I'm not even sure who is selling it. I thought it was a private owner, but it might still be the Catholic Church. They don't part with much, especially these days, with attendance so poor."

Sylvia pushed the key fob, locking the vehicle out of habit, not any real threat of the rental car being stolen or anything taken. The chances of anyone even seeing the red Camry before spring were slim if she slipped and tumbled off the cliff into the roiling water or was taken down in an attack by a pack of coyotes or trampled by a moose. If something unfortunate happened to her, no one would come to her rescue—even by Friday evening, after Kent realized she was missing. No one would send a search party to this remote road. Perhaps DNA testing years from now, when her bones were found by some hiker or kayaker, would reveal that the author Sylvia Drummond Wright had met her maker on this remote property.

She would keep a safe distance from the edge of the cliff.

She knew body retrieval from a drowning was not pretty. Nan had had the horror of identifying her daughter weeks after she jumped off the Reversing Falls Bridge. But neither Papa's body nor the other two fishermen who went down with the *Sylvie D* were ever found.

Sylvia unfastened a rusty gate and pushed the metal against the snow, opening it just wide enough to get through. No roadway was evident, but the tree line indicated the way in. A RE/MAX sign dangled from a post. Sylvia had never walked with snowshoes, and as she lifted one, keeping clear of the other, she recalled the discussion with the woman at Canadian Tire the day before.

"Are you looking for wood, plastic, or metal?"

"I don't know."

"Do you plan to snowshoe groomed trails or wooded areas?"

"Wooded areas, I guess."

"Do you have the boots you'll be wearing with you?"

"Boots? No."

"Well, these ones are good. They are easy to fasten and will adjust to any boot. They are popular and in a middle price range."

After paying, Sylvia had gone to the Mark's Work Wearhouse next door. She picked out a pair of high, lace-up boots and a three pack of below-zero socks. She grabbed a fleece-lined knit toque, a scarf, and down-filled mittens.

"You're all set for the elements," the cashier had remarked.

Private, natural beauty, and wooded splendour.

The wind picked up and the air was biting as Sylvia continued her trek along the tree-lined roadway, wondering what she would find when she got to the clearing where she supposed the building would be. A Catholic girls' home, the lady behind the counter at the Irving had called it when she'd inquired about the property. It had closed in the early seventies, apparently, and had been used after that as a retreat of some kind. The woman didn't know if the church still owned it.

Irving. The familiar blue lettering with red parenthesis top and bottom was to any New Brunswicker a magnetic pull, a beacon of convenience, milk, bread, gas, chips, pop, and those long hot dogs on the rotisserie. Papa had always bought her one at the Irving in Black's Harbour. She'd pulled into the parking lot and gone in, walked up and down the aisles before approaching the cashier to ask for directions.

"We used to go there as kids. They had bonfires and hootenannies on the beach. My aunt cooked there for a while. She wasn't too complimentary of the ones who ran the place. Priests, I guess, or Brothers and a nun or two. Nasty pieces of work, whatever they were, according to my Aunt Cecelia. As kids we never saw that side of it. It was just a good chance for some fun and free food. There were always hot dogs, marshmallows, and ice cream Revels. We never had treats like that growing up."

Sylvia heard the flapping as she rounded the corner and looked up to see a large section of the rusty tin roof lifting in the wind. The log building was large, long, and sprawling, with a middle gabled section. Four windows were spaced evenly on the main floor, six on either side of the upper level, and there was a large arched window in the gable. Unruly bushes grew high, almost hiding the front veranda, and a big, leafless tree leaned precariously, one large bough broken off and resting on the veranda roof.

Sylvia bent down, unfastened the snowshoes, stepped out of them, and stuck them upright in the snow. She stepped onto the first of three wide steps leading to the veranda, not sure it would hold her weight. The window pane in the wooden door was cracked. The door was probably locked.

"That property would scare a person off this time of the year," the Re/MAX agent had said. Would a warm summer day make this building any more inviting? Sylvia wondered as she turned the knob and the heavy door opened.

<center>~~~</center>

Sylvia Drummond stepped into the front foyer hoping to catch a breath of fresh air and be out of Sheldon's sightline for a minute or two. She reached up to the bulletin board to reattach the corner of a Prince poster. Lovesexy Tour, Maple Leaf Gardens, October 5, 1988. She'd been in this city for over two years.

Lovesexy. *Oh please,* Sylvia thought as she brushed the loose strands of hair from her face, trying to tuck them back into what had started as a tight ponytail. "Hair must be pulled back off the face" was the number one edict at Blackburn's Social Club. Tight skirts and lots of cleavage expected, but God forbid any unruly hair. And these damn shoes. Nothing sexy about comfort, apparently.

"Why Toronto?" Nan had asked the day Sylvia packed her suitcases. "If you moved to Saint John, at least you could come home to visit once in a while. Toronto is so far away. You don't even know anyone there."

"I don't know anyone in Saint John either, Nan. And there's no boy waiting in Toronto to ruin my life. You've always told me that's what happened to Mom. And you've told me my whole life what a terrible place Saint John is. Now all of a sudden Saint John is just fine?"

"Fredericton or Moncton, then. Somewhere close so you can at least come home to see us at Thanksgiving and Christmas and maybe for a few days in the summer."

"Toronto is where all the big publishers are, Nan, and I'm going to get a job at one of them. I'll work there in the daytime and finish my novel at night."

Working at Random House and sneaking her debut novel into the slush pile had been her plan. But what a pipe dream that had been. Blackburn's was her third serving job, but at least the tips were decent here.

"Drummond, what the hell are you doing out here? You've got a full section and we've got people waiting for tables. Table eight is ready for their bill."

Table eight might be big tippers, Sylvia thought as she began totalling the separate bills. Usually a table full of men with good appetites played the game of one-upmanship to see who could spend the most and leave the biggest tip. That was, of course, if they didn't get overserved. That was the challenge: the right amount of attention, a bit of flirting, and knowing when to close the table down.

The two couples at table nine had been there forever. Only one of the four had even ordered a drink. The redhead had sent her Caesar salad back, claiming she'd ordered Greek. Sylvia had brought her a new salad, explaining that she would comp it, which meant of course the money would be taken from Sylvia's wages. Then when Sylvia set a baked potato down in front of the woman, she insisted she'd ordered garlic mashed. No profit from that table.

Table eight was six guys in shirts, ties, and suit jackets. They were obviously professionals of some kind, and their relationship, judging from the interactions she'd overheard, seemed business-like—not the ridiculous banter she heard between Connor and his buddies. Bankers, accountants, or tax guys, maybe; guys Connor and his eclectic friends would find boring. Boring, maybe, but she guessed none of them were being supported by some poor girl working minimum wage.

"Table six is ready to order."

"Okay, thanks, Monica. Can you give table eight their bills?"

Monica had started the hostess job two nights ago. She was just a kid, still in high school, for God's sake. High school seemed a lifetime ago. Long bus rides across the ferry on those dark, cold winter mornings. It had been on those bus rides she'd started writing the first pages of her still-unfinished novel. A story of a young girl arriving on a remote island after her mother's untimely death. The names, the city, the circumstances of the death changed, of course. Fiction.

Sylvia took the drink orders and rattled off the specials while forming her first impressions of the four women at table six. Childhood friends, maybe sisters; four women who obviously knew each other very well, had a history and a familiar comfort with each other.

"It's Margie's fiftieth. She's the first of us to turn the big five-Oh. We're celebrating tonight. Is the lobster East Coast?"

"No, Lisa, it's Toronto lobster," interrupted the woman wearing a *Look Who's 50* button and a tiara.

"The only lobster worth eating is from the East Coast. I've had the lobster they serve at Red Lobster. I don't know where it comes from, but it is nothing like what you get on the East Coast. If I'm going to pay for lobster, it has to be East Coast."

"Are you from there?" Sylvia asked.

"Yes, PEI."

"I'm from New Brunswick."

"Well then, you know what I'm talking about."

Sylvia nodded. As usual she kept her interactions and conversations with customers brief, never bothering to expand or tell how she might really feel about any topic. As it was, Sheldon gave her a hard time for talking too much to her tables.

Yes, she knew all about East Coast lobster. What was such an extravagance to most people was a common meal served when she was growing up. Papa always brought a few home after each day out. The ones he brought home were usually the deformed ones, claws missing or shell a different colour than normal. He brought a blue one home once. Sometimes they were freakishly big or had barnacles or weird growths. Whatever Papa couldn't sell on the dock made its way into Nan's kitchen. Sylvia hated watching the lobsters squirming in Nan's hands before she dropped them into the boiling water, but she loved sitting around the table while Papa cracked open the claws and pulled out the tail meat for her and Nan. She could almost taste it and feel the juice and butter dripping off her chin.

"My grandfather was a lobster fisherman," Sylvia added.

"Oh, lucky you."

Right, lucky me until his boat capsized. Came apart, really. All that ever surfaced was the section of the hull bearing the name. Nan said the letters Sylvie D *were almost as bright a red as they'd been the day she and Papa had painted them.*

"She'll bring good luck, Sylvie girl," Papa had said that day. "Good luck like you brought Nan and I the day you came to live with us. Keeping two old folks young, you are, my love. Two old codgers keeping young bringing up a darling girl like you."

"I'll get your drinks and give you a bit more time to decide."

"Table nine says you haven't been back to take their dessert order," Sheldon spat at her as she headed toward the bar. It was a nightly task, keeping her distaste and revulsion for Sheldon at bay. It seemed wherever she worked there had been a Sheldon; a weaselly little man with a mega ego. Stuck somewhere in 1953, Sheldon thought he was superior to women just because he had a penis and the title of assistant manager.

"I may as well just pick one and take it to her," Sylvia muttered under her breath. "She'll say she didn't order whatever I take her anyway."

"I took table eight's money," Monica said. "One of the guys left this for you."

Kent: 416-857-2378

Call me.

Chapter Two

The air inside seemed colder. It was dark, and Sylvia was unsure she should venture in any farther. The floorboards could be rotten. There could be racoons or other creatures inhabiting this empty old building. What was she hoping to find, coming way out here by herself? It was one thing to walk the property on a blustery, cold day, but to actually come inside this dilapidated building as if she were at a downtown open house was really dumb.

The windows in the big room beyond the entryway were providing some natural light even with the heavy snowfall. Sylvia closed the door behind her. She made a noise, a loud, ridiculous "Hello!" in the attempt to scare away anything that might be living here. She had never been the courageous one. Kent always checked the dark places, took the garbage out at night, went to the girls' room to get the bat that one time when it was flying franticly around their bedroom. He was the brave one, the take-charge parent. Sylvia kept walking, knowing Kent would think it was dumb.

She knew he would think it was dumb of her to come here in the first place. Obviously she knew that, or she would have told him about it. She would have mentioned just how interested she was in seeing the property from the small ad. She hadn't shown him the ad or talked to him about it at all. What would she have said? Why had the ad gripped her? At first she figured it was a reminder of Grand Manan, of her childhood; a place she could own that took her back there in some way without actually going back.

They'd sold Nan's house and property years ago. They had not even considered keeping it for a summer place. Kent said the house was not worth putting any money into. And why did it matter so much that she see the inside of *this* building? It was nothing like the small two-storey house Papa had built for his bride. Why had it mattered that she come here in the first place?

Kent, the take-charge guy. She had called him the first time, but he'd decided everything that followed. Their first date had been in a small bar on the ground floor of Kent's office building. At thirty-one he already had his own office in a large accounting firm. He hadn't talked much about himself but filled that first evening with compliments and encourage-ment. He made her feel beautiful, smart, and capable, and he told her she had to leave Connor.

Sylvia had opened up to Kent right away. She talked at length about her dream of writing, of being published, of hav-ing a career as an author. He instantly filled up her reservoir of hope and positivity and refuelled the confidence Connor had drained from her. And he understood her grief and guilt.

"You have to go home. Your grandmother needs you and

you need to say a proper goodbye to your grandfather. You cannot run away from who you are. Until you take the time to work through your feelings, your writing will be stalled."

They slept together on the second date. Kent had taken her to his twelfth-floor condo on Yonge Street, small but modern and clean. So organized and uncluttered. As she lay in Kent's arms, everything seemed perfect. A dream come true.

Two days later Sylvia moved her clothes into Kent's closet, unpacked a small box of her possessions, and quit her job. Kent booked her flight to Saint John and her return flight for the first week of January.

"Three months will give you some time with your grandmother. You can decide if she should stay in her home or move to the mainland. You can mourn your grandfather and clear your head. You can get back to your writing and see how that goes, and you can always write once you get back to Toronto."

❦

Sylvia pulled her suitcase off the carousel of the only baggage claim area in the small Saint John airport. She'd watched it go around at least twice before she remembered that the set of Samsonite luggage Kent had brought home from Eaton's the night before was bright turquoise. The set included one large suitcase, one medium, and a small cosmetic case. She'd only brought the large suitcase, checked it, and apparently forgotten what colour it was during the two-hour flight.

Her mind was a muddle. Kent had carefully gone over the steps she'd need to take to get the rental car at the airport. He'd given her his Chargex card along with a letter giving her permission to use it. He had tucked an envelope of cash into her purse as they said goodbye, explaining that it would be enough to rent the Datsun coupe he had booked for her if for some reason they wouldn't accept his credit card.

"You have the car for one week. I've arranged for a university buddy to meet you in Black's Harbour and bring it back to Avis next Saturday. That should give you enough time to check out the possibility of a neighbour picking you up when you come back across the ferry. And you'll have a car to use for a few days while you see how your grandmother is getting on and what needs to be done. I assume it will be an automatic transmission, but you can drive a standard, right?"

Sylvia had learned to drive in Papa's old Chevy truck. Three on the tree, a clutch that stuck, and roads where you seldom met another vehicle. And Papa sitting in the passenger's seat telling her when to shift.

She had nodded. Most of their conversations after that first night had been one-sided. It was almost as if she were just watching this two-week whirlwind relationship happening to someone else. Had she in fact left Sylvia Drummond behind in the loft apartment when she packed her things and walked down the fire escape? The damn elevator had been down, which added a bit more drama to her departure. Leaving Connor and all the disappointment behind was the point, after all; leaving it and going to a new life. So why did it feel so shitty?

She'd figure it out once she got to Nan's. She hadn't even told her she was coming. Thoughts of the surprise and happiness on Nan's face when she opened the door had pushed out all the other worry and apprehension she was feeling.

"Is this your husband's credit card?"

"My fiancé," Sylvia replied. "He called and booked the car yesterday. Kent Wright."

"Oh, yes. Here is the reservation. No problem. I just need your driver's licence and we'll have you on your way."

Sylvia passed the woman her licence. It had been Nan who encouraged her to take the driver's test. Papa had driven her to Black's Harbour and waited while the examiner took her out in his car. Luckily there had been no opportunity for parallel parking, and she got the licence on her first try.

"Can you tell me how to get to the west side of the city and onto the highway to Black's Harbour?" Sylvia asked as she took the keys.

"The road is well marked once you get into the downtown. When you leave the airport, just keep going once you turn left onto the main road. I'm sure you'll have no trouble."

Sylvia did not share the woman's optimism. All she could hope for was not to get too badly lost, not to have an accident, and to get to the Grand Manan ferry in time for its last crossing.

～⁓～

Sylvia pulled open a cupboard door. Canned goods still stocked the shelves, the labels looking antique, like props on a movie set. She imagined the contents bulging with bacteria. A deep sink of ridged enamel showed rusted lines of years of hard water. Leaves lay in the drain, no doubt blown in through the missing pane in the window above the counter. The pale pink countertop was grimy, large sections broken off revealing the water-stained plywood beneath.

Sylvia pulled out a straight-back wooden chair and sat at the large dining table. Her writer's imagination began conjuring up the crowd around this table. Kids, all girls, a range of ages. Large platters of food being passed, or bowls of thin, watery soup set in front of each diner. Was this a happy, nurturing place, or one of fear and tension?

Nan's kitchen had always meant comfort, delicious smells and tastes. Warmth radiated from the wood-burning cook stove and from the words and actions of Nan and Papa. To a little girl coming from an existence of fear and unpredictability, Nan's kitchen meant nourishment, safety, and love. Tears ran down Sylvia's cheeks.

～⁓～

The ferry crossing was rough, which added to the nervousness Sylvia was already feeling. She could hardly wait to wrap her arms around Nan. The emotion of knowing Papa would not stroll up behind them waiting patiently to deliver his bear hug was sitting in her throat and she was just barely keeping it together. She didn't know anyone on board, but several people struck up conversations with her. Twice, the talk had revealed enough details for the person to deduce she was Evelyn Ingalls's granddaughter and that brought words of condolence each time.

"Oh, such a sin about Paddy. God love you. A crying shame that was."

"My uncle fished with Paddy Ingalls years ago. Never a better man, my uncle says. And a better fisherman never sailed from this island. But the sea will claim what it takes, and not a thing we mortals can do about it."

Sylvia stared out at the cresting waves. Swells any higher would have cancelled the run, and as thankful as she was to have caught this last trip, a night at the Granite Town Hotel in St. George might have helped to calm her nerves. A good night's rest might have made her feel stronger for the reunion ahead. Sylvia leaned back and shut her eyes. Maybe if she appeared to be sleeping no one else would speak to her before this crossing was over.

When she drove off the White Head Island ferry, the setting sun made the scene eerie and strange. Nothing had changed, though. She was sure Donald Green was wearing the same jacket and cap he'd been wearing the day she drove off the island more than two years ago. He waved like he always did, but she figured he had no idea who the woman driving the gold-coloured Datsun was. He'd find out, though; you could be sure. No one came onto the island without Donald Green knowing who they were and what their business was here.

As Sylvia rounded the bend she could see the lights of Nan's house: downstairs lights and the porch light. That had always been a thing with Papa. "We'll leave the porch light on for you, Sylvie." He always turned it on in the early morning hours when he headed down to the harbour, and at dusk Nan made sure it went back on for his return.

Evelyn Ingalls stood in the doorway, her grey hair uncombed and sticking out in all directions. A full apron covered a pale blue dress and a variegated brown cable-knit sweater was draped over her shoulders. She let out a small gasp. Sylvia enclosed her grandmother in her arms, the woman melting into her for several seconds before she straightened up to speak.

"Dear God, Sylvie. You scared the life from me. I was dozing in Papa's chair and the knocking woke me up. Startled me senseless. Thought I was dreaming, then I open the door to you. Best sight I could imagine. Let me give you a good looking over. You're thin."

"Sorry I scared you, Nan. I should have called."

"If I'd have known you were coming, I'd have baked a cake," Nan said in a singsong voice, pulling Sylvia in and closing the door.

"You say those same words to every visitor who darkens this door, and you always have something baked."

"Have you had your supper, love?"

"No, I had a coffee and muffin on the boat, though."

"Hang up your coat. I'll heat you up some supper. Dear Lord, it's good to see you."

"I'll get my luggage out of the car first."

"Luggage? Hope you've got lots of it, darling girl, and that you're staying a spell."

"I'm here for a while, Nan."

"Well, bring it in, we'll get caught up and I'll get you fed."

Sylvia brought in her suitcase, hung her coat on the hall tree by the front door, and sat down at the kitchen table. Minutes later Nan set a steaming plate of vegetables and chicken in front of her. While she ate, Nan scurried around, sweeping the floor, filling the dishpan, cutting a generous piece of apple pie and topping it with a scoop of butterscotch ripple ice cream.

"You finish eating while I go upstairs and air out your bedroom. I'll strip the bedding and make it up fresh."

Sylvia felt the tension of the frenetic dance she was watching her grandmother perform but knew there would be no point trying to stop it. She was just taking her last bite of pie when Nan came back into the kitchen.

"Just set your dishes in the pan and come sit with me. *Jeopardy* is coming on."

Sylvia sat on the couch across from her grandfather's brown recliner. She'd never seen Nan sit in Papa's recliner before, and the emotion of it caught in her throat. The theme music and Johnny Gilbert's "And here's the host of *Jeopardy*, Alex Trebeck!" transported her back to the hundreds of times she'd sat in this exact spot, listening to the opening of the only show her grandparents watched, a nightly ritual that gathered the three of them together. Papa always answered the most clues, impressing her with his scope of knowledge. That a man who lived his whole life on a small island in the Bay of Fundy knew so much about world geography and history always amazed her.

"Books, Sylvie. If a fella has books the whole world is his. My folks couldn't give me much, but they gave me books."

Sylvia had considered the three floor-to-ceiling book-shelves in the upstairs hall a treasure trove from the first day she arrived. No book within her reach was out of bounds, and Papa's only rules were don't fold down the pages, don't scrib-ble in the book, and don't bend back the spines. He'd told her to look at the pictures, read any words she could, and "every one of these books will wait patiently for you. The books and all the mysteries they hold will be the same, unchanged and constant."

"Should I make a pot of tea, Nan?" Sylvia asked on the first commercial break.

"We watched some Bob fella win his fifth game on our last night. Your papa got the Final Jeopardy answer right and was pretty puffed up."

"Do you remember the question, Nan?"

"Yes, I remember it. The heading was Twentieth Century Literary Characters."

"That would be right up Papa's alley."

"The clue was, 'His first name refers to the ancient district where you'd find the Greek capital; his surname is a bird.'"

"Atticus Finch."

"Your Papa would be so proud of you."

Sylvia batted the tears from her cheeks. Would he, though? Or would he think she was a self-centred, thoughtless bitch, too caught up in her own life to worry about her grandmother?

"I sat down to watch the show the night he didn't come home. I thought if I started watching it your grandfather would come through the door, cold, hungry, and shook up, but alive. I figured they'd been taken aboard some other vessel and the storm kept them from radioing the coast guard. I truly believed he'd be home by Final Jeopardy. I turned off the television that night and went to my bed still not believing what I knew to be true in the core of my being. My Paddy wasn't coming home again. I didn't turn the show back on until one month later. It was December 3, I remember, and it was a Teen Tournament. Foolish, isn't it, but the night I turned it on it felt like at least for a half an hour a day he was back home with me."

"I am so sorry, Nan. I am so sorry I didn't come home when Papa died."

"You're home now, aren't you? Who is Winnie-the-Pooh?"

"That was a *Daily Double*, Nan."

"And a pretty easy one. How about that pot of tea?"

Sylvia wiped the tears off her cheeks while wiggling her fingers inside her mittens, realizing how cold they were. Was she to sit here and freeze to death? Had she run away from a life so bad that becoming a block of ice in a deserted building near a body of water in New Brunswick was a better option? Was Kent's plan of moving to a bigger, more impressive house in Rosedale that terrible? But a five million dollar house with five bedrooms and six baths did not have enough room for Nan, apparently. He'd brought home the Clarmount Seniors' Home brochure months ago and kept offering it up like a salesman expecting a generous commission.

Sylvia stood up and walked to the big window. The snow was still coming down, and as she stood there, she realized she could barely feel her toes. It would be foolish to stay much longer. She looked toward the stairs, imagining how she could make this place livable. Heat and electricity first of all, but right now she needed to get back to the car.

She'd written her first book during her three months back on White Head Island. It had come fast and furious and had nothing to do with the pages she'd brought with her. It was actually a story Kent had suggested the night before she left. It was a marketable story, Kent said, and when Sylvia stepped back from it after its publication, she didn't even recognize it. It was as if it had been written by someone else. Someone Kent had created or she herself had fashioned to fit what she thought Kent wanted.

"So that's the reason for such a short engagement?" Nan said, coming through the arrivals gate.

Sylvia reached out to hug Nan, then stepped back. "Hello to you too, Nan. There are two in there, so I guess it's already pretty obvious. Not due until September, but I'm getting bigger every day and we figured if I was going to get a dress on and not look like a whale going down the aisle we'd better do it now. How was your flight?"

It had all happened so fast. Five months of whirlwind changes: a publishing contract, a husband, pregnant with twins, and buying a house. Kent surprised her with the deed at the reception and in his speech invited Nan to move to Toronto to live with them.

It had been Nan who got Sylvia through the first few years with the twins. The five of them spent the next years squeezed into a small bungalow in Rexdale. But sometimes, especially since Sophie's accident, Sylvia had felt like she had no control in any of it. It was as if someone else was writing the screenplay of her life.

⁓⁓⁓

Sylvia strapped the snowshoes back on and began the walk out to the car. She had never voiced these thoughts out loud. Instead she allowed herself to get caught up in the whirlwind of her first book tour and the demands of two more books for the same publisher. The third book had made the *Maclean's* bestseller list, and she had no trouble finding an agent and a more prestigious publisher for her fourth book.

The fourth book was finished as she languished in bed during the third trimester of her second pregnancy. Writing, resting, and praying that the baby she was carrying would be viable. Fuck, she hated that word and all the medical terms given for the devastation of delivering a dead baby. Placental abruption. A boy, a beautiful, perfect boy with no breath, no heartbeat, and no future. Patrick Ingalls Wright, the son she held for twenty minutes and never got to mother.

But life had gone on. She had so much to be thankful for, after all. She was a published author with some notoriety, had two beautiful healthy girls and a husband who was now a named partner in a large accounting firm. She'd managed to put her grief aside somewhere and get on with things. Her growing girls kept her busy, her fifth and sixth books came out, and life went along year after year until it all came crashing down five years ago the day Sophie tumbled down a ski hill in Quebec.

Kent could go ahead and sell the house. He could even buy his big house in Rosedale, but she would not be moving into it with him. She was buying this property. In the spring she would bring Nan and Sophie here. For the first time since dialling Kent Wright's number, she would decide her own future. And that future would include reclaiming this old building and bringing Nan back to the sea.

Sylvia brushed the snow from the driver's side so she could slide in and start the car. She turned the heater on full blast and sat for a few minutes, allowing the warm air to penetrate her cold body. She would clean the car off in a few minutes and head back to Moncton if the car wasn't stuck. She glanced at the gas gauge, thankful she'd taken the time to fill up before leaving the city.

The plan had taken shape on her walk back to the car, but she'd known the moment she walked through the door of the old building. She would call the real estate agent in the morning and make an offer. She would offer forty thousand—twenty-three thousand below the asking price. Paying cash, plus buying in the off season, would likely be a good incentive for the seller to accept. Kent didn't even know she had Papa's life insurance money in an account in New Brunswick. She and Nan had gone to Saint John and opened it in December, 1988, and Sylvia had added to it over the years. There was enough in that account to pay for this place and do some renovations to make the old building habitable.

As Sylvia stepped out of the car and walked around to the trunk, her gaze went to the snowshoes propped up in the snowbank. What would she do with snowshoes in Toronto? Would they even fit in her suitcase? She looked toward the yellow cottage. She gave a brief thought to putting the *Luna Sea* sign back on the post but instead just moved it to grab the snowbrush. Closing the trunk, she began removing the blanket of snow from the roof.

She picked up the snowshoes and walked up to the cottage door. She did not expect it to open, and it did not. Walking around to the side, she discovered a storage box. Using a snow-shoe, she cleared off the snow and ice from the top of the box and lifted the lid. Two lawn chairs, some beach toys, and a few empty flower pots left just enough room for the snowshoes. Another mystery for the owners to ponder upon their return.

Her first move would be to suggest early retirement to Kent. If they sold the Rexdale house they could put that money into this place too, or possibly a new house could be built instead of renovating the old building. She would present it all to Kent, but whatever choices he made, she was coming here and Nan was not going into any nursing home.

Sophie could have her therapy at the Moncton hospital. She would settle into a different facility and get used to new workers if care was taken to provide all the familiar routines and comforts she clung to. For the most part her thirty-year-old daughter's world revolved around her collection of stuffed animals and her favourite show on Netflix. The theme song of *Spirit Running Free* usually calmed Sophie, and she happily watched the same episodes over and over. Sophie's needs were simple.

Olivia's needs, on the other hand, were not as clear, and something Sylvia hadn't had much to do with for quite some time. Olivia's angry accusation when they'd last spoken seemed unfair but not completely untrue. The years since Sophie's accident had not been easy. Maybe she had forgotten Olivia in all of it.

Sylvia stood looking toward the horizon. The expanse of the Northumberland Strait seemed endless, but she knew from elementary school geography that Prince Edward Island was across the waves. No trace of land could be seen today, with the water and sky melding into a drab palate of grey. There was something so soothing about the sound and sight of it. The smell and the damp feel of the air reminded her of sitting on the shore when she was a kid straining her eyes imagining she could see Papa's boat bobbing on the waves.

Part of her wanted to just stay right here. Maybe she could break into the small yellow cottage. Perhaps there was a wood-burning stove or electric baseboards and she could heat up the small building. Of course, she would need supplies, but she could wait until morning and go to the Irving for a few things. She could, for tonight at least, pretend that this little cottage was hers and that she lived in this remote, amazing place all by herself. Maybe here she could even start writing again.

Ridiculous. Running away today was just a fantasy. Breaking and entering and pretending was totally out of character. Sylvia Drummond Wright went along with things. She didn't rock the boat or make a fuss. She smiled and nodded, fell in step with her husband's view of things, and played her part in the Wright family story. She had long since stopped writing her own.

Sylvia got behind the wheel and put the car in drive. The car lurched a bit, and for a second Sylvia thought it might be stuck and maybe her plan would need to be orchestrated out of necessity. She imagined a call to CAA for a tow truck would take hours, if she even had reception. The Camry, however, moved slowly onto the road, and Sylvia accelerated a bit. She would cautiously make the drive back into Moncton, and tomorrow she would fly back to Toronto. Staying was not in the cards, but Sylvia was determined that returning would be.

Chapter Three

Kent didn't often take the time to focus on the Toronto skyline. The view he saw from his office window had not changed much in the twenty years he'd inhabited this same office. Today, however, he was mesmerized, as if he had for the first time noticed it. The Goodenham building stood in its red-brick splendour, dwarfed but not diminished by the glass and concrete surrounding it. The CN Tower reached toward the sky like a giant concrete tree trunk. The sunlight shimmered off the sea of windows and metal surfaces.

Such a different view from where he'd been two days ago. He'd been back and forth to New Brunswick several times in the last five months. The fourteen acres on the Northumberland Strait that Sylvia had purchased on a whim had quickly become an albatross around his weary neck. Giving up this job to fully embrace his new venture was long overdue.

Last week he'd gone to supervise the final stage of the renovations. Arriving on site, he'd been sure the contractor would fail to meet the negotiated completion deadline. The accountant in him quickly calculated the payout they would be entitled to if things were not ready for the finish date, but the retreat coordinator he'd become panicked at the thought things wouldn't be ready when the ten writers arrived on opening day.

It was a brilliant plan. The lodge was opening on August 10 and would provide writing opportunities for up to ten participants at a time. The Wright Retreat was being offered in various durations. Kent had given the business plan careful thought, consulting with several successful writing-retreat organizers before finalizing the details. He had engaged a PR and advertising firm that had peppered the writing community with information about this prestigious New Brunswick retreat.

Writers could sign up for the ten-day "Hide Away and Write" retreat. Accommodation and meals would be provided. No workshops or mentorship offered. Another option was the two-week "Strength in Writers" retreat, and it offered accommodations, meals, writers mentoring writers, group readings and critiques, goal setting, time management tips, and professional advice.

The big one, the main drawing card, was the one-month retreat. Kent hadn't given it a catchy name; attaching Sylvia's name to it was enough. Accommodation and meals were provided, of course. Participants could write in solitude and determine how much interaction they wanted with other writers, sliding into existing groups. The main draw of this retreat would be the five one-on-one sessions with renowned author Sylvia Drummond Wright. She would also instruct them on query-letter writing and provide submission assistance.

Once advertised, the first ten spots filled quickly, and several deposits for further openings had already been accepted. Three of the ten participants arriving on August 10 were signed up for the one-month retreat, which was the most lucrative. They had paid in full, shared all their dietary details, and sent in their writing samples. Two women and one man were taking advantage of the opportunity to be mentored by Sylvia Drummond Wright.

Everything was coming together, Kent thought as he continued his steady gaze. Renovations were done, a housekeeper and a cook had been hired, supplies were stocked, flights booked. The house had been sold and packed up. Sophie, Evelyn, and Sylvia were already settling into the apartment at the back of the lodge that had been renovated to be the family's living area. One week from today he would be gone from this office, from his career, and be in New Brunswick to welcome the first round of writers.

Kent bowed his aching head, resting it in his hands. He took a deep breath before looking out the window again. His eyes zeroed in on a plane descending toward the Toronto Island airport. His only worry, the worry that was keeping him up at night and causing his ulcer to flare up, was the troublesome detail that Sylvia had no intention of having anything to do with the Wright Retreat. He'd been sure her initial resistance would have fizzled out by now. She had been so angry when he'd put everything in motion, even as she opposed the idea so strongly. But lately she'd been silent on the subject, putting all her attention and energy into the move.

Kent's gaze went back to his computer screen. He stared at the empty page he'd brought up in preparation for the group email he would send with last-minute details and encouragements.

Cc: Veronica Savage, Benson Grant, Kitty Forsythe, Grace Wanamaker, Jonathan Cameron, Janice Knockwood, Gavin and Irma Church, Abby Trenholme, Tyler Woodhouse, Darcy Lawson

Kent had had more correspondence with Gavin Church than with any of the others. Gavin had been the first writer to sign up and was bringing his wife. He'd waffled between the two-week retreat and the one month, finally deciding to commit to the two weeks with the option of extending it. He'd already sent his writing sample in case he took advantage of the one-month option. Maybe by the time Gavin's two weeks were up Sylvia would be ready to give the one-month participants what they'd signed up for.

⚬

Being in the kitchen alone after lunch was not something Irma Church took for granted. Since Gavin's retirement she got very little time away from his constant chatter. Naptime after lunch, his walk to the corner store for the *Globe and Mail*, and hours here and there when he actually went to the den to write were the only morsels of reprieve she got these days.

Irma scrubbed at the cast-iron frying pan. Gavin had eaten enough for three men who'd been in the woods all morning. "That man could eat the arse out of a low-flying bird," she muttered to no one, chuckling with the memory of her mom saying that about each one of her sons just about every day. It surprised Irma just how often she found herself sounding exactly like her mother, and her forty-two years gone, along with the others.

Irma's thoughts returned to the discussion she and Gavin had had at the table over lunch. "Quit your fighting," Daddy used to say when a heated debate would flare up at the Doyle dinner table.

"We're having a discussion, Daddy."

"Is that what you're calling it, Irma Jean? Alls I know is your Mama goin' be some vexed with ya if you don't stop your discussin'."

It hadn't been a fight at the table today, but Irma had certainly given her opinion to Gavin's announcement that not only had he signed up for that writing retreat he was interested in, but he'd also booked their flights to New Brunswick.

"Dear God, Gavin. I thought you said we could drive there. Paying all that money to fly sounds fucking stunned to me. I am quite sure we could find a cheaper way to die."

Gavin's eyebrows had lifted in that slight manner it always did when his wife used the F-word. It was a wonder his eyes hadn't fluttered right out of their fucking sockets by now.

"For heaven's sake, Irma. You're more likely to meet your maker being hit by a bus crossing Yonge Street than in a plane crash. Renting a car and driving to New Brunswick seems no safer to me. There are no guarantees in this life."

"Like I don't fucking knows that. What I don't know is just why you have to go all the way to New Brunswick for a writing retreat. I'm sure you could find one in the GTA, which would eliminate flying or driving. Jump on public transit and go write your fucking head off."

"It's with Sylvia Drummond Wright."

"Can't say that means a flipping fuck to me."

Irma ran more hot water into the sink. She'd heard the name Sylvia Drummond Wright before, even tried to read one of her books after Gavin read it. He had to go right out and buy it the day he saw it had been longlisted for the Giller Prize. It hadn't won, so what was the big deal? And for damn sure the East Coast was no drawing card. She'd seen plenty of the Atlantic Ocean, fishing boats, and rocky outcrops.

Downtown Toronto suited Irma just fine. She blended in here, even though Newfoundland showed up every time she opened her mouth. Gavin had tried for years to tone that down, even though he'd found it lovable at first. What he found so refreshing and entertaining early on soon became an embarrassment for him.

They'd met when she was waiting tables at the George Street Diner. George Street Diner; what better place for a girl from St. John's to find work when she arrives in the big city alone. She wasn't actually a townie, but no one in Toronto cared about that distinction. Easy on the eyes and willing to work her ass off were the attributes she brought with her from Petty Harbour. There was nothing else to bring, after the fire.

Gavin had been a regular, and it seemed she always got his table. She flirted a bit with him, like she did with everybody. "Lay that Newfie charm on, girl," Marnie used to say. The flirting went on for over a month before he'd asked her on a date. They'd had three more dates when he invited her to meet his mother. The dinner hadn't gone too well, but despite her Newfie charm, he stuck around.

"My God, Irma, did you have to tell my mother she was as stunned as the quilt?"

She *had* been as stunned as the quilt, and maybe even the comforter, thought Irma as she dried a plate and placed it in the cupboard.

The rest of the *discussion* at lunchtime had zigged and zagged a bit, but in the end it was clear that she and Gavin were flying from Pearson to Moncton next Saturday, meeting the other retreat participants, and going someplace called Petit-Cap. And just before going for his nap, Gavin had thrown in the fact that instead of staying two weeks they might stay for a whole month.

⁓✼⁓

Benson Grant had gone to great lengths to reinvent himself. Grecian Formula had removed any trace of the greying hair he'd grown out a bit, allowing his thick childhood curls to reappear, and he'd shaved off his signature mustache, but former students were still recognizing him. After retirement he'd considered moving from this town, where he would always be

Mr. Grant, high school principal, divorced and disgraced by a stupid affair with a bus driver.

At first Nancy would have been happy to see him go, but she probably couldn't care less now that she was remarried and had weathered the shitstorm he'd created. She came out pretty damn good, actually, with the house and half his pension. And the kids were long gone. Not one of the three stayed in Fredericton. But he chose to believe they would have left even if their father hadn't screwed their bus driver.

No, he had decided to stay in his hometown. He still had a few friends and had found a group of new ones who fuelled his childhood dream. The Windsor Street Wordsmiths met every Tuesday at the library. Corny, maybe, but it didn't feel that way when he got to read his week's work to the others. His work was gorier, more graphic and raw than what the others were writing, but crime fiction had always been his passion. He'd just finished his first novel and was working to self-publish. Visions of seeing his own name on the cover were that much closer to coming true.

His pen name, really. He'd chosen Cormier, his mother's maiden name, to publish under. *Benson Cormier* had a ring to it, and maybe people in Fredericton might buy the book if they didn't realize it was his.

Doris had brought the advertisement to a meeting of the Windsor Wordsmiths in June. They'd all talked about the possibility of signing up for the retreat. It was just outside Moncton, not real expensive, and there were three options. In the end he'd been the only one to sign up and had decided on the two-week retreat, feeling pretty confident he didn't need Sylvia Drummond Wright to guide him, especially since she did not write crime stuff. He would take his guidance from Harlan Coben, Dick Francis, and Elmore Leonard.

~~~

Grace Wanamaker was now older than both her parents had been when they passed. Hobbling around in this old house trying to keep all three floors and the huge lawn and countless garden beds up to the standard her parents had maintained was getting to be more than she could handle. She hadn't actually been to the top floor in at least two years and now hardly went to the second floor after getting Wallace to move her bed to the small bedroom off the parlour.

Luckily, Wallace came around once in a while. She knew part of the reason he didn't come by more was probably the lengthy list she met him with every time he came. A few errands, a fix it or two, didn't seem too much to expect of a son. She had hired a boy to do the lawns, and her neighbour's cousin Donna did all the garden work. All of that would have been way too much for Wallace. He had his own life, after all.

His own life. Had she ever had a life of her own? Most would say having only one child was a light load. Her sister Velma had raised eleven, having gotten herself hooked up with a good Catholic man. Vincent was the opposite of a good Catholic, with his strong atheist views, but a good man nevertheless. He never kept her from going to church, though. He'd even tolerated all the God talk and giving thanks at every meal once they moved in to care for her parents.

Last month Grace had called the young Fudge girl, who'd just started selling real estate, asking her to come do an appraisal. It was time to let this house go. There was no one left to argue that the house needed to stay in the Montgomery family. Not a Montgomery left in the town they'd help build. Better it sell now than after they found her decomposing body in the cellar. Wallace had given her a stern talking-to when he realized she was still going down to the basement. Her washer and dryer were down there, and her big chest freezer. She didn't go down every day, and when she did she took her time and always held on to the handrail.

The timing had worked out perfectly. The sign was going up today. She'd had the Duncan woman come to clean top to bottom last week, and she planned to be gone for a month. People could file through and see the *mansion* on Lakeside Drive without the old lady who lived there or her clutter being around. Maybe by the time she got back from the retreat the house would be sold, and her name would have reached the top of the waiting list for an apartment at Empire Crossing.

Grace crossed the room and pushed down the button on her kettle. The catalyst for selling had come from a brochure she'd picked up at the library in May. A life of her own and finally getting serious about her writing came to mind as she leafed through the colourful brochure with details of a writing retreat in New Brunswick. She and Vincent had driven through New Brunswick the year they drove to Halifax for his sister's wedding. They'd stopped for gas outside of Moncton and Grace had convinced him to take the time to visit Magnetic Hill.

Magnetic Hill, an unexplainable pull causing cars to coast uphill. A retreat with Sylvia Drummond Wright was the magnetic pull Grace felt reading the details of the month-long retreat.

She had started the book the first year they'd moved in with Mother and Daddy. She hadn't told anyone, not even Vincent, but found time almost every day to add a bit to the story. Horror, not the type of story most would expect from a sweet little old lady who never said boo and dutifully did all that was asked of her. The little lady who sat at the organ every Sunday at St. Mark's United Church had a dark side, and Grace was going to let that side come out in spades in the month holed up in a lodge in New Brunswick.

~~~

"It's the Northumberland Strait, Nan."

"Right. You keep telling me that. I think I dozed off, which always muddles me a bit. I was dreaming, I think."

"That's okay, Nan. If you want to pretend it's the Bay of Fundy and you're sitting on your porch at home, you go right ahead."

"It's lovely here, Sylvie. The fix-ups are beautiful. That Kent can get things done, can't he?"

"Yeah."

Sylvia picked up Nan's mug with the premise of getting her a fresh cup of tea. Walking inside, she choked back the emotion Nan's words had elicited. Early on she'd thought she had enough fight in her to shut Kent down. She'd been so proud of herself when she'd come back from the trip to New Brunswick in January and made all the necessary arrangements to buy the property. The sale had gone through before she shared any of it with Kent.

"What the hell were you thinking, going ahead with such a major purchase without telling me?"

"It was my money, and I knew damn well what you'd say about it."

"So you think we are just going to pull up roots and move to some godforsaken spot in rural New Brunswick?"

"I don't know what you're going to do, but I am, and so are Sophie and Nan. You've made every other goddamn decision in our marriage. I made one for a change, and I don't give a rat's ass what you think about it. And my roots are in New Brunswick, by the way."

"So I don't get a say in any of this? Are you asking for a divorce? Friggin' weird way to go about it, buying a piece of rock not worth half of what you paid."

"Oh, you know all about real estate value in Atlantic Canada, do you? I should have known that, since you know everything about everything. An Ontario thing, I guess, if you want to regionalize all this."

"What the hell are you talking about? Is this menopause?"

"Oh fuck, now my choices are hormonal."

"Well, what the hell is it, then?"

"I'll tell you what it is. I want to move out of this city. I want to breathe fresh air and see the sky at night. I want to live in a place I picked that means something to me. I want my daughter to feel the salt air, to feel her bare feet in the rippling waves, to watch birds fly and hear the wind. I want my grandmother to live out her days with me in a place that brings us happiness, not in some fuckin' old folks' home where she can sit in a chair drooling all day."

"Wow, you've really thought this out. You have no idea what will need to be done to make a rundown shack in the middle of nowhere into this paradise you've dreamt up."

"Of course I don't. Kent Wright is the only one who knows anything. I couldn't possibility figure out how to hire someone to put a new roof on a building or build new kitchen cupboards. Go fuck yourself."

Sylvia looked around at the apartment kitchen, a part of the huge restoration that had taken place since her first step inside the old lodge. She waited for the tea to steep before returning outside. Setting the tray down, she unfolded a fleece blanket and draped it over Nan's legs.

"I made fresh tea, Nan. Let's sit out here a while longer before we go inside. I think it's going to be a beautiful sunset tonight. I put Sophie's show on, so she's good for an hour."

"This has been a lot for you, moving your old grandmother

down here and getting Sophie settled. You must be so tired, Sylvie."

"I'm fine. Sitting here with you and looking at that water and sky takes away any weariness I might be feeling. I'm good."

"You're just like your papa. He could be half dead, but once he got outside he'd perk up. He loved the water and the sky, the rougher and darker the better. Makes me think he died happy, being in the middle of a storm and ending up in the sea. Once he gave in to the terror, of course. I hate to think of the terror he must have felt. Fear of leaving us would have been the worst for him."

"He sure did love his Evie."

"And his Sylvie, and his baby girl, of course. Losing your mother was almost his undoing."

"I've thought about her so often since moving here. I spent such a long time not thinking about her at all. For years she was just a name to me. At four years old I had so few memories, and they were all bad. As I got older, I told myself she was weak. She let a man use her, lead her down a path to addiction, and she took a cowardly way out by climbing up on the rails of a bridge and jumping off. I was angry at her but at the same time so grateful that she got out of the way so I could live with you and Papa. That's terrible, isn't it?"

"Oh, sweetie. We should have told you more about who your mother was as a little girl. But because it was so hard for Papa and me to talk about her, we let her be invisible to you. That wasn't right."

"I have done exactly what I was so angry at her for doing. I followed a man, thinking he could meet my needs."

"Don't be ridiculous. Kent is nothing like your father. He has been a wonderful provider, has loved you and the girls, and has been a wonderful grandson-in-law to me."

"I think I hear Sophie hollering. Netflix must be circling. I am going to have to get better internet here."

Sylvia got up quickly, hoping Nan hadn't noticed the tears filling her eyes. Walking in the door she could see Sophie enthralled, glued to the TV screen. It wasn't being tired, stressed, or overwhelmed by the move that was making her so vulnerable and quick to tear up. In two days Kent would arrive, and the day after that ten strangers would descend on her quiet getaway. After all the fighting, all her determination, Kent had managed to take over—and she had let him.

Kent had found a way to go along with her idea of moving here by making it into something he was completely in charge of. He had mutated the future she'd envisioned, and she had let him. By the time the Wright Lodge and the Sylvia Drummond Wright writing retreats materialized, Sylvia had lost her fight. She watched the wheels he put in motion without a word of opposition. She'd put all her energy into getting Sophie, Nan, and herself moved in, rather than climbing a bridge railing and jumping into the depths below.

⌒⌒⌒

Veronica Savage squatted down to fill the bottom shelf. Stocking the top shelves was fine, but her sixty-three-year-old body did not squat well. She was not going to kneel or sit right down on the floor and let customers see the spectacle she'd create trying to get herself up. When had she become this old and this creaky? Four more shifts and she could leave this behind for a while.

In April, when Veronica had seen the spread in the newspaper supplement, she had started shaking. The photograph of the seaside retreat looked so beautiful. She had folded the supplement up and stuck it in her pocket before returning the newspaper to the rack beside her cash register. Tanya had told her more than once to buy her own newspaper, but there hadn't been a customer in sight and Tanya was in Florida. This wasn't a bad place to work when Tanya was on vacation.

Veronica had been working at the Quispamsis Shoppers Drug Mart for twenty years. She'd taken an early retirement from the bank thinking she'd be able to write full-time with Robert still working. Her small pension would give her enough income so she wouldn't have to beg for money to buy the few things she wanted.

Collections; she'd always had collections. Snow globes, bells, cups and saucers, owls, and salt and pepper shakers, to name a few. A hoarder, Robert called her, and at the end he wouldn't stand for it. His tolerance and affection had dwindled gradually, she realized when she was finally able to look at the trajectory of their marriage from a distance. A distance, all right, once she'd moved out of their Kennebecasis Park home into a one-bedroom apartment in Quispamsis. Her space had been reduced and so had her collections, along with her aspirations.

Since seeing the ad she had saved every cent she could. She was determined to live on Robert's paltry alimony cheque and save her salary for three months so she could pay for the premium retreat and afford to take a whole month off. She'd known as soon as she saw the Wright Lodge spread that she was going and staying for a month. She was going to do what she had dreamed of doing since she was a teenager. She was finally going to find the courage.

—✤—

Tyler Woodhouse never tired of seeing his name on the dust jacket of the hardcover book he kept on the card table in his sister's basement. He was grateful for this small room in her cramped basement and for her wifi. He'd let his apartment go after being laid off from his pathetic job. At least now he'd have a believable excuse for not making his child-support payments every month as well as more time to write. Darlene never let him see Henry anyway. A bad influence, she said, as if everyone she knew didn't smoke a little pot.

"You're forty years old, for God's sake," she'd hollered during their last altercation. "Nobody can make a living writing books about dragons and wizards."

"So you've never heard of the nobody named J. K. Rowling?"

"Oh shut up. Like your book is Harry Potter."

"Actually, my protagonist's name is Victor."

"Oh, well then."

Tyler booted up his laptop. He was hoping the edits for his next book would be in his inbox. The house was quiet, Dan and Maryanne at work and the kids in school, making it a perfect day to work. Sometimes the only chance he got to write was at night, and he was no Richard Brautigan, who was said to write at midnight, carrying his words like a dreaming child into the darkness of the pages.

Tyler had gone through a Richard Brautigan phase, an obsession really, in his first year of university. The tattered copy of *Trout Fishing in America* that he'd borrowed from his high school library and never returned was always in his backpack and certainly formed his early aspirations.

Oh good, Tyler thought as he clicked on Matt's subject line: *2nd Round Edits*.

What came up after the click was not the pdf Tyler expected.

> *Almost done with second round.*
> *Shouldn't take too much to get them to*
> *the copyedit stage. Some retreat info*
> *crossed my desk and thought you might*
> *be interested. New retreat in New Bruns-*
> *wick is offering a one-month retreat*
> *that might just be what you need to get*

*your groove back. Seaside accommoda-
tion, meals and a roof over your head
for a whole month. Cost is less than one
month's rent in Halifax. I know living
with your sister is getting old. And it's
with Giller-longlisted author Sylvia
Drummond Wright. That would look good
on your CV, buddy. Think about it. I'm
attaching the info.*

<hr/>

Maybe Keto will do the trick, Kitty Forsythe thought as she typed it into Google. *Take the Weight Loss Quiz* caught her eye and she chuckled. She had done it all. She could give a Weight Loss 101 course, but it would have to be a year-long program to cover all the plans she'd followed, all the special food and supplements she'd bought, and all the failure she'd absorbed. All while putting on at least ten more pounds than what she'd lost each time.

A twenty-eight-day meal plan. Something to consider after the two-week retreat she was going on. No point in trying to begin a strict eating plan while holed up in rural New Brunswick trying to finish her latest hot lesbian romance novel by the deadline. She was so much better at imagining herself a lesbian than she was at imagining herself thin.

Chapter Four

Jonathan Cameron began the e-transfer, relieved that his bank account finally had the funds to cover it. A published author with four books should be able to pay for a short retreat in New Brunswick. God, the cost was equivalent to a meal in one of Toronto's fancy restaurants. Jack Rabinovitch, who'd started the Giller to honour his wife, was quoted as saying a person could buy all the novels on the Giller shortlist for about the same cost of a meal in Toronto.

Four published books, and he got a yearly royalty cheque that might buy three or four such meals. A kids' book writer, not a term he used but one he'd heard so many times in a condescending way, as if writing kids' books was a hobby anybody could have. He was proud of his work, but he had an adult novel beating at the gate, and when he saw the retreat ad in the Writers' Union of Canada *Write* magazine, it seemed exactly what he needed to get to work on it. The one-month retreat would have been ideal, but the ten-day was all he could afford.

His boss acted like Jonathan taking twelve days off would bring the Toronto Transportation Commission to a complete standstill. He'd started as a ticket taker at a TTC booth ten years ago, but when it looked like everything would soon be

automated he'd trained as an operator. In his new position
he had no vacation time yet; twelve days with no pay, and the
retreat registration fee was going to be a sacrifice. But how was
he going to write his Giller-prize-winning novel without some
sacrifice? He pushed *send* and left the break room.

~~≈~~

Kent accepted the e-transfer, depositing it in the account
he kept exclusively for retreat expenses. Most of the actual
renovations had been paid for with Sylvia's money, with a bit
of money from the sale of the house thrown in. It had shocked
him that the Rexdale house went for as much as it did, but
he'd invested the majority of it, mindful of the fact he might
want to buy a small condo downtown so he'd be able to get
away from the remoteness of rural New Brunswick when he
needed to. He would wait on that purchase for a while, first
making sure the retreat could maintain itself financially.
The main factor would be building a good reputation so that
people would continue to be willing to pay the steep cost of a
reputable retreat.

Only two writers had registered for the ten-day retreat, the
cheapest. In fact, after having offered it, Kent had questioned
his wisdom. He would have lost money if all ten rooms had
been filled with writers on ten-day retreats. Having the three
one-month signups helped to give the overall bottom line a
boost. Having five two-week participants was good too. And he
had six future participants already registered, one for a one-

month retreat. Kent was confident he could keep the momentum going and make this business work.

Janice Knockwood had told no one her plans. Lee had sent her details about the retreat outside Moncton, offering to lend her the money for the ten-day registration. Very nice of him, but Janice Knockwood did not take charity. Not unless that charity included interest rates. She would pay off her Visa next month or the month after.

"You need to get back to your book, Janice. Your story needs told, and who better than you to tell it?"

She'd started working with Lee five years ago, after meeting him at a writing event. She'd read a short excerpt from her memoir, and afterward he'd approached her, offering to edit what she had written so far and help her finish it.

Jesus, Janice thought, *I could write an entire manuscript on the turn my life took in those five years.* Change the names to protect the guilty, of course. But what would protect her embarrassment at having made the stupid choice to take up with Marshall Redmond? Oh, how amazing he'd seemed at first. Ruggedly handsome and four years her junior. A leap of judgement, a wild and crazy love affair, and a huge payout of misery.

But she had survived it, just as she'd survived all the other crap she'd had thrown at her, and she was stronger than ever.

Stronger and more determined to get on with whatever life she had left to live—and at seventy-five, chances were there wasn't a whole lot.

<center>~~~~</center>

"I can only take ten of you with me."

Abby Trenholme pulled her suitcase off the top shelf. "I'm not putting you in this, you silly puppies. Donavan, you be brave for the others. The mesh bag will be fine and allow you to breathe."

Abby looked around the room. Stuffed dogs lined shelves, covered her bed and the top of her dresser. It had been a while since she'd counted them, lined them up smallest to largest, or looked at the alphabetized list of their names. A name for each letter had been her goal initially, but there were now way more than twenty-six, and she didn't try to equalize the use of letters. She now gave each new stuffie a name that best suited them.

Rex was her newest and her only Dalmatian. Black labs held the highest number, Huskies a close second. Donavan was her oldest, and he got to sleep with her every night. She didn't leave the house without him. She rarely left the house, actually, because not everyone understood the need for a twenty-nine-year-old woman to carry stuffed dogs everywhere she went. She never took all of them, of course; that would be ridiculous. She tried to be fair and give them all turns.

Luckily, three years ago she was given the option of working from home. It was ideal for her because when her quota was met she could spend the rest of the day on her writing. Four of her middle-grade dog stories had been published, and her publisher wanted four more in the new easy reader series they were promoting.

Her routine was working just fine, and Abby wasn't sure why she started googling writing retreats in April. She had no intention of attending any of the retreats she looked at. She didn't go places, didn't drive, and had never flown. But for days she kept going back to the website for the Sylvia Drummond Wright retreat, which was located on the other side of the country.

Slackers, her great-grandfather had always called East Coasters. Abby wasn't sure why. It apparently had something to do with the time he spent in Halifax during the war. He still used the word when talking about people from the east, even after his grandson married a girl from New Brunswick.

Abby walked across the room and picked up Slacker, her big Basset Hound. He was a lazy old fellow who usually just slept on the chair near her bed. "You're a slacker, old guy. Do you want to go to New Brunswick?"

She had emailed Kent Wright in June inquiring about the accommodations, the meal plans, and what transportation he could provide from the Moncton airport. They had a few back-and-forth emails, but Abby had never believed she would actually go. She made lists of questions to ask, researched nearby tourist attractions, and priced her flight, still not thinking she would go through with it.

That was what she remembered from the weeks before the explosion. Her mother had talked constantly about the vacation they would take in August. She hadn't been back home for ten years, and she was determined to take the whole family, even Donavan. Dad went along with her talk but kept saying he couldn't get that much time off.

"Maybe you and Abby will have to go without me."

"I'm not going home without you. I want everyone to meet you. I want them to see what a catch I got."

"We'll see."

Abby picked up two pugs next. "You two can both come. You'd cut up an awful fuss if I left one of you behind. Lucky for you my next book is about a pug, so I'll need you for inspiration."

Abby took her time selecting six more dogs. It would be so hard to leave the others, but it wasn't as if she needed someone to come feed or water them while she was away. She might be a bit weird, but she wasn't crazy. She knew these dogs she loved so much were not real. They were not alive. But they were her friends, and she would be happy to return to them after her two-week retreat was up.

<hr>

Sylvia put the lasagna in the oven, set the timer, and went outside. She had no intention of eating in the big kitchen when the retreat began. She would continue to prepare meals for herself, Nan, and Sophie in the small kitchen, in her own apartment. Dorothy Fleming, the local woman Kent had hired to be the cook, had started today. When the woman arrived this morning Sylvia had watched from the window as she walked back and forth carrying bags of food and supplies into the lodge. She hadn't seen her again, but as she walked around the corner of the building Sylvia could see Dorothy sitting at the far end of the front veranda.

"You must be the missus," Dorothy called out.

Sylvia approached as Dorothy continued to talk. "That is one fine kitchen in there. I've worked in plenty, but that one takes the cake. Did you design it?"

Sylvia walked the length of the veranda and leaned on the post across from the woman. "No. My husband had someone do that."

"Well, it is lovely. Those double ovens are great, and that commercial dishwasher will be a godsend. I've fed larger crowds, but not three meals a day, day after day, week after week. I was happy to get the work, though, I tell you, and a decent wage. Most people want you to work for nothing. I've been cooking at the Legion for twenty years, and lucky if I get a thank you. Every event they just assume Dot's going to make rolls, Dot's going to cook the turkeys, Dot's going to make the soup and chili. They'll find out real soon just how much Dorothy Fleming did around there now that she has a job. Mind if I light a smoke? I'll blow the smoke the other way. I cut back a lot but can't seem to quit all together. Yeah, I consider myself real lucky landing this job. All year round, your husband says. Two weeks off at Christmas, but he plans on running retreats all year. Well, that suits me just fine. All my kids flew the coop years ago and I'm lucky if the grandkids come around. Jennifer's at UNB in Fredericton and she comes to visit some, usually looking for a care package. Oh, they all like my cooking.

"Your husband thought I might cook *and* do the house-keeping, but I set him straight on that. I just told him if you want your guests fed real good and the meals served on time I need to be in the kitchen. I can cook up a storm and I guarantee they'll be no complaints, but I don't have time to be changing beds and cleaning while I do it. Had my fill of all that raising six kids and looking after a husband. I don't have him to worry about anymore, God rest his soul.

"I gave your husband my sister-in-law Marjorie's name, and she's tickled to be working three days a week. That brother of mine is a tightwad. Marjorie will be real glad to have her own money. Now, will I be cooking for you all as well? Your mother and daughter live here, right? And Mr. Wright, of course. Will I be adding four more potatoes to the pot?"

"She is my grandmother, actually," Sylvia said. "No, I will cook for us and we will eat in our apartment. Kent will eat with the others."

"He said you were a famous author. He sounded right proud of you."

"It was nice meeting you, Dorothy. Mr. Wright will be here tomorrow, so if you have any other questions he'll answer them for you."

Sylvia walked into her small kitchen, took a quick look in at the lasagna, then sat down at the small table. Dorothy Fleming was right about how nice the kitchen was. The whole lodge was lovely. Renovations had turned the rundown old building into an inviting facility. The large kitchen had all new cupboards and new appliances. The large table had been refinished and fifteen new chairs bought to replace the mis-matched ones. New windows had turned the dingy first floor into a bright space, and sliding doors led out to the rebuilt front veranda facing the strait. The fireplace had been resur-faced and a gas insert installed, making the sitting area in the great room very cozy.

The top floor had been gutted and reconfigured into five single bedrooms sharing two bathrooms and five ensuite bedrooms. A lovely sitting area tucked into the large gabled section had been furnished with armchairs and tables where people could write looking out at the stunning view of the Northumberland Strait. Sylvia had to admit the building had been transformed into a perfect writing retreat.

Dorothy Fleming could talk the hind legs off a donkey. She'd give Kent a run for his money and hold her own. *No flies on her*, thought Sylvia, chuckling at her stream of clichés. Nan would really like Dorothy. And maybe Nan would like to go to the Legion Dorothy was talking about. It would be nice to grad-ually get to know people and fit in to the community they were now a part of. Nan still missed the closeness of living on White Head Island, so making some friends would be good for her.

The knock at the screen door startled Sylvia. She turned and saw Dorothy in the doorway.

"I'm leaving. I'll be here in the morning bright and early, and Marjorie will be with me. She'll get the beds made up and have everything shipshape by the time the first guest arrives. I'm cooking a roast of beef for tomorrow night's supper. Mr. Wright left the menu planning to me. A roast beef dinner seems like a good opening night supper, don't you think? I make a lovely Yorkshire pudding. And I'll have a few pies to give folks a choice. I'll drop one in to you if you like. Would apple be okay, or would you prefer a lemon meringue? I make a lovely lemon meringue."

"Oh, you don't have to worry about feeding us, but my daughter does love lemon meringue pie. Maybe just this once, Dorothy."

"Dot, please. I get a bit nervous when folks call me Dorothy. We're going to be like family as far as I can tell, with me hanging around here every day."

"Okay, Dot it is, and you'd better call me Sylvie. My Nan is Evelyn, and my daughter's name is Sophie."

"I'm not the best with names. I remember folks' faces, though. Figure I'll have lots of names to keep straight. Mr. Wright said ten writers are coming tomorrow. I'll try my best with those folks, but for sure I'll remember your name, Sylvie, and I look forward to meeting Evelyn and Sophie. Goodnight now."

Veronica opened the closet. Three suitcases sat piled on the top shelf. The top one was smushy enough to squeeze in above the other two in the limited space between shelf and ceiling. The cloth tapestry of the top one was worn and threadbare, hardly holding together, and the clasp had long since broken. She would pack the other two for the retreat and return the top one to the shelf. This apartment had very little storage space, but she had no intention of throwing the old suitcase away.

"I don't know why you don't throw that old thing out," Robert used to say.

They had had several discussions over the years regarding her refusal to discard what to him seemed like a useless old suitcase. She saw it as much more. She could recall the first time it had been packed, brand new and sitting on the bed beside her mother's red leather case. Her mother had folded each item of clothing she'd taken off hangers in her closet and placed them carefully in the red case. Three cotton house-dresses folded perfectly and set in on top of her full slips, the silk and lace so pretty to look at and touch. Then her mother had folded her one good dress. She placed several pairs of cotton pyjamas, brassieres, underpants, and hosiery neatly on top.

Then Mother began packing Veronica's bag. Veronica paid no mind to the items Mother was packing in her excitement to be going with Mother wherever it was she was going. *TB hospital* meant nothing to her; she just felt the relief that she would be going too. She had been so afraid she'd be left behind with Daddy and cranky Grandma Helen. Sweet Nanny Gladys had gone to that other hospital, and Veronica had never seen her again.

The second time the tapestry bag was packed came to Veronica's mind as she closed the closet door. She had packed it herself. Two pairs of blue jeans, her new white peasant top, shorts and tops, a dress for Mass, nightgowns, and underwear. Her only bra was way too small, but Father would not take her to buy a new one. And her swimsuit barely fit either, but Father said the nuns would take her shopping.

"I've paid a clothing allowance, so they damn well better supply anything you might need while you're there. Stop your blathering. Lots worse places you could be going. Sea air and the great outdoors. Always thought that was part of your mother's problem. She stayed holed up inside too much. Hated the outdoors, your mother did. You would have thought a mosquito bite would have killed her, the way she carried on.

"Your mother was so frail and sickly. Took a lot out of her, giving birth to a mammoth baby like you. Her lung sickness settled in shortly after your birth. Could have been that hospital too. Things weren't sterile like they are nowadays. Anyway, she never recovered. Wouldn't wish the hand we were dealt on anyone. It wasn't easy having a wife cooped up in that TB place for almost two years and then to die anyway. Damn shame she didn't die quicker."

Veronica opened the biggest suitcase. Through tear-filled eyes she lifted a stack of journals off the floor. "Damn shame he didn't die *sooner*," she mumbled.

Chapter Five

The next morning it wasn't Dot's silver Ford Focus Sylvia saw pull up to the lodge first thing but a red SUV of some kind. An attractive young woman stepped out of the passenger side, opened the back door, and pulled out a laptop bag, a suitcase, and a big designer purse. Sylvia considered ignoring the woman, letting her walk up to the main door of the lodge, where no one would respond to her knocking. Kent should be here if he expected one of the writers to arrive so early. As far as she knew, Kent arrived on an early flight from Toronto and was picking up a rental van to wait for all the authors in Moncton.

Sylvia walked into the yard and across the lawn to the walkway up to the main door. She coughed so she wouldn't startle the woman, who had her back to her, knocking loudly while trying to look through the frosted glass in the door.

"Are you looking for the retreat?"

The woman whipped around. "Yes. I overestimated how long it would take us to drive from my cousin's house in Shediac. Are none of the others here yet? I'm in the right place, though, right? My name's Darcy."

"Yes. This is the place. Mr. Wright won't be here until this afternoon. The cook and housekeeper should be here soon, and they can let you in. I don't have a key to this door."

"Oh, that's okay. The water looks so beautiful and calm. I can sit on the bench and wait. I am just so happy to be here. Are you one of the writers?"

"No."

"I'll let my cousin know she can leave. I just wanted to make sure I was at the right place."

The woman turned to wave to the driver of the SUV and added, "The *Wright* place," with a chuckle.

Sylvia stood somewhat awkwardly. This young woman may have come to the retreat because of some familiarity with the name Sylvia Drummond Wright, but she obviously was not familiar with what she looked like. But to be fair, Sylvia thought, standing here in yoga pants and a sweatshirt, her hair pulled back in a messy bun and no makeup, she certainly didn't look like any of her author photos.

"Do you think the wifi will work out here?" Darcy asked.

"I'm thinking not, but I'll leave you to try. The cook's name is Dorothy. She should be here in ten minutes or so."

"Thanks. And what's your name?"

Sylvia walked away, pretending she hadn't heard the question.

Darcy Lawson pulled a journal and pen out of her purse. She wouldn't try her laptop. There would be lots of time to get online, and there was probably a password. The woman who'd greeted her didn't offer that up when she asked about the wifi. She would just go old school and write in the new journal she'd bought just for this retreat.

It was so wonderful being here. She'd made a New Year's resolution that she would write every day and do all she could to make her dream of getting published come true in 2019. As part of that resolution, she had applied for a sabbatical from her teaching job. She hadn't gotten it but was put on a waiting list. Last week the school board office called, saying someone had cancelled and she could have the first term off if she still wanted it. She'd had to scramble to get registered for the creative writing course at Queen's and quickly emailed Kent Wright to take the last spot, signing up for the two-week retreat, which would get her back to Kingston in time for classes.

Darcy had flown to New Brunswick four days ago and spent some time with her cousin Amanda and Amanda's new husband. They spent two beautiful days sunbathing at Parlee Beach, which had been delightful even with the swimming ban. Usually by the double digits of August Darcy was prepping for the high school English courses she taught and spending time getting her classroom ready.

<hr />

Kent Wright pulled out of the Chevrolet dealership. After considering the cost and inconvenience of renting a van each time, he had decided buying one was the best option. In the long run it would be more cost effective. Sylvia had her Rav 4, and perhaps he would buy himself a small car depending on how much running around he would need to do while in New Brunswick. Mrs. Fleming had agreed to look after all the grocery and supply purchasing, but there might be times he'd need a car. He would wait on that decision, though, since he hadn't even discussed buying this van with Sylvia.

Sylvia hadn't shown any interest in the financial aspect of running this retreat. She hadn't shown any interest in any of it, and Kent was hoping that would change once the first group settled in. This was a viable business. He'd received seven more registrations in the last two days and was very optimistic that he could keep the lodge filled with enough writers each week to more than cover the expenses. Profit was made any week the lodge was at full occupancy. And there were several weeks like that in the next few months. Sylvia would see what a good idea this was as time went on. Possibly it would even get her writing again.

Kent did worry about what would happen if Sylvia continued to refuse to participate. He needed writers to come away from the Wright Retreat with rave reviews if it was to keep up the momentum. Word of mouth among the writing community would be its strongest asset, and he could not afford to have writers leaving with less than they'd signed up for.

Before leaving yesterday, he'd tied things up in Toronto and was confident he'd thought of everything on this end. Despite his poor sleep at the airport hotel last night, he'd awoken with energy and optimism. He was ready to meet the authors and see this business unfold. Traffic in this city was certainly easier to navigate through. Maybe there was something to Sylvia's claim that a slower life in New Brunswick was what they needed. Launching the inaugural retreat was exciting but just a tad daunting, with the tension between him and Sylvia. It would be good to see Sophie and Evelyn, though.

The Churches, Kitty Forsythe, Grace Wanamaker, Jonathan Cameron, and Abby Trenholme were arriving on the same flight from Toronto. Janice Knockwood was meeting them at the airport, and he would pick Veronica Savage and Tyler Woodhouse up at the bus station after meeting the 12:50 flight from Toronto. Benson Grant was driving himself to the lodge and Darcy Lawson was being dropped off sometime today.

⁓〜⁓

Benson pulled into the Irving Station on the main street of Cap-Pelé to check the Google map directions on his phone. He'd taken the correct exit and was on the right road, but he was worried he'd missed the turnoff he was supposed to take. This old car had no such thing as a GPS system, but at least it was still running. Nancy got the good vehicle, and he'd had to settle for the old Corolla. Keeping the old girl going was getting to be a challenge, but at least she had passed inspection last month.

Thinking about how different his life would be if he hadn't fucked up was something he tried not to do very often. Retired with his full pension, a mortgage-free house, money to travel, and time to enjoy these years with Nancy would have been the perks of remaining faithful. And he would have been the only grandfather to the baby Kayla was having in January. Nancy's new husband, Ron, would no doubt get top billing, and the loser, cheating grandfather will probably be given limited visiting rights.

Benson passed the lady behind the counter his bag of chips and bottle of Coke and asked about his destination.

"You haven't quite driven far enough. About two miles down the road you'll see the sign for Silver Sands Campground. Follow the signs and it's at the end of that same road. That Wright lady is lovely. She comes in quite often. Sophie loves the Slushies. Too bad about her daughter, isn't it? Such a shame to see a sweet girl like that in the prime of her life with such an injury. Must be so hard."

*

Janice had gotten up early and caught a ride to Moncton with Hank. He didn't have a delivery at the airport, but after making his other stops, he'd offered to drive her there.

"Nobody picks up hitchhikers anymore, and especially not an old Indian."

"We're Indigenous now, Hank. Keep up."

"We're still Indians to most folks, and that's among the nicest words they use. Where you headed? Flying somewhere?"

"I'm meeting a ride."

"Top secret, is it? I haven't seen that bastard in a while, and even if I did, I wouldn't tell Marshall Redmond anything about you."

"No, it's not top secret, but I didn't tell anyone where I was going, not even the kids. They don't need to know everything about their old mama. I'm going to a writing retreat. I got a book about my life started and I figured a fancy writing retreat might be just what I need to get it finished."

"You writing about *The Resi*? Jesus, girl, don't you think it's best to leave that hellhole alone, let it rot just like those sons of bitches have done by now? Rotting in hell is the best they could hope for. We've been gone from there a long time, girl. Don't you think it's best we forget it and not stir up all that shit?"

"I thought that for a long time, Hank. God knows we had that beat into us. Thought I could forget it all, but you know as well as I do what it takes to forget."

"Oh, sweetie. We were so hopeful those first few years. We were warriors, survivors, indestructible, we thought. We weren't going to give in and take the path we watched others go down. No, *we* were going to be different."

"It was no more your fault than mine, Hank. At least we got the kids from the years we had together. Maybe if we'd gotten help, talked about it or written it down, we could have done better. But we ain't dead yet. Writing my story is something *I've* got do."

"Try not to be too hard on me Jan. God knows I loved you. Still do, truth be told, but there's way too much water under that bridge."

"Don't you worry. Of all the villains in my past, you sure aren't one of them. I never would have survived if you hadn't been there. No regrets when it comes to you and me. Well, that's not true, of course, but we can't relive the past or get back the years we wasted. For the most part the kids forgive us, except Casey. She's forgiven you, but me not so much. Every bad thing was my fault, as far as she's concerned."

"She's just got some more growing up to do, Jan. She'll come around."

"Listen, I really appreciate the ride. I'm only going to this Wright Retreat for ten days, or as I like to call it, the 'White' retreat, as I figure I'll be the only Indigenous person there. I'll likely see you when I get back. Maybe even let you read my book. You can read, can't you?"

"Don't be such a smartass, girl. I could pick you up if you want. Maybe we could even go visit Casey."

"I'm sure your wife would not be too thrilled with us taking off together on a road trip to Ontario. I'll find a way home. Don't worry about me."

"I wish it was that easy. I always worry about you. It's in my blood, I guess."

❦

Kent Wright pulled the *Wright Retreat* sign out of his briefcase. He walked closer to the arrivals gate and held it up, as he'd seen them do in movies. From the corner of his eye he saw a woman stand and approach him.

"Kent Wright? I'm Janice, Janice Knockwood."

"Oh yes, Mrs. Knockwood. Hello."

"Janice will do just fine."

"The others should be coming through the gate momentarily. The arrivals board says the Toronto flight has landed. Have you been waiting long?"

"No, just got here myself. How many coming from Toronto?"

"Six. Three live in Toronto, one in Port Hope, one from Manitoba, and one coming from Alberta."

"Wow. Folks are coming from all over. I just live in the Miramichi, though I don't reckon you know where that is, since you're from Toronto, right?"

"Yes, that's right."

"How'd you end up running a retreat in New Brunswick?"

"My wife grew up in New Brunswick, a place called Grand Manan. It was her idea to move here."

"Right, your wife is Sylvia Drummond Wright. My apologies, I haven't read any of her books, but I've heard of her."

"Here they come. Let's move over a bit, get out of everyone's way and let them come to us."

One by one the writers noticed the sign and clustered around. Irma and Gavin were among the last passengers to file in. Introductions were quickly made and Janice led the way to the baggage area. Keeping the names straight was going to be a challenge, but Kent noticed Janice had mastered them all right away and had already fallen into leadership mode. That was fine with him. He had his strong points, but crowd control wasn't one of them.

Sylvia heard the car. She'd come to the shore right after breakfast and sat in the damp sand, extending her bare feet into the rippling water. Sophie had had a terrible night. Whatever had haunted her last night, it had taken a long time to settle her down. Sylvia had resorted to sitting Sophie in front of the television and putting Netflix on, hoping not to wake Nan. Turning the volume as low as Sophie would tolerate, Sylvia had stretched out on the couch and drifted back to sleep.

Sylvia turned her head to see a black Toyota pulling into the yard and watched as a man got out. She wasn't moving to go greet him. Dot or Marjorie would be out the door in a jiffy and show him to his room. Only eight more to arrive, and as far as she knew, Kent was picking them up in Moncton. She was going to enjoy the peace and quiet as long as she could. She was dreading the arrival of eight more strangers, but the real source of her dread was having Kent arrive. This time he was staying.

⁓⁓

Veronica Savage entered the Via station and made a beeline for the ladies' room. The bus had been a bit behind schedule, but she would still have time to walk to the Tim Horton's in the Avenir Centre and grab a bite to eat before Mr. Wright picked her up at two. He'd said another writer, a young man, would be coming from Halifax and was getting picked up at the station as well. She would look around the terminal to see if anyone looked like a writer, whatever a writer looked like. Maybe she'd wait until she came back from Tim Hortons. A young man would not want to accompany an old woman to lunch.

"Any chance you're a writer waiting here for Kent Wright?" Tyler Woodhouse asked as he held the door open.

Veronica had a large satchel slung over her shoulder and she was trying to manoeuvre two suitcases through the door.

"Yes, I am. Are you the young man from Halifax?"

"Yep. I'm Tyler. Just got here. Is there anywhere cheap to eat around here?"

"I'm walking to the Tim Horton's a couple of blocks away."

"Great. Why don't we get a locker and leave our bags? You look as if you have your hands full. How long are you staying?"

"I'm staying for the month-long retreat, and I never have been one to pack light. It sounds like a good idea to leave this stuff here. You young folks are so smart."

"Well, I'm not so sure about that. I'm staying for a month too, and all I brought was my backpack. Let's find the lockers. Hopefully we can cram everything into one."

⁓

Evelyn Ingalls ran the brush through her snow-white hair. Oh, how Paddy had loved her long wavy hair. "My black-haired beauty," he'd always called her, even when hints of grey crept in. She recalled the Christmas he'd given her the pearl hair clasp. Walking to her jewellery box, she picked up the clasp,

Susan White

running her fingers along the smooth stones before twisting her hair, fastening it into a bun.

Seventy-four years had passed since the early days of their love. She was not quite eighteen when she'd walked down the aisle of the North Head Reformed Baptist church, toward a young Paddy Ingalls, only one year older, waiting at the front of the church. Both had been so anxious to begin a life together.

Paddy had already started building their house on White Head Island, and they'd moved in the day after returning from a short honeymoon in Maine. There had been much left to do, and together they worked away at it for years. And for five years they waited for a child. When it finally happened, Evelyn had been sure she was imagining the symptoms, just wishing it to be true. But five months later she gave birth to a beautiful baby girl.

Valerie had been such a joy, which made the change in her personality at sixteen so difficult to take. Overnight she became moody, nasty, and constantly in a rage. Her main focus was how much she hated the island and her life. Two days before her seventeenth birthday, Valerie had stormed out the door directing a torrent of anger at her mother.

"I hate this fucking island. I'm not you, Mom. I'm not getting married like you did so I can be some guy's slave. I am going to live. Just because you never left this shitty place doesn't mean I want to stay here."

74

All Valerie's hurtful words were fired at her mother, her father having gone out on the boat hours before. Paddy never said it, but Evelyn always felt he thought she hadn't tried hard enough to keep Valerie from leaving or to convince her to come back home. He never understood the tension between them.

Evelyn had witnessed the same tension with Olivia and Sylvia for months before the big fight, and Kent had never been around for the battles. Daughters put a different face on for their fathers. All their anger and nastiness seems to be reserved for their mothers and comes as such a surprise to their fathers. It is the mother who carries the sorrow deep in her heart, managing the guilt, the regret, always questioning how they could have done better.

And on top of that tension, Sylvia had the sorrow of Sophie. Last night had been difficult, and the stress was obvious in Sylvia's eyes and voice this morning.

"I'm fine, Nan. The coffee's on. I'm going to the beach. Sophie is sound asleep and will probably stay asleep for a while."

Maybe with Kent coming, some of the pressure would be lifted from Sylvia's shoulders. Evelyn always tried to mind her business, but Kent needed to know just how hard this was for Sylvia. It would have been so much better if they'd just moved here and relaxed, letting the fresh air and beautiful surroundings fill up their hurting souls. But Kent had gotten the idea for this retreat thing he was doing. More pressure for Sylvia, as far as Evelyn could see. She might just have to say her piece.

—◦◦◦—

Abby Trenholme was the first one in the van, taking a window seat and belting her stuffed dog into the seat beside her.

"His name is Donavan. He's friendly."

Okay, thought Kent as he helped Grace Wanamaker step up into the van.

"Sorry I'm such a nuisance. You must be wondering what an old lady like me is doing on such an adventure."

"Oh, it's an adventure all right," said Irma Church. "What odds our ages? We're all here now and I'm a bit gut founded if I do say so."

"She means she's hungry," Gavin explained. "It might take a while before you have a clue what she's saying."

"Good thing you're here to translate for me, Mr. Church," Irma snapped. "Oh, wait, b'y, I wouldn't be here if you hadn't dragged me along."

"Don't figure it matters what any of our ages are," Janice added. "I'm no spring chicken myself. We'll all get along just fine, I expect."

"Donavan is seven, which is forty-nine in people years."

Kent hoped no one saw his eyes roll in the rear-view mirror. He was familiar with Sophie's obsession with her stuffies, but she had brain damage as an excuse.

"There will be a nice lunch when we get to the lodge," Kent interjected.

Veronica Savage and Tyler Woodhouse were standing

outside when Kent pulled up in front of the Via station. He jumped out and opened the sliding door. Tyler threw his bag in and reached to take the suitcases from Veronica.

"Wow, this one's really heavy," Tyler said, gesturing for Veronica to climb into the van.

Janice quickly introduced herself before asking them their names. She then introduced the others. After a bit of chatter things got quiet as the van left the downtown and got onto the highway. About twenty minutes later Kent took the exit off the highway and pulled onto the scenic secondary road.

"The countryside is beautiful," Kitty said. "I am so excited to see the ocean. I've lived in Manitoba all my life."

"Actually, the lodge isn't on the ocean," Veronica said. "It's the Northumberland Strait."

"That's good enough for me. Can you swim in it?"

"Sure," Kent answered. "It's cold, I've been told, but my wife swims in it. She grew up on the Bay of Fundy, so she is used to swimming in freezing cold water."

"I thought your wife might have come with you to pick us up," Gavin said. "I suppose she's busy back at the lodge. I must tell you, I am so excited to meet her."

"So the flight was good, was it?" Kent asked not directing his question at anyone in particular.

"Oh my God," Irma said. "Don't get me started."

"Not a fan of flying?" Jonathan asked. "I thought it was pretty uneventful, actually. I could tell you some horror stories."

"Please don't," Gavin said. "I'll be lucky to get her on a plane again when we have to go home."

"How long are you all staying?" Grace asked.

"Veronica, Tyler, and Grace are doing the one-month retreat," Kent answered. "Gavin, Kitty, and Abby are here for two weeks, as well as Benson and Darcy, who are already at the lodge. And Jonathan and Janice are with us for ten days."

"We're the cheap ones," Jonathan joked, turning to Janice.

"Or the fastest writers," Janice replied.

"Well, what matters is that we are all together now," Grace said. "I think it will be real nice to get to know you all."

Kent zoned out the chatter paying close attention to the landmarks. He was still not familiar with this drive and didn't want to embarrass himself by getting the van full of excited writers lost.

⌇

Sylvia saw the van turn the corner just as she got to the back door. She'd go inside until everyone got out and went into the lodge, but she'd be damned if she was going to hide away avoiding them. This was her home, her property, and somehow she would find a way to tolerate this whole retreat shit.

⌇

"This soup is amazing," Grace said. "And your biscuits are as light as feathers. Biscuits were something I never mastered."

"Oh, thank you," Dot replied. "The key is not to handle them too much. I figured you people would have an appetite. I do like to feed folks with an appetite."

"An appetite's never been my problem," Kitty said. "What a beautiful view. Anyone want to go for a walk after lunch? I assume it's all right if we walk along the beach."

"Yes, of course," answered Kent. "Our property goes a fair way along the shore, but I understand there is public access a distance in from the water anyway. There are a couple of trails in through the woods on the property too."

"I've already done a bit of exploring," Darcy said. "I think I'll do some writing this afternoon. There's a perfect little nook upstairs. Oh, and the wifi password is wright88. It seems the strongest in the sitting area upstairs."

"I suppose that sort of thing matters to you young folk," Gavin said. "I do all my writing on a portable Olivetti Underwood."

"What about research? I'd be lost without Google," Jonathan said.

"I use the good old public library," Gavin said. "I think I've got all the research done for the novel I'm working on. Good research and a pretty good memory is what I rely on."

"I'd love to go for a walk with you, Kitty," Veronica said. "What about you, Irma?"

"Sounds great to me. Not sure exactly how I'm going to put my time in. I did bring my crossword books, and I see there are some puzzles over there on the shelf."

"My mother-in-law loves puzzles," Kent said. "She'd love to come in and do some with you."

"I thought maybe your wife would have had lunch with us." Gavin said.

"Our daughter Sophie gets a bit overwhelmed in crowds, so I'm sure she fed her in our apartment out back. Sylvia will probably be in for supper. I know she's anxious to meet you all."

"Oh, that was your wife I met this morning?" Darcy asked. "I asked her if she was one of the writers. How embarrassing."

"She's a bit shy." Kent said. "You know how writers can be."

~~~

Dot knocked on the screen door before entering even though she could see Sylvia sitting at the table. "I brought you some biscuits."

"You don't need to worry about us. Sophie loves the pie, though. She's already eaten over half of it."

"Listen, I know having all these folks around isn't going to be easy on you."

"What makes you think that?"

"I'm not blind or stupid. Your husband seems like the one fired up about all this. I'm not getting the same vibe from you."

"Let's just say none of this writing retreat stuff was my idea. But when Kent Wright gets an idea, there's not much point opposing it."

"What's your plan?"

"What do you mean?"

"You know they came because of you."

"Yeah."

"So what's your plan?"

"I don't have one. I'm not staying holed up in here avoiding them, so I guess I will have to talk to them."

"Well, they seem like a nice bunch of folks. Interesting bunch actually. One of the young women has a stuffed dog. I had to give him a bowl of water. Quite the mix, really, but just folks trying to find their way like the rest of us. I am cooking a feast tonight. Roast beef, gravy, lots of vegetables, and Yorkshire pudding."

"Roast beef, eh? Well, I should at least meet them, I guess."

"My supper will be worth coming over for, if nothing else."

"Okay, Dot. I'll come for supper."

⟿⟾

Sylvia turned from the sink when she heard the screen door opening, thinking it was Dot coming back in. Kent walked up and reached out to hug her.

Sylvia pulled back. "Hi. Sophie is inside. She will be so excited to see you. I didn't tell her you were here."

"Is she the only one excited to see me? Sorry I didn't come in sooner. I had to settle everyone in, and Dorothy had lunch ready. It would have been rude not to sit and have lunch with them."

"Is that a dig at me?"

"No, I made your apologies. I realize Sophie requires your attention. Where's Evelyn?"

"She is lying down."

"You'll join us for supper, won't you? Evelyn could stay with Sophie."

"You're starting to shit yourself now, aren't you? You've got all these people here and they think they're getting me as part of the package."

"Can you at least come meet them?"

"Oh, relax. I'm coming to supper and I will be civil. I won't tell them they have been brought here on completely false pretenses. I won't drop that bombshell on the first night. And you might consider giving Dot a raise," Sylvia said, picking up a biscuit and starting to butter it.

<hr>

Veronica shut her bedroom door, taking several deep breaths to quell the emotion. Blinking her eyes, she attempted to dissipate the tears welling up. She knew how to combat the urge to give in to emotion. She'd learned that handy skill early on. A tuberculosis hospital ward did not offer much privacy, and a little girl was expected to be quiet. No outbursts of emotion or temper tantrums were tolerated. She was told to be strong and good if she ever wanted to see her sick mother again.

Kitty and Irma were still walking along the shore when Veronica had climbed the stairs from the beach and headed across the open field toward a path into the woods. The emotion hit her as she walked further in, thinking perhaps she could keep walking, find a spot to sit, and let the tears come. Instead she cut through a thick stand of birch trees and ran to the lodge, oblivious to whether there was anyone on the veranda or in the great room or kitchen.

Veronica lifted the smaller suitcase to the bed and unzipped it. Journals; all sizes, several plain ones in various colours, lots with inspirational quotes, some with puppies, sunflowers, roses, landscape scenes, mockup novel covers, some leather with embossed designs, and lots of black-and-white composition books. She spread each one out on the bed. Thirty-three journals, just a fraction of her collection, but a suitcase full, a heavy suitcase full.

Veronica picked up a pink journal, the embossed word WRITE in gold lettering. She clutched it to her chest and sat on the wingback chair in the corner of the room. She remembered buying each journal. Not the exact date or store, but with each purchase she remembered the feeling of hope, of optimism and possibility. Each journal had been bought with the belief it would be the one she'd fill with the words waiting to be written.

She released her hold on the journal and opened the front cover. Inside a geometric design of gold on a white background, calligraphy lettering read *This book belongs to*. Veronica had written her full name. She had written the date she purchased the journal, just as she had in all the other journals. Opening to the first lined page, the tears began to flow.

A pristine page, the fine blue lines unwritten upon. This pink journal was empty, as were all the other journals spread out on the bed. A collection of unused journals, each one a volume of nothing, of foolish dreaming and naive believing that Veronica Savage would ever release the deep pain she pushed down every day.

But she had come to this place. She had packed each journal and her collection of fountain pens believing this was where she needed to be to write the first word. She had to believe that this was where the first word would be written and that first word would break open the dam to the deluge that would follow.

⌒⌒⌒

Sylvia was the last one to the table. The smells hit her as she opened the front door, and she thought back to the cold day she'd entered this building for the first time. So much had happened since then, and she felt a flicker of pride in the fact that she had put all of it into motion by driving here that January day, even if the future she'd imagined had been tampered with, adjusted and changed into what met her eyes as she walked through the great room to the dining table where the retreat participants were seated.

Kent rose and welcomed Sylvia to the table. Dot set the platter of roast beef in front of her. The woman to her right passed her a bowl of steaming mashed potatoes. The man directly across the table introduced himself.

"Gavin Church. I'm a big fan. I've read all your books. I was rooting for you to be shortlisted. Thought your book was better than the winner. I sometimes wonder what those judges are thinking. I've bought every Giller book, and most of them I can't even get through."

"Well, thank you."

"Here's the gravy. I'm Gavin's wife, Irma. I'm stunned about all that writing stuff. I do like that Jodi Picoult though."

"I'm Grace. Your lodge is lovely. I had a short nap after the delicious lunch Dot fed us, but I've been sitting on the front veranda just staring at the sea since I got up. Something about water, isn't there? I live by a lake, but there's something about the sea. And such a beautiful day."

"How about we go around the table and everyone can introduce themselves to Sylvia," Kent suggested. "I'm not great with names and could use the reminder myself. Maybe some of you could too. Janice, we'll start with you."

"Janice Knockwood. You can call me Jan."

"Jonathan Cameron."

"Benson Grant. I write under the name Benson Cormier. But just Benson is fine."

"Darcy Lawson. I am so sorry I didn't recognize you this morning."

"That's okay," Sylvia replied.

"Kitty Forsythe. Yeah, that's my real name."

"Tyler Woodhouse."

"Abby Trenholme. And this is Donavan. He's too big to set

on the table, but he behaves himself on my knee. I don't let him beg at the table."

"I'm Veronica," said the woman who had passed the potatoes. "Very nice to meet you, Ms. Drummond Wright."

"Sylvia, please."

"You live in an apartment out back, right?" Veronica asked.

"Yes. My grandmother, Evelyn, and daughter Sophie live there too. Sophie doesn't come outside much, but my grandmother loves meeting new people."

"Kent says Evelyn loves puzzles," Irma said. "I dumped a big one out earlier. Maybe she can come help me. I only found a few pieces for the bottom edge so far."

"She would love that. I'll send her in after supper."

<center>~~~⚸~~~</center>

Irma hopped up to help Dot clear the table. "You may think by the end that I've more lip than a coal bucket, but I don't sit by getting waited on. While I'm here I mean to help out, if for no other reason than to save my sanity. Won't go bossin' ya or nothing, but hope you'll let me help out."

"For sure, Irma," Dot said. "I'd love the company, truth be told. And you know what they say about many hands."

"Make light work," Sylvia interjected. "My papa always said, no one can whistle a symphony. It takes a whole orchestra to play it."

"I don't whistle, and lord thundering, you don't want me singing," Irma chuckled. "But I can damn sure dry a dish."

"We don't have to wash many dishes with this dishwasher," Dot said.

"Some nice piece of stuff, this kitchen, that's for sure," Irma said before lowering her voice to a whisper. "Now don't that one with the dog appear a bit stunned?"

Benson joined Tyler and Jonathan, who were sitting out on the veranda, a crimson tinge in the sky a precursor of the sunset to come. "I love this time of the day. Most of the murders in my work happen just as the sun is going down."

"Should we be nervous?" Tyler asked.

"I got a lot of writing done this afternoon," Benson said. "Just happened I killed someone off right before supper."

"Did you shoot them or stab them or was poison involved?" asked Jonathan.

"Strangled, actually. What do you guys write?"

"People die in my books too," Tyler answered. "But usually in large, bloody battles, or as old men on their deathbeds."

"I write kids' books about poop and pee," Jonathan said. "A selective audience, and my publisher would veto any killing if I threw it in the storyline. I'm writing something a bit more mature while I'm here though. The great Canadian novel, perhaps."

"Is there such a thing?" Gavin asked, coming out the screen door.

Chapter Six

Rain beating on the window woke Jonathan up. He reluctantly left the warmth and comfort of the bed and crossed the hall to take a shower. No imposition, really, although an en-suite room would have afforded him more privacy. But sharing a bathroom was something he was used to.

The house on Bloor Street had one small bathroom, and with seven kids he'd been lucky to get a trickle of hot water by the time his turn came. A trickle of water that could quickly disappear if the electric bill was unpaid. Feast or famine, as unpredictable as the rest of it. A childhood filled with unpredictability and disappointment.

Squeezing the shampoo into his hand, he traced the line of the scar. Mom had rushed to his side, wrapping the deep gash and carrying him next door. She held him tightly in the back seat of Mr. Ferguson's car as he drove them to Victoria General. Jonathan hadn't blinked, watching the needle penetrate the flesh as the long piece of nylon closed the wound.

Afterward he'd fallen asleep in his mother's arms. Her rocking and tender voice quieting his fear and lessening the pain. Mom was always there, fixing the shit his father left in his drunken wake. He'd never blamed Mom, unlike Bev.

"Fuck, Jonathan. Fart, poop, and pee jokes don't change any of this shit. And God forbid we blame anything on Mom. Saint Delores can do no wrong in her baby boy's eyes. Christ, she could have left the old bastard long ago and we wouldn't have been any worse off."

⌘

Waking up before sunrise, Kitty had tied her unruly hair into a tight ponytail, dressed quickly, and gone downstairs. Stepping out onto the covered veranda, she stood watching the sheets of rain, a grey veil over the vast horizon of water and sky. Even with the dawning light, it remained dark and grey but the air was warm and the quiet peacefulness so amazing.

She'd set her laptop down on the large pine coffee table in the great room before stepping outside. She would write in this quiet, early morning. She would pretend she was alone here, this place, her sanctuary; her own place. Would she conjure a husband, a couple of kids, or was her imaginary life one of solitude? Perhaps her success as a bestselling author afforded her this log building as a summer home. Perhaps it was here she wrote the novel which had been turned into a Hollywood movie or popular Netflix series.

This was her fantasy, and she could embellish it any way she chose to. She would be thin, of course; not dangerously thin but shapely and gorgeous. She would come down every morning in a robe and walk down the stairs to the shore. She would drop her floral robe in the sand and walk naked into the water. She would plunge into the deeper water and swim with long strokes far out, where she would float on her back allowing the waves to embrace her.

The crunch of tires on the gravel driveway interrupted Kitty's imaginings.

"Good morning, Dot."

"You're up bright and early, Kitty."

"Do you swim?"

"I can swim, but can't remember the last time I did."

"Have you ever swum here?"

"Not right here, but I've swum in the strait, if that's what you mean. We always swam at Cooper's Point when we were kids."

"Is it cold?"

"Yeah, I guess it's colder than a river or lake, but you get used to it real quick. Are you going in?"

"No, not right now, anyway. I'm a bit of a chicken. Do you need any help?"

"No. I just have this basket of hot muffins. I better get inside and start cooking breakfast. The others will be up before I know it."

"I'm just going to sit in the corner of the great room and do some writing."

"I'll put the coffee on right away."

*

Darcy could smell the coffee as she stepped out into the hall. She felt some relief seeing no one else had settled themselves into her spot. She'd parked herself there right after supper last night and left behind her dictionary and thesaurus, hoping to indicate her intention to work there again today. "Book bags don't hold places" was the silly chant they'd used in elementary school when she'd done her practise teaching in a grade two classroom. High school kids used other indicators to mark their territory.

It was a Windsor chair, although she wasn't sure how she knew that; a Windsor chair with arms and a soft cushion on the seat. It had been against the wall, but she'd pulled it up to the rectangular pine table that was just the right size for her laptop and the books and papers she always laid out when she started working. The angle allowed her to see out the large arched window and the view last night had been stunning. Moonlight had shimmered across the dark, still water, and the night sky had been alive with starlight. As she worked she'd watched the cloud cover spread across the sky.

That cloud cover brought this morning's heavy rain and grey sky. Not much light was coming in the large window. She would need to bring the lamp over from the small table in the corner to illuminate her work station. She would set everything up before going downstairs for coffee, just in case someone else saw the prime writing spot and claimed it for the day.

❦

Sylvia picked up a magazine and absently leafed through it. Sophie had been restless on for the drive to Moncton and had refused to get out of the car when they arrived at the hospital. Not liking the outdoors much anyway, Sophie's determination to stay in the car was compounded by the pouring rain. What a difference from the girl who couldn't get enough of everything connected with outdoor adventure. This of course was just one of the differences between the before and after Sophie.

Sylvia rarely let herself go to the what ifs—what if the girls had chosen a different vacation, heading south to the sun and sand instead of east to the cold and snow. What if Kent had never encouraged skiing lessons? What if Sophie had been pregnant when she thought she was that January? If that whole drama hadn't caused Sophie and Mark to break up, maybe Sophie would have stayed home with Mark and Olivia would have gone on the ski trip alone. What if Sophie had died on that hill?

That was the huge *what if* that Sylvia seldom allowed herself to think about. The idea that it would have been better for Sophie or easier for her was unthinkable. What kind of selfish mother would wish for the death of her daughter? Sophie was happy in her own way. She smiled, laughed a lot, and had more good days than bad. She gave hugs freely and never held a grudge. Most upsets were forgotten quickly. She was different from before, but her kind, loving heart was still beating.

Sylvia had convinced Sophie to get out of the car with the promise of buying her the stuffed rainbow-coloured unicorn she'd spotted in the gift shop on her last trip to the hospital.

It was funny how Sophie could remember that sort of thing. Running from the parking lot to the hospital door, Sophie shouted the word *unicorn* repeatedly, which probably seemed strange to people hearing her but was a very welcome sound to Sylvia.

Sophie's language was so limited. She said *Mom, Dad, Nan, drink, no, done* and a few other words. She could sometimes repeat words, and once in a while completely surprised them with a random string of words. None of it was predictable. Right from the beginning, several doctors gave completely different prognoses. One said Sophie would never function past a catatonic state. One overly optimistic doctor had predicted a complete recovery. And there had been several doctors with predictions somewhere between the two extremes.

Sylvia had given up taking much stock in what any of them said. She relied on the OT and speech therapy professionals, the kindness and understanding of the people who patiently worked with Sophie and gave Sylvia the encouragement to simply take one day, one hour at a time. She was thankful for the special moments she had with Sophie and didn't let herself think too much of the what ifs and the what could have beens.

⁓

Only Kitty and Dot were downstairs when Jonathan grabbed two muffins and a cup of coffee and headed back up to his room. He had wasted yesterday. He'd gotten caught up in the social aspect, allowed himself to sit outside with some of the others after supper, and hadn't gone upstairs until after midnight. He wasn't here to make friends. This was not a vacation. He came here to write. He would meet with the others at suppertime, but the rest of the meals he would take in his room, and he would keep focused on what he'd come to do.

A shitty first draft was his goal. He would do the revising and structuring later, but these days were for the slogging out, page after page. Sitting around gabbing was not going to get in the way of that. He opened his laptop and clicked on the file. Chapter seven. "Let's get at it," Jonathan said aloud and began his hunt-and-peck typing.

<hr />

Dot poured the pancake batter onto the hot griddle. Bacon sizzled in the pan and the water bubbled in the pot of boiled eggs. The table was set, and Gavin and Irma had already taken their seats. Breakfast required juggling to ensure everything was hot when served at the best of times, but having eleven people on their own morning schedule made it even more of a challenge. She would do her best to accommodate the group, who seemed to be taking their good old time coming for breakfast.

"I'd just tell this crowd it's not a restaurant you're running here," Irma said. "My mother fed nine of us every morning, and if your arse wasn't on the chair when she flopped your egg in front of ya, you were shit out of luck. Someone else would take your breakfast as fast as look at 'er. Way I figure it, it's not every day Morris kills a cow. If someone's willing to put my breakfast on the table, I'll damn well sit down and eat it."

"Well, everyone's got their own morning routines," Dot replied.

"Too damn bad. Tell them breakfast is served at eight thirty sharp, and if they want it they better get their sorry arses to the table."

Benson, Tyler, Janice, and Veronica entered the room just in time to hear Irma's last words.

"My sorry arse is here," Benson said.

"I slept so soundly last night," Veronica said. "Woke up and couldn't believe it was almost eight thirty. Must be the fresh air."

"I had to wait for the shower, Tyler said. "Has Jonathan been down yet?"

"He came and grabbed a muffin and some coffee," answered Dot. "Says he's staying in his room all day and we won't see him until suppertime."

"And Darcy's upstairs working," Kitty said as she sat down at the table. "Some of us have more discipline than others, I guess. I don't miss a meal, though, as you can plainly see."

"I heard you up bright and early," Grace said as she sat down.

"Maybe we should all just be responsible for getting our own breakfast instead of you trying to figure it all out, Dot," Janice suggested.

"That's what I was saying," Irma added.

"In your roundabout Newfoundlander way," Gavin said.

"Only way I've got," Irma snapped.

Kent sat down at the table, greeting each person by name and only making one error. "Oh, sorry, Tyler. For some reason I get you and Jonathan mixed up."

"Yeah, young white men all look alike," Tyler said.

"I realize you all have different morning routines," Kent said, "but Dot will make a full breakfast every day. She'll have it ready for eight thirty, and you can make up your mind about joining us. There are lots of snacks available as well and you are more than welcome to help yourself whenever you get hungry. Your meals are part of your retreat, and I do not want anyone going hungry."

Dot set the platter of blueberry pancakes in the centre of the table. "Nobody goes hungry in my kitchen, Mr. Kent, and if you get any complaints from folks about not getting something they paid for at this retreat, it won't be the food, if I have anything to do with it."

Abby walked up to the table, four stuffed dogs clutched in her arms.

"It's raining cats and dogs," Tyler joked as he stood to pull out a chair for Abby.

"It might be the old teacher in me coming out, but how about we all get together later this morning for an impromptu writing workshop and tell each other what we're working on?" Benson said. "I don't mind reading a bit of my work and you guys might like to do the same. Our retreat is called Writers Helping Writers, is it not?"

"Actually the two-week is called Strength in Writers," Kent replied. "I apologize for Sylvia not being more involved yet. Our daughter has a bug of some kind, so Sylvia is pretty busy looking after her right now. She will be around more when Sophie is feeling better. She's really anxious to meet with Tyler, Veronica, and Grace to start your mentorship. She'll have a handout for the two-week participants soon with goal-setting and time-management tips. I was thinking we could have our first reading tonight, which I'm sure Sylvia will attend. I'll put out a sign-up sheet. Let's have five readers tonight."

Dot continued to work, her back to the table, not offering anything to the conversation she was overhearing. Her lack of interaction was not keeping her from responding in her head though.

That Benson fella is so full of himself he's likely to implode. Grace is sweet but she looks as if she might nod off at any time. Kent is doing some serious bullshitting, covering his butt big time. He sounds so convincing you'd think he almost believed what he was saying. Sophie sick, my ass. He's some piece of work.

"I won't read tonight," Veronica said. "And I'm sorry I don't have anything ready for Sylvia yet. I will get my sample to her as soon as I can, and I do look forward to her input. I'll sit in on your session this morning, Benson. I probably won't add much, but I look forward to learning from the rest of you."

"I'm not ready to read anything yet either," Janice stated.

"I could use some feedback on my work for sure," Tyler said. "I only have the first chapter written, but I'm sure you'll indulge me. I'll give you a summary of where I think it's going."

"Funny how it never quite goes the way you think it's going to. At least, my work never does," Gavin said.

"I outline chapter by chapter and stay right on track," Benson added. "Crime genre follows a formula."

"I suppose the horror genre does too," Grace said, "but I still get surprised."

"That's the fun of it," Gavin said. "I write historical fiction and have to be accurate, but I never know exactly where my story is heading. I have a plan, but it changes sometimes."

"That's what Sylvia always says," Kent said.

Oh please. He uses her name to sell this retreat and thinks dropping her name enough will do the trick. Good luck with that, buddy.

⁓

Irma ran off the front veranda, around the building, and up the stairs to the back apartment, trying to dodge raindrops. She knocked and opened the door, sticking her head in to get out from under the dripping water overhead.

"Anybody home?"

"Yes, come on in," Evelyn said.

"That's a mausy ol' day out there," Irma said. "I'm Irma."

"If mausy means raining hard, you're happy right. We could use the rain, though, I figure. I'm Evelyn Ingalls, Sylvia's grandmother. What are all the writers doing today? Staying inside, I suppose."

"Oh yeah, they're all wrapped up talking about writing. Don't interest me in the least. Figured I'd venture back here and make my introductions."

"I'm glad you did. I've been meaning to go in and say hello to everyone myself. Sylvia said it was a nice supper last night. She's not home; she took Sophie in to Moncton for her appointment this morning."

"Yeah, supper was great. Dot's a good cook and I must say I don't mind having someone cooking for me. Don't think I need a month of it, though."

"Oh you're one of the one-month folks."

"Signed up for two weeks, but Gavin says we might stay for the month. Doesn't appear I have much to say about it. No point in being biniky about it, though, I suppose."

"You're from Newfoundland, right?"

"How'd you come to that?" Irma laughed.

"I'm a Grand Manan-er, and we're said to have our own way of talkin' too. Makes us who we are, I figure. And you ended up in Toronto too, I hear."

"Spot on, buddy, and I means buddy in a good way. Showed up there when I was just a girl and never saw no reason to leave."

"You don't have any family still in Newfoundland?"

"Well, that's a sorrowful story for another day."

"How about a cup of tea?"

"That would be right nice."

<hr>

Darcy came downstairs for her second cup of coffee and politely declined the invitation to join the group at the table. "I'm going to keep working upstairs. I hope no one minds me hogging the spot up there. I kind of laid claim to it and I have all my stuff spread out. I find for me being out there is better than closing myself up in my room. If I'm in my room I feel like I'm missing something. Up there I can see the water, and there's natural light, although this morning it's kind of dark, and up there I can hear you all talking but still get some writing done."

"That's fine," Kitty said. "I'm glad it works for you. I never could write with other people around, and I'm surprised I got as much done as I did sitting down here before breakfast. It does really help to be with a group of people who get it. I think it's great we can decide what works for us and there is not a lot of scheduled stuff. Kent put out a signup sheet for the reading tonight. I will read tonight and I'll choose something not too X-rated. I write lesbian romance novels, by the way. Not a lesbian bone in my body, excuse the pun, but I write pretty hot girl-on-girl stuff."

"I'll read tonight," Gavin said. "And I'll stay for this workshop for a bit, but I've got a scene calling to me. Dreamt about it last night. Any of the rest of you have dreams about your writing?"

"Dreams are my best entertainment these days," Grace added. "Still see my husband Vincent most nights, and he's been gone for twenty-two years."

"Well, let's get started then," Benson instructed. "I have a handout about my strategy for creating a story arc, and I'll tell you how I develop a character."

✦

Kent opened the car door, greeting his daughter. "Hi, Sophie girl."

Sylvia walked around the car, opening an umbrella and passing it to Kent. "Tell Sophie her unicorn won't get wet if she gets out quickly and stays under the umbrella."

"Umbrella, umbrella," Sophie chanted.

"How was her appointment?" Kent asked, holding open the door for Sylvia and Sophie while closing up the umbrella.

"It was fine."

"Some of the group are having a writing workshop session. They would love it if you stopped by and offered something."

"I'm tired, Kent. I was up at six and got our daughter to an eight o'clock appointment after practically wrestling her out to the car and into the hospital. I haven't even eaten anything. And Sophie needs her medication, but of course you have no idea how hard it is to get it into her. Let me at least take my jacket off and get some coffee before you start whining to me about what the damn authors need."

"I'll make a new pot, Sylvie," Evelyn said as she entered the kitchen. "We've got company. Irma came over to introduce herself."

Sylvia walked into the living room. Irma was sitting on the couch holding the unicorn.

"She's gone to get her other friends to show me."

"She said that?"

"Yeah, pretty sure that's what she said. She told me to look after this one."

"Wow, I'm impressed. She doesn't usually open up to new people."

"I don't always either. Not to all those dammed authors, for sure."

"Oh, you heard me? Sorry."

"Don't be sorry, love. I'd have to be some stunned to think it's the authors you're angry with. Some husbands are stunned, no doubt about that. Mine has dragged me here, but I think folks like Evelyn and Dot are going to make it bearable. And your sweet Sophie, too."

⁓⁓

Veronica felt a headache coming on as she headed up to her room. The room was lovely. The yellow walls and the bright colours on the patchwork quilt gave the space a cheery, warm feeling. The good-sized bed, wingback chair, and roll-top desk fit nicely. The full bath had a clawfoot tub as well as a corner shower stall. The whole upstairs was so nice. So different from what it had been before the renovations.

She had heard Kent talking last night about the condition the log building had been in when Sylvia bought it. The upstairs had been broken up into several small rooms, each one with two sets of bunk beds separated only by a narrow path between them. Small barred windows set high on one wall were the only light.

Veronica reached into her cosmetic bag to the pharmaceutical selection she always carried with her. A sinus headache, no doubt brought on by the barometric pressure. Or a stress headache brought on by the drone of Benson Grant's self-adoration. Or maybe the dull headache was a result of the effort she put into pretending she was a writer. It was excruciating to be here. What had made her think she could just show up and confront what she'd been hiding from for so long?

~⁓⚬⁓~

Janice had revised her opening page more times than she could count. Coming to her room, she brought up her manuscript on her tablet and imagined herself standing in the great room reading the first page aloud. After rereading it several times, she turned her tablet off and headed outside. The rain was steady but warm as she walked along the beach, her bare feet digging into the wet sand.

What had made her think she would ever be able to read out loud to this group? She hadn't even been able to put into words what she was working on when Benson had asked the question to everyone around the table. Grace had outlined a concise description of a bloodcurdling cat-and-mouse game set in a cabin by a lake. Tyler explained the world-building he was focusing on, and despite the strange names and convoluted storyline, it sounded intriguing. Gavin had read a prologue, but she'd stopped listening three or four words in. Kitty had told them how successful her lesbian romance writing was and said her plan during the retreat was to finish her seventh book in the series, a book she'd already been given an advance for.

Veronica passed and Janice felt the tension in her words. She sensed Veronica's work held raw pain and she knew how hard that was to manage in her own writing. Lee said to just let it rip. Write it as you feel it and let the chips fall where they may. Speak your own truth and the hell with everything else, he'd told her over and over again.

But what was the truth? Had time and misery distorted the truth? Had she even known what was true at the start of it all? How could she even believe the truth of it when she had been brainwashed right from the beginning to erase everything she knew to be true? Her own name, her language, the people she loved, and the pride she felt in being who she was. She was just six years old when it had been stripped from her in every possible way. How was she to return to that little girl and speak the truth of what had happened?

And even if she could, would English words explain it? How could that little girl stand with her head up and read those words without the deep fear of being struck down and punished, erased and eradicated again as if the wet, urine-soaked sheets were still draped over her cold, trembling, terrified body?

"What is it you are working on and what do you hope to accomplish while you are here?" Benson Grant had asked.

Janice stood in the pouring rain. She stared in at the light she could see through the great-room window and felt the dripping hair on her face. She squished her bare feet deeper into the sand. Her drenched T-shirt and pants clung to her body. She allowed the gasps to come and the sobbing to take over. She would dispel the hurt while she was here and she would find a way to give a brave voice to that scared, silent little girl. This place would wash her and the rest be damned.

Chapter Seven

The early morning light beamed through the window. Irma shielded her eyes from the sunlight. She reached her arm over and found the space beside her in the bed empty. Sitting up a bit, she noticed the closet door open and Gavin's shoes gone. It had been a restless night; a night of jumbled dreams, with each one taking her to the red house with the yellow door in Petty Harbour.

There was seldom a warning for the nights that brought such misery. She could go months without the kind of night she'd just had. It was as if her brain were like her mother's old pressure cooker. Mother always warned them to stay clear when she filled the pot with the ingredients for the Jiggs dinner, locked the lid down, and waited for the temperature to rise. Irma kept her lid locked just as tight, but some nights the pressure built and the lid blew off.

The exhaustion she felt the morning after such nights was debilitating. She often stayed in bed for hours sleeping it off and getting her sorrows put back carefully where she stored them. Gavin used to hold her and help with the filing. He would offer loving words and encouragement. But he had long ago given that up, offering at best a dismissive, "You are fine,

Irma. Why you get yourself in such a state is beyond me. It's been forty-two years, for God's sake."

In the first years they were together he would hold her as she gasped for breath feeling as if her chest would collapse. "Just breathe, sweetheart."

Irma never woke Gavin anymore. Now she would cry quietly, keeping her shaking at bay as long as she could. If she happened to call out in her confusion, claiming she couldn't breathe, Gavin would roll over angrily and state that she was breathing or she'd be dead. If the emotion overwhelmed her she would leave the room and go to the spare bed until the shaking and terror subsided.

Last night she'd kept it quiet. The tears flowed, but she choked back the sobs and muffled her panic. But she felt the exhaustion this morning and was considering going back to sleep. Gloria Louise would be older than Sophie. Sweet Sophie had brought out an armful of her stuffed animals, and as Irma cuddled each one she thought of her baby daughter and played in her mind each year she never had.

"Are you coming down for breakfast?" Gavin said, poking his head in the bedroom door.

⚊⚊⚊

"Did you get lots of writing done yesterday, Jonathan?" Tyler asked.

"I did, actually. I figured this morning I'd come to break-fast then hide away again and see what happens. I'm at kind of a crossroads, after a bit of a glitch so to speak."

"I suppose the ten-day people feel more pressure to get writing done," Benson said. "Two weeks seemed perfect to me, but I get lots of writing time anyway. But you guys work, right?"

"Unemployed right now," Tyler replied. "Mooching off my sister and her husband and getting a bit of unemployment, but I'll need to find something soon. This month is kind of my last hurrah before I step up and get a decent job."

"I'm a transit operator for the TTC, which means night shifts, split shifts, overtime, and not a whole lot of writing time," Jonathan said. "You're living the dream, Benson."

"Oh yeah, the dream. Don't wish your life away, guys. Worked for thirty-five years. Can't believe how fast it went by. You blink and it's gone."

"That's the truth," Grace said. "I'll be eighty next month."

Irma sat down between Gavin and Veronica. "Saved my place, I see. I'm a bit slow getting around this morning. Sorry, Dot."

"Never you mind," Dot replied. "Nobody took your egg. I made a breakfast casserole this morning and there's plenty of it. Would you like a cinnamon bun?"

"Those cinnamon buns are amazing," Kitty said.

"I slept like a log again last night," Veronica said. "I'm telling you there is something about the salt air."

"I thought maybe my reading put folks to sleep last night. I might have gotten a little carried away," Benson said. "It's so hard to narrow down what to read. Once you get started you just want to keep reading."

"Thought we'd have five more readers tonight," Kent said. "Pretty sure Sylvia is going to join us."

"Is Sophie feeling better?" Dot asked.

"I'm going for a swim today," Veronica stated.

"Won't it be awful cold?" Grace asked.

"Worth it once you get in," Veronica replied.

"Sylvia swims almost every day," Kent said. "You ladies should ask her if she'd like to join you."

"Let's have a good old swimming party," Irma said. "Don't suppose you birds would go skinny dipping."

"What kind of retreat is this?" laughed Kitty.

"I might just march right into the water as naked as the Good Lord made me," Janice stated.

～⁂～

Sylvia reached for the lamp on the bedside table. She'd slept in and with the blinds drawn the room was still dark. A dream had woken her in the middle of the night, and she woke sobbing. It had taken her a while to calm down and get back to sleep. The dream had faded, but her thoughts were still on the March day that had changed everything.

Olivia had been right behind Sophie, their constant rivalry and competitive natures likely the motivator to tackle the challenging hill that day. Both were experienced skiers and very confident in their abilities. They'd come with a group of friends to the Quebec ski hill, and they'd never skied those slopes before.

Olivia said she'd veered to avoid her sister, thinking the fall a harmless one, letting out a holler of triumph. But her feelings of victory and superiority quickly vanished when as she reached the bottom and saw the rescue team rushing up the hill. Her panic hit when an unconscious Sophie was brought down on the stretcher.

"It's Sophie." When Sylvia picked up the phone and heard Olivia's trembling voice she was sure her daughter was dead. She passed the phone to Kent. Nan had rushed across the room and caught her before she fell to the floor. The dream had been a mixed-up nightmare including Papa's *Sylvie D*, her yellow cat, Micah, that Papa gave her on her tenth birthday, the woman behind the counter at the Irving station, and rolling waves hitting the shore. A great big jumble, but the sobbing came when the dream took her to the first moments standing beside Sophie's hospital bedside.

They had taken the first available flight to Quebec City and then a cab to Saint Francois. They were not prepared for what they saw walking into Sophie's room. Her head was wrapped, her face swollen and bruised. Several tubes connected her to loud machines. It looked like a scene from a nightmare. Their beautiful girl had been unrecognizable.

"Where's Kent sleeping?"

"What?" Sylvia answered.

"I came out for a glass of water last night and he was asleep on the couch."

"He's fallen asleep on the couch for years, Nan. Nothing new about that."

"He had a pillow and blankets. He is sleeping on the couch."

"Well, did you really think things would be all lovey dovey when he got here? And you have to realize I bought this place to get away from him."

"I knew you two were having a rough patch, but what couple doesn't?"

"You and Papa, for one."

"Do you really think we never had our troubles?"

"You never considered leaving him, did you?"

"My options were pretty limited. I never worked a day in my life, for pay that is. If I had left, where do you suppose I would have gone?"

"But did you ever want to?"

"Maybe, but I figured early on that running from a problem doesn't make it go away. Staying and working at fixing it brings better results. Do you think your mother was better off running to Saint John? And what about Olivia, do you think her leaving has made everything all right for her?"

"I try not to think about Olivia. Maybe it is easier for her to be away from her sister and put all her energy into hating me."

"She doesn't hate you."

"Oh, Nan. I am such a mess. I am tired and so sad all the time. I don't even know who I am anymore. I thought coming here was what I needed. It finally felt like I was taking charge of something and by making it happen I would find what it is that's been missing for as long as I can remember. I want that girl back who used to sit on the shore of the Bay of Fundy and dream. I'm not even sure what it was I dreamt about, but I just know I damn well didn't find it."

"I wish I knew what to tell you to make everything all right, Sylvie. All I know is as long as a person still has breath, a beating heart, and a clear mind, choices are ours to make. You have to do what feels right. I do believe bringing us here was the start of that. The fourteen-year-old girl is still in there, you know. Believe it or not, there is still a young, dreaming girl inside this old body of mine."

"Oh, Nan. I love you so much. You have always been my compass, the voice of reason in all my turmoil."

"Sophie is settled and calm. Her video is good for an hour anyway. Why don't you go put on your bathing suit and go for a swim?"

Sylvia arrived on the beach just as Janice, Veronica, Grace, and Irma got there.

"A good old swimming party," Grace declared. "I put my suit on, but not sure I'll get up the nerve to get more than my toes wet."

Veronica pulled her loose dress up over her head and

threw it to the ground. Without a word she turned to the water and rushed in.

"Proper t'ing, Veronica," shouted Irma. "Seems like you done this before."

Sylvia ran in and dove under close to where Veronica had surfaced. "Come on, girls," she hollered. "Don't stand there gawking. No point in wading in slowly, just take the plunge."

"I didn't bring a fancy bathing suit, and I got nothing the rest of you haven't seen before, but the nuns did a real good job of making us ashamed of our nakedness," Janice said. She pulled off her jeans and rolled up her shirt sleeves. She twisted her long hair into a bun and ran in the water.

"Dear lord," Grace said. "A bunch of swimming dervishes. Come on, Irma. Let's not be candy asses."

Irma pulled her dress over her head. "God love your cotton socks, Grace. Let's go."

Dot stepped out onto the front veranda after hearing the screams coming through the screen door. She counted five bobbing heads in the water. *If they can do, it so can I*, she thought as she walked toward her car. For some reason she'd thrown a bag with a change of clothes in the back seat before leaving home this morning. There was no way she was stripping down to her undies, but she would wear her shorts and shirt in and change into her dry clothes afterward.

She placed her glasses on the dash and pulled her arms out of her T-shirt so she could slip her bra off. She wasn't going to flop those things around naked all afternoon, and it would take the rest of the day for that massive thing to dry if she got it wet. She tucked her bra into the bag and headed to the beach.

⌇

Jonathan heard the screams and laughter through the open window. Standing to look out, he could see the women in the water and Dot walking down the stairs to the beach. Funny how the scene he'd been working on since breakfast was a swimming scene. A near drowning scene, actually; a memory that had come to him from out of nowhere. He was shaping the remembered scene to fit his character and the fictional story he was creating. But he could clearly remember it as it had played out on the last day of school in grade eleven.

A bottle of lemon gin shared between just he and Len. Even as he took big swigs he'd recoiled at the disgusting taste. He'd felt sick from it and from the pitiful fact that he was choosing to follow in his father's footsteps. What other excuse would there be for swallowing this swill? The scene he was building had his character recalling the day he'd decided that he was not going to end up a drunk like his father.

Had it been that day he'd made the same decision? He drank alcohol afterward but never got that drunk again. And he never came as close to dying, either. It had been euphoric, not frightening. He'd swum out over his head in a trance as if he were all alone in a world where there was just water and the vast blue sky.

Len was sitting on the shore, dopey and heavy-headed with the effects of his share of the gin, but somehow he became aware of his friend's struggle. Len ran into the water and swam out, pulling Jonathan from the water before his head went under the dreaded third time. He'd felt no panic, no fight to live or save himself, and had Len not looked up and realized he was in trouble, he would have slipped under the surface and been gone.

The panic came as he lay spitting and sputtering on the sand. His head cleared of its drunken stupor, and the terror of his near death hit him with force. Truth and revelation came threefold: he would not let alcohol cloud his judgement again, he was not infallible, and he would choose living over dying.

⁓⁓

"That made me feel like a teenager again," Dot said as she sat on the sand laughing, minutes later. Grace and Irma had come back to the shore with her, but the other three were still swimming.

"I know. It felt wonderful," Grace said. "I thought when I first went under the cold water I was going to have a heart attack."

"Lord thundering, it was cold. I thought they all were fucking stunned, but in I went, just like a lemming jumping off a cliff."

⁓⁓

Tyler opened his window to escape the stifling heat of the upstairs room. He felt a breeze off the water as he sat back down at the table. Sounds penetrated the room along with the fresh air. He could hear the distinct sound of Irma's voice and Dot's laughter. Another sound accompanied the outside voices and laughter and it took him a few seconds to discern they were coming from next door. It was a singsong tone that at first he thought was laughter. He walked across the room to hear it better.

It was crying. A soft cry with sporadic gasps. Abby, the strange, stuffed-dog-toting girl, had barely spoken a word to him anytime they passed in the hall. It was Abby crying. Should he go next door and ask her if she was all right, or put his headphones on before sitting back down at his desk? The sounds seemed in opposition to each other. Laughter and camaraderie outside, solitude and anguish inside, and neither really involved him.

"Are you okay?" Tyler asked, knocking gently on Abby's door.

～～

Veronica had woken up with the determination to take to the water, but she'd envisioned the swim as a private one. She saw it as being a first step. She wanted to plunge under that cold water and come back up, ready. She pictured a release that could possibly involve screaming, swearing, or a long, steady, cleansing cry. She was sure the deep waters could contain the emotion she needed to expel.

She should have kept her intention to swim to herself, but she hadn't thought her after-breakfast announcement would encourage others to join her. Even Dot had come. This swim was not what she had pictured, but there was something supportive about having the other women with her. Maybe she could take advantage of that support and they could in some way help her with the difficult business she had come here to do.

The women she could see on the shore were all older than her, except Sylvia. Dot and Irma were a few years older, Grace the oldest, and Janice somewhere in between. These women had experience, years of living under their belts. Maybe they would have something to offer her if she were able to tell her story and share her pain. Maybe swimming this morning wasn't meant to provide a private beginning, pushing her toward the words she longed to give voice to. Maybe these women would be the listening ears and hearts she longed for, the mother she'd been longing for most of her life.

<hr />

"Are you okay?" Tyler asked again.

Abby opened the door a bit wider. Tyler could see the stuffed dogs lined up on the trunk at the foot of the bed. Abby was clutching the big one she called Donavan.

"I'm fine," she answered in a whisper without looking up.

"Do you want to go for a walk or something? It is such a

nice day, and we probably both could use some fresh air and a break."

Abby turned, scanning the room as if looking for permission.

Tyler continued. "Writing can sometimes get pretty emotional. I find the best thing is to just walk away and separate yourself from it sometimes. You write dog stories, right?"

"Yeah."

"Did you hear the swimmers? They seem to be having quite a time."

"Yeah."

"Let's just take a walk along the beach. We could stick our feet in the water and cool off. It's hot up here."

Abby set the dog down beside the others, slipped on her Birkenstocks, and walked out into the hall, shutting her door behind her.

⌇

Veronica quickly towelled her hair off, draped the towel around her shoulders, and sat down with the others on the shore.

"I was raised a good little Catholic girl," Irma said.

"My sister married a good Catholic," Grace said. "I chose the United Church of Canada. They seemed more tolerant and open minded to me."

"Don't get me started about the Catholic Church," Janice said.

"This property used to belong to the Catholic Church," Sylvia said. "It was a summer camp or something, right, Dot?"

"A home for girls," Dot replied.

"A girls' prison," Veronica muttered under her breath.

"Oh, the Catholic church was good at building places to contain children," Janice said. "Especially kids who 'needed the Indian beat out of them.'"

"Terrible what they did in those residential schools," Grace said.

"I'm going to read tonight," Janice said her voice a bit louder than she meant it to be.

Tyler and Abby walked down the stairs and on to the beach. "How was the water, ladies?" Tyler asked.

"Damn cold," Irma replied.

"Amazing," Veronica answered.

"I need to get to the kitchen and start lunch," Dot said. "I don't get paid for sitting around gabbing."

Benson pegged out, winning the second crib game in a row.

"I've met my match, I guess," Kent said.

"My wife and I used to play a lot," Benson said. "She'd get so pissed off at me for winning. *Anybody but Benson* was the mantra in our house. We played a lot of games, and I seemed to win a lot. I wonder if she plays games with Ron."

"She remarried, did she?"

"Oh yeah. Mr. Perfect, apparently. A better husband, a

better father, and soon to be a better grandfather. Maybe not a better crib player, though."

"I'm not the best husband or father myself these days," Kent said. "Want another game?"

"No. I think I'll go try to get some writing done. Maybe after supper."

<hr />

After walking quite a distance in complete silence, Tyler suggested they sit down awhile. They'd gone around the bend and could no longer see the lodge.

"Do you swim?" Tyler asked.

"No."

"I took lessons one summer when I was a kid," Tyler continued. "It might be like riding a bike, but I haven't gone swimming for years. My ex-wife always wanted to go somewhere hot in the winter, but we never did. We never did much of anything, except fight. You're not married, are you?"

"No."

"My son Henry takes swimming lessons. I haven't seen him in a bit. We are in the middle of another custody hearing thing. I'll never get custody, but I hope to get some regular visiting worked out. The poor kid must be so mixed up. He's only three, but it's important for a kid to have his father. You don't have kids, do you?"

"No."

"Where you from?"

"Alberta."

"Oh, wow, you came a long way for this retreat."

Abby stood up and zipped up her hoodie. The air was still warm, but the breeze coming off the water felt chilly. Why had she left her room? *A long way to come for this retreat* was an understatement of monumental proportion. She looked down at her Birkenstocks, concentrating on the placement of her feet on the uneven rock surface. She pictured herself bolting, turning around, and rushing back to her room.

It was exhausting enough when she made herself come out of the sanctuary of her room to sit with the others at mealtime. She consciously had to focus as hard on the act of walking through the great room and sitting at the table as one might on completing a marathon or the climb up Mount Everest. She knew how dumb it was to sit Donavan up on a chair beside her and use him as a buffer, a focal point for others to zone in on so they didn't really see her.

What the hell had she been thinking, leaving Donavan behind and coming outside with Tyler as if she was normal and going for a walk with a person was normal? As if she could carry on a conversation and in any way open up. She always had to push herself to speak when spoken to, unless the conversation centred on one of her dogs. All she'd been able to manage were one-word answers to Tyler's questions.

The panic welled up, and Abby felt a fever-like heat envelope her body. She quickly unzipped her hoodie and whipped it off. She kicked off her Birkenstocks and headed to the water's edge. She waded into the rippling water. Taking deep breaths, she stared toward a distant object on the horizon: a boat.

"Are you okay?" Tyler asked.

"No, I'm not," Abby said.

"Maybe you're dehydrated. I'll run back to the lodge and get you some water."

"I'm getting water for Abby," Tyler called out to Dot after making his way back up to the lodge. "She's had a weak spell of some kind."

"Here, take this juice and a cookie. The girl eats like a bird. Good for you to get her outside. The poor thing needs fresh air."

Tyler took the juice and cookies from Dot. It was nice that Dot seemed concerned about Abby, but at the same time it struck him as a bit condescending. He felt the need to defend Abby but did not say a word. People always thought they knew what another person needed when they had no idea what was really going on.

People saw Abby with her stuffed dogs and didn't look any further. People were great at giving labels and putting people in categories so they wouldn't have to look any further. He was not going to do that with Abby. He was going to treat her the way he himself had longed to be treated all those years he spent feeling invisible.

Tyler set the drink and cookie down and headed upstairs. Maybe he had no business doing this, but he was going to do it anyway. He opened Abby's bedroom door. Marjorie looked up from her vacuuming, nodding as Tyler picked the big dog off the chair. Donavan, Abby called him. He would take Donavan to Abby.

⌘

"Sylvie, I think now that you are back I'll go see if Irma wants to work on the puzzle. Sophie fell asleep a few minutes ago. How was your swim?"

"It was great. Irma and some of the others went swimming too. Even Dot came."

"Oh, that's nice. Maybe you are going to like having people here after all."

Sylvia let Nan's words hang without responding. It wasn't as if she didn't like people. She closed her bedroom door and slipped off her wet suit and started getting dressed. While swimming she'd actually had the fleeting thought that she might read tonight. Her eyes went to the grey trunk at the end of her bed. A World War One footlocker, actually, that had belonged to Nan's father, her great-grandfather. It had always been in her bedroom growing up, and as a kid she'd kept all her dearest treasures in it.

When she packed up her office to move, she had culled so much. She had kept galleys and copies of her books, and some posters and promotional stuff, but had thrown a lot away. So much of what had seemed so important over the years seemed valueless when it came right down to deciding if it were to come to her new life.

That thought made Sylvia chuckle. Her new life was just her old life in a different setting. What had she really thought this move would bring? The initial attraction was escape, rebellion of some kind, independence. She had craved freedom and a new start. Or, as she had said to Nan earlier, maybe what she had really been looking for was a return to something.

Sylvia knelt down and opened the trunk. A pile of composition books and some yellowed file folders. A small pink music box. Two photo albums and a baby's striped green-and-white sleeper. And the blue Hilroy notebook, its cover faded and wrinkled. Wrinkled from the tug-of-war battle she'd had with Bennett Small on the school bus the day he'd snuck up behind her and grabbed the notebook. He'd started reading from it at the top of his lungs.

She had lost her mind and viciously attacked him, jumping repeatedly, trying to take back the notebook he was holding just out of her reach. When she finally got hold of it, Bennett wouldn't let go, and it was the bus driver who had retrieved it, breaking up the tussle. Amid sobs, she had screamed for the notebook back. A week's suspension from the bus was the result of her actions, and Bennett just got a reprimand with a warning to stop teasing her.

That's what they had all thought her overreaction was about. An older boy teasing her, a crush and her embarrassment. She had seethed with the words they all had used to account for her outburst. Even Papa had made wisecracks about young love.

Sylvia picked up the blue notebook and opened to the first page. The cursive writing was so juvenile, a full, round, exaggerated script. The name at the top of the page was the name she'd created and imagined as her famous penname. The first sentence was still frozen on the page, and in her mind Bennett Small's voice reading each word aloud made a mockery of the words that still held such gnawing pain.

Reading in public was always a double-edged sword. Giving the words on the page a voice and sharing them with a listener or an audience was both thrilling and frightening. Sometimes as she read from a page in a book holding her name, she was taken aback with the thought of it. Even more overwhelming were the times she would be at an event and a reader would read something from her work that had impacted them.

She'd get so emotional thinking of the full-circle moment that began with the crafting of a story, the task of creating something word by word, the process of it coming to publication to the moment a perfect stranger held the book in their hands, turned to an exact page and a precise sentence, and read her words back to her. It was possibly the most rewarding part of being an author, and the part she missed the most.

The notebook she was holding held so much more than the beginning attempts to tell the story her sixteen-year-old self felt driven to tell. It held the layers of dreams that had piled up since she stood in front of the bookshelves in the upstairs hall holding tightly to Papa's hand while he told her the magic and wonders each book held. The variety of spines, the block letters of titles and author names. The cascade of colour and possibility.

Papa gave such value to the books filling the shelves. The emotion and adoration so strong in his voice as he shared his feelings about reading and having books in his life. The blue notebook held her desire to someday have a book on Papa's shelf of wonder. A book with the name Bridget St. John. How ridiculous, the penname she'd created. How very transparent when the bridge in Saint John loomed so greatly in the story. The name and the story a fabrication of a teenager's overly dramatic imagination.

Papa had not lived long enough to hold a book with his granddaughter's name on the spine, but Sylvia remembered holding her first book and whispering Papa's name as she turned to the dedication page. Her first book had been dedicated to Paddy Ingalls, her beloved Papa, but she'd never truly been proud of it. Papa would not have been so dismissive of it, though, and she knew the first thing he would have done was place it on the bookshelf in the upstairs hall.

Chapter Eight

Kent's outstretched legs hit the arm of the couch. He rolled over a bit, letting his feet dangle as he repositioned his pillow. *This damn couch is so uncomfortable*, he thought. *When one of the ten-day people leaves I should move into a bedroom in the lodge, unless by then I've managed to get back into my wife's bed.*

Sylvia seemed more herself last night than he'd seen her in a long time. Janice had just begun her reading when Sylvia entered the great room, an old blue notebook clutched in her hands. When Janice finished, Sylvia stood to read, without any preamble or introduction. She simply opened the notebook and read, not looking at anyone in the room. She'd read, closed the notebook, and left.

As she walked away, Kent was overwhelmed with how much she looked like Olivia. Even as she read, it didn't seem like his wife of thirty years standing in front of him. She seemed young and vulnerable. Her words were raw and powerful, and he'd never heard them before. What he heard was the writing of a stranger. The rest of the writers sat in silence after Sylvia left until one of them stood to say goodnight and they all quickly dispersed.

He had been so eager for Sylvia to get involved, to participate and be a part of this whole retreat venture. She had done that last night, so he should be feeling some relief, but instead her reading had left him shaken and confused. It felt like by doing exactly what he'd asked her to do, she had clearly shown him her intention to do just the opposite.

<center>~~~⚬~~~</center>

Sylvia knocked lightly on Janice's door. Dot hadn't even arrived yet, and she knew it was too early to be waking someone, but Sylvia had been lying awake waiting for the sun to rise so she could go to talk to Janice.

Janice opened the door a crack, pulling on her colourful robe. Her long hair was dishevelled and her eyes squinted, adjusting to the light streaming in the hall window.

"Did I wake you?"

"Yes, as a matter of fact, you did, but come in. I was a while getting to sleep last night."

"So was I," Sylvia said.

"Sit down."

"Are you on the ten-day retreat?" Sylvia asked.

"Yeah," Janice answered.

"Is the work you were reading from last night finished?"

"No, not quite. I've been struggling with it—avoiding it, maybe, if the truth were told."

"I know all about avoiding. Would you stay for a month if you could?"

"If I could, I guess, but I was hard pressed to scrape up the money for ten days. I'm not even sure why I thought coming here would get me on track, but I am glad I did. Just to be with other writers helps. But permission to be a writer isn't the demon I'm battling. And not sure being here a month would win that fight."

"Is your demon believing you have the right to tell your story?"

"Kind of, I think. But even more than that, it's convincing myself it makes any difference. Telling my story won't change a damn thing, so what's the point?"

"That's the question, isn't it? Why tell any story, and who the hell are we telling it for? Creative writing courses teach writers to know their audience; publishers gauge the market and tell writers to write what's popular, what's selling. 'Write what you know' is another mantra. 'Write what scares you the most,' I heard an author say once. There's lots of advice and wisdom out there, and no doubt some people come to retreats like this looking for some magic formula."

Sylvia wiped tears away before continuing. "I have not written one word in over two years, but last night I filled ten pages in the old notebook I'd started writing in when I was sixteen years old. And my frenzied writing felt more real and more important to me than anything I have published. My Giller-longlisted novel is shit, it's nothing, it's nowhere near the writing I heard from you last night."

Janice stood and reached for a box of Kleenex from the bedside table. She sat across from Sylvia, offering her the box but staying silent, sensing she had more words that needed saying.

"I am such a fake," Sylvia continued. "*Sylvia Drummond Wright.* Hope you didn't buy into that bullshit. I don't know shit, and I'm in no position to be anybody's mentor, but I was wondering if you'd be mine. I will pay for the month-long retreat, shit, I'll pay for two months if that's what it would take for you to finish and get your book ready for a publisher. And at the same time you can get me on track, keep me writing. Together we can figure out what the hell we need to write and what story we need to tell."

"In Grade Four, Sister Mary Grace passed me back a story I'd written. The first thing I noticed was the colourful butterfly sticker on it; then I saw the word *excellent* written in red ink. But after setting the paper down on my desk, Sister Mary Grace leaned in close and whispered *a'tugwewinu*, the Mi'kmaw word for storyteller. I have never forgotten the kindness and generosity of her whispered word."

"Well, maybe I can be another Sister Mary Grace for you."

"And who will I be for you, my friend? Who declared you *a'tugwewinu*?"

Sobs erupted from somewhere deep within and Sylvia did nothing to stop them. Janice wrapped her arms around her and let the crying ebb and flow.

"I always thought it was Papa or maybe even Nan, as she always praised everything I did. But just now when you asked that question, it was my mother who came to mind. I was almost five when my mother died, and all my memories of her got thrown in and mixed up in my life with Nan and Papa. I held on to a few bad memories, thinking that was all I had of my mother. I believed everything that mattered came after she died.

"I brought a tattered copy of *The Snowy Day* with me to Nan and Papa's. They read it to me many times, but before they would turn to the last page I would shut them down. I'd ask for a different book or a drink of water to keep them from turning the page and reading me the last line: *And they went out together in the deep, deep snow.*

"I remember that line and the sound of my mother's voice reading it to me. And I remember when she finished reading it I would begin a long, detailed story that was different every time, telling what adventures they found in the deep, deep snow.

"'You're my little storyteller,' she would say, tickling me and hugging me before tucking me in wherever we found ourselves sleeping that night."

⌇

Dot stirred the pancake batter, listening to the morning noises upstairs. Something about a quiet kitchen made her feel lonely and sad. But who would want to return to the years when mornings were hectic and crazy? Feeding six kids and trying to get them out the door in time for the bus had never been an easy task. Feeding them and distributing their lunches and marching them out the door took military precision, and she'd always been very proud of how efficiently she managed it.

Had she taken the time to enjoy those days? Had she paid enough attention to each child, to each special quality and the quirks they possessed? Had she paid enough attention to Donald? Theirs had been a whirlwind romance, her sixteen and him twenty. His rugged handsomeness near took her breath away, and apparently she caught his eye too. Young, naive love had them walking down the aisle three months after they'd started dating, and them without a pot to piss in. Then six babies in ten years, with Donald away driving truck most of the kids' growing-up years.

Something about yesterday's shenanigans had jarred her. She'd surprised herself by joining in and allowing herself to have fun. She'd managed to prepare lunch, and baked all afternoon, but for a little while she'd felt like a young girl just hanging out with friends and having fun. She wondered if the girls who had been here years ago ever had such fun on this shore.

Foolish old woman, letting her mind wander. All water under the bridge now.

⌒⌒⌒

Abby stepped into the shower, letting the hot water wash over her. She felt a flicker of excitement knowing she would see Tyler at breakfast. He had touched her shoulder last night.

They'd walked upstairs together after the reading and he had touched her shoulder and said, "See you in the morning."

She was being ridiculous. A brush on the shoulder and the words *see you in the morning* were not such a big deal. But Tyler had been so kind, so nice to her, and she hadn't felt his judgement or pity. He'd come with juice and cookies and he had brought Donavan. He'd sat down beside her and passed Donavan to her, as if needing a stuffed dog was perfectly normal and not batshit crazy.

Gavin pulled on his trousers and tucked his shirt in. "Looks like another nice day."

"I'm going to do a load of laundry this morning," Irma said. "Evelyn said I could use the clothesline on their back step. No need of a dryer on a day like this. I've missed a clothesline all these years living in downtown Toronto. My mother's clothesline was her pride and joy. Washing for the nine of us meant carrying water and heating it on the cook stove, washing and rinsing, putting each piece through the old wringer, and taking the heavy basket out to the yard. Father strung the lines between the maple tree and the shed and Mother hung her wash in the same meticulous way every time. She'd start with father's dungarees, his good pair and his work ones, then each of the boys' pants, oldest to youngest."

"Are you going to list every item, Irma? For God's sake, your mother hung her laundry out in a particular way. You've been deprived all these years with no clothesline. And like I haven't heard for years that your mother was a saint."

"I listen to you going on and on about that damn book you're writing and never say a word about it. My mother might not have been a saint, but she was a damn sight closer to being one than your mother ever was."

"Dying didn't make her perfect, you know. Them all dying didn't make them perfect."

"Fuck off," Irma said, slamming the bathroom door behind her.

Irma clutched the side of the sink, willing herself not to cry. There'd be no point telling Gavin about last night's dream. He was becoming more and more hardhearted and dismissive of her feelings. How was it that something still so painful and raw for her had become just a tool he used to hurt her?

She'd been banging on the front door trying to wake them up. The step beneath her feet was the same flat rock she'd watched Daddy drag up and put in place at the front door. Mother had painted the door yellow after the rock was settled into place. The bright yellow door still intact in her dream, her pounding on it as flames took over the top story. And Gloria's cries rising above the loud knocking.

"Dying didn't make them perfect," Irma mumbled. Mother, Father, Thomas, Travis, Sandra, Faith, Debbie, Fenton, Wendell, Sharon, and sweet baby Gloria were not made perfect in their dying, but they were loved and mourned as much on this day as the day she'd lost them. Feeling that sorrow still was the truth of it, whether that was right or wrong, and she was less and less willing to stay with a man who didn't get that.

⌇

Kent met Sylvia coming across the yard. "Where were you this early?"

Sylvia didn't answer but kept walking. Kent turned and started walking with her, toward the back of the building.

"Your reading was good last night."

"Thanks. I don't need your approval, you know."

"I know that, but I can compliment you, can't I? I was glad to see you getting involved."

"Janice is staying for the month. I am going to pay her registration."

"Okay. Money doesn't have to change hands. This is your venture too. The retreat money is your money."

"I don't want it to be. This retreat business is yours, Kent. You do the accounting and managing and I'll keep my finances separate. It will make things easier in the long run."

"Why? Are you planning a divorce?"

"I'm not getting into that right now. This whole thing is your baby, and I want to remain separate from it. I'm writing again, and that's what I'm going to concentrate on. That and looking after our daughter. I'll e-transfer you the money for Janice."

"Okay."

Sylvia opened the screen door and walked into the apart-

135

ment, leaving Kent on the landing.

"I'm glad you're writing again, Sylv."

⋯⋅⋙⋅⋯

Jonathan came out into the hall and nodded to Darcy, who was sitting at her spot by the large window.

"Good morning. You're back at work, I see."

"Yeah, I didn't get much writing done yesterday."

"I got a fair amount done. Can't believe how quickly the days are going by."

"You're only here for ten days, right?"

"Yeah, that's why I'm feeling the pressure to write. I didn't pay to come here to make friends or socialize. I came here to get some writing done."

"So did I, but it is nice getting to know other writers. Are you going to read tonight?"

"Yeah, I might. I've been working on a section that is pretty intense. I'd like to read it out loud to see if it works, but I'm not sure I can read it without falling apart."

"Seems to me it's a good group to fall apart in front of. Everybody's got their own stuff going on. Writing is a leap of faith at the best of times, don't you think?"

"Is that what it is? How about I'll read tonight if you will."

⋯⋅⋙⋅⋯

Instead of joining the others for the nightly reading, Janice and Sylvia had decided they would spend the time at Sylvia's kitchen table sharing their afternoon's writing. As she ate supper with Sophie and Nan, Sylvia anticipated her time with Janice; an excitement she couldn't remember feeling for a long time, if in fact she had ever felt it. She never was one to collaborate or network with other writers. She had developed a good working relationship with her editor, but there was something different about letting a professional, who was paid to clean up and improve your writing, see your revised work, compared to allowing another writer to look at your rough, first draft.

What was this she was writing, anyway? It was a return to the story she'd started at sixteen, but it was so much more. She had thirty-six more years of life and writing experience behind her, which definitely changed her perspective from the naive approach she'd had originally. But the bare bones of the story remained, as well as its personal draw. It felt like the writing was controlling her, not her manipulating the writing, and it was exhilarating. She couldn't wait to read this afternoon's writing to Jan.

"I'm going to go to the lodge tonight if you don't mind," Evelyn said as she rose to begin clearing the table. "Irma and I thought we'd work on our puzzle while the readings are going on."

"That sounds great, Nan. I'm going to give Sophie her shower and get her ready for bed. She can snuggle in and watch her show in her room, and if she falls asleep she'll be in bed already. She hasn't been sleeping well, so whatever works. Janice is coming over here after her supper. We're going to read our work to each other."

"I think it is wonderful you've started writing again, Sylvie. Maybe Kent had the right idea making this a writing retreat."

"It has nothing to do with him, Nan. The right idea, or the Kent Wright idea, has nothing to do with me writing again."

"Well whatever the reason, I'm just glad you are. You have always been a writer, and it's been hard to see you unable to do what you love."

"Do you remember the book *The Snowy Day*?"

"Yeah, I think so. A little picture book, right? A bright, colourful cover with a little boy in a red snowsuit. You loved that book when you were little."

"Yes I did."

⌇

Benson scanned the opposite page, careful not to lose his place. He had almost read the entire chapter, and another minute or two would wrap it up. But as he read each line he became aware of the sound of his own voice.

"Dad, quit talking to us in your principal's voice," the kids used to say. "We are not your students or your teachers. We are your own kids, talk normal and stop the friggin' act."

Was the boring, monotone voice he heard echoing in his head right now his author's voice? If it was, it needed work. If he was boring himself, he could only imagine how the others were feeling. He finished the sentence, not even bothering to build the crescendo or complete the chapter with his deliberate cliff hanger.

Benson sat down, despite the fact he'd rather have bolted and left his uninspired audience behind. He would be courteous enough to stay and listen to the readers who were following him. The Windsor Wordsmiths had a hard and fast rule about supporting each other, and he had developed a good game face and a repertoire of positive responses.

Jonathan stood to take his turn. He scrolled down on his phone screen, finding his desired passage. He paused, thinking of the emotion writing it had elicited, hoping he could mask that emotion while reading it.

"I am not going to give you any preamble or explanation about plot, characters or setting. I am simply going to read you a passage I wrote yesterday, or at least I am going to try."

<center>~~~⚭~~~</center>

Sophie consented to having her hair washed, and Sylvia got her showered quickly without incident. Sophie chose her favourite pyjamas and settled into bed, happily swaying to the theme song of her beloved show. Sylvia lowered the volume a bit, mouthing the words of the beginning scene of episode one, season three. She had heard these shows so many times she could mute the TV and recite every scene line by line, not that Sophie would tolerate that.

Jan was already sitting at the table when Sylvia came into the kitchen.

"I made tea," Jan said. "Hope you don't mind me making myself at home."

"I don't mind at all. Nan made banana bread. Do you want a piece?"

"Not right now, thanks. Dot had gingerbread and whipped cream for dessert, and the pieces she cut were massive. I'm going to gain twenty pounds staying here for a month. Small price to pay for the writing I'll get done. I was on fire this afternoon. How about you?"

"I wrote quite a bit too. Do you want to read first?"

"Sure," Jan replied. "I've been bawling all afternoon. Maybe I'm all cried out and can read it without tears."

It was Sylvia wiping away a steady stream of tears and trying to compose herself after Janice read the handwritten pages in front of her.

"Oh my God, Jan, that's awful. I can't believe how cruel they were. You were just little kids. Who would treat little kids like that? How the hell did you survive?"

"We all survived, but barely. We're all still living, which is even more unbelievable. Six of us, and each one more messed up than the next. Took turns being the most fucked up, but every one of us damaged and dysfunctional. And the saddest part is how powerless we were and still are to help each other."

"You were forbidden to talk to each other?"

"It was part of their plan to wrench the 'Indian' out of us.

From the day we arrived, we were kept separated. *Nuelewumg*, Christmas, was the only day we were allowed to spend time with our siblings. The nuns would walk back and forth in front of us as we sat together for the hour or so we were given to visit each other. They were so afraid we would speak the Mi'kmaw language to one another. The rest of the year we would steal glances and take whatever opportunity we could to check on each other, quickly asking one brother if another was okay or asking a sister where another sister was.

"I remember always watching any line of boys being paraded in front of us for punishment, hoping none of them were Harold, Noel, or Teddy. I especially feared one of them would be among the runaways filed in to be humiliated in front of everyone before they were locked up in the dungeon."

"There was a dungeon?"

"Not like in fairy tales. It was a windowless closet under the kitchen stairs. A broom closet filled with cleaning supplies, and only the light seeped through the crack under the door; cramped and small, especially when more than one runaway was locked in there at a time.

"And family extended to more than just our siblings. The Mi'kmaq are raised knowing the actions of one affect us all. People from the same reserve were extended family, so if someone from your reserve was punished, you became part of their shame. Our shame is still what weighs us down the heaviest."

"My God, Jan. I've got myself all wrapped up in the tragedy of my own story, but I've got nothing to tell compared to you."

"It is not a scale of suffering we need to have in mind when we write, but a release from our own suffering, whatever it is. A writer cannot mask their own story with another's trying to meet some level of despair that will make his or her writing superior to another. It is authenticity that creates good writing, and each writer must search for their own and allow their own story to surface. That is what success is."

"You amaze me Jan. You see life with such clarity and wisdom and you have more to teach me about writing than I, with six published books, could ever teach you."

"Yeah right. Tell that to my kids who watched me empty a bottle every day and end up barely able to speak a word of sense."

"But you speak it now."

"Hard come by, but maybe, finally, I'm able to find the right words."

"Seems to me addiction is the cause of a lot of pain. For my mother, it was heroin."

"Is it the cause or the side effect? Mine was alcohol, as was my ex-husband's and my three brothers', but other crutches take over when one has trouble walking the path they were meant to walk. For my sister Vivian it was anger, and my sister Rose, fear. Rose has spent her life hoping to blend in and be invisible, not allowing anyone to ever hurt her again. She barely eats enough food to stay alive."

Evelyn entered the room and sat across from her granddaughter.

"Liquor seems to be the topic of the night. Jonathan just read something that pretty much left the room silent and I now come in to you guys talking about it. Liquor, I was taught that liquor was the root of all evil. Cut and dry was the wisdom of the Reformed Baptist church. My mother belonged to the Women's Christian Temperance Union.

"The philosophy of the WCTU was just don't let a sip of alcohol pass your lips and you'll be fine. *Lips that touch liquor will never touch mine.* I believed it, even signed a pledge when I was twelve years old that liquor would never pass my lips and that I would never marry a man who drank liquor. Pretty straightforward and pretty damn naive, but I stuck to it."

"Papa never drank, did he?"

"Paddy was not a drinker. It was his choice, but I might have had something to do with it. I only recall one drunken night. He and Harry Green got into the whiskey the last night of lobster season our first year married. My rage and how miserable he felt the next day probably convinced him to leave the booze alone."

"Just damn lucky as far as I can see," Janice said. "And those temperance ladies might have had something in the *don't let it pass your lips* advice. Wish I'd never took the first sip and let the follow-up sips lead me to believe the more I drank the less pain I'd feel. First you take a drink, then the drink takes a drink, and then the drink takes you. Oh I've got all the clichés; I could keep you up all night with them, but I think I'll head to bed instead. Sober nights and clear mornings are a gift

I appreciate every day, and especially after a day of unloading like I just put in. Thank you, Sylvia, for listening."

"Thank you for letting me, Jan. Goodnight!"

<center>~~~~⚡~~~~</center>

After turning out all the lights downstairs in the lodge, Kent sat himself on the wide veranda facing the dark expanse of the Northumberland Strait. The cloud cover pretty much hid the moon and stars, but the air was warm. Kent had no desire to head around back. Maybe he would let himself fall asleep stretched out on this lounge chair. He'd likely wake up in the chill of predawn once the dew settled in. He should go back inside and grab a throw off the couch but chose not to move.

Kent felt rather immobile both in body and mind. Everyone had seemed to be in a stupor after Jonathan's powerful reading. The emotion was raw and penetrating. It had certainly hit a mark with him. He seldom allowed himself to go to the place Jonathan's words had taken him. Sons of drunken fathers; he used to think he could pick them out of a crowd, usually because they were following in their father's footsteps.

Kent had chosen the opposite approach. An occasional glass of wine with a meal, a beer or two at a summer barbeque, but for the most part Kent stayed away from what he always considered the evil that made his father into the monster he'd watched while growing up. The devil he had been relieved to watch drink himself to death, if it could be called drinking yourself to death when a forty-three-year-old man steps in front of a bus.

What kind of a father leaves a teenage son to look after his mother? But no amount of looking after could save a woman already completely destroyed by the man who had claimed to love her.

Chapter Nine

Dorothy Flemming slowed in front of the last cottage before turning onto the driveway to the lodge. This little yellow cottage stood out from the others. It looked so cared for, so loved, but for some reason was still boarded up this season. Who owned it, and what kept them from coming this summer? No sign hung from the chains on the post at the end of the little drive. Unnamed and unclaimed. The little yellow cottage made her feel sad for some reason.

She felt tired this morning, which was probably the reason for her melancholy. She'd been so glad to get this job, but already the pace was catching up with her. Omelettes this morning would be easy enough to prepare, and she'd made a red pepper soup last night that she'd serve for lunch with cold cuts and buns. Feeding people came easy; it was the interacting and socializing that wore her out. But of course, that was not what she was here for.

❦

"You scared the life out of me," Dot said when Kent sat up as she entered the lodge. "Wild night, was it?"

"Not exactly," Kent replied. "I fell asleep on the deck, actually, but woke up near frozen before daybreak and slipped in here so I wouldn't wake anyone out back."

"Going to be another great day by the looks of things," Dot said. "What are all the seaside scribes up to today?"

"Seaside scribes. Catchy name. Maybe I should use that in our promo ads."

"Evelyn came up with it. What a lovely lady she is."

"Yes, she is."

"She's pretty with it for her age."

"Yeah. She has always been a crackerjack. She's been such a huge part of our lives. Both Sylvia and I lost our mothers at a young age, so Evelyn has been mother, grandmother, and great-grandmother wrapped up in one."

"You have another daughter, right?"

"Yes, Olivia. She and Sophie are twins. Sophie's accident was hard on her. Olivia hasn't dealt well with it."

"Not my business, but it seems it's been rough on all of you."

"Well yeah, of course it has. Our daughter went from a vibrant young woman with a promising future to a helpless child."

"That kind of trauma is not easy on a marriage."

"Do you have anything else in the car that needs to be brought in?"

"I have a pot of soup in the truck, but I can go get it. You probably want to go shower and change before breakfast."

"Do I look that bad?"

"No worse than any of us first thing in the morning."

~~~

Grace Wanamaker sat down on the side of the bed to buckle her sandal. Waking up she'd been confused and for a few seconds didn't know where she was. She remembered that happening for a while after she'd moved into her parents' house. She and Vincent had taken a different room from the one she'd grown up in. The room they'd moved into was right beside Mother and Father's, so she could hear them in the night if they called out.

She sometimes heard them still, through the thin veil of sleep. All her people came to her in the night, leaving her with a sadness in the morning when she realized she was all alone. She had spent a lifetime serving others, planning her days around the needs and desires of the people she loved. It was a strange feeling to be on her own, answering to no one. It was nice getting to know the folks on this retreat, though.

Grace was finding most of the writers friendly. Kitty was chatty and very funny, her sense of humour blunt and slightly risqué. Benson was never at a loss for words, and if she made the mistake of sitting near him she could be sure he would steer the conversation his way with barely a chance for her to get a word in edgewise. Vincent's brother was like that. Everything was all about him.

Janice was quiet, although kind and welcoming. Jonathan and Darcy had been keeping a lot to themselves, very disciplined and driven with their writing. Tyler was a lovely boy, so caring and respectful. She'd noticed him walking with the introverted girl yesterday. She was so glad he was reaching out to her. She had tried to talk to Abby, but unless she was saying something about her dog, Abby made no effort to respond. Gavin seemed fine, but Grace did not like the way he spoke to Irma. That was something she'd always hated about her brother-in-law, David. He talked down to Velma and would embarrass her in front of others.

If there was anyone in the group who might need her attention and care, Grace felt it was Veronica. Veronica carried a sadness so deep it seemed to be seeping out her pores. She put on a careful front, hid behind a smile and courteous words, but Grace sensed a deep, debilitating sorrow that she couldn't quite put her finger on. It was lovely being here and having the time to work on her writing, but during the month they were together maybe she could reach out to Veronica.

"Stop mothering me," Wallace had said angrily the day before she left home.

"How do you expect me to stop mothering you? I am your mother," she had replied.

"And I'm a grown man. Maybe you'll find someone to mother on that ridiculous retreat you're flying off to."

"Maybe I will," Grace said aloud now as she headed down for breakfast.

Olivia Wright stared out the window from her regular stool at Magnolia's. Coming to this coffee shop was a daily thing, even after she'd stopped using the place for free wifi. She usually stopped for a latte on her lunch break or sometimes on her way home from work. Today she'd taken the afternoon off for an appointment. Time off from being the mail girl, the coffee girl, the run-to-the-dry-cleaner's girl, or Richard's in-a-pinch babysitter. A ground-floor position, her dad called it. A make-work position for the loser daughter of a partner. But it paid two bucks an hour more than minimum wage.

After Sophie's accident Olivia didn't finish her master's degree or follow up on any of the job offers she'd received before the trip. "A promising future," the interviewers had said. Sophie had no future, wouldn't return to her career or climb the corporate ladder. And as Olivia became more withdrawn and unmotivated, the tension between her and Mom escalated. It seemed the more miserable she felt the meaner she became. After one particularly nasty fight, she'd left home and moved in with Ryan, a guy she'd just started seeing and barely knew. He didn't care whether or not she contributed to the expenses and it had taken her a while to figure out the line of work that gave him such deep pockets. She would like to have been able to say that she took a moral stand and left on principle, but the truth was, Ryan's unexpected incarceration dried up her cash cow.

So next she'd moved in with three high schools friends and even got a job waiting tables for a few months. But one by one her roommates left; one got married, one got knocked up, and the last one just got pissed off at her and she couldn't swing the rent alone. So she called Dad. That seemed a better option than crawling back home.

The small bachelor apartment Dad had rented her came with the condition she take the job he'd arranged for her in the mail room of his office. He had topped up her salary and she managed to pay rent, buy groceries, and have a bit of disposable income. The job was far from challenging or fulfilling, and sometime in the first few months there she'd gotten it in her head she could prove her worth by becoming a published writer like her mother. But it really couldn't be called writing, because what she was actually doing was taking her mother's second book and copying it word for word, except for the deliberate changing of character and place names. It quickly became an obsession, and she often worked long after midnight.

Even as she wrote, Olivia knew the obsession to copy her mother's book was a strange if not psychotic undertaking. But the more she wrote, the more determined she was to complete the writing and then attempt to have it published. She would not use her own name, of course; any connection to her mother might invite an editor to compare her work to her mother's. An especially astute editor might even realize the similarity or dig a little deeper and discover the deliberate plagiarism.

Her appointment today had been with a small Toronto

press interested in publishing her manuscript. While waiting to be called into the editor's office, Olivia had picked up the brochure for the Wright Retreat. She read through the details and paid close attention to the photographs, thinking how weird it was she didn't know anything about this undertaking. She'd known Dad had retired and his office was now inhabited by a pushy woman only a year older than she was who felt quite entitled to treat the mail girl like a piece of trash. But Dad had mentioned nothing about buying a lodge in New Brunswick and starting a writing retreat.

Olivia had picked up the brochure again on her way out of the office, tucking it in her backpack beside the contract she'd just signed. The small press had accepted her book, and that should have made her happy, but she felt like she would vomit as she walked out onto the sidewalk. What had she been thinking? Did she really think the book could come out, even under her pen name, and that no one would sooner or later figure out it was just her mother's book in disguise?

Olivia took a long sip of her now cold latte. She read through the details in the brochure. She stared at the bio and photograph of her mother. It was the one on the back cover of the very book she'd spent months copying. Putting her drink down, she picked up her phone and typed in the email address on the brochure. She would register for the month-long retreat beginning September 1. She'd mail a money order so her father would have no clue the author registering was his daughter. She would give her notice at work and break the lease on her apartment.

She wouldn't reply to any calls, texts, or emails from the publisher, which would put a stop to the process. She wouldn't cash the one-hundred-dollar advance she'd been given and she'd rip up the contract. She would stop this craziness now and do what she'd been longing to do since the day she'd left in a rage.

She would go to her mother. She'd never really been angry at her but was too afraid to face who it was she really blamed for Sophie's accident. She needed Nan, and she needed her twin sister. She needed to be forgiven. Olivia Wright needed the Wright Retreat.

～◦～

Sylvia slowed in front of the yellow cottage on her way back. An hour ago she'd left the apartment, the sun just peeking up over the horizon, the morning dew still fresh and the air cool. Something had propelled her to head out and walk along the gravel road leading from the lodge and turn left onto the main road. She'd driven out the gravel road, turning right toward the highway many times, but had never chosen this route on any of her walks, always walking the shoreline or the wooded trails.

The post still stood, chains dangling where the sign she'd stolen had been. She remembered having thoughts of what the owners might think upon their return. *Luna Sea.* She'd packed the sign into her suitcase before flying back to Toronto and had stashed it away in a closet. She'd made sure to bring it when she moved but hadn't dug it out of the box. Several of her boxes remained unpacked. There was limited space in the apartment, and for some reason it didn't feel like her permanent home yet.

The yellow cottage was still boarded up, unlike the other cottages along the road that were bustling with seasonal occupants. She'd heard the revelry on the shore most nights and seen the flames rising from a communal bonfire. She'd been tempted to go over and introduce herself but had never gone to join them. She stopped in front of the yellow cottage and imagined attaching the oval sign back onto the dangling chains.

~~⚬~~

Veronica stood at the closet looking over her choices. It looked as if it was going to be another warm day. Her first urge had been to put on her bathing suit and head down to the water before the others gathered for breakfast. A dream last night had put her out into the deep water at dusk. The setting sun was bouncing off the rippling water. Noises of the others gathered around a bonfire that had just been lit, smoke rising instead of flames, seemed muted, foreign, yet familiar. One voice called her out, beckoned to her to swim into shore, but she swam out further with desperation to escape, as if it were possible to reach the distant shore and walk out in a different place.

Tears ran down Veronica's cheeks and she grabbed the flowered shirt off the hanger. She'd wear her beige capris and this shirt. It had been pink, striped seersucker that day. A sundress with an empire waist falling full like a feed sack. The morning she'd pulled it on over her head, she'd had no idea what was coming. The pain, the agony, and the fear. And the sorrow that had outlasted all the rest, the sorrow and the anger; an anger she'd pushed so far back and never allowed herself to feel.

Kent rounded the corner just as Sylvia came into the yard.

"Another early morning," Kent said. "This country air seems to be agreeing with you."

"Where did you sleep last night?"

"Speaking of country air, I guess it's changing my habits too. I fell asleep on the front deck of the lodge."

"I've been for a walk and it's given me an appetite. I might just come over and let Dot feed me one of her big breakfasts."

"That would be great. I know the one-month people are anxious to see more of you."

"You still don't get it, do you, Kent? I'm not part of this grand scheme of yours. I have no intention of providing the goods you advertised."

"You are mentoring Janice, aren't you? And you paid her one-month fee, so it looks to me like you're on board."

"Keep thinking whatever you want, Kent. You always do

anyway. God forbid anyone deviate from a plan you've put into place."

"When did you get so angry? I don't remember you being so opinionated and hard to get along with. I've given you a good life, haven't I? I don't remember any complaints."

"Since when did you notice anything? You have always seen exactly what you choose to see. You have been so busy controlling our lives trying to make up for not being able to save your mother that you never saw what was really going on."

"Oh, so now you're the expert on messed-up, motherless children. I suppose it takes one to know one."

"When did you become so angry?" Sylvia said walking away.

<center>~~~</center>

Tyler fell into step with Abby as they descended the stairs.

"Another great day, Abby. Smell the coffee and whatever else Dot is cooking up. Must say, I could get pretty used to this life. What about you?"

Abby clutched Donavan a little closer. Before leaving her room, she'd vowed she was going to talk to Tyler, if he bothered to talk to her today. He'd been so nice again yesterday and all she'd managed were her usual one- or two-word replies. She had a brain in her head. She was more than capable of writing intelligent sentences in her work and carried on lengthy conversations with her dogs, so surely she could say something meaningful out loud to Tyler.

"My mother was from New Brunswick, but I'd never been east until now. I really like it so far."

"Good morning," Jonathan said to everyone sitting at the table. It was fiction he'd read last night, he'd reminded himself before leaving his room, and nothing to be embarrassed about.

Benson reached over and filled Jonathan's coffee cup. "It's a great morning. Glad to see you're joining us for breakfast this morning. Is Darcy writing already?"

"She's not at her spot yet?"

Sylvia walked into the room and sat down at the table. "Hope you don't mind if I mooch some breakfast this morning, Dot."

"Are you kidding? I've cooked plenty, and you're more than welcome at any meal I serve."

"You own the place," Gavin said.

"Yeah, I guess, sort of," Sylvia said. "Where's Irma?"

"Oh, she's coming. She woke up on the wrong side of the bed so I stayed out of her way. God forbid I should say anything to her."

"Yeah, God forbid," Dot said, flopping an omelette on Gavin's plate.

Grace picked up the pitcher of juice and poured some into her glass. "Not everyone's a morning person. Always took my husband at least one cup of coffee before he spoke a civil word. Can't imagine Irma being out of sorts. She's so funny and easy-going."

"No comment," Gavin said. "We missed you last night, Sylvia. What were you and Janice up to? Didn't know the ten-day retreat included a one-on-one with you."

"She's staying for the month, actually," Sylvia said. "She's not downstairs yet?"

Kitty slid in behind the table. "Looks like another beauty day. How's everybody this morning?"

"I'm fit as a fiddle," Grace answered. "Can't see why I wouldn't be in this lovely place, surrounded by such lovely folk and being fed these lovely meals."

"Wow, she went from a ten-day to a one month," Gavin said. "And you've started mentoring her already. I guess I better make my intentions known."

"You'll have to talk to Kent, Gavin. I don't have anything to do with the running of this retreat."

"Really? It's your name attached to it."

"You sure it wasn't you who got up on the wrong side of the bed?" Dot said to herself, loud enough for Gavin to hear.

Seconds of silent tension were broken as Veronica and Janice got to the table.

"Good morning. We were just saying what a beautiful day it is," Kitty said. "Grace is fit as a fiddle and the rest of us have no complaints either. How did you two sleep last night?"

"Fine," Janice answered. "Great day. The way I look at it, any day this side of the sod is a day to be celebrated."

"I suppose that's one way of looking at it," Benson replied. "Although some days my aches and pains make me question this gift of getting old."

"Not everyone is so lucky," Abby said.

"That's right, dear," Grace added.

"What did I miss?" Kent asked, opening the sliding doors and entering the great room. "Sure hope I haven't missed breakfast."

⁓⁓⁓

Irma stared at her face in the mirror. It was startling just how much she looked like Grannie Doyle. If she grew her greying hair and pulled it back into a tight bun, she would be the spitting image. She had the unhappy martyr look down pat, and that was what hit Irma so hard seconds ago.

Grannie Doyle had died when Irma was just ten years old, but she remembered so clearly the deep lines of unhappiness and the scowl of misery she saw on her grandmother's face every day.

Grampie Doyle had always looked the opposite: teasing and laughing, grinning and cajoling like a Cheshire cat, her grandmother always said. How could one couple have faces and demeanours of such extremes? It wasn't until years later Irma was told the reason behind Grannie Doyle's unhappiness.

"Your Grannie Doyle had a hard go of it, Irma. Your Daddy was born after a long string of dead babies and a whole lot of disappointment. Your granddad took to the bottle, and the more babies she lost, the meaner he got toward her. He was the life of the party to everyone else but a mean, nasty son of a bitch to his wife. How she put up with him, I don't know.

I'd have smothered him with a feather pillow."

Irma never believed her mother would have resorted to murder if she'd had to live the life her mother-in-law did, but something in her words and the way she always delivered them gave Irma the strong message that a woman didn't have to take such abuse from her husband.

Irma stared at her own wrinkled face and unhappy eyes. Gavin was not a drunk or an abuser, but he was not the loving husband he'd been at the beginning. Should a woman have to stay married to a man who no longer loved her or treated her with respect?

Irma walked back into the bedroom and picked up the pillow. She hugged it tightly to herself and let the tears fall. What would her mother say? What would her sisters say if they were still here to offer counsel? It was Sharon she'd confided in when her period didn't come for the second month in a row.

"You're not the first girl in Petty Harbour to be saddled with a bastard child, Irma. And yours isn't the first that that slimy Kenneth McNeil planted the seed for, neither. But the hell with him and all the rest. You know Mother and Daddy will do right by their own. And Mama always says the babies bring the love with them."

And Gloria had brought a ton of love with her. She came into the world with a crown of brown curls, a full, sweet face, and a disposition like an angel. *Like an angel*, they'd all said so many times in those first few months of her little life, not knowing, of course, how short her earthly life would be.

And Sharon had been right about her parents. They had supported Irma right from the start, accepting their daughter's condition and willingly making room for a new baby. The only requirement was that Irma make a plan to raise her daughter on her own and live an independent life in the future.

"This mistake will not ruin your life, Irma Jean," her mother had said. "You are not damaged goods, and you will not hide away under your parents' roof. You are a strong, healthy girl with your whole life ahead of you. We will help, and the baby can stay here with us until you are on your feet. You'll go to St. John's, get a job, and make your way. Once you've got some money saved, you can take Gloria and make a life for the two of you in town. God willing some fine man will come along for you and love Gloria as his own. You will not wither away in Petty Harbour, letting the shame of one bad decision weigh you down."

One bad decision, Irma thought now, clutching the pillow tighter. Was being away working in St. John's that fateful winter night when the old red house caught fire and burned like a tinder box, not sparing a living soul under its roof, her worst decision? At least if she'd been home that night, she would have perished with the lot of them and not had to live the last forty-three years in such misery.

It had been a slow winter's morning at George Street's Bridie Molloy's, with just a few regular customers and a tourist or two. She'd been taking a couple's order in the corner booth, the morning sun streaming through the window, when

Claudine beckoned to her, her face ashen white, her words jumbled and senseless. Through the clatter of vowels and consonants, one word reverberated. Gone.

"They's gone, m'dear. They's all gone."

～◦～

Darcy looked up to see Kent Wright walking toward her. She'd slept in this morning and had grabbed a muffin and coffee before heading to the shore. She passed Sylvia and Janice, who were sitting on the front veranda deep in discussion and only nodded. Tyler and Abby were farther over on the beach, throwing stones into the waves. Grace and Veronica had been sitting in the great room. She wasn't sure where the others were.

"We missed you at breakfast," Kent said. "I suppose you were busy writing."

"Actually, no. I slept in this morning and can't seem to get going. I thought I was on a roll, but I'm not feeling it today."

"It's okay to have a down day. Maybe you just need to take a rest and not force anything."

"I thought I knew where my story was going, but this morning everything I've written just seems like crap to me. Does that ever happen to your wife? Crisis of confidence, I think they call it."

"Yes. I think it happens to every writer. Every person, maybe. We all second guess ourselves at times."

"I keep thinking that maybe I should be back home getting ready for school. That I know. I can make lesson plans and map out a semester, but what the hell makes me think I can write a novel?"

"Do you know anything about hot tubs?"

"What?"

"Hot tubs. Last night when I was out on the deck after everyone had gone to bed I thought how nice it would be to have a hot tub here. I think after a long day it would be pretty relaxing for people to have the option of getting in a hot tub. They're good all year round, and I figure having one would be value added to an already nice retreat package. What do you think? If we had a hot tub, would you use it?"

"Well, yeah, I guess so."

"I'm going into Moncton to look at hot tubs. Why don't you come with me? Maybe an outing is just what you need."

"Sure, why not? I don't know anything about hot tubs, but I'll come with you for the drive."

⋙⋘

Irma led Sophie by the hand and down the back stairs.

"We're going to get some fresh air, sweetie. We'll take a little walk and get the stink blown off us."

"Stink, stink, stink," Sophie repeated, a wide grin on her face.

Evelyn fell in behind them. "You're a godsend, Irma. We can never seem to convince her to go outside. You seem to have a magic touch with her. I swear she'd do anything you ask her."

"I don't know about that, but sometimes a person will do for a stranger what they won't do for family."

"The way I see it, you're pretty much family, even in the short time we've known you. I do believe things happen for a reason, and you happened along for us just when we needed you."

"Just when I needed you too, my dear."

Chapter Ten

Darcy opened her eyes to the sun streaming through her window and practically jumped out of bed. The slump she'd been in yesterday seemed to have passed. Actually, it had passed by the time she and Kent got back to the lodge at suppertime. Apparently she had needed the pep talk he'd given her. To be complimented and encouraged by such a successful, self-assured man was the boost she needed. He wasn't hard on the eyes, either.

Robin had always accused her of being a pushover when it came to older men. There had been a bit of a pattern, but as far as she was concerned, men her own age had nothing to offer. One downside was being mistaken for the daughter on occasion. Not yesterday though.

"And what do you think, Mrs. Wright?' the salesman had asked after delivering his pitch on the selling features of the Odyssey six-person tub with twenty-one jets and LED "Moon Glow Waterfall" lights.

Kent hadn't bothered to correct the man.

"I can have it delivered in a week. We can also provide an electrician and a plumber to install the same day as delivery. You and the missus can be relaxing in this beautiful tub by nightfall one week from today."

Everyone was seated at the table for supper when they got back from Moncton, and no one seemed to notice that she and Kent had even been gone. Not that their excursion had been some clandestine thing, but neither she nor Kent offered up details regarding their outing. Kent hadn't even mentioned ordering the hot tub.

✿

Irma was determined to make it down for breakfast this morning. Dot hadn't asked any questions yesterday when she'd entered the kitchen after everyone else had left. It would have sounded stupid to tell Dot that she'd gotten to the top of the stairs and overheard Grace say she was fit as a fiddle and the waterworks had started up again. Instead of attempting to stop them and disguise her red eyes from the others, she'd gone back to her room and had a good old pity party. Mother always said sometimes that's the best you can do.

Mother always added that once the pity party was over you needed to put your feet on the floor and get your sorry arse back out the door. She had done that. After a cup of coffee and some toast, Irma had gone over to visit with Evelyn and Sophie. She'd even got Sophie to go outside for a walk, which had done the world of good for both of them. It had certainly helped Irma rid herself of the thoughts Grace's words had stirred up.

Grandpa Doyle was a fiddle player. Wasn't a day went by he didn't take out his old fiddle and rosin up the bow. His tunes ranged from upbeat, toe-tapping jigs to the downright mournful, take-your-heart-right-out airs. Everyone loved to gather in to hear Tommy Doyle play his fiddle.

Everyone but Grannie and Irma, it seemed. Every time Grandpa played the fiddle, Grannie would take to another room or leave the house altogether. Irma was only five or so when she first noticed that and followed her grandmother down the lane to the boathouse. She'd stood outside, somehow knowing her presence wouldn't be welcome.

Irma had thought it was laughing at first. A deep, guttural laugh, frightening and foreign. Pressing her ear closer to the slatted door, she realized it was sobbing. She'd run back to the house because she felt her grandmother's sorrow was not her business, but mostly because the anguish she heard in her grandmother's weeping was more than a little girl knew what to do with.

The happy, social, fiddle-playing man who brought cheer to others was never able to offer an ounce of compassion to his wife, and on more than one occasion raised his hand to her, causing her even more misery. Fiddling became a sound Irma detested. *Nero fiddled while Rome burned* was a line Irma heard once, and right away she changed it in her mind to *Tommy Doyle fiddled while his poor wife withered up and died.*

She'd be damned if the same was going to happen to her. For Gavin it was the pen, or the typewriter, she supposed. He was more than willing to take to his typewriter, putting down words with the hope of charming the masses, but wouldn't take the time or the energy to notice his own wife fading away in front of his eyes.

Irma Doyle Church was not going to take to the boathouse or hide in the attic and cry her tears in private. She'd done enough of that. She knew she could manage the sorrow she carried deep within her; she had done so for years. But she didn't need to stay with a husband who was unwilling to love her through it all.

⌇

Tyler and Abby had started a bonfire farther down the beach last night and sat talking until well after midnight. Abby had no grand visions of a romance coming from this, but it was monumental, and she smiled as she headed to the shower. She had spoken more words to Tyler in the last couple of days than she'd spoken to another human being for a long time.

At first she supposed she talked some. The first foster home wasn't even too bad, and there had been younger kids, which she loved. Rebecca was the baby, and Abby had loved helping to look after her. And there'd been a dog. She was a bit snappy, which was fine, because Abby was not ready to love another dog like she'd loved Donavan. But once in a while Nellie would get up beside her on the couch and snuggle in and Abby would scratch her behind the ears. Ted and Betty were kind and they tried to get Abby to talk about things, but she never let her guard down.

Abby learned early on to tell Mrs. Best, her first social worker, what she wanted to hear without ever really telling her anything. How could she ever say out loud how she felt? How could she tell anyone how guilty she felt for not being there? She would have heard Donavan bark if there had been a noise or smell before the explosion, and maybe she would have been able to wake her parents. Donavan always slept on her bed, but that night he was probably in his kennel in the laundry room, and no one would have heard him when he barked a warning.

She had begged for the sleepover at Sadie's that night. Mom said no, she was overtired and should stay home and get a good night's sleep in her own bed, but she'd had a hissy fit until Mom gave in and let her go. She hadn't kissed her mother goodbye but ran out the door when Sadie's dad picked her up. And she hadn't hugged Donavan goodbye. Abby couldn't believe she'd told Tyler all that last night.

<center>~~~</center>

Veronica searched through the pile on the floor, looking for the journal that had come to her mind as she was waking up. On the day she bought it, she'd stood in front of the journal display at Indigo, allowing her eyes to peruse the choices. She'd believed, as she always did, that finding the right journal was the key. The key; she forgot who gave her the five-year diary that Christmas, a red vinyl diary with a little lock and key. It was probably Aunt Marjorie. Veronica had loved it right away.

She'd filled each little section faithfully every day, chronicling the important details of a thirteen-year-old's life.

Each night after writing the day's details, she would carefully turn the little key in the lock, making sure her thoughts, dreams, and desires were locked away privately. Then she would tuck the diary in under the bottom of her mattress. She hid it away every night, even though there was no one in the house that gave a hoot about any of her secrets or what her dreams were.

Veronica sat at the table and read the Eleanor Roosevelt quote on the cover: *The future belongs to those who believe in the beauty of their dreams.* It was this quote that had caught her eye that day, causing her to purchase the lime green journal with the magnetic flap cover. The quote had spoken to her because she was still under the naive illusion that she could barrel toward the future without facing the past.

Facing the past was what she had come to the Wright Retreat to do, but was she any closer to doing that? Could she take one of her fountain pens and pull the cap off and begin to fill the pages of this journal? Could revisiting the past finally open the way to the future? Did her dreams still matter?

<hr />

"Kent, I've decided to stay the month. Can you let me know what I owe to cover the difference? And when can I expect to start my sessions with Sylvia?"

Kent stopped and turned to respond to Gavin, who had followed him out the door into the yard after breakfast.

"What? Oh, right, you did say you might stay the month once you settled in. Sure, we can register you for the month and for sure you can take advantage of the month-long retreat features. I'll just subtract the two-week fee from the one-month and add Irma's cost, of course. I won't charge her the full amount. I'll work out a cost for her meals and accommodation. I'll have to check with Sylvia and get back to you."

"She's already working with Janice. What about Tyler and Veronica? Have they had any sessions yet?"

"She and Janice kind of hit it off, I guess. I don't know if you realize it, but Sylvia's had a bit of a dry spell lately. It happens to a lot of writers. Janice seems to have helped her start writing again. You just never know, right? I will talk to her and get right back to you."

"Maybe it's the change. I know the whole hormonal thing has hit Irma hard."

"Oh, I made the mistake of mentioning that once and I certainly won't again. We men have to be careful with that sort of thing."

"Oh, I hear ya. Marriage doesn't come with a manual."

﹏ゑ﹏

"Do you suppose they even realized we were sitting here?" Janice said.

"Probably not," answered Sylvia. "I knew this was coming.

Gavin seemed pretty pissed yesterday when he asked about you getting one-on-one time. I told Kent this was going to happen sooner or later. It'll be interesting to see how he handles this. Tyler and Veronica don't seem as intent on getting their money's worth."

"A dry spell, hormones, woman's moods and fancies," Janice said. "Don't you love how dismissive men can be? A marriage manual. I could write one and they wouldn't like it, I can tell you that."

⁓

After breakfast Tyler and Abby headed down the beach together, leaving the others milling about in the great room or sitting out on the veranda. Benson had suggested another group session, and most had agreed to meet back in the dining room in an hour.

"Do you think things happen for a reason?" Tyler asked.

"I don't know," Abby answered. "What do you mean?"

"Well, here we all are at a retreat in New Brunswick. None of us knew each other, but something drew us all here. For ten days, two weeks, or a month, we are in this place together. Meeting you happened because we both made the choice to come here. And think of all the things that could have gotten in the way."

"There was a lot in the way of me coming. I hardly ever leave my apartment. Buying groceries online is a real thing, you know. I do just about everything online. I work out of my apartment and go days, sometimes weeks, without seeing another person. Getting on a plane and coming here was as far from my mind as flying to the moon."

"That's what I mean. Something made you come here. It seems to me you either believe things happen for a reason or you believe everything is random."

"What would be the reason for my parents dying and not me? What would the reason be for me to get passed from one foster home to the next and ending up so socially inept I fill my life with stuffed dogs instead of people?"

"I don't have answers for all that. I'm the question guy. But something brought you here and got you talking to me, right here, right now."

"Something made you knock on my door. Nobody else did."

"Oh, I'm a good guy. Just ask my ex-wife."

"I think you are."

<hr />

Kitty hit *send*, letting out a little holler, causing Grace to look up from her writing and Veronica to put down the book she was reading.

"I just sent my manuscript to my publisher," Kitty announced. "I needed these few days to finish it and get it ready for her to look at. God knows it will need some editing, but it feels so good to finish it."

"Have you got anything else started?" Veronica asked.

"Oh yes, I've always got something on the back burner."

"Another lesbian love story?" Grace asked.

"Yeah. That's what I do."

"Have you ever considered trying something different?" Veronica asked.

"Why fix what ain't broken?"

"That's kind of how I feel about the horror genre," Grace said, "but sometimes I think I should try my hand at something a bit more personal."

"A memoir?" Veronica asked.

"Not exactly, but a story that more reflects my life. I never have been stalked by a murderer or forced to hide out in a remote cabin to get away from an ex-lover."

"What do you write, Veronica?" Kitty asked.

"Kind of floundering. Haven't actually done much writing yet, but I hope to."

"Everyone has to start somewhere, sometime," Kitty said. "Have you had a chance to meet with Sylvia yet? Maybe she could encourage you and get you started."

"I don't like to bother her, but maybe."

"And you can talk to us too. Strength in Writers, right?" Grace said.

Chapter Eleven

"It is hard to believe Jonathan leaves today," Kitty said. "The ten days flew by. I remember thinking there wasn't much difference between the ten-day and two-week retreat."

"Four days, actually," Irma said.

"I know that. But four more days seems like a lot now that we have to say goodbye to Jonathan. I don't feel ready to leave, so I can't think he does either."

"Janice would be going too if she hadn't snagged the one-month somehow," Gavin piped in from across the room. "And she's had almost a week of nonstop mentoring from the author who is supposed to be the drawing card of this retreat."

"Oh, stop being such a spoilsport," Irma said. "Kent told you she's reading your sample. Maybe she's finding it a bit cumbersome and boring. You don't write light and fluffy."

"Like you know anything about writing."

"She knows about storytelling," Veronica added. "I've hardly stopped laughing, listening to her and Kitty."

Kent walked into the apartment kitchen just as Sophie was sending her cereal bowl hurtling across the room.

"Not a fan of the Cheerios?" Kent asked.

"Not a fan of anything this morning," Sylvia said.

Kent bent to pick up the biggest piece of the broken bowl. "Don't suppose this is the time to ask if you've read Gavin's sample piece?"

"I have, actually, and I jotted a few comments. Maybe that will keep him happy for a day or two. It's funny how you always get your way sooner or later."

"It doesn't have to be a battle, Sylv. This retreat can work for both of us."

"I'm not arguing with you this morning."

Sylvia passed Kent some paper towel, the broom, and the dustpan.

"I didn't come to ask you about Gavin, actually. I figured I should tell you what I bought before the delivery truck comes. A hot tub. I bought a hot tub."

"A hot tub. Okay, whatever."

"Why don't you take a break and I'll entertain Sophie? Should I try to get her to eat something else?"

"Oh, just give her a piece of Dot's chocolate cake. That's what she wanted in the first place. Don't know why I fight her; it's just as much a waste of time as fighting you on anything."

"Take an hour or so. I have to leave around eleven to get Jonathan to the airport, then wait for a writer coming in from Montreal. I should be back by late afternoon. I've told Dot what she needs to tell the guys when they come to install the hot tub."

Tyler rolled over and gently brushed the hair from Abby's face.

Abby opened her eyes, feeling panic at having Tyler so close in the light of day.

"Oh my God," Abby said, pulling herself to a sitting position.

"I didn't mean to wake you. You looked so beautiful lying there."

"Right, scary, you mean."

"I don't mean scary at all. I'm sorry I startled you."

"You slept here all night?"

"You fell asleep in my arms and I didn't want to disturb you."

"Oh my God, Tyler. I'm such a mess. You don't need my bullshit."

"I don't think you're a mess. I think you are brave and amazing."

"I can't believe how much I told you. I talked your ears off last night and now you have to deal with me first thing in the morning. Bet you're kicking yourself now for knocking on my door. You didn't come to this retreat to babysit me."

"I came to this retreat because I was meant to. It's a

crossroad in my life, and I believe in yours too. I believe we came here to meet each other."

"I have never woken up beside a guy before."

"Well, there you go. It's been a while since I've woken up beside a woman."

"We didn't have sex, did we?"

"Oh God, I hope I'm not that forgettable. No, we didn't. We just talked and you fell asleep. I don't know about you, but that felt perfect to me."

⁓⁓⁓

The post was new, not the one that had held the oval sign and stood empty since the January day she'd first stood in front of the yellow cottage. A new post and an Exit Realty sign had been installed at the end of the drive. *Exit strategy* came to Sylvia's mind. That was, of course, what had brought her to this location in the first place. From the moment she'd cut the small ad from the supplement, her mind had begun forming an exit strategy. It hadn't gone quite the way she envisioned it, but maybe there was a second phase, a next step.

Sylvia hurried back to the apartment, thinking Sophie's lunch would need to be prepared and Nan checked on. Nan had seemed off this morning, a bit weak and muddled. Perhaps she shouldn't have stayed away all morning. Kent was there when she left, but she'd seen him drive out at least an hour ago. Maybe being alone with Sophie was getting to be too much for Nan, although Sylvia knew she would never admit that. Admitting Nan was slowing down was not easy either. What would she ever do without the woman who had always been her strength and support?

Sylvia heard the laughter and talking as she got to the steps. Sophie's laughter usually only came when watching her shows. But what Sylvia heard coming from the kitchen was Sophie's laughter and words intertwined with Nan's voice and Irma's distinct cadence. Sylvia stood still for a few seconds, enjoying the sound, considering turning away so as not to interrupt the pleasant interaction.

Irma opened the screen door. "Come in, my love. Sophie's right good this morning and we're having a time here. Evelyn made her cheese biscuits and I mixed up some chocolate chip cookies. Sophie's having a tea party for her little ones."

<hr>

Melanie Hargrove settled into the window seat in the small plane. Not a fan of flying, she'd slipped an Ativan into her mouth in the security line, swigging the last of her water before disposing of the bottle. It wasn't leaving the ground and taking to the clouds that frightened her as much as it was the containment. Having control and the ability to run were always the foremost considerations in her cluttered and roiling mind, and being closed up in an airplane took away both.

It seemed lately the only time her mind quieted was when she stood in front of a canvas with a brush. Even the pen or the computer keyboard did not offer that same reprieve. The brush calmed her agitated mind and allowed her to zero in on a place more tranquil, a safe place where she could breathe. After years of so little control, those moments were welcome and she craved the peace they provided.

She was headed to a writing retreat, not a painting one. But along with her laptop she had brought watercolours, pastels, some sketchpads, and a couple of canvases. She was going to take the next two weeks and explore both sides of her creativity. And no one knew where she was. What better freedom could she ask for?

<center>~~~⁓⁓~~~</center>

Kent got to the arrivals gate just as the flight from Montreal was unloading. He'd given himself lots of time to get Jonathan to the airport for his flight, leaving just a few minutes to wait for Melanie Hargrove. He had almost forgotten he had a two-week participant coming today. Organizing arrivals and departures might prove to be a bit of a challenge. Then he panicked, realizing Janice's room would not be available, since she was now staying for the month.

But Melanie Hargrove could take Jonathan's room, and the next writer wasn't coming until the two-week people were gone. A one-month person was registered to arrive on the first of September. And a week later three two-week registrations were booked. Hopefully he could keep all this straight. Sylvia was so much better at juggling that kind of stuff. She had always kept the girls' busy schedules straight.

⟶⟨⟶

Sylvia pulled another box from the shelf. Sophie had fallen asleep curled up with Irma on the couch after lunch, and Evelyn had gone to her room to nap. Sylvia had sat down at the kitchen table to do some writing when the Luna Sea sign came to her mind. She'd gone to the closet and started pulling cardboard boxes from the shelves as quietly as she could. She had no idea which box it was in. And what did she need it for?

Sylvia pulled the folded paper from her pocket. Does a writer always carry a pen? She'd been asked once when she pulled a small pen and a sticky notepad from her pocket to jot a thought down. Lately she'd started making sure she was equipped in that way again.

EXIT Realty
382-3946
Dennis Walker

⟶⟨⟶

Irma sat down on the step, reluctant to enter the lodge. It was a wonder Gavin hadn't sent out a search party. She'd left the lodge just after helping Dot clean up after breakfast and had stayed the whole day with Evelyn and Sophie. She'd even had supper with them and had helped get Sophie ready for bed. Sophie had been trying to say "Irma" all day and somewhere along the learning she'd settled for "Ma" and then it morphed into "Mama." A few minutes ago as Irma tucked all Sophie's stuffies into bed beside her, she had reached up, wrapped her arms around Irma's neck, and clearly said, "Love you, Mama."

Tears streamed down Irma's cheeks as she recalled the words Gavin had hurled at her this morning: "Evelyn is not your mother and that girl is not your precious Gloria. For God's sake, Irma, pull yourself together. She's just using you for free babysitting and senior care. They are not your responsibility."

Irma knew who Evelyn and Sophie were, but Gavin didn't understand that her desire to be with Evelyn and Sophie had more to do with her than with them. It wasn't who they were but who she was when she was with them. For the first time in such a long time, she was hopeful and happy when she was helping to care for Sophie and while spending time with Evelyn. She knew she wasn't family and that the elderly woman and that sweet girl did not belong to her, but it felt right nevertheless. She felt more accepted in their presence than she had felt with her own husband for a long time.

"We're getting in the new hot tub," Kitty said, stepping out onto the veranda. "Do you want to join us, Irma?"

"No."

"Where the hell have you been?" Gavin asked, coming up behind Kitty, a towel draped over his arm.

Not answering, Irma got to her feet and walked into the lodge.

It took a few seconds for Kent to realize the pressure he felt between his legs was not being caused by the jets. The light pressure changed to a stroking, and it was taking considerable effort to keep the pleasure of the sensation from registering on his face. Kent turned slightly to verify who this invitation was coming from, still trying to appear engaged in the conversation around the tub.

"I hope this doesn't give me a rash," Gavin said. "They put a lot of chemicals in these things, you know."

"It is beautiful," Grace said. "First time in one of these for me, but I plan on getting in any night you have it up and running."

"Me too," Kitty said. "Thought my big arse might not fit on the seat, but I guess they build these things for all sizes. One size fits all doesn't always ring true."

"It's pretty relaxing, that's for sure," Benson said. "Not that these days have been too taxing. I'm going to hate when my two weeks are up. Can't believe us two-weekers only have four more days."

"I plan on being a repeat customer," Darcy said.

Kent flinched. "That's good to hear, Darcy."

Chapter Twelve

Sylvia sat across the table from Gavin, unsure how to begin. She had passed him his thirty pages with the notes in the margins, as well as a page of her general comments. This collaboration was definitely out of her comfort zone. It hadn't felt like that at all with Janice; all their interactions had been back-and-forth discussion, mutual observations, and genuine support. This felt the extreme opposite. Kent had set her up as some sort of guru, some experienced expert, and she certainly didn't feel like one.

"Your story is captivating. You have certainly put a lot of effort into the research."

"Is it publishable?"

"With a bit of revision, I think it is ready to submit to a publisher. That is a complicated process, and you need to be prepared to send to several houses."

"I was told you would help me submit."

"I can offer some suggestions."

"You don't like Mavis?"

"I didn't say that. I suggested you flesh Mavis out a bit."

"What the hell does that mean?"

"I didn't get a sense of her. She seems flat."

"That's why I stopped going to all those creative writing

courses. They all used lines like that. I expected more from you."

"I am just suggesting that you show the reader a bit more of who Mavis is. What are her motivations? Share a bit of her back story, maybe."

"Can you help me write a query letter?"

"Why don't I give you a chance to look over my comments, and we can meet again in a few days. Maybe decide which publisher you would like to approach first and let me know when we have our next meeting. I will talk to you about the submission process then."

"Fine. I don't do all that internet stuff. Do you have a handout of some kind with publishers' names on them?"

"Sure, I'll compile a list for you."

⌒⌒⌒

Sylvia was swimming back to shore when she spotted Kent coming down the stairs to the beach. She hadn't seen him yet this morning but assumed he'd spoken to Gavin and was coming to give her feedback on their meeting. She considered turning back and swimming farther, staying in the water long enough to wait Kent out. She was in no mood for his criticism.

Kent sat down on the bottom step. Sylvia got to her feet and walked toward him. She grabbed her towel, slipped on her sandals, and sat down beside him.

"What happened to us, Sylv?"

"What?"

"I slept with Darcy last night."

"Wow. You lead with the top story, don't you?"

"We haven't had a marriage in a long time."

Sylvia took a deep breath.

"You know what, Kent? I don't care. I stopped caring a long time ago. You were right, this move was my way of asking for a divorce, but I was too damn spineless."

"I'm not a bad guy."

"No, I know you're not. I haven't got the energy or the interest to tell you what you are or why I think you do what you do. But one thing I do know is you always need a project, someone to fix. I guess Darcy fits the bill."

"I will go along with whatever you want to do."

"Great. I'll keep you posted on what my plans are. Maybe we can end this marriage and both get what we need."

<hr />

Irma was tucking a tea towel into the neck of Sophie's shirt when Sylvia came into the apartment kitchen.

"You can feed yourself your spaghetti, sweetie. The messier the better, my mudder always said."

Sylvia sat at the table, lowering her head into her hands. She felt the rush of tears and angrily wiped at them.

"Are you okay?" Irma asked sitting down beside her.

"I thought I was. I guess it is a bit upsetting when your husband tells you he's screwing someone the age of his daughters. Kent slept with Darcy last night."

"Lord thundering. Can't say I saw that coming, but not much surprises me. That brown-haired mousey slut knows you're right out back. She's got some nerve."

"Her loss, the way I see it. She didn't know who I was the day she came, but it seems to me not knowing who Kent is will be a bigger mistake for her. She's welcome to him."

"I'm putting the kettle on. You need a cup of tea, girl."

"Where's Nan? I never even thought about her when I sat down and blurted out to you. She thinks the world of Kent."

"Evelyn went to the city with Dot. I hope you don't mind her leaving Sophie with me."

"Are you kidding? You are amazing with her. Better than I am. More patient, I think."

"That's not true. God love you, you have her all the time. I breeze in here and spend an hour or two and make it look easy. There is nothing easy about what you've been given."

"I'm just so weary. The last few days I've felt like I have to make a move. I have to step up and figure out where I'm headed and what I need to do about things. Maybe Kent just gave me the push I need."

"Dear Jesus, you and me both. I've been like a simmering pot, bubbling with anger and so afraid of it boiling over."

"We are in control of our own futures, Irma. Nan says as long as we have breath and a beating heart, we can dream and we can make choices."

"Wise woman, that grandmother of yours."

"Do you think she's getting any of that spaghetti in her

mouth?" Sylvia asked, looking at Sophie.

"Oh yeah. She's chewing, and look how happy she is."

~~~

Melanie Hargrove rolled over in the bed. She was shocked to see that the clock on the bedside table said 12:05. She hadn't slept this late since she was a teenager. She looked around the room at the mess she'd made unpacking last night. She knew the organizing of things needed to start in this space that would be hers for the next two weeks. It was a starting place for the choices she had come here to make. She was not going back to Montreal, but she had no clue where exactly she would go.

Traumatized, the therapist called her. PTSD was the diagnosis, as if a diagnosis made any of it easier. It had been in the therapist's office she'd picked up the brochure advertising the Wright Retreat. The cost of the two-week registration was just about the same amount she had in her chequing account, and her Visa handled the flight. So here she was, safe and sound, holed up for two weeks with room and board and possibilities.

When the two weeks were over, she would figure out her next step. Whatever that next step was, it didn't include Dawson. Bordeaux Prison was providing his room and board for a minimum of two years. Surely in that time she could re-establish herself and begin a life somewhere he would never find her.

Melanie's stomach rumbled. She could hear talking downstairs and figured people were gathering for lunch. As hungry as she was, the thought of food made her nauseous. She would get up, take a quick shower, and go make toast or something. She didn't want anything more than that, and she wasn't keen on having to talk to the others. She'd done her best last night, feeling overwhelmed by the friendliness and constant chatter at suppertime. She'd made herself eat enough to not appear rude before leaving the table.

Melanie got up and took the sketchbook off the chair across the room. Opening to the first page, she recalled sitting on the bench at the far end of the lawn looking back at the lit-up lodge, hearing the chatter and laughter coming from the hot tub. With charcoal and pastels she had sketched the lodge, the dark treeline behind it, and the night sky above. It looked so peaceful but somehow foreboding, as if it held secrets.

<center>~~~</center>

Kitty finished setting the table while Veronica ladled the soup into bowls.

"That Dot is a marvel," said Veronica. "I hope I don't mess everything up. This place never saw meals like this before, I tell you."

"Were you here before?" Kitty asked.

"I'm just going from what I've been told. Some sort of Catholic children's home. Stark and cold, nothing welcoming about it. Watery soup with scarcely a scrap of meat in it, un-like this amazing pot of deliciousness Dot left for us."

Benson, Tyler, and Abby came in and sat down at the table.

"Two new cooks today?" Tyler asked.

"Dot and Evelyn headed into Moncton this morning, and I told Dot not to rush back," Veronica answered. "Figured I was able to put lunch on the table. She made it before she left, of course. I'm not much of a cook."

"And I'm her trusty assistant," Kitty said. "I'm going to let out a holler to anyone else who wants to eat. Have you seen the others?"

"Grace and Gavin are sitting out on the veranda," Benson replied. "Not sure about the others. Haven't seen the new girl yet this morning."

Kitty walked to the bottom of the stairs and hollered, "Soup's on!" and repeated the announcement at the open front door.

Darcy had no intention of stalking Kent or appearing needy, but when she looked out her window and saw him sit-ting on the steps leading to the shore, she dressed quickly and headed outside. She was halfway across the lawn when she re-alized Kent was waiting for Sylvia to get out of the water. Darcy quickly turned and headed in the path leading into the woods.

She had dated married men before, but never with their wives so close by. Maybe calling it dating was a stretch. First date was buying a hot tub together, and second date tumbling into bed like frenzied, caged animals desperate for sex. That's what it had felt like. No foreplay, no chatty repartee, just sneaking upstairs, shutting the door, and going at it. And why had she initiated it? She hadn't been wrong, though; Kent Wright needed no more prompting than her giving his penis a rub under the frothy water of the hot tub.

Most of the married men she'd had relationships with had been the same. Unhappy, unfulfilled, sexless marriages. Or at least that's what she always told herself. At first, anyway, until the truth of her role became more evident. None of the men ever left their wives and families. She was a sideline, a brief distraction, a temporary entertainment. She was the flavour of the week until they realized the menu they wanted was what they had at home. Robin told her that each time, but for some reason married, older men were the demographic she gravitated toward.

Would Kent Wright be any different? Was his marriage over? Was the fact he was willing to cheat in such close proximity to his wife a good sign? Maybe she had finally chosen a man who would be willing to put her first, leave his previous life and make one with her. She had her looks and her youth, and she knew how to use them to her advantage. And the sex had been mind-blowing.

Darcy walked back out the path. She could see Sylvia rounding the corner of the lodge and Kent now sitting on the bench by the beach steps. Time for her next move, she figured, if she were to stay in the game and maximize her chances.

She only had four more days here, and she intended to leave an impression that Kent Wright would not soon forget.

❦

Grace liked to think she was pretty good at reading people. She'd noticed a few days ago that Darcy Lawson seemed to always settle herself near wherever Mr. Wright was. In her almost eighty years on this earth, Grace had seen girls like Darcy many times. Stella Richards had been the one who nearly made Vincent disregard his wedding vows permanently, but luckily Grace had been able to nip that in the bud.

Now from her spot on the veranda Grace could see Darcy plunk herself down on the bench, cozying up to Kent. Sylvia had just come across the lawn and gone around back to her place. And something had been going on in the hot tub last night. Men can be led around by that small head between their legs, letting it take over any common sense in their big head.

Not her business, thought Grace as she rose to her feet. Not her business, but maddening just the same. What was wrong with men?

"Lunch is ready," Grace hollered toward the shore before going inside.

Chapter Thirteen

An eleven o'clock appointment was set up, and Sylvia paced anxiously from the kitchen to the living room. She was bursting to tell Nan and Irma what she was considering but would wait until she met with Dennis Walker, had a tour, and was given all the details about the property. Beach rights, probably, but no land to speak of. The cottage was small but, she assumed, winterized, as she had seen the outside apparatus for a heat pump around back.

The more Sylvia thought of the small yellow cottage, the more excited she was about the idea of buying it. Maybe she had known from the moment she parked in front of it in January that the small building had a place in her future. Or maybe it was when she walked away with the sign. And it had occurred to her a few days ago that she could move into the cottage by herself. She could have Nan and Sophie in the apartment next door, while having a place all her own.

And Irma had made that idea even more possible yesterday when she'd told her she was considering not returning to Toronto with Gavin when the month was up. It had instantly come to Sylvia to offer Irma a place to live and the job of caring for Nan and Sophie, but she hadn't shared that yet either.

It somehow seemed too good to be true, but Sylvia kept telling herself there was no reason why both women couldn't use the arrangement to get what they wanted.

And Kent had assured her he would do whatever she wanted as they figured out the termination of their marriage. Sylvia felt all the balls were in her court at this point and was going to take advantage of that. During the last few days it seemed like maybe the relationship between Kent and Darcy had ramped up, and he was anxious to have some options.

⋙⋘

Janice froze in front of the mass of stone she'd almost tripped over. The trek into the woods had been the result of the passage she'd forced herself to write when she returned to her room after breakfast. It had been the part of her story she'd avoided the most vehemently, always knowing she would have to go to it sooner or later if the whole truth was to be told. The writing had cascaded on to the page. Four handwritten pages, which would probably revise down to two, but when she finished she'd dropped her pen like it was oozing poison and rushed out the door. She felt the need to cleanse herself.

It was not your fault, it was not your fault were the words roiling in her head as she headed to the cover of the wooded path. Her eyes were heavily filmed with the tears she was angrily resisting. *I did nothing wrong. It wasn't my fault. Damn you, you sick bastard. I was seven. Fuck you, you bastard son of a bitch.*

Janice stared at the moss-covered statue; a similar statue

had sat on the mantel in the room with the heavy oak door that closed with a thud every time she was led inside. Some statue of Mary that supposedly protected and sheltered her precious children. Every time her eyes fell on the angelic face of the holy mother, Janice was reminded that a little Mi'kmaw girl was not among Mary's flock.

Janice pulled moss from the crumbled face and screamed her curses, not caring if anyone heard. "You did not protect me, you lying bitch, you stone-hearted Madonna. Why have you not rotted and disappeared? Who dragged you to this place and let you cover with dirt and decay? Who did you stand over and not protect when you stood erect? Why do you still haunt my waking and sleeping dreams? Mary, mother of God. Come to me in my time of trouble. Mary, mother of God."

Janice beat her fists on the granite, feeling the flesh tear and seeing the blood surface while she continued to scream curses and condemnation.

≈

Melanie stood before her makeshift easel. She had propped the canvas on the arms of the Adirondack chair, letting it rest against the post on the veranda. She turned it a bit to get the proper lighting and began to set out her paints, allowing the inspiration to come.

She could see a line of clothes fluttering at the back of the lodge. She wanted a clothesline to be the focal point in her painting but wanted an expansive view of the lodge and the wide blue water in the background. She sat down to begin a sketch to get that perspective in order before she committed paint to the surface of the blank canvas.

For some reason Melanie envisioned the clothesline to contain similar items, not the varying array on the line in her sight. She would paint the line with all the same type of garment: loose, flowing, sleeveless dresses, the same in style but made with a variety of fabrics.

⤙᳁⤚

Veronica opened her window to get a clearer idea of what it was she was hearing. She had come up to her room to put on her bathing suit and had been ready to go out the door when she heard what sounded like a low, mournful chorus. It was coming from the woods. Was someone hurt? She rushed out the door.

⤙᳁⤚

Sylvia approached the black car, an Exit Realty logo displayed on the side. Did it really matter what she found on the inside of this cottage? What about the price? Was she willing to pay whatever the asking price was to get this little building, which had become a symbol of her freedom, her independence and the future she was imagining? Would room size, floor coverings, the year the roof was put on, the tax bill, or monthly power costs matter? Did anything Dennis Walker have to tell her even matter? Had she made up her mind to buy this cottage months ago, or at least the day she saw the *For Sale* sign?

From the walkway Sylvia noticed that the shutters had been pulled back from the windows, giving the little cottage an even more welcoming look. As she got to the door a strange sound echoed in the distance, but a tall man stepped out, introduced himself, and invited her inside, distracting her from trying to narrow down what it was she was hearing and from where it was coming.

~~~

Veronica got to Janice at the same time Benson and Gavin did. Janice did not move as they approached. Her wailing and cursing continued. Veronica lowered herself, sat on the ground beside Janice, and motioned for the two men to leave. Both turned and walked away quickly.

"You're okay," Veronica whispered repeatedly, reaching out and touching Janice's shoulder, waiting for the cries to subside.

After a few minutes Janice pulled herself to a sitting position, her face streaked with paths of dirt, leaves, and grasses. Blood pooled on her scraped knuckles. Her expression was distorted, her body shaking, her eyes a dead calm of sorts.

Veronica wrapped both arms around Janice, bringing her in close. Janice allowed her head to rest on Veronica's shoulder. Words did not seem necessary, but Veronica wanted Janice to know that what she'd heard in her outburst and saw in her eyes was an emotion she was more than familiar with.

"It is not our fault. We did nothing to deserve what was done to us. We are more than our pain."

As Veronica whispered these words, a dam of emotion gave way and she did nothing to stop it. Janice seemed not the least surprised by Veronica's sobs and reversed the embrace. The two women rocked each other.

Grace stood a distance away, not wanting to intrude or interfere with the intimacy of the interaction. She would not speak until they were ready. She would help pull them back to the now when they were able to let go of the painful grip of some past heartache. Whatever that heartache was, Grace knew it was deep and insidious in its grip, and the need to expel it was what both woman had in common. She did not know that pain firsthand, but she felt genuine compassion for it and would wait to comfort them as best she could.

～⁂～

"The owners are anxious to sell," Dennis Walker said. "It is the grandson of the couple who own it that I am dealing with. Apparently the wife had a stroke last fall and the husband is not well either. They have gone into nursing care. Up until her stroke they were living here year-round. They winterized it a few years ago. Patrick says it is a cottage that has been in the family for years and it is hard to let it go, but he lives in Vancouver and at this point does not see himself using it enough to make keeping it worthwhile.

"The grandson's name is Patrick?"

"Yes."

Sylvia quickly pushed down thoughts of her grandfather and her infant son. She certainly wasn't offering this emotional connection to a total stranger. Good negotiating skills did not come with the admission she had already pretty much decided to buy regardless, and now the name of the seller emotionally sealed the deal.

"The asking price is reasonable, but Patrick did indicate some wiggle room."

"How soon could I take possession?"

<hr />

Melanie heard the commotion but purposefully shut it out. Some of the others were attending to it. She had seen the woman rush out the door and head to the wooded path a while ago and only nodded at her. She didn't know the names of everyone yet. Social interaction and small talk had never been her forte, even before the two years she'd spent with Dawson, which had isolated her even more and rocked her self-confidence.

She spoke through her paintbrush and the words of her poetry, whether or not anyone saw it or listened. And right now a long line of colourful dresses was what she had to say, and she would ignore whatever else was going on around her. She was really good at doing that.

⁓⁓⧫⁓⁓

Benson popped the K-cup into the machine and set a mug on the tray. He felt a bit shaken by what he'd just witnessed. He and Gavin had been in the great room when they heard Janice, and they couldn't ignore it. She'd sounded like a trapped animal, except of course her agony had been expressed in words. He'd recognized the words from his years as a choirboy at St. Dunstan's. The rote memory never disappears, even when a person has not darkened the door of a church in fifty years. Grandmother Cormier would be rolling in her grave at the lack of Catholicism in her descendants. And for sure she would be horrified to hear Janice's curses.

Thank God Veronica had shooed them away. What good could he or Gavin have been to the situation? He expected Janice might have slugged either one of them had they come close enough. He felt bad for her, though. Gavin mumbled something about hysterical women and went upstairs immediately, but he would make a cup of coffee and calm his nerves.

⁓⁓⧫⁓⁓

Right after breakfast Kitty had gone to her room, taken a headache pill, and put in her ear plugs. But sleep had not come. In two days she would be leaving this place, and the thought of that had hit her hard. What had she believed two weeks hiding away in a remote part of New Brunswick was going to do for her? She had met her goal of finishing her manuscript. But she had come here for more than that, and she didn't feel ready to leave. Going back to business as usual was not something she was looking forward to.

<center>~~~~~~</center>

Tyler and Abby stopped walking, and looking back realized how far they had come. Instead of joining the others at lunchtime they had decided to pack a small picnic and head along the beach in the opposite direction from where they usually walked. It seemed as if they needed to get away from the lodge to make some important decisions, with the time getting so close to when Abby would leave and fly back to Alberta.

"Let's sit here and have our picnic," Tyler suggested.

Abby spread out the blanket and kicked off her Birkenstocks.

"My mom made a big deal of picnics. Sometimes in the dead of winter she would pretend our family room was the beach and spread out a blanket, bring lunch down in her grandmother's red basket, and we would have a picnic. She'd put on her sundress and wide-brimmed sunhat and we would imagine we were at the beach."

"You are at the beach today."

"Is it weird if I pretend she is here with us?"

"Are you kidding? We are writers. Imagination is what we do. Would Donavan come to the picnics?"

"Well, yes. He hogged most of the blanket and always got most of my sandwich."

"I have been thinking that maybe I should cut the retreat short," Tyler said. "I don't know if Kent would refund some of my money or not, but I think I should get back to Halifax and get a job. It doesn't have to be Halifax. I could come out to Alberta and look for something there."

"First of all, I think you should stay for your month," Abby began. "I need to go home and look after a few things. I don't want you to come to me. I have nothing to stay in Alberta for. I want to leave my life behind and come here. Coming to New Brunswick seems right to me, but I don't want you to jeopardize your relationship with Henry. Wouldn't it be harder to get regular visitation if you were in a different province?"

"I have to get a job first and get my life together. We can figure out that part later. Could you work from here?"

"I think so, but if not I can get something else. I feel for the first time in forever that I can do pretty much anything I set my mind to. Getting rid of an apartment full of stuffed dogs will be my first task."

"You don't have to get rid of all of them."

"I know."

"You can just figure it out as you go."

Abby reached over and kissed Tyler. "*We* can figure it out as we go."

"Is that Sylvia?" Darcy asked.

Kent slowed the van and turned his head in time to see a tall man reach out and shake Sylvia's hand.

Chapter Fourteen

Benson pulled his chair out and stood up, clearing his throat and taking in a breath as if preparing to deliver the morning announcements.

"August 24. Two weeks is up and some of us leave tomorrow. This has been quite the experience and hopefully has made us all better writers. I know myself I've learned a thing or two by listening to you all. Let's make the best of this last day some of us have together with a final workshop this morning. I propose we meet around this table again in an hour with something we wrote since coming and state why being here helped you write it. The four of you who are staying are welcome to join us. I'm sure Dot will put on another pot of coffee and maybe even whip us up her famous cinnamon buns. I'm going to miss her cooking, I'll tell you."

"I'll join you, Benson," Kitty said. "And I'll put a vote in for those buns, Dot."

"Go home, yer mudder's got buns, we used to say as kids," Irma said.

"We should make sure Sylvia comes in for your last workshop, Benson," Gavin said. "You two-weekers haven't gotten much from her. Some of us one-monthers haven't got much either. Maybe you could go ask her, Janice, since you seem to be her pet."

"Wow, you sound like an entitled teenager, like one of my students, Gavin," Darcy said.

Grace stood up and began clearing off the table. "I just hate it when folks leave. Maybe it's my age, but I try to see the good in everyone. Not an entitled teenager, for sure, and don't think I ever was one. I'd love to join you for a workshop, Benson. Let's all just get along today."

"Let's make it a party day," Tyler said. "Maybe a bonfire and hootenanny, like they say used to go on here."

"Who says that?" Veronica asked.

Melanie entered the room. She set her canvas and supplies down in the great room while she made her way toward the coffee pot. Veronica rose from her chair and walked closer to the partially completed painting. She took a gulp of air and steadied herself.

Outlines of the building, horizon, and water were obvious. It was clear more detail was to be added, but the clothesline stretching along a good part of the painting was the focal point and already had most of its detail, colour, and texture. Sleeveless sack dresses, each one different in colour and adornment. A red checked one, a pale blue one with yellow sunflowers, one with a green geometric design, a yellow one with purple polka dots, a pink-and-white-striped one. A pink-and-white-striped one.

Veronica slumped to the couch, feeling her body spin and her head pulsate. How had this girl known about the dresses, about the very dress she'd been wearing on that terrible day? She felt the panic erupting and knew she should be taking refuge in her room but felt nailed to the spot. Through blurry eyes she saw Janice and Grace approach.

"Are you all right, dear?" Grace asked.

Janice sat down, pulling Veronica toward her. "Take a deep breath. Deep breaths."

"Must have been something I ate," Veronica said weakly. "Shouldn't have taken that second sausage."

"Let's get the dear girl a cold cloth," Irma barked. "Clear out and give her some space, for God's sake. Open that front door and let some fresh air in Gavin. Lord thundering, people, have you never seen a woman go faint before?"

❧

"They're all having a workshop right now. Most of them anyway," Janice said. "Veronica had a bad spell after breakfast and went to lie down, and the new girl barely speaks to any of us. She's out on the veranda painting. Not my place to judge. She paid her money for the retreat, so she can paint or knit a scarf for all I care. Gavin had his knickers in a knot. Thought I should be dragging you over for the workshop. I didn't tell him to bite my arse, but I wanted to. My dirty look might have said something similar."

Sylvia poured iced tea into Janice's glass. "I won't be sorry to see him leave, I'll tell you."

"You'll hate to see Irma go, though. Sophie's sure taken a liking to her."

"We all have. Look at them out there. And listen to that laughter. You can't imagine how I love to see Sophie so happy. I couldn't get her anywhere near that swing, but Irma suggests it and she's out the door like a bullet. She's been such good company for Nan, too."

Sylvia continued lowering her voice a bit. "Actually, she's not leaving, but that's just between you and me for now. She hasn't told Gavin yet."

"What a smart woman," Janice said. "I'd have put a pillow over his head long ago."

"Funny, that's what Irma's mother used to say about her grandfather. Men should really be more afraid of us."

"My ex never had to worry about me murdering him in his sleep. The opposite might not have been true, though. He was a saint. Not perfect by any means, but awful good to me."

"Is Knockwood your married name?"

"No, Hank's last name is Perley. My kids are Perleys, but I never changed my name."

"So you'll publish under Knockwood."

"Now, ain't those nice words. Yeah, if I get published it will be Janice Knockwood on the cover."

"I have no doubt you'll get published."

"Thank you."

"I remember practising signing my name after my first

book was published. I wanted to be sure I knew just how I was going to write each letter so my signature would be impressive and consistent."

"Do you remember doodling as a kid?" Janice asked. "My friends and I used to see just how different we could make the writing of our names."

"Oh my God, yes. I went through a stage when I made the *a* at the end of my name a heart. Then of course with each crush I would practise writing my name as Mrs. Whoever. It was Mrs. Kenny Small for a short time, and then I had a long stretch of writing Mrs. Burton Green on everything. Nan picked up a Kleenex box once and every inch of it was covered. I had written *I love Burton Green* or *Mrs. Burton Green* on every square inch of it."

"I had a friend named Sue who signed her name Sioux for our entire Grade Eleven year," Janice added. "Didn't matter to her it wasn't her tribe."

"I knew I wanted Sylvia Drummond Wright to be the name I published under, but I did go through a penname phase in high school. Bridget St. John."

"Fancy."

"Not really. Kind of sad and pathetic. It was a play on words and a dark comment on my past. My mother jumped off a bridge in Saint John and died."

"Oh, Sylvia. I am so sorry."

"Isn't weird how when you say the words out loud to someone they sound flat, like you're making it up for attention? Yeah, poor me, my mother jumped off a bridge. 'Go jump off a bridge,' kids used to say in elementary school, until Mrs. Carpenter heard them one day and put a stop to it. Somehow it was worse when they knew. Just words, but not just words when it really happens."

"So you decided against Bridget St. John?"

"Yes. Olivia found a loose-leaf sheet with that name all over it one day when she was rooting though a drawer in my office. She was around ten, I think. She loved the name and went through the next few months insisting we call her Bridget St. John. Nan, Sophie, and I complied, but Kent was oblivious to it and kept calling her Olivia, and of course she never corrected him.

"I never told her the significance of the name. The girls knew my mother died when I was four, but I never told them how. Each time she used the name it was a pinprick of pain for me, like some kind of acupuncture. Maybe it was healing after all. Saying the words can lessen the pain."

"Isn't that what we've been telling each other?" Janice said.

<hr />

Darcy opened the door of the storage shed.

"I wondered where you took off to after breakfast," Darcy said.

"Aren't you joining the others for the workshop?" Kent asked.

"I read my piece and then slipped out. Benson is reading, so he didn't notice, and the others are in a bored trance. I'm not wasting my last day here on that shit. I was hoping we could do something."

"Well, I do have to go in to Moncton for a few things if you want to go for the ride."

"I want to go for a good old-fashioned backseat fuck, if you want to know."

"Well, that could be arranged. The back seat goes down in the van."

"Now you're talking dirty. Like I wasn't horny enough."

"Give me five minutes and I'll meet you at the van," Kent said.

"Not a problem," Darcy said moving closer, her crotch gyrating against Kent's thigh. "You don't have to ask me twice."

⌒⌒⌒

Dot pulled the car into the Legion parking lot.

"This is the social hub of our community, Evelyn. At least for us old folks. *Keenagers*, this group is called. Stupid name, but I guess most of them are pretty keen to still be breathing."

"Oh Dot, you are so funny. It was nice of you to invite me to come with you this afternoon. I miss the small community I was used to on White Head Island. I belonged to a couple of groups in Toronto, but it wasn't the same."

"Small communities are great, but everybody knows everybody's business. You'll be surprised how much folks will know about you in there. Not much goes unnoticed or ungossiped about around here."

"I know how that works in a small place. It seemed the minute Valerie stepped on the ferry, the whole island knew the Ingalls girl was leaving home. Then you become the mother of the dead girl, the poor dead girl who jumped off a bridge. And of course most people knew Paddy's boat had gone down before I did."

"Nobody will likely tell you right away, but sooner or later as you get to know these folks better they'll let slip the most repeated fact told about Dorothy Flemming over the last fifty years. I may as well tell you before we go in."

Evelyn looked over and saw tears dripping off Dot's cheeks.

"We killed a girl. Hit the poor thing with our car. God love her. I see her still, lying on the road gasping for her last breath."

"Oh my God, Dot. That's awful."

"Thought when I took the job it wouldn't haunt me so much, but every time I drive along that road I relive it. The poor dear girl was running away, they figured. Not running, I'm sure, as the poor thing was nine months pregnant. The lodge used to be a home for unwed mothers, pregnant girls some barely in their teens. God love them.

"It was such a dark, foggy night, and at first we thought we'd hit a deer. I hear the thud still. Donnie wasn't going to even stop, but something made us pull over. We watched the poor girl die, knowing her unborn child would die too. There was no such thing as cell phones or 911 in those days. We had no ambulance service even. I ran to the home and woke them up. They hadn't even known she was gone. Patricia, her name was."

"Oh, Dot, we don't have to go in if you're not up to it."

"I'm fine. I just needed to tell you for some reason. It's coming up to the day, so I guess that's why it's on my mind. Let's go in and put on our *keen* faces. There will be fancy sandwiches, and Faye Clark always brings a pan of her lovely tweed squares."

~~~

Tyler dragged more wood onto the pile. He and Abby had spent the last hour placing rocks in a big circle and gathering wood along the shore.

"When we've got enough wood gathered, let's drag some of those logs over to make seats around the circle," Tyler said.

"Wow, you know what you're doing. Had a lot of bonfires in your day, did you?"

"Actually, only one I remember. I lived with my mother's cousin one summer before I went into care. Guess I was more than she was willing to take on, but she was nice. Hebert and Connie, their names were. Well, Hebert's folks owned a cottage on a lake somewhere. We went there for a weekend once and I helped him build a fire."

"Why didn't you tell me you were in foster care too? You let me go on about it and never said."

"It's something I try not to think about. Not that they were all bad. A couple of them were pretty good, actually, but in some ways that was worse. The good ones always made me hopeful. But in the end I always chalked it up to the fact I must have been too big of a pain in the ass for anyone to consider keeping me around long term."

"So you aged out too?"

"Yeah. Never quite understood that logic. How many kids do you know reach eighteen and no longer get anything from their parents? Christ, Darlene's parents still dish out money and have a say in just about everything she does. I blamed that for most of our problems, actually, so maybe Social Services has the right idea. On your own at eighteen to sink or swim."

"What about your sister? Was she in foster care?"

"Mary Ann hit the jackpot. The first home she got sent to adopted her right away. She was younger and cuter."

"That must have been hard. But you guys stayed close?"

"I guess so. Her parents are nice. They invited me for Christmases and shit. Let's finish getting this bonfire set up."

⁓

Kitty began taking some clothes off the hangers in the closet, folding them and placing them in the open suitcase on her bed. She might as well pack some this afternoon and not leave it all until morning. Veronica's panic attack had flustered her, and she'd spent the last couple of hours in her room. It always floored her when a situation could not be handled with a snappy comeback.

She'd felt the tension around the table when she, Tyler, Abby, Gavin, and Grace had met for Benson's workshop. She'd taken the piece she'd written the day before but hadn't offered to read it. Instead she read a section from the manuscript she'd sent to her publisher, making up some elaborate story about how the sunset two days ago had prompted her to write it. Bullshit.

Bullshit, just like most everything else she wrote or said. Same bullshit, different day, and different location. She had loved being here, but what change or impact had it really made on her? She would pack, sleep one more quiet night here, and in the morning she would leave. She would return to her previous life with all the previous bullshit.

Kitty scrolled down to read the first paragraph of the passage she'd taken but hadn't for one minute considered reading out loud to the group.

The girl's screams were silent, her arms limp, offering no fight. Instead she went quickly to another place, her grandmother's house. Her grandmother's cherry pie, turkey dinner dressing, pasta shells with Nan's special sauce, Mr. Big bars. Soon this would be over and she would get up and walk away.

She pulled a sundress off the hanger. *Fuck*, she thought, *this thing looks more like a tent than a dress.* She pulled it over her head. Good, heavy cotton reaching almost to her ankles. She'd wear it down for supper and no one would know she was stark naked underneath. *Nothing to hide under there,* she thought, chuckling.

᭞

"What's cooking?" Benson asked. "It smells amazing."

"Lobster Thermidor," Dot answered, "corn on the cob, and roasted red potatoes. Peach and blueberry cobbler for dessert. A last supper for some of the folks. I wanted to make it extra special."

"Do you mind if I go invite Sylvia and Evelyn to come for supper?" Irma said. "I'll stay with Sophie and have mine later."

"It would be lovely if they could come. I'll dish yours up and you can eat it there. Do you suppose Sophie would eat any of it?"

"I think her taste goes more to peanut butter than lobster."

"I'm allergic to lobster," Darcy called down from upstairs.

"What a shame she told us," Irma whispered. "I'd love to see her swell up like a bloated fish."

"I'll fry her a hotdog." Dot said with a grin.

"Oh, she's getting a hot dog already," Irma added.

᭞

Kent stood, picking up his wine glass to raise a toast.

"Thanks for the lovely meal, Dorothy. Two weeks have flown by, and we are sorry to see more of you go. We hope you will return and we hope you will tell others about our little retreat here and what we have to offer. To Benson, Abby, Kitty, and Darcy."

Janice kicked Sylvia's leg under the table and smirked at her friend. They had laughed earlier when Sylvia made a comment wondering if Kent would add sex with him as a feature of the two-week retreat.

"To the Wright Retreat," Benson added clinking his wine glass.

"To Dot's cooking," Kitty toasted.

"To you all," Grace said, raising her teacup.

Abby stood and took a deep breath. "You have all been so kind to me. This retreat has been the best thing in my life and I won't forget any of you."

Tyler stood beside her and put an arm around her, leaning in to kiss her cheek. "Not me, at least. She's moving to New Brunswick. That's how much she's liked being here, and me."

Cheers rose from around the table.

"That's great," Kent said. "Might have to add the chance of romance to the attractions of the retreat."

Janice kicked Sylvia again before standing up to make a toast. "To friends. I am so thankful for the friends I've made here."

Another cheer came from around the table.

Sylvia stood. "To your friendship, Janice, and to Dot, Irma, Grace, Veronica, and Kitty. All of you."

"She doesn't mean me, I'm sure," Gavin said to no one in particular.

"We've got a bonfire ready for later," Tyler said.

"Look at the beginning of that sunset," Veronica said.

"Bonfire and a late-night swim. Sounds amazing," Kitty said. "Let's keep this party hopping."

~~⁘~~

Veronica stood mesmerized by the changing sky. The rocks along the shore looked a purple grey as they met the shades of orange consuming both sky and water. The sky was a deep tangerine shaded only with the wisps of floating clouds moving slowly. The water was a light peach rippling below the skyline. Connecting both was a blazing lemon-yellow sun gradually dipping out of sight, leaving a bright line of reflection in the water.

With squinting eyes, Veronica saw the setting sun as a large, encompassing cross. She would enter the water under that cross, a cross of forgiveness and redemption, not the cross of judgement and condemnation that had once hung above her and left her wanting. Barely aware of the others following behind, Veronica walked toward the water's edge, stripped off her cover-up, and bounded into the waves.

Grace spread out a blanket and settled herself. Kitty pulled up a lawn chair and sat down beside her. Tyler and Abby were starting the bonfire and Benson and Gavin stood nearby. Sylvia and Janice joined Veronica in the water. Melanie stood before a blank canvas set up on the veranda, anxious to capture the shades of the sunset before they disappeared. Kent and Darcy had just entered the hot tub. Irma walked around the corner, taking in everyone's whereabouts. She was weary but would go to the bonfire for a while before heading up to bed.

The shades of orange had faded and darkness was offering up the shadows of the still night. The three swimmers were out of the water, dried off, and sitting in front of the heat of the bonfire. Grace, Irma, and Kitty had come over to sit around the fire as well. Abby and Tyler sat in a tight embrace, seemingly oblivious to anyone else in the circle. Benson and Gavin had left the beach a few minutes ago.

Sylvia stood to throw more wood on the fire and looked toward the lodge just as Kent and Darcy left the hot tub and entered the side door together.

"I bought the yellow cottage next door," Sylvia announced.

"I'm not going back to Toronto with Gavin," Irma added. "I'm moving in with Evelyn to help look after Sophie."

Chapter Fifteen

Kitty jumped out of bed. The dress she'd been wearing last night was in a crumpled pile on the floor and she was as naked as she'd been last night. Only Sylvia, Janice, and Veronica were still around the fire when the urge had hit her. She'd stood up, pulled off her dress, and headed to the water. Wading in to up to her knees, she'd stopped and raised her arms. Had she hollered?

If no sound had come out, an internal noise erupted. She had reached her hands to the sky as if she could grab the moon and felt the eruption coming up from her toes. The release of shame, self-hatred, and disgust. She screamed the anger she'd felt, the screams she'd kept silent that day and forced down the years that followed. She had dropped into the water, and as her head went below the surface, she was not sure she would come back up.

But the holler she let out when she stood back up was real. It was loud, and it echoed across the still, dark water. Veronica was at her side first, Sylvia and Janice shortly afterward, and the three of them guided her back to the shore. She stood, still naked, while the sobs erupted and the final release came.

"My name is Kathleen."

She kept repeating that over and over, as if that fact was the one she'd kept hidden all these years. Veronica had walked her back to her room, gotten her into bed, and covered her shaking body. Veronica pulled up a chair close to her bed, held her hand, and waited until the rest of the story poured out.

～❦～

"My Aunt Marjorie cries really loud," Veronica said.

Marjorie Wilkin's cries were echoing off the walls and down from the high ceiling of the Coverdale Baptist church, where most pews were filled and the last of the family was filing in.

"Shh, Ronnie," Mrs. McDonald said as she pushed Veronica into the seat, releasing the tight grip she had on the six-year-old's hand. Mommy was the only person in the world who called her Ronnie, but Veronica didn't correct her neighbour.

"She's too young to go to the funeral," Veronica had heard her Aunt Marjorie say to Daddy last night.

"She might as well face the fact her mother is dead, for God's sake. Never was one to baby the child. No one babied me, and I turned out just fine."

Veronica stared at the big wooden box at the front of the church. She could still hear Aunt Marjorie's crying and wondered why no one was telling her to shh. That is all anyone had said to her since she got out of Daddy's car. Since three days ago, actually, when they told her Mommy was dead. She wanted to let out a loud scream. She wanted to squeeze out of this pew and run to the wooden box. She wanted to cry and holler and say some of the bad words she always heard Daddy say. She wanted to beat her fists on the wood so that they hurt as much as her heart did.

Mrs. Flanagan walked onto the platform, sat herself down on the round stool, and pulled knobs out on the organ, and the creaky music started. Everyone stood up, and Veronica could no longer see the wooden box or the picture of Mommy on the table beside it.

Veronica had gone to sleep last night with the words of a hymn stuck in her head. This morning the melody was still there, but the words kept evading her. Shall we gather at the river was all she could remember but knew the song said something about angels and saints.

She would get up quickly and go check on Kathleen.

⁓⤙⁓

Tyler sat on the side of the bed, waiting for Abby to come out from her shower. He would prefer a more romantic setting, but he wanted to ask her before he lost his nerve. He held the tattered book, thinking of the day he'd pulled it off the shelf at the library. The crude tracing of the author's printed name along with the simplistic drawing of a fish gave the book an amateur look. The typed title seemed almost an afterthought put there so readers would take it seriously.

Tyler had signed the book out and read the whole thing that same night. Right away there was something in that little book that gave him permission to be what he'd imagined himself being as long as he could remember. Never a poet but a writer, someone able to write down the thoughts that constantly beat around in his head but he never gave voice to. There was no one who would listen anyway, but maybe if he rounded up all his thoughts and ordered them in sentences and story, someone would see him and hear what he had to say. He would maybe matter to someone.

Tyler had considered returning the book when it came due, maybe signing it out for another week, but he never did. It was his. It belonged to him. He would run his fingertips over the laminated barcode label and look at the library stamp on the inside cover and feel a sense of bravery and rebellion. Richard Brautigan had written *Trout Fishing in America* just for him.

Tyler knew a proposal with the gift of a stolen library book was dumb, but he didn't care. The book was valuable to him and he believed Abby would get that. A ring could come later.

Irma was up and dressed before Gavin this morning. She knew there was no hurry, but something about this day, this day when Kitty, Benson, Abby, and Darcy were leaving, seemed like the day to tell Gavin her plans. She realized telling him when he still had two more weeks here might make those two weeks uncomfortable. But really, what had been comfortable in the last two weeks with regards to Gavin? He might as well know her plans and get used to them. Might make it easier in the long run.

Darcy rolled over and ran her fingers along Kent's naked back and down to his buttocks. He'd fallen into an exhausted sleep last night after two good workouts. She had lain awake entertaining thoughts of him asking her not to leave today. She could, like Gavin, extend her retreat registration to the month, but she wanted it to come from Kent. She did not want to appear to be begging, to be needy and weak.

Robin always accused her of showing her hand too soon. "Play hard to get," she would advise. Darcy hadn't wanted to play hard to get in the sex department, as that was her ace in the hole. If last night had been any indication, her theory was correct. Hopefully her leaving today would not end Kent's desire. She would play the morning cool and wait to see what her next move was.

Benson zipped up his suitcase and set it out in the hall. For some reason he'd woken up thinking of the hotel in Maine where he and Nancy had spent the first night of their honeymoon. Bar Harbor in September was quiet and romantic. They'd arrived late, checked in, and gone at it like rabbits. They had been going at it like rabbits last night in the room next door, by the sounds of things.

A part of him wanted to take Kent aside today and tell him not to be an asshole. He could tell him short-term gain made for long-term pain. Speaking from experience, he could tell him you pretty much lose from every angle when you throw away a marriage. But what good would it do? Would he have listened to anyone? Hindsight's 20/20, they say.

⁓⌇⁓

August 25, for the last fifty years, was a date on the calendar to dread, find her way through, and get past. Donnie had never seen her need to dwell on that date, but every year Dot acknowledged it in the same way.

"What good is getting yourself in a state every August? Not a damn thing you can do to change any of it. Won't bring that poor girl back. You're just torturing yourself as far as I can see."

Dot listened to Donnie's rant for the first few years, but went about her rituals on the day anyway. Every year on August 25 she went into Moncton, bought one yellow rose, drove to the spot, and laid it on the side of the road.

"If you need flowers, why the hell don't you just pick some out of your garden or along the side of the road and go lay them there? Don't see why you have to go all the way into MacArthur's to buy a rose."

"It's my way to remember her. Someone needs to. Her life and the life of her child are worth a bit of time and a rose."

"Well, you're going to do what you're going to do. I'm not spending the rest of my life feeling guilty. It was an accident, for God's sake. She shouldn't have been in the middle of the road on a dark, foggy night. Maybe she ran out in front of us on purpose. Can't see where it was my fault."

After a few years there had been no discussion when August 25 came. She would just go do what she did every year and Donnie would ignore it. The years since he passed were the same. But something about this year felt different. Maybe it was being here every day and driving the road every morning, but this year she felt closer to Patricia. This year she laid a dozen yellow roses on the side of the road before continuing on to the lodge and starting breakfast.

<hr />

"I told some of them about buying the cottage last night," Sylvia said as she sat down beside Nan. "I suppose I should tell Kent next."

"And what about Irma? When is she telling Gavin her plans?"

"Today, I think. Do you think we could make room for her even before I move into the cottage? She might not want to be sleeping in the same room as Gavin once she tells him."

"She can move her things into my room. And she can sleep in my bed with me for now if she doesn't mind."

"We can ask her this morning."

"Don't you think you should be trying to contact Olivia? This will be the second move you've made without her knowledge. It breaks my heart thinking she might go to the house and not find us there."

"Kent has been in touch with her. He got her a job in his office a while ago. She knows he retired, and I assume he told her about the move."

"We were two years not knowing where your mother was, and it was terrible. Then she called your grandfather to come to Saint John and meet her at the Diana restaurant by the city market. She was pregnant with you. He tried his best to convince her to come home until at least after you were born, but she wouldn't. She stayed clean for a full year, and we were so hopeful."

"And you took me for a while, right?"

"Yes, we had you for six months just after you turned two. We would have fought to keep you, but your mother was clean again, working, and had a nice apartment. She'd left your father and again we were hopeful."

"I don't remember living with you and Papa then, but I do remember the picture of you my mother always kept nearby. I used to cry for you sometimes, and she would let me sleep with your picture beside me. That's why I wasn't afraid when they brought me to you and Papa. I already knew you."

"Oh dear, I wish things had turned out differently. We loved you so much, but raising you was never how it should have been."

Sophie bounded into the kitchen, interrupting the conversation. Sylvia got up and emptied the rest of her coffee into the sink. The piece she had read from her blue notebook was about those two days, those two long, frightening days. Her memory of being alone and waiting in that little apartment, constantly going to the window, hoping to see her mother walking along the sidewalk and enter the front door. She kept listening for the bell, her signal to open the door and pull the long cord that would unlock the bottom door and her mother would come upstairs and everything would be all right.

~~~

Abby took the book from Tyler.

"You love this book."

"And I love you."

Abby walked across the room. She picked up the stuffed Basset Hound.

"Did I tell you why his name is Slacker?"

"Because all East Coasters are slackers?"

"I will take your book and accept your proposal if you will take this guy. I'll look after *Trout Fishing in America* and you look after Slacker until I come back, and then we'll look after both together."

Tyler wrapped his arms around Abby, pulling her in close to kiss her.

"We are engaged, Abby Trenholme."

"Yes we are, Tyler Woodhouse."

~~~

Veronica knocked lightly on the door in case Kitty was still sleeping. She would have to get up soon anyway, but letting her sleep a bit longer after the night she'd had seemed kinder than waking her. Kitty opened the door and invited Veronica in. She was up and dressed and putting the last few things in her suitcase.

"Good morning, Kathleen."

"Thank you so much for being there for me last night. You were an angel."

"Well, I don't know about an angel, but I am glad you felt able to confide in me. Keeping such a painful secret takes its toll."

"You're friggin' right it does. It's not like I haven't tried to deal with it. I've been to therapists, read lots of books about surviving rape, but I had never actually said the words out loud to anyone before. I bullshitted every therapist I saw. Bullshitted myself for a long time. Do you really think the mind can blot trauma out?

"Yes, I know it can. But listen, this morning is not about me. I want to make sure you are all right. I wish we had more time to talk before you leave. You can write to me if you'd like. Writers are good at writing stuff, or at least we're supposed to be. It hasn't worked in my case, but maybe if we start writing letters back and forth it will help me as much as it could help you. I brought you an empty journal, and my mailing address is on the inside cover. I really think last night was just the beginning of the healing that words will be for you."

***

"So just like that, you're ending a thirty-five-year marriage. You meet a brain-damaged girl and an old lady and decide to trade me in."

"You don't get it, do you? Have you even noticed how unhappy I have been? Being here with Sophie and Evelyn has been like a breath of fresh air."

"Divorce is not cheap, and don't even think I'm going to sell the house and give you half. I'd never get another house for what we paid for it. Do you have any idea what Toronto real estate is like nowadays?"

"I don't care about a divorce. I don't want anything from you. You can pack my stuff up and give it to Goodwill for all I care."

"Are they going to pay you?"

"Yes, they are. Imagine, I am going to get paid for cooking and cleaning. God knows I've done it all these years for barely a kind word. Feeling appreciated seems like more than enough of an attraction to stay, if you want the truth of it."

"Oh my God, Irma. Like I've been such a bastard to you."

"I am not saying that, Gavin. I'm staying here when you go back to Toronto. Let's just leave it at that."

***

Dot stepped out onto the veranda and watched as the suitcases were being put in the back of the van. She had packed bagged lunches for Kitty, Abby, and Darcy, and packed Benson some snacks for his drive. It had been different watching Jonathan leave, probably because he left alone. This time, with four leaving at the same time, it seemed more emotional for everyone. Darcy for sure was not taking it well. But Dot was pretty sure the conversation she'd overheard between Kent and Darcy outside the open kitchen window was meant to be private.

"When will I see you again?"

"I don't know, Darcy."

"Will I have to register again and come back if I want what we have to continue?"

"What is it we have?" Kent asked.

"We have great sex, for one thing."

"Yeah, you're right there. I suppose we could meet in Toronto in the fall sometime."

"I need more than a sometime. Do you plan on staying here forever? Couldn't you move back to Toronto and run the financial part and let Sylvia keep things running here? I could move to Toronto for a few months, anyway, and we could be together."

"I don't know yet, Darcy, and I don't want to be pressured. I have to figure some things out."

"I need you. I can't bear the thought of leaving today without at least having a plan in place to see you again."

Dot closed the window, not wanting to hear any more of Darcy's grovelling or Kent's pathetic responses.

⌐∾⌐

"You're not going out for the goodbyes?" Irma asked, stepping into Sylvia's kitchen.

"I said goodbye to Abby and Kitty last night. Kathleen, I mean."

"Kathleen?"

"Oh, you'd already gone to bed when Kitty went for her swim. Poor thing. I knew she was fighting a demon of some kind. She had a breakdown. Went for a skinny dip and completely lost it. I'm surprised you didn't hear her hollering."

"I thought Kitty was more quiet than usual at breakfast, and Veronica seemed to be watching out for her. It seemed a little odd."

"Yeah, Veronica took her to her room. She was very comforting with her."

"I have the feeling Veronica has a deep sorrow of her own. It seems to me we all have fought some battles in these last two weeks."

"My mother always said that everyone has their own sorrows to bear," Evelyn said. "The longer I live, the more I see the truth of that."

"The first day I came to meet you, you asked if I had any family in Newfoundland," Irma said. "I said it was a sorrowful story for another day. I hope you don't mind if that day is today."

"Of course we don't mind," Evelyn answered.

Sylvia put a cup of coffee down on the table in front of Irma and sat down.

"It was a fire. God knows how it started, but the devil knows how quickly that old house became an inferno. Folks said it was like nothing they'd ever seen before. Started in the night and not a soul got out. Not a soul. My prayer is that it happened so fast they never knew and didn't suffer. My baby girl was among them. Gloria, her name was, and she was only seven months old. My baby, my mother, my father, four brothers, and four sisters, all gone. My family, my home, and my whole life gone in the time it took for that old house to burn to the ground."

"Oh my God, Irma, that is horrible," Sylvia said. "You weren't home?"

"No, I was in St. John's working."

"Terrible loss, just terrible," Evelyn said. "And to lose a child, no loss like it. Both Sylvia and I know that loss."

"But thank God you still have your sweet Sophie."

"Yes, I do, and I am so grateful for that. I was not spared the loss of my sweet boy, though. My sweet boy Patrick. He never took his first breath. I never looked into his open eyes and felt his heart beating next to mine. He was gone before he was even here."

Irma stood and reached out to hug Sylvia. "God love you. God love us all. I told Gavin my plans this morning."

"How did he take it?"

"He ranted a bit. Mostly about money and how he didn't do anything wrong."

"You can move in here if you want, if you don't mind sleeping with Nan until I move into the cottage."

"G'wan, I used to sleep in a double bed with two of my sisters growing up. I've had to sleep with Gavin for years and his snoring near got me drove. Evelyn will be a delight I'm sure. Now, Sophie girl, let's you and Irma go outside and wave to the folks who's leaving. And you got through two weeks with those damn authors, Sylvia."

"I did, didn't I?

Chapter Sixteen

"I gave the empty rooms a good cleaning and now I just have to make up the beds," Marjorie said, sitting at the table while Dot poured her a cup of tea. "Do you know when more writers are coming? I'll have the rooms ready, but I was wondering if anyone is coming today."

"Mr. Wright is away for a few days. Last-minute trip to Toronto, I guess. I don't think anyone new is coming until the first of September. I'll only be feeding seven or eight in the next few days. Not that it really matters to me. I've never been one to ration food or measure it out by portion size."

"You're like your mother in that way. She put on some meals back in the day, didn't she?"

"That's for sure. No one darkened Mother's door and went away hungry. I hope the same can be said of me."

"You doing okay, Dot? I know August is a hard month for you."

"I'm fine. Thanks for asking. This year feels different. I finally feel like I can lay Patricia to rest. It's weird, but being here every day and cooking hearty meals in this kitchen feels like I am caring for her in some way. I know that's crazy, but even with all the changes the building has seen, I feel the presence of the poor frightened girls who lived here while going through the most vulnerable time of their lives. Young girls hidden away here, waiting to give birth to their shame. It was such a disgrace back in those days to be pregnant out of wedlock. But most of the girls were just kids, too young to be going through what they were going through, too young to be mothers and too young to be married."

"Did we even know as kids what this place was?" Marjorie asked. "I knew the Catholics had some kind of camp at the end of this road, but until the accident I didn't know what it really was. What were you and Donnie doing on this road that night, anyway?"

"Oh, for God's sake, Marjorie. Use your imagination. Don't tell me you and Walter never drove down this road to go parking."

"You guys were married, for God's sake. Why the need to go parking?"

"Donnie's mother was living with us, and we had four kids by then. Finding the quiet time or place to be together wasn't easy, so that night instead of heading right home after the dance we came down here. That always made things worse in my mind. If we'd gone right home that poor girl would still be living."

"You know what Walter says *if* is?"

"Oh, I know. He got that from Dad. If I heard him say it once I've heard it a million times: '*If* is a mighty small animal and it doesn't live in these parts.' Now, if you don't get back to work and leave me alone, I won't have lunch ready when the writers come in."

⁓ᵧᵣ⁓

From the kitchen window Sylvia noticed Gavin approaching the steps. She went out the door and stood on the landing, ready to cut him off.

"I am not here to see Irma, if that's what you think. Seems she's made up her mind and isn't going to listen to me anyway. I am here for that list you promised me. Surely to God with just four of us left you can find the time to deliver what the one-month retreat promised. Oh, I suppose there are five of us, but of course Janice has had lots of attention from you already. I heard her say this morning that she is ready to submit her manuscript. I'm ready too."

"Did you do any revisions from the notes I gave you?"

"I said I was ready. Have you got the list?"

"I'll get it," Sylvia replied, stepping inside and closing the screen door behind her.

"Bring it over to the lodge," Gavin hollered in through the screen. "Once I've looked the list over, I want you to help me write my query letter. Kent said I could print it on his computer and he would mail it for me when he gets back."

"Some of the publishers want electronic submissions."

"What part of 'I don't do the internet' do you not understand?"

Sylvia closed the inside door without responding.

"Oh, me nerves," Irma said, walking into the kitchen. "Plain to see who knit him. His mother was as fucking stunned as he turned out to be."

Grace and Veronica slowed in front of the yellow cottage. A *sold* banner hung from the Exit Realty sign.

"This is a sweet little place," Grace said. "I am so glad Sylvia will have her own little nest while still staying close to her daughter and Evelyn. It's a godsend that Irma came along. You know what they say about God working in mysterious ways. It's as if this little cottage was put here just for Sylvia. I know that's not true, though, since I'm sure it was built years ago."

"All these cottages were built sometime after 1969."

"Oh, did Sylvia tell you that?"

"Maybe. I heard it from someone. Apparently the lodge was the only thing on this road. In the middle of nowhere, private and hidden from the public, which was probably what the people running it wanted."

"I hope Kathleen is all right. It was sweet of you to comfort her the other night. You were sweet with Janice, too. Isn't it a sin that so many women have suffered, and usually at the hands of men? I was spared such suffering."

"Let's try to look in the windows," Veronica said. "Sylvia says it's roomier than it looks. I'm so glad she'll get to move in before we leave. Maybe we can have a little housewarming for her."

Melanie looked at the finished paintings. She felt pride in the fact that she had been inspired and followed through with the inspiration, actually finishing two paintings since arriving. Follow-through had been lacking with her art in the last two years. When she moved in with Dawson, she was so happy to have a space for her work and the time. He suggested she quit her job and dedicate her time to her work. How generous and loving he was at first.

A pattern of attention and dependence, her therapist called it. Abusers build up reliance and limit your outside contact with other people. They fill the bank with positive feelings, giving you a false security before they begin their controlling behaviour.

The sunset and the clothesline paintings both held a mysterious aspect Melanie couldn't exactly name. The reaction the woman had had to the clothesline one had almost made Melanie not finish it. She had gone about filling her coffee cup and sat at the table, not appearing to even notice the panic attack the woman was having. She knew that feeling, when you think you will stop breathing and die from a fear so debilitating you see no escape from it.

She had escaped. She had left in the night when Dawson slept soundly after exhausting himself with rage. She had walked down the street, called a cab, and had the driver take her to the emergency department. The next day she had laid charges and allowed her injuries to be photographed and her shame to see the light of day. Weeks later the landlord had let her into the apartment and she had taken her possessions and all her unfinished paintings. She had thrown the canvases in the dumpster, not wanting to have the reminder of the early days, when she believed the fantasy Dawson had created to control her.

⌒⌒⌒

Tyler kicked at the loose rocks, sending a spray into the still water. Yesterday's goodbye had been difficult. Thinking of being here for two more weeks without Abby was so depressing. He was anxious to get back to Halifax and get a plan in place, but Abby had made him promise to stay, concentrate on his writing, and enjoy the rest of his retreat time. He would do that, but this afternoon he was just going to wallow in some self-pity.

"Hi, Tyler," Grace said. "Lovely day, isn't it? Veronica and I have been for a walk, and she's gone in to put her bathing suit on so she can go for a swim right after lunch. It was hard for you to let Abby go, I'm sure. You were sweet to her. She was lucky to meet you."

"I was lucky to meet her."

"And she's coming back to New Brunswick. That's great."

"We're engaged."

"Engaged! Oh, how lovely. Congratulations."

"I gave her my favourite book and she gave me a stuffed Basset Hound."

"Oh, sweet. What a special thing for both of you. It seems to me a book instead of a ring is perfect for getting engaged at a writing retreat. And she gave you one of her precious dogs. That is lovely."

"Thank you, Grace. Being here without Abby for the next two weeks will be easier with you around."

"Oh, that's sweet of you to say. Thank you. If I had a grandson I'd want him to be just like you, Tyler."

"Never had a grandmother either. How about we be stand-ins for each other?"

"Sounds like a great plan."

~~⚬~~

"You went all out making lunch today, Dot," Grace said.

"Well, I had some lobster still and thought a good East Coast lobster roll would be perfect today."

"And a chocolate cake with boiled icing," Tyler said. "It isn't anyone's birthday, is it?"

"I'm sure it's someone's birthday. Not any of us, though."

"A special day for someone," Grace said. "We saw a dozen yellow roses just lying on the side of the road on our walk. Suppose someone dropped them there by mistake?"

"No, not by mistake," Dot answered. "A young girl died there fifty years ago yesterday."

Veronica froze, her teacup partway to her mouth. With shaking hands she set the cup down and rose to her feet. "Oh my God, Patricia," she cried before running from the room.

Veronica could barely see as she ran toward the water. Her heart was beating violently in her chest. Earlier when she'd knelt to look closer at the bouquet of roses on the side of the road it had not even dawned on her that that was where Patricia died. They hadn't been told exactly where the car had hit her, but they knew it was not far from the home. She remembered the coroner's car driving up and they'd all been shooed inside. Later she had watched Sister Dorcas shoving Patricia's things in a cardboard box and taking the box to the burning barrel out back.

Reaching the water's edge, Veronica sped up, plunging herself into the waves. She thought briefly of Kathleen and knew in the moment the same desire to allow the water to take her. This pain was unbearable. She was so damn tired of keeping it in its place. The release had to come one way or another. She opened her eyes underwater, wondering if the need for air would save her.

⚬⚬⚬

"I had the feeling Veronica had been here before," Dot said. "That poor girl must have lived here, probably at the same time Patricia died. Makes sense now why that painting spooked her so. Those loose dresses you painted, Melanie. Had you known this was a Catholic home for pregnant girls?"

The moment Melanie stepped out of Kent Wright's van, a dark feeling of sadness and pain had hit her like a wall of hot, stifling air. She knew nothing about the history of the large,

sprawling log building, but she felt a veil of misery and suffering surrounding it. She felt called to paint something with
hope and colour to lift that veil. How could she explain that
to the people who were now staring at her, waiting for her to
answer Dot's question?

"I will go to her," Grace said. "I think the rest of you should
stay in here and give her some space. She needs to let something very painful go and doesn't need a crowd to witness
it. She might be able to do that if just one of us waits on the
beach for her. Do you think that's all right, Janice?"

"You go to her, Grace. The rest of us will be there for her
when she's ready. God love her. I hope she can let it out. She's
built a mighty fortress to contain her pain, and it is not easy to
break that down. I speak from experience."

～⁊～

Sputtering and gasping for breath, Veronica instantly
thought of plunging her head below the surface again. How
long would it take before her body stopped resisting and
allowed the water to drown out its craving for air? But Grace
was sitting on the grass just above the sand, and the sight of
her felt as if a lifeline had just been thrown into the waves.
Veronica stood in the chest-high water and began walking to
shore.

Grace enclosed Veronica in her arms, oblivious to the dripping water. The sobbing began and Grace rocked her, cooing
comforting words of reassurance until Veronica's crying sub-

sided and her body slumped to a resting position. Grace cradled Veronica's head in her lap and began a gentle prodding.

"You need to let it out. As hard as it is, the words must be spoken aloud. Your story needs to be told."

Veronica shook violently, and Grace thought the crying would start again, but she heard the first words come instead.

"He sent me here when I started showing. Questions would be asked, and he knew he would be blamed. I was a kid, young for thirteen, and they would have known. He brought me here and never showed a smidge of remorse or sympathy. I wailed and he sat and watched as they dragged me from the car. He drove away in such a hurry rocks flew up from his tires. He died while I was here, at least, so I never had to see my father's vile face again."

Grace felt rage and disgust but said nothing. This was just the beginning of what Veronica needed to say out loud if the poison she carried inside was to be expelled. Grace would offer no platitudes to quiet or cap those words. She would offer her listening ear and all the time Veronica needed to complete this excruciating task.

"My baby was born on August 19. The morning was normal. I had no twinge of anything and I wasn't due until September. I was hanging out clothes, dresses. We all wore those dresses. That day mine was pink-and-white-striped seersucker. It was cracking tight. Water gushed from between my legs and I was terrified. Patricia took me inside, but they made me come back out and finish hanging the laundry. By then the pain had started.

"While I writhed in pain the sisters stood around me praying, chanting the rosary but not offering any comfort. Father Golding stood outside the door chastising me, spewing words of condemnation and offering up prayers for my dark soul. My thoughts of hellfire were directed to the bastard who brought me here, the one who put me in the throes of such misery, but I kept silent through the long night of agony and exhaustion.

"She came just as the first sliver of light broke across the foot of the bed. I felt near death, but her cry brought me back. She was the most beautiful creature I had ever laid eyes on, and when they laid her across my chest I felt a happiness like no other. I felt as if my beloved mother had returned in the form of this tiny, sweet child and she would be my salvation."

Veronica sat up. Tears fell in a steady stream down her cheeks, but her voice did not waver as she continued.

"Her name was Elizabeth. I was repeating her name softly and telling her how much I loved her when Sister Dorcas entered the room and lifted her from my chest.

"'There is no need to name her,' she spat at me. 'She is too small to live. Incest planted her seed and she was cursed from the beginning. God's judgement will overcome evil.'

"I never saw my baby again. I am sure I heard her weak cries for days afterward, but I was told she died before nightfall.

"That is why Patricia was running away. She knew they killed my baby and buried her in the woods and was afraid they would do the same to hers. She was hoping to be far away before her baby came."

"Oh my lord, Veronica. You were just a child, a poor, motherless child. So much was taken from you, and none of it was your fault. You were not to blame."

The two women sat in each other's arms, silently accepting the gifts they had both just received.

<hr>

"Veronica's time has come," Janice said entering Sylvia's kitchen. "Grace is with her."

"What happened?" Sylvia asked.

"A crack broke her pain wide open. A dozen yellow roses and a fifty-year-old tragedy broke down the walls she built to protect herself. I pray for her deliverance."

"A dozen yellow roses?" Sylvia asked.

"Is the fifty-year-old tragedy the girl that Dot and her husband killed?" Evelyn asked.

"What the hell are you all talking about?" Irma asked.

"Veronica was here as a young girl," Janice continued. "I had a sense of that. There were a few things she said that made me wonder. I think I knew the day she came to me in the woods, but maybe I was too caught up in my own struggle to see that hers was tied to this place. This place was a Catholic home for pregnant girls. I should have known the damn Catholics had something to do with her pain."

"You said Dot and her husband killed a girl?" Sylvia interjected.

"An accident," Evelyn said. "They were driving along the road leading here and hit the poor thing. She was running away from this place."

"Grace is with her?" Irma asked. "Nobody sweeter than that lady to give comfort."

"Yes, Grace thought she should go to her alone, give her a chance to let her guard down and let her story come out."

"We should all go now," Irma said. "She needs to know we are all here for her. This place that tore her down and broke her is now the place to build her back up. I'm not a clever writer, but a person would have to be fuckin stunned not to see that."

"Oh my God, I love you Irma," Sylvia said.

⟿⟾

From the kitchen window Dot could see everyone coming from Sylvia's and heading across the lawn toward the beach. She threw off her apron and stepped out to join them. Melanie, just setting a canvas on her makeshift easel, felt drawn to head down to the beach and followed behind Dot.

Tyler stepped out on to the veranda and sat on the lounge chair, his coffee and laptop situated to begin working.

Gavin looked out the big window in the great room. "This place is a loony bin," he grunted and headed upstairs.

Grace and Veronica looked up to see the women walking toward them. Even Sophie was in tow.

"I think Kathleen would suggest a ritual for this particular moment," Sylvia said as she pulled her loose dress up over her head.

"As naked as God made us," Janice added. "Who's with us?"

Chapter Seventeen

Sylvia had been up since first light, anxious to work on a scene she'd dreamt about. The rapid progression of this book was surprising and so refreshing. Yesterday in a reply to her publisher's email regarding a couple of festival offers, she had declined, using the excuse she was busy working on a new novel. Tara's reply was positive and encouraging. She was anxious to have another Sylvia Drummond Wright novel.

Sylvia wondered if when Tara read it she would still be as pleased. Surely her voice was present, even if the storyline was so different and so personal. For the first time she completely understood the compelling reason to write. For years she thought it was for notoriety, praise, a market, monetary gain maybe. But her writing had changed, and for the first time she felt she had something to offer other writers.

Kent had been gone for a few days, and the feeling of freedom without him around was palpable. Sylvia hadn't realized how tense she'd felt watching Kent with Darcy. It wasn't jealousy, she didn't think, but she was glad not to have a front row seat to her husband's affair.

Yesterday she had met with Gavin and pretty much dictated a query letter for him to send. She had kept silent otherwise, allowing him to vent in his usual manner before excusing herself for her scheduled meetings with Grace and Veronica.

Grace read Sylvia a passage she wrote describing the very brutal murder of a father who had sexually abused his young daughter. That sweet elderly woman had channelled her anger and compassion into a powerful piece of writing. The story arc of her current work had completely changed. Grace asked for a bit of advice and Sylvia was happy to give it.

Next she met with Veronica and was so delighted to hear how excited Veronica was with her newfound ability to put her thoughts and emotions into writing. She opened a pink journal, showing her the pages she had filled in the last few days.

"I have written everything I can remember. I am so surprised what has come to me as I write. I thought all the memories of the time I spent in the children's ward of the TB Hospital were gone, but the more I wrote, the more I remembered. And it came to me how I was going to write my story as fiction."

Veronica picked up another journal and opened to the first page. "I have a title already. 'Fifty Yellow Roses.' Do you ever start with a title?"

"I usually know the title quite early on. It changes sometimes. I had a title once that my publisher refused to go with. In retrospect, she was right. A title gives you focus, though, so I think it's great you have one already."

"I suppose I'll want a computer or laptop, but for now I

have no shortage of journals to write in," Veronica said. "I'm going to use aspects of my story but change a lot. I jotted down my characters, and some of my ideas. Then I just got started."

"That is a great approach. Some writers like to outline everything and map it all out, but I start with a basic plan and let it unfold as I go. You will be surprised how the story will lead you."

"I am excited to see that too. What a few days ago seemed so dark and heavy seems the exact opposite. My baby doesn't die in my story."

Sylvia got up and walked across the kitchen to make a fresh pot of coffee. Veronica's words reverberated in her head. *My baby doesn't die in my story.*

Sylvia had almost told Veronica about Patrick yesterday but couldn't. It would have sounded trite, opportunist, and insincere, as if she were matching one dead baby story with another. Irma, Veronica, and she could form the Dead Baby Society, with Nan as their Robin Williams.

⟿

"Welcome," a woman said, rising to greet her. "Come take a chair. We're just getting started."

The chairs were in a circle in the basement room, and Sylvia's first thought was to turn around and run back to her car. It had taken her a while to find Stone Church on Davenport Road and had nearly given up. The meeting started at seven and it was already seven fifteen when she'd pulled into the parking lot. Somehow she'd made herself go in, so leaving now would be ridiculous.

Sylvia slipped into the chair and accepted the box of Kleenex from the woman beside her. She could see that several people already had tissues to their eyes. Apparently it didn't take long to open up the waterworks. There appeared to be some kind of introductory, soul-exposing exercise going on.

"My name is Lydia, and I lost my son Tate three years ago to leukemia. I have been coming to this group for two years. I don't know what I'd do without it."

"Hello, Lydia," the group chanted.

"I'm Thomas, and this is my wife, Andrea. Our daughter Rachel died three months ago of a heroin overdose. This is our first meeting."

"Hello, Thomas and Andrea," the group chanted.

"Welcome to Gentle Path," said the woman who had shown Sylvia to her seat. A mass of greying dreadlocks adorned the woman's head. She was outfitted in colourful layers of flowing cotton dresses topped by a crocheted granny-square vest, giving her an aging hippy, Woodstock vibe.

"My name is Beth. I lost my oldest son, Levi, in a car accident six months ago. I want to thank Rochelle for inviting me tonight. I have been having a really difficult time."

The hippy woman walked across the circle and hugged Beth. Sylvia realized there were only two people between her and Beth, which meant of course her turn would be soon. She felt nauseous thinking she would have to actually say Patrick's name out loud. What had she thought coming here would be?

Maybe Kent was right when he told her it was a stupid idea to go to some grief group.

Kent's approach was to not talk about it at all. She wasn't sure he had even wanted to name their son. He just wanted to leave the hospital and forget all about it. She had been the one to disassemble the crib and pack away all the baby things. He had quickly turned the nursery into his home office, as if it had all just been a bad dream.

"My name is Sylvia. My baby was born dead. His name was Patrick. He would be five months old today."

<hr/>

Dot stepped outside to greet Sylvia. She had her pies in the oven and had the stew meat simmering on the stove. Sylvia didn't need anything more on her plate, but Dot needed to tell her anyway.

"Good morning, Dot."

"Good morning, Sylvia. How is everyone out back? Must be a relief to have Irma with you now."

"It is. Sophie adores her, and she's such good company for Nan."

"I wanted to talk to you about Evelyn. Have you noticed anything with her lately?"

"What do you mean?"

"I don't want to be an alarmist, but I've been a bit concerned about Evelyn in the last couple of days. Has she been to a doctor lately?"

"I haven't gotten us a family doctor yet. I did all I needed to set up a team for Sophie but haven't even thought about us."

"Is she on any medication?"

"She takes one pill for blood pressure. Why?"

"Well, I thought maybe some of what I'm seeing might be from her medication."

"What are you seeing?"

"She seems off a bit, confused, and I thought her speech was slurring a little last night. I don't want to panic you, but she might be having some TIAs, mini strokes."

"Oh Dot. Have I been so caught up with Sophie I haven't even noticed? Or maybe I just want to believe she will live forever, or as long as I need her, anyway. What the hell is wrong with me?"

"Don't beat yourself up. Sometimes a stranger sees what family doesn't."

"You are no stranger, Dot. I don't know what I'd do without you and Irma. I'm damn lucky to have such caring friends."

"I'm going to call my family doctor and see if I can get him to take you and Evelyn. My niece is his receptionist, so I might be able to pull some strings. I may as well try for Irma too. I wanted to talk to you before I went ahead and did that. Would it be all right?"

"Of course. Thanks. That would be great. And thanks for telling me your concerns. I'll watch Nan more closely until we get her in to see a doctor."

Veronica sat on a chair opposite to where Melanie stood painting.

"I'd like to buy the clothesline painting from you," Veronica said.

"Really?"

"What do you charge for your paintings?"

"To tell you the truth, I have never sold one. Haven't even finished one until I came here."

"Well, isn't that funny. I hadn't written a word until three days ago. Something in the salt air, I say."

"You were here when you were a teenager, right?"

"Yes, I was. It was a secret I kept well-guarded. Your painting almost did me in, though. The day I saw it was a very important date to me, but somehow I kept it together. Practice, I guess. I had years of not letting that date overwhelm me."

"I'm sorry my painting was painful for you."

"No apology necessary."

"I got a sense of this place the moment I got here. I felt such a dark sadness, and the painting was my way of lifting that feeling with colour and hope. The thought of sundresses came to me, so I filled the clothesline with some colourful ones.

"We wore loose dresses like that all year round. They gave us scratchy sweaters to wear over them in the colder weather. I think one of the nuns made the dresses, and believe me, they weren't as pretty as the ones you painted. Your painting was the beginning of an unravelling I needed, and I am thankful for that. Irma keeps telling me how fitting it is that this place that nearly killed me is the place where I can recover. My decision to come here was deliberate. I knew it would either make me or break me. I am so thankful for the people here who have helped make sure it was the making, not the breaking."

"Then I will be happy to give you my painting and hope you will always look at it and recall this time of healing. I know how hard healing can be, and I'm glad I can be a small part of yours."

"Did you want to go for our walk now, Veronica?" Grace asked, stepping out onto the veranda.

"Sounds good. I was trying to negotiate a price for Melanie's painting, but she's not much of a salesperson."

"How about you give me a copy of the book you're writing when it gets published?"

"God love you," Veronica said. "That's a perfect plan." Turning to Grace, Veronica added, "Let's go. I'd like to walk along the road. If Patricia's roses are still there, I'm going to take one and press it."

"That would be nice."

"I have been back and forth with how I'm going to write the fictional story that in some way frees me up to tell aspects of my own story. I think the girl who gets hit by a car will be me, kind of. But my baby doesn't die. They tell me she's dead and that my father is coming the next day to pick me up. I run away. The main character in my book raises my little girl and gives her a yellow rose every year. When the girl turns fifty she comes back and uncovers her mother's story. I think that's how it's going to go."

"I have no doubt you will manage to tell a powerful, touching story, and in doing that tell the painful aspects of your own. Are you afraid to tell it as your own?"

"Like in a memoir, you mean? I have thought about that, but I want to explore more of this place and some of the girls I knew here. I can do that through fiction. Writing it as a memoir limits me to only my truth."

"Your truth is a difficult one. Your father robbed you of so much, and you must really hate him."

"Funny, I do and I don't. Once in a while a good memory sneaks in and I realize how badly I wanted him to be who he was in those good memories. He wasn't all bad."

"Nobody is, I suppose. But he took something from you he had no right to take."

"I know that, and I suffered greatly because of it. My marriage was doomed from the beginning because I could not love normally. I never stopped being the hurt little girl trembling in the dark. And I was never able to have another child, which might have kept Robert and I together."

"Was there a physical reason you couldn't have another child? Did your daughter's birth do damage?"

"No, not that the doctors ever told me. I was never given a medical reason for not getting pregnant again. Sporadic sex might have been the main reason. It was never pleasurable for me. You just had one child, right, Grace?"

"Yes. Wallace was an only child. I was never told a medical reason either, and it wasn't for lack of trying. Some things are just meant to be, I guess. I learned to live with the disappointment."

"I wanted so badly to have a child to love. Became a bit of a crazy hoarder, thinking the more knick-knacks I had, the less sorrow I would feel."

"Oh Veronica, my heart breaks for you,"

"I'm okay, Grace. It feels as if a huge weight has been lifted and I am finally going to be who I was meant to be. Some folks don't get that chance, you know. Some people are destroyed by their troubles."

"We are pretty lucky, that's for sure. Here we are in this beautiful place on this lovely day. I think it's wonderful that you got to see the building where you suffered such loss changed into a place which now encourages creativity and self-expression. And just like Melanie said, there will be a book come of it, and I believe it will help others face their own sorrows."

"The roses are still there," Veronica said. "I love that Dot put a rose here every year. I am so glad Patricia and her baby were not forgotten. I think I'll take two, one to press and one for Elizabeth's grave. Do you think Dot would mind?"

"I'm sure she wouldn't mind at all."

Veronica bent down, taking two roses from the bouquet on the side of the road.

"Let's head back," Veronica said. "I want to take you to the place where they buried Elizabeth. I wasn't ready the other day, but I'm ready now."

⁓✧⁓

"It's Kent on the phone," Irma said.

"Tell him I'm not here," mouthed Sylvia.

"I'm sorry, she's not here right now. Can I give her a message?"

"He's flying back on Friday," Irma said after hanging up the phone. "He left the van at the airport, so he doesn't need picking up, but he wondered if you needed anything from Toronto."

"What would I need, for God's sake? I knew he'd be back. A one-month writer comes in on Sunday, so I figured he'd be back for that. Part of me was hoping he would just stay in Toronto. I've pictured him and Darcy holed up in a little love nest. I sound jealous, don't I? I don't think I am."

"Of course you're going to be a little rotted by it all. But at least him coming back will give you a chance to work a few things out. And the brown-haired mousy slut won't be with him."

"You crack me up, Irma."

⁓✧⁓

Veronica led Grace along the path in the woods, stopping just a few steps past the upturned statue where Janice had collapsed. She placed one of the yellow roses on the ground.

"Oh my goodness, dear. You came to Janice and held her, giving her comfort in her anguish, the whole time knowing you were only a few feet away from your baby's grave. Your strength is staggering. God love you."

"I don't know about that. My ability to put on a good face is staggering, might be more like it. Smiling, simple Veronica Savage with her stupid collections and not a thought in her head. That was the part I played so no one would see anything else."

"But you got yourself here. I think that took strength."

"She's not the only one buried here. We were not supposed to go anywhere near the woods, but we did, and often there would be fresh dirt days after one of the girls gave birth. Then sometimes a woman would come, the same woman, driven up in the same car. She would go inside and come out with a baby in her arms and leave. None of the girls ever left with their babies unless their families came back to get them, but that rarely happened. It was the woman, which meant adoption, or a fresh grave in the woods."

"That is terrible. Against the law even then, I'm sure. Babies can't just be buried in the woods as if they never existed."

"The church was the law. In this place, anyway. We were just kids. We had no rights and nobody spoke for us."

"How long were you here?"

"I came in April and left just before Christmas. The

months after were worse than the months before. It was torture watching the others get to their time, knowing what they
had ahead of them. And most of the work fell to the girls who
had already had their babies."

"Where did you go after you left?"

"I went to my Aunt Marjorie's, and you would think that
would have been a good thing, but it wasn't. My Aunt Marjorie
had bad nerves—mental illness, we'd call it now. She would
have really dark times and I arrived in the middle of one of
her darkest. She barely knew I was there."

"Oh, what a shame, dear."

"I stayed with her until I finished high school. I left and
moved to Saint John to attend Modern Business College. I met
Robert in Saint John and got married when I was nineteen,
thinking I finally had someone who would love me. That didn't
work out so great. But enough of this, Grace. Let's go see what
Dot has for supper."

Chapter Eighteen

Your Dad was just here was all Kayla's text said yesterday. It had been enough to kick Olivia into gear to finish packing up her things. Her lease wasn't up until the 31st, but she didn't want to be here if her father showed up to see why she'd quit her job. What the hell was he doing back in Toronto?

With not much to pack in a furnished apartment, Olivia quickly threw her things into two suitcases and a backpack. She booked a room at the Super 8 in Mississauga for two nights. The room was cheap and the hotel provided a shuttle to the airport that she could take on Sunday. Getting out of the downtown would make the chances of running into her father unlikely.

Secrecy and sneakiness were not foreign qualities for Olivia Wright; they were qualities that had not always served her well, though. The major secret still haunting her was Mark. Had she always wanted something just because it was Sophie's? The dark-haired Cabbage Patch Olivia got that Christmas had not been as desirable as the blonde one Sophie got. Blonde braids and a cute freckled face that Olivia had taken a permanent black marker to, giving it a mustache and heavy, evil-looking eyebrows.

Sophie probably would have just traded with her if she'd

asked. Sophie was always the sweet one, the generous one, the peacemaker. Eventually Sophie might have even forgiven her and welcomed her nephew or niece and accepted Mark and Olivia's relationship if they'd stayed together. But secrecy and sneakiness had prevented any of that happening. Olivia hadn't given Sophie the chance to be her generous, sweet, forgiving self.

And during their fight Olivia had thrown the terrible truth in Sophie's face. Why had she fired the hurtful truth at her sister in their chalet room that night? Sophie's anger had caught her off-guard. But even more than Sophie's angry words it was the hurt in her sister's face she would never forget.

"You selfish, heartless bitch. Did you have any idea how badly I wanted that baby? I heard its heartbeat two days before I lost it. I was devastated. I don't give a fuck about you and Mark, but I'll never forgive you for holding me while I cried, all the time knowing you were carrying what I was so desperately grieving for. And you already had an appointment at the Cabbagetown Clinic for the next day.

⤛⤜

Darcy rubbed her fingertips along the granite countertop. An L-shaped kitchen with an island big enough for two stools facing the large window that looked out on Lake Ontario. The two-bedroom condo was small but modern and efficient. White walls would need a splash of colour, but Kent said he'd leave his credit card and she could do some decor shopping while he was in New Brunswick.

She was surprised how quickly Kent had come to the decision to rent a condo and how willing he was to sign the paperwork when they came to see this one. Lease to own, and they could take occupancy right away. Once Kent Wright made up his mind about something, he made it happen. He had even rented her a car so she could go to Kingston and get her things while he was in New Brunswick.

Kent set the suitcases down and came up behind Darcy, wrapping her in an embrace. "Let's walk down the street to that little bistro and have lunch before we go furniture shopping. Have you thought how you'd like to furnish the second bedroom? A desk, of course, but do you think we need a spare bed in there?"

"I don't think we'll have any company, do you? Did you see your daughter?"

"She wasn't there. Apparently she quit a week ago. I tried her cell phone, but no answer. I don't know if I'll bother trying to go by her place before I leave or not."

"How long are you staying?"

"I don't know yet. You've got to let me figure it out. I have to make sure the retreat is successful and running well before I come back for any length of time. Sylvia never wanted it in the first place, so she just might let it run itself into the ground if I leave things up to her."

"So am I just going to be a kept woman who sits around waiting for you to come to Toronto?"

"I told you from the start that I needed to look after a few things before I can commit to anything. I got us a place, which I thought you'd be happy about. At least now you can be here while you decide what you want."

"I want you. I am quite happy to cancel my fall plans and be in Toronto until Christmas at least. I am anxious to have the time to write, and you have given me that confidence. Whether I go back to school second term will entirely depend on whether you have settled in Toronto by then or not. I am not going to give up everything to be a lonely mistress pining for my lover."

"How about your lover takes you right now on the bare hardwood floor in our empty bedroom?"

"Yeah, that sounds more inviting than the ceramic tile in this room or on this granite island."

"I am a middle-aged man, for God's sake. I don't think I'm up to sex on the island."

"Tell that to someone who hasn't seen what you can do," Darcy said as she led him down the short hallway.

⌇⌇⌇

"I think your writing is amazing, Tyler," Sylvia said. "Is this book in a series?"

"Yes, it's the third in a trilogy. I am enjoying bringing the story to an end. I'm actually looking forward to going in a completely different direction with my next book."

"Have you been talking to Abby?"

"Yes, I call her every night and text her all the time. I am missing her like crazy."

"I'm sure she's missing you too."

"She says she is."

"Any idea what you'll do when she comes back?"

"I keep trying to come up with a plan. I wish I could just write full-time and make enough money to support us. Abby found out she can keep working at her job as long as we live somewhere that has good internet."

"It will all work out, I'm sure."

"Irma's staying to care for your daughter, eh?"

"Yeah. We are all very happy about it. Except Gavin, maybe. Sophie loves her. It works out nicely for all of us."

"I am so glad I heard about this retreat. It's changed my life, you know."

"I was not on board with the idea, but I am starting to see its value. I'm so happy it was a good place for you and Abby. And Veronica has benefited from coming back to a place that held such sorrow for her. Janice has done some amazing writing here. It was a good place for Kathleen to come to terms with some things. I'm glad the retreat offered them that chance. I guess we'll just have to see what the future brings. I'm not going anywhere, and the lodge is all set up for a retreat, so it might as well keep being a place writers can come to."

"I think it's a very special place, and a large part of that is because of you, whether you know it or not."

"Well, thank you, Tyler. It's been great having you here too. Maybe the Wright Retreat has a place in your future as well."

"Who knows?"

Dot was in the kitchen mixing up a batch of brown bread rolls while Irma and Evelyn sat around the two-thousand-piece puzzle that was quickly taking shape.

"Did you ever see so many cats?" Evelyn said.

"My mudder always had cats," Irma said. "Usually a tabby or two, a jet black one and a calico."

"Sylvie had a yellow one named Micah. Her papa gave it to her on her tenth birthday."

"All kinds of cats and colourful balls of yarn. Here's some green pieces that probably go there somewhere, Evelyn."

"The two of you have more patience than me for doing that," said Dot. "I never saw the point of all the time it takes to put a puzzle together just to tear it apart and put the pieces back in the box when you're done."

"But yet you go to all the trouble of cooking something just to see it devoured," Evelyn said.

"That's true, I guess," Dot replied.

"Dot got us in with her doctor, Evelyn. You have an appointment this afternoon."

"Sylvie said you were going to do that. I was never one for going to a doctor much. Paddy either. Too much trouble. We had to go to the mainland to see a doctor. But I guess an old lady like me should get a checkup once in a while, although the way I look at it, living to my age is already a bonus. My Paddy was only sixty when he died, and my girl only twenty-two."

"I feel that way too, Evelyn. Every day a blessing. Dear God, I got forty-two years past everyone in my whole family."

"I'm not one to run to the doctor every time I get a little ache or pain, either," Dot said. "But sometimes it is necessary. You don't want to just ignore things that a doctor could make better."

"But really, can a doctor make a ninety-two-year-old woman better? My time will come, and plugging me full of pills isn't going to change that."

"But you'll go and let him check you out though, right?" Dot asked.

"Well, yes, of course I will. Sylvie wouldn't let me hear the end of it if I refused. Maybe a trip to a doctor will be a good thing. He can break the news to her that sooner or later I'm going to die."

"We all are, my dear," Irma said. "We've got a puzzle to finish and there'll be buns to eat."

⤙⤚

Tyler pulled the lawn mower out of the shed.

"What are you doing?' Gavin asked walking up behind him. "Have they got you doing free yard work? They've got my wife cleaning and caregiving. We paid to come here, for God's sake."

"I offered to mow the lawn. I don't mind at all."

"Give them an inch, they'll take a mile. "

"We learned metric growing up. 'Give them a centimetre, they'll take a kilometre' doesn't sound quite as good."

"Whatever. I'm just saying we paid good money for this retreat. Have you even gotten your five one-on-one sessions?"

"I've met with Sylvia a couple of times. I find her very helpful and supportive."

"Whatever. I won't be raving about how great this place is, I tell you. Wish I'd kept it to two weeks and left when the others did. Maybe my wife would have left with me. Now I get to sit around waiting to go home by myself. Paid for two extra weeks for a damned query letter I could have written on my own."

Tyler reached down and pulled the cord to start the mower. He nodded at Gavin and began mowing.

Tyler loved watching the swath of cut grass getting wider and wider. There had been a big section of lawn in front of Connie and Hebert's house. That summer it had been his job to keep it mowed. Once a week Hebert would get the mower out of the shed, fill the small gas tank, and pull the cord to get it running. He'd hold down the throttle and motion for Tyler to come take the handle. Connie made him wear goggles and ear defenders and tie up his sneakers with a double knot.

"I'll not have you losing an eye or a toe. Lawn mowers are very dangerous. Pay attention to what you're doing. Tuck those laces in."

Connie went over the same list of cautionary reminders every time and every time when Tyler was done she would say the same complimentary things.

"That lawn looks wonderful Tyler. Such a big boy, mowing this lawn all by yourself. Looks just great. Like a golf course, don't you think, Hebert? What a big help you are, Tyler. No problem having you around."

And every time he'd bask in her praise, thinking if he did a good job at the lawn and the other chores they would keep him. He was always careful to be polite and say his pleases and thank yous. He didn't eat too much and always carried his dishes to the sink. By the end of the summer Tyler was so sure they would keep him. But they didn't.

⁓ৎ⁓

The sound of Sophie's giggling was coming from the other room. That happy sound always filled Sylvia with conflicting emotions. On one hand, she was glad when Sophie was enjoying whatever was making her laugh. It was always a relief when her mood was good and she was content. But on the other hand, Sophie's childlike glee was a sharp reminder that her adult daughter had severe impairments and always would.

Irma and Nan had gone to the lodge to visit Dot and work on their puzzle. Irma had been reluctant to go, knowing Sylvia was writing, but Sylvia had insisted. It was wonderful having an extra person to help care for Sophie, but she wasn't going to take advantage of Irma and not do her part. That wouldn't change when she moved into the cottage.

And Dot's concerns were on Sylvia's mind. She needed to be mindful of her grandmother's age and not take advantage of her either. She was anxious for the appointment Dot had gotten for them to see if there were any serious health issues. Just being ninety-two came with issues, and it was time to admit that. At least she hadn't gone along with Kent's plan to put Nan in a home for her final years.

Olivia had been on her mind a lot lately too. Maybe when Kent got back he would have some news about her. Hopefully they got together while he was in Toronto and he could tell Sylvia how their daughter was doing. Both girls had had such potential, honour students throughout junior and high school, and both had enrolled in the University of Toronto after graduation. Finishing her first degree, Olivia had started her master's degree in English Literature with hopes of eventually becoming a professor. Sophie completed her law degree and began articling at a large firm, where she'd met Mark.

Sylvia had never understood what Sophie saw in Mark. He was nice enough, but she never felt he was good enough for her daughter. Seemed a bit of a flirt, and Sylvia had always thought Sophie was more invested than he was. She'd been glad Sophie's pregnancy had been a false alarm. They would have managed, but she and Kent had been concerned a baby would end Sophie's career plans.

Sylvia recoiled from the emotion of that thought. An unplanned pregnancy was nothing compared to a traumatic brain injury, which had done more than cause a detour in her path. The tumble down that ski hill had destroyed Sophie's future plans and totally sidelined Olivia's as well. Olivia never went back to school and never returned to normal, even though she had not been the one injured.

Chapter Nineteen

Kent Wright looked at the departure board, annoyed that another hour had just been added to the delay. A direct flight from Toronto to Moncton should be uncomplicated, but apparently staffing issues come up on the last day of the month. He would keep this in mind for future trips and avoid last-day-of-the-month flights. If he'd known he would have stayed at the condo instead of getting himself to the airport two hours before the scheduled flight.

The goodbyes had been dramatic. You'd think he was going off to a foreign war, the way Darcy went on. To calm her down he had made the promise to be back in ten days. Even as he said the words he doubted that would happen. He had a one-month writer flying in tomorrow and on the seventh, three two-week writers were coming. The one-month people already there would leave on the tenth, and he certainly wanted to be there to send them off. Maybe by the middle of the month, if everything was going smoothly, he could come back to Toronto.

Sylvia planned to move into her cottage on the day the two-week writers came. Irma was already living in the apartment with Evelyn and Sylvia. There was one ensuite bedroom empty right now, but he should leave it empty for the one-month writer coming tomorrow. For now he would move into one of the empty single rooms and share a bathroom. Once the one-month people left he would claim an ensuite room and keep his things there while travelling back and forth to Toronto.

He would check the rest of the fall schedule, making sure he could juggle the rooms while still keeping one for himself. Getting back to his wife's bed was now permanently off the table. Starting a relationship with Darcy had put the final nail in that coffin, but he had known for a long time the romance in their marriage had died. These next few days would be all about making the end as amicable as possible. He wanted the freedom to be in Toronto most of the time but needed to know the retreat would not go belly up. It was a good investment. Surely Sylvia could see that now and would cooperate in running it.

Sylvia was writing again and enjoying some mentoring activity. She had help with Sophie and was settling into the routine of things. She and Dot had hit it off and Evelyn seemed settled as well. Sylvia was as invested in the Wright Retreat as he was. Surely they could work out some terms, making the divorce and running of the retreat friendly and beneficial for them both. He would be careful not to appear too eager to get back to Toronto and wouldn't mention renting the condo at this point.

Finally, they were calling his flight to the gate. At least the flight was less than two hours. The van was in long-term parking, and the drive from the airport was short. He would be at the lodge by suppertime. An evening to relax, maybe some solitude in the hot tub and a good night's sleep before heading back to the airport tomorrow to pick up Bridget St. John. Keeping up with the libido of a thirty-year-old was exhausting.

~~⚬⚭⚬~~

Sylvia plunged under the water again. She and Veronica had been back and forth in the water all afternoon, swimming and enjoying the heat of the day. There would not be many more swimming days like this as August came to an end. Swimming was helping to quiet worrisome thoughts of yesterday's doctor's appointment with Nan. It had gone well, really. Her blood pressure was good. The doctor had tested her reflexes, her mobility and strength, and was not overly concerned with anything he saw. He filled out a requisition for bloodwork and was booking an MRI and CT scan. He said there was a possibility of some TIA activity, and if a blockage showed up he would prescribe a blood thinner.

Sylvia knew she should be pleased with how the appointment went, but there had been something so upsetting about seeing her feeble grandmother through someone else's eyes. The questions Dr. Keating asked were suitable for a ninety-two-year-old woman, but it was as if Sylvia had suddenly seen Nan as if she were looking at a stranger. It seemed like Nan had aged without her even noticing, or with her in complete denial.

"You seem worried," Veronica said, sitting down on the shore beside Sylvia.

"I'm fine. A bit preoccupied, maybe."

"How was Evelyn's doctor's appointment?"

"It was good. He's ordered a few tests, but he was pleased with her health overall."

"God, yes. She's amazing. If I'm that healthy at her age I'll be thrilled."

"I don't know what I'd do without her. I feel a bit guilty saying that, knowing you didn't have a grandmother growing up and lost your mother when you were so young. Then there's Irma. I have nothing to whine about."

"You are perfectly entitled to feel whatever you are feeling. Other people's losses don't change your own emotions around losing a loved one. And the number of years you have them doesn't matter. Loss is difficult no matter what."

"I think I'll get a dog."

"What brought that on?"

"I've been thinking about it since I bought the cottage. I've always wanted a dog. Nan used to say we'll see, but we never got one. Kent claimed he was allergic, but I think he just didn't want to be bothered. I'm going to get a dog. No reason I shouldn't."

"Sounds like a plan. Do you have a breed in mind?"

"No. I don't want a little yappy thing, but I don't want a great big horse either. I think I'll know my dog when I see it. I'm going to take a trip to the Animal Rescue League in the next while and check out the dogs they have there. I would like to take a dog that needs me as much as I need him or her."

~~~

Gavin pulled up a chair beside Tyler on the veranda. "I'll be glad to have Kent back tonight. We're outnumbered by all these women. Listen to them carrying on in the water. They sound like a flock of geese, for God's sake. Nothing worse than a bunch of squawking women."

"I love to hear women laughing and chatting."

"Really?"

"I love being around women. I'm like a baby who was weaned too soon."

"Whatever the hell that means," Gavin said, taking the manila file folder from his lap, then standing and making his way across the lawn for the privacy of the bench at the edge of the woods. He'd still have to hear the foolishness on the shore, but he wouldn't have to see them. And he wouldn't have to talk to Tyler.

Sitting down, Gavin took the pages of his manuscript from the folder. It seemed in the last couple of days he carried the pages around like a small child carries a blanket. Were they comforting to him? His query letter was ready to go, and he had no intention of making any changes to his manuscript. He took the page of Sylvia's comments off the top of the pile. Her comments still grated him, and he wasn't sure why he hadn't thrown them in the garbage.

Mavis was flat. Whatever the hell that meant. *Flat, one-dimensional, cold hearted, emotionless.* These words came to Gavin like a torrent, a deluge he certainly wasn't expecting. *Give her a back story.* As if he knew one! Making up one was more than he was willing to do. Mavis needed to be exactly the way he wrote her. He had no intention of exploring who Mavis was and what any of her motivations were.

Shit, he thought. *Mavis is my mother.* Why had that never occurred to him before? There was a good reason he hated those creative writing courses when instructors would go on about the layers in writing, the probability of a person writing what grips them personally. Bullshit. He purposely kept his writing completely separate from his own life. It was why he was so meticulous in his research and always wrote unfamiliar settings and historical periods he had no personal experience living through.

He had given Mavis no personality, *no agency*, as an instructor might say. He had no intention of changing that, even though Sylvia had said that even if a publisher accepted his manuscript, an editor might urge him to expand Mavis.

Cold hearted, emotionless, a granite, unmoving statue standing where he needed a mother to be. One of his first memories was of running toward his mother, his chubby arms outstretched, and her shooing him away as if he were a disgusting bug.

Gavin Henry Church, you're fine. You scratched your knee, for God's sake. You'd think your leg was dangling from its last sinew the way you're carrying on.

Gavin Henry Church, stop that caterwauling. A big boy like you doesn't need to wake his mother. It was just a dream. What I have told you about the threshold to my bedroom?

Gavin Henry Church, if you turn out to be half the man your father was, it will be more than I ever expected.

Gavin Henry Church, you can do better than some simple Newfoundland orphan who can barely speak the Queen's English and wears her sad story like a badge of courage.

Gavin Henry Church, I can't believe you won't even take in your dying mother. After all I've done for you.

Gavin recoiled at the sound of his mother's voice reverberating in his head. "Stunned as the quilt," Irma had said that day. Irma used the word *stunned*, but maybe *stunted* would have been more on the mark. His mother had been stunted by something. He'd never explored what it had been that left his mother with no capacity to show love. Not a hug, a kiss, an embrace of any kind could he remember receiving. The word *love* had been forbidden, never spoken or written. Never a word of praise or encouragement.

Irma had been such a breath of fresh air. Her quick humour, loud laughter, and unfettered weeping were all welcome. Emotion and passion were like an addiction for him at first, and he could not get enough. But somehow he had reverted back to the habits of his boyhood. He had gradually built the walls back up around his own emotions and allowed his fear of rejection to determine his behaviour.

Gavin almost jumped from the bench when he realized

tears were streaming down his cheeks. He quickly looked to see if anyone was close enough to see his vulnerability.

"Jesus, man, pull yourself together," he muttered under his breath. "This place is getting to you. Maybe booking an earlier flight is what you need to do. The last thing you need are thoughts of suckling your mother's breast or crying over spilled milk. Dried-up, curdled milk from a breast that never nourished me."

Gavin crumpled the page holding Sylvia's comments and stuffed it into his shirt pocket. He then scooped up all the pages of his manuscript, placing them carefully back in the folder. Standing and looking around again, Gavin quickly made a beeline for the lodge.

❦

Kent woke up with a start when the pilot announced they were preparing for landing. Foggy from the dream he'd been absorbed in, he looked to his left to see if the twins were beside him. Little girls with missing front teeth and colourful Blossom hats. His girls always turned heads. Identical twins with sweet little faces and bubbly personalities. And his attractive wife, who was more and more being recognized after the success of her third book. This was the stage of his life the dream had taken him to.

Kent quickly set himself back in the present as the rows emptied and he stood to get his carry-on out of the upper compartment. He pulled the parking slip from his pocket. This

airport offered a straightforward exit, and he had no checked
bags. He would pay for his parking, make his way to the long-
term lot, and be on the highway in minutes.

Passing one of the souvenir kiosks, Kent noticed a carousel
of stuffed animals. *I should get the girls something*, he thought,
then quickly recalibrated. He would stop and get a stuffed
lobster for Sophie and lobster-trap salt-and-pepper shakers
for Evelyn. No gifts for Sylvie and Olivia. The thought of that
brought a lump to Kent's throat as he passed his purchases to
the cashier.

⁓⁓⁓

Janice and Sylvia sat alone at a dying bonfire. Remnants
of a vibrant sunset had faded in the dark sky, and the air was
still. The previous chatter had gradually faded as well. First
Grace excused herself from the circle, followed by Tyler, Irma,
and then Veronica. Melanie had lagged behind for a few minutes before heading up to the lodge.

"Kent was wound up tonight," Janice said.

"Yeah, he took over from Benson playing the master of cer-
emonies. I wanted to puke when he kept going on about how
good it was to get back to this rugged beauty after a few days in
Toronto."

"Gavin didn't say much," Janice added.

"No, he was very quiet. No complaints or sarcasm at all. He
told Irma earlier that he's rescheduled his flight and is leaving
tomorrow."

"Oh, really? How is she feeling about that?"

"Some mixed feelings, I'm sure, but relief among them."

"That Tyler's a nice kid. I'm so glad he and Abby found each other," Janice said.

"Yeah, they seem so good for one another. I'm not sure Kent and I ever were. What about you and Hank?"

"Oh, at first we had something special. We'd both been through hell and were determined to survive together. We had a few really good years before things fell apart. And we got six kids out of it."

"Do you ever just think it's too much?"

"Fuck, yes. Life is too much. We've got to keep slogging through it, though. But I suppose we could bungee-cord bricks to our arms and go for a swim."

"I always thought my mother took the easy way out."

"Nothing easy about any of it. It can get to be too much. Life comes with layers and layers of pain. And healing is hard work. Wounds can be pretty deep. Scabs are crusty and gross, but they keep a cover on the wound. If you pull a scab off too soon you bleed, the wound is still raw and tender. After the bleeding stops you have to wait for it to scab over again. If you let the scab fall off when it's ready, the wound underneath will look as if it's healed, but if you dig too deep at the wound it will start to bleed again. The best healing comes when all that's left is a scar, the wound healed completely. But scars are hard to come by. You have to wait, be patient, and be willing to let the deep wound heal right to the core. Some folks aren't able to do the work."

"And we all have scars, don't we?" Sylvia said. "Jesus, just at this retreat alone we could make a list that sounds fictional."

"My youngest daughter, Casey, was a cutter. Her wounds were hidden, and she gave herself visible ones so we would have to see her pain. She finally got help and is in recovery, but she still hasn't forgiven me."

"Forgiven you for what?" Sylvia asked.

"For not seeing what she was going through. A male relative was sexually abusing her, and I was too drunk to see the signs. I was a long time taking any responsibility for that. I felt that I was doing the best I could at the time and that she should understand that. Sometimes the best we can do is just acknowledge another person's pain and ask for forgiveness for whatever part we played in it."

"I don't know exactly what Olivia's pain is, but I know her anger is directed at me."

"Maybe that is deflective on her part. Anger is often a mask."

"Maybe the first thing I need to do is reach out to her and tell her I'm sorry for anything I've done or haven't done."

"Apologies are a start. Just ask the Canadian government. But only a start. Healing is a journey, and the apology is just a place to leave from. I'm done for today. My bed's my destination for now."

Chapter Twenty

"Sylvia, would you mind coming over to breakfast with me?" Irma asked. "I don't expect a big dramatic goodbye, but I figure if I show up for breakfast and everyone is around, he's not going to make a scene. Figure he'll have to at least say his piece about not being able to refund my return flight. I'll keep my lips closed and smile sweetly, waving as I watch his sorry arse driving away."

"What time is his flight?"

"Not sure, but he said he'd go to the airport with Kent when he leaves to pick up the author who's coming."

"I'll just put coffee on for Nan, then get dressed and come over with you. I'll check and see if Sophie's still sleeping."

~~~

Gavin pulled everything off hangers, not even bothering to fold anything, and tossed his clothes in the suitcase. Irma always took great care with packing. He would only need the one suitcase but considered taking the other one for spite. He'd paid for the set of luggage, and thoughts of Irma packing it for some enjoyable trip she might take pissed him off. But paying to check an empty suitcase was stupid, so he closed the closet door, leaving it there.

Thoughts of returning home and seeing all of Irma's clothes neatly folded in her dresser and hanging on her side of the closet reminded him of the conversation they'd had the day she dropped the bombshell that she was staying. Easy for her to say "just give my stuff to Goodwill." Purging the house of all her things was going to be a big job. Maybe he'd hire the woman next door to do it. More money that he'd have to spend. He had to pay a change-of-flight fee, which almost dissuaded him from leaving today. Then he'd waited on hold for twenty-eight minutes, only to be told Irma's flight couldn't be refunded without trip insurance. He hadn't bought trip insurance. How the hell could he have known his wife would lose her mind and decide to stay? She hadn't even wanted to come.

Gavin walked into the bathroom and grabbed his toiletries off the vanity. Irma had taken the bag she always put them in. With his luck his shaving-cream can would explode in his suitcase. He threw the shaving cream in the garbage before returning to his suitcase and throwing in his other things. He zipped the suitcase and carried it out of the room.

⁓

Dot was preparing waffles with fresh blueberry compote along with fried ham, scrambled eggs, and fried potatoes. She'd been grinning since realizing this breakfast was a goodbye meal for Gavin. She would not be sorry to see him go and had just said so to Grace.

"My brother-in-law David was just like him," Grace said. "Always snarky and mean to Velma, and a nicer woman you'd never meet. I don't know what makes some men so nasty. Velma always blamed his mother. She was a piece of work. Not a loving bone in her body. Velma ended up looking after her for fifteen years and never got a kind word from the old battleaxe."

"Grace, I've never heard you say a mean word about anyone," Dot said. "Here I thought you were all sweetness and light."

"Well, it's hard to be sweet and kind to folks who don't deserve it. What really gets my dander up are men who mistreat woman. I've been in such a state thinking about what Veronica's father did to her. And he never had to pay for it. I don't know what killed him, but whatever it was, it wasn't bad enough. I wrote a real nasty ending for him in my book, but of course it wasn't him. That's the fun of writing fiction. I pretended it was him."

"Again, not a side I expected from you, Grace."

"Oh, speak of the devil," whispered Grace as Gavin came to the top of the stairs.

Gavin stomped down the stairs, dragging his suitcase behind him like a sulky kid.

"The devil, all right," mumbled Dot.

Irma and Sylvia came in the sliding door as the others came down the stairs behind Gavin.

Just regular conversation took place while everyone en-joyed the delicious breakfast Dot served. As people were get-ting up from the table, Gavin cleared his throat to speak. Irma turned toward him and Sylvia sat back down, ready to support Irma if need be.

"What time are we leaving, Kent?" Gavin asked.

"I plan on leaving at ten thirty. The flight Bridget St. John is coming on from Toronto gets in at twelve thirty."

"Who?" Sylvia asked.

"The one-month author."

"What did you say her name was?"

"Bridget St. John."

Sylvia stood up, gripping the table. Janice noticed the co-lour drain from her friend's face and walked around the table toward her.

"I'm going to the airport with you," Sylvia said quickly while walking away.

"I'll come too," Janice said, following Sylvia out the sliding doors.

"It has to be Olivia," Sylvia said as she and Janice headed across the lawn. "That name cannot be a coincidence."

"Well, we'll go and see. You said you've been thinking a lot about her lately. Maybe she feels the need to fix things too, and she's coming to do that."

"Oh my God, Jan. I feel like I'm going to be sick. I can't stop shaking."

"You're okay, Sylvie. You'll be fine. You will go to the airport, and if it's her you will bring her to this place. I will be right beside you."

"How can Kent not even realize it's her?"

"You said he never called her Bridget when she went through that phase."

"I know, but you'd think he would make the connection. I don't even want to tell him why I'm going to the airport with him. God he probably thinks it's some breakthrough in my attitude to be on board with this damn retreat."

"Well, it might be the retreat that's bringing Olivia here."

"Maybe. I never told her we moved here, but if she saw the brochure she would know it's ours. Nan just said the other day that I should be telling her about buying the cottage. Maybe Kent told her about the retreat, but obviously she didn't tell him who she was when she registered. A one-month writer, for God's sake. It's his own daughter coming."

"Okay, for right now just calm down and breathe. Go in and tell Evelyn what's going on and relax. You will muster all the strength you need when the time comes. I'll meet you at the van at ten thirty."

"Thank you, Jan."

⁓

Gavin was already in the passenger seat and Kent was just sliding into the driver's seat when Janice came out the door and Sylvia walked around the corner. Kent automatically opened the sliding door, and the women climbed into the van, going to the very back seat. Nobody spoke as the van drove out of the yard. Irma and Sophie stood waving from the landing of the apartment stairs. If Gavin saw them, he did not let on.

"So, you have my query letter to mail, right?" Gavin asked a few minutes later.

"Yes. Good luck with that, by the way. Hope you feel you've had a successful retreat experience."

"Well, considering my wife decided to leave me while I was here and I'm cutting it short, you might conclude it wasn't all good. But don't worry, I'm not going to fill the internet with bad reviews. I don't do the internet, and don't expect to start anytime soon. I'll be too busy for a while cleaning the house out of reminders of my wife and the life I had before coming to your retreat. Didn't expect to go home to that."

Kent stared ahead and did not respond. Sylvia looked over at Janice and kept silent too. Nothing more was said until Kent pulled into the airport parking lot.

"I assume you will calculate a refund for the ten days left to my retreat," Gavin said. "I suppose the cost of the ten-day retreat is a bit much to expect back, but I will look for a cheque to come in the next while. I do have contact with other authors, and I'd rather not have to badmouth the Wright Retreat. You want all the good publicity you can get, just starting up."

Again, Kent said nothing, and Sylvia was surprised at his restraint. Janice, however, leaned ahead, making sure Gavin could hear what she had to say.

"Okay, tightwad. How about you consider the fact that your wife who cooked and cleaned for you for thirty-three years is not asking for a damn cent? She is not demanding a divorce with a fifty-fifty split of all your assets. She is just choosing to live in peace without you. So suck it up, buttercup, and shut the hell up."

Sylvia and Janice walked ahead and into the airport, going right to the arrivals area.

"I am a mess," Sylvia said. "I'm excited and scared to death. She's my own daughter, for God's sake, but I'm so nervous to see her. Wouldn't it be a hoot if it wasn't her, if there really was a writer named Bridget St. John? Oh my God, I can't stop shaking."

"Come over here and sit down. Take a deep breath. You've got a few minutes to pull yourself together and get ready. She's probably just as nervous. It will all be fine. Do you want a coffee or anything?"

"No. Thanks. And thanks for coming with me. Nan offered to come before she heard that you said you would. Funny, she didn't think it was enough that my husband, Olivia's father, would be there. And she thought I should see Olivia without her to complicate it. I'm sure Olivia has been missing her grandmother and sister. If Nan were here the reunion would be very emotional."

"Here comes Kent. He'll be digging out his Wright Retreat sign, watching out for the author," Janice said.

Sylvia looked up to see the arrival board light up the word *arrived* beside the Air Canada flight from Toronto. She stood and moved closer to the gate.

~~~

Veronica stared at the page she had just written. Her handwriting was sprawling and messy, but hopefully she would be able to read it later. She could feel the confidence beating in her chest. She knew the writing would continue, evolve, and become something. As she wrote there was adrenalin pulsating that propelled her to keep going without regard for anything but the release. She knew the unfettered words would need to be waded through, revised, rewritten, weighed and balanced, but the initial outpouring felt euphoric.

On the first day of January she had starting writing in the little red five-year diary Aunt Marjorie gave her that Christmas. Each page was divided into five sections, leaving only a small space for each day's entry, so she'd very carefully choose the important aspects of the day to be recorded. Every night for almost a year she had faithfully uncapped her fountain pen and neatly chronicled her days. But in mid-October the entries stopped.

The next day she could not even bring herself to pull the diary out from between the mattress and box spring where she kept it hidden. Hiding it was a ritual, an exercise in maintaining privacy. Privacy, the sanctity of her own bedroom and her own bed, had been violated, and in those October days she dreaded nighttime and floated through the daytime. Veronica never entered another word in the red leather diary.

Years later, reading the diary entries she'd written before that night was like reading about the life of a stranger. Each time she stood before a selection of journals, it was the words telling who she became on that dark night that she dreamed of writing. But not a word had been written in any of those journals. Not a word had been muttered to anyone until she'd let the words escape on the shore in Grace's arms. So many words to free up and put to paper. The process would be excruciating, but she would not hold anything back. She would just let the words cascade, and when she was able, she would fashion them into the story she needed to tell so that someone would finally listen. This had been the release she'd dreamed of.

<center>~~~</center>

Sylvia watched each person filing through the door into the arrivals area. An elderly couple, the man leaning on a cane, the woman scanning the crowd looking for whoever was meeting them. A harried mom, an infant strapped to her chest and three kids trailing behind her. A handsome business man, his suit so starched and pressed it looked as if it could stand alone if he were to slip out of it. Two chatty teenagers, sports team jerseys and jeans full of holes. Olivia, her hair pulled back, her face thinner than her sister's but so similar it was jarring.

Sylvia felt the huge gulf that time, distance, and Olivia's angry departure had created. Frozen, she made no move as

Olivia came closer. Their eyes connected, and Olivia rushed toward her mother. Sylvia felt her knees buckle. Olivia's backpack dropped and her arms reached out to steady her mother.

"Olivia?" Kent's voice echoed behind them.

Kent awkwardly passed Janice the sign.

"There is no Bridget St. John," Janice said.

"What do you mean?" Kent asked.

Janice backed away, letting the family drama play out. She sat down in the rows of seats along the wall to wait.

"Do you honestly not remember me being Bridget St. John for almost a whole year, Dad?"

"No."

"When I was eleven I decided to change my name. I insisted everyone call me that. I can't believe you don't remember. I almost used a different name to register, but maybe I wanted you to guess it was me. "

"You knew right away when I told you the author's name this morning, didn't you, Sylvie?" Kent asked.

"Yes. I could tell it didn't ring any bells for you. And I don't suppose you have a clue where she got the name."

"From a soap opera, maybe. It sounds like a soap opera name. *General Hospital* or *All My Children*?"

"No, not a soap opera," Sylvia said choosing not to elaborate.

"You didn't have to pay to come to your own parents' retreat, Olivia." Kent said.

"I know. But when I saw the brochure it seemed like a

perfect way to make a surprise entrance. I figured Mom would pick up on the name and know right away."

"I don't have anything to do with the registrations. This whole retreat thing was your father's idea."

"She is warming up to it, though."

"And you are one of the writers?" Olivia asked turning toward Janice.

"Yes. I came as a ten-day and ended up staying for the month. Your mother has been a huge help to me."

"I always wanted to be my mother. Funny story there, but not for now."

"Lots of stories coming out at the Wright Retreat. A young woman who talks to stuffed dogs got engaged to a dystopian fantasy writer; a lesbian-romance writer had a skinny-dipping, life-changing moment. A historical fiction writer comes with a wife and leaves alone when she decides your mother, sister, and grandmother are more of a family to her than he ever was; a woman returns to the lodge where she lived as a teenager when it was a home for pregnant girls. I could go on, but you'll get caught up once you settle in. You've come to the right place if you've got stories to tell."

Olivia turned to gaze out the window of the van once they were on the road. It had been so great hugging her mother. Even Dad had welcomed her with such enthusiasm and hadn't even mentioned her job. It felt like a homecoming, and she was anxious to see Nan and Sophie. But the stories she needed to share were a weight she was weary of carrying no matter how hard they'd be to tell.

"Did you bring a bathing suit?" Sylvia asked. "Wait until you meet Irma. Wait until you taste Dot's cooking. The rooms are nice too. Oh, this retreat your father created is top of the line. I'll have to take you to the Irving for Slushies. It will freak the lady out who works there. She always makes such a fuss over Sophie. Remember all the tricks you two played on people over the years? No one could tell the two of you apart."

"I wish that were still true," Olivia said.

"Nan and Sophie will be so happy to see you, Liv," Sylvia said.

⤳✥⤝

Evelyn scooped a dollop of the frothy white frosting onto a chocolate cookie, picked up another, and squeezed it on top. Shortly after Sylvia left she had started making Olivia's favourite childhood treat. Baking did not come as easy as it once had, and she got Irma to read the recipe to her and check her measuring as she mixed up the batter.

"The recipe says whoopie pies, but one time Olivia called them whoopee cushions by mistake and the name stuck. The girls would make farting noises when someone would take a bite. Isn't it funny the things a person remembers? Little girls giggling, their faces covered in white icing, sprays of chocolate crumbs coming from their mouths."

Evelyn finished putting each pie together, placing them in the cookie can, feeling the excitement build. She wondered how the reunion at the airport had gone. She wondered what changes she would see in her granddaughter. Olivia would definitely see changes in her. How had they let the years go by?

"Gavin will have landed by now," Irma said.

"Are you having regrets?" Evelyn asked.

"No, not really, but there is something sad about it all. I do feel sorry for him sometimes, and of course I wish things had turned out differently."

"My Paddy used to say, 'If wishes were horses, beggars would ride.'"

"My father used to say, 'Wishing Thursday was Friday is a waste of a day,' and Mudder used to say 'Wishes won't wash dishes.'"

"Your parents sound like wonderful people."

"They weren't perfect, but they were damned close as far I'm concerned. Gavin says their dying didn't make them perfect, and I know that's true. But they loved us and gave us a good life. They built a home where we could laugh and cry and make mistakes. Gavin didn't have that."

"That's it, isn't it? It's knowing we're still loved even when we make mistakes, because God knows we all make them. Olivia coming here is the best I could wish for, because there's no point wishing for what's already passed to be any different. Let's take Sophie outside so we can see them when they drive up."

"I'll go in and get some lemonade for this party," Dot said. "Want to come help me, Sophie girl? Dot'll give you a treat."

"Treat, treat," Sophie repeated.

"I hope we haven't done the wrong thing getting Sophie all wound up," Evelyn said. "I'm not sure how she'll react when she sees her sister."

"They're twins?" Melanie asked.

"Yeah. Identical twins. No one could tell them apart growing up. We could, but to most people they moved as one, two sides of the same coin until they were in their teens. And then the accident. That changed everything."

"I'm sure the bond will still be there," Irma said.

"God love them," Grace said.

"What time was Sylvia's daughter's flight coming in?" Tyler asked.

"Twelve thirty," Evelyn answered.

"When did Sylvia figure out the one-month writer coming was her daughter?" Veronica asked.

"Just this morning at breakfast," Evelyn answered. "Kent said the author's name and she knew right away. It was a made-up name, but a name Sylvia is very familiar with."

"I'm glad Janice went with her," Grace said.

"Here comes the van," Tyler said.

The van stopped and Olivia was the first one out. As she closed the door, Sophie came back out onto the veranda. A screech of some description came from Sophie's throat and she began shaking. Dropping the pink Popsicle from her hand, she pushed past the others and ran down the stairs. The screech had changed to a scream.

Irma and Sylvia quickly fell into step, following Sophie around the corner as Olivia collapsed into her grandmother's arms, sobbing. Kent walked around to the back of the van and pulled out Olivia's suitcase.

Sophie was already in her bedroom when Sylvia and Irma entered the apartment. The screaming continued but had morphed into a recognizable word, the same word Sylvia remembered Sophie hollering while running through the hospital parking lot in the pouring rain a few weeks ago. Sophie kept screaming the word as she pawed through the collection of stuffies on the bench until she found the one she was searching for.

Sophie came out the door of her bedroom calmer, the sound a gentle mewing as she cradled the rainbow-coloured unicorn in her arms. Tears were streaming down her cheeks, but as her mother tried to reach out to comfort her, she pushed her out of the way.

"Liv, Liv," she hollered, running out the door and down the apartment stairs.

Sophie came running across the lawn, shaking a stuffed toy in the air. Olivia had just released Nan from the long hug, and Sophie stood bouncing in front of her, hollering her name over and over. Sylvia and Irma walked up behind.

"Liv, Liv, Liv!"

"Sophie," Olivia managed, emotion choking any other audible word.

Sophie stopped moving, took a few calm breaths, and began cradling the unicorn in her arms while making soft cooing sounds. Everyone was silent and transfixed in the interaction between the sisters. Sophie brought the unicorn up to her lips and kissed it sweetly before passing it to Olivia.

~~~

Sylvia and Olivia sat alone on the shore in the quiet stillness. The setting sun was just about out of sight as if the water was swallowing it.

"I feel like I've been crying nonstop since Dad pulled the van up in front of the lodge," Olivia said. "My God, Mom, Sophie just breaks my heart. It must be so hard for you day after day. I should have stayed around to help you."

"We're not getting into the should haves or could haves, especially not tonight. Tonight I'm just going to enjoy having my other girl here. Irma has been a godsend. She is so patient with Sophie. You saw how easily she can calm her down. Sophie was getting to be too much for Nan, so I couldn't really leave her for very long."

"Nan has aged a lot," Olivia said.

"She is ninety-two years old, Liv. It was bound to happen. But I've just come to terms with that myself. I was so determined that she would always be there for me, I couldn't entertain the possibility she might not."

"Do you think you could sleep with me tonight like you used to do? Remember, Sophie and I would take turns having mother-daughter sleepovers. You'd make a tent in the family room and we'd drag the cushions off the couch and lay our sleeping bags on top of them."

"Of course I remember. Hope you don't want me to sleep on the floor. I'm getting too old for that. Your room has a perfectly good queen-sized bed. I'll just go tell Irma what I'm doing and grab my pyjamas and housecoat. I'll meet you in your room in a few minutes."

Olivia watched as the very last flicker of sunlight disappeared. Would she muster the courage to tell her mother tonight? She clutched the unicorn and let the tears start up again. What she needed to finally tell her mother couldn't wait any longer. The truth needed to be told right away. She could not go another day without letting it out. She needed the forgiveness her family could give if she was ever to forgive herself. Sophie had in her own way made that clear.

<center>~~~~</center>

"It's been quite the day," Sylvia said, fluffing up the pillow under her head and settling comfortably to face her daughter. "I don't know how long I'll be able to stay awake. It's been pretty emotional all round, right from the moment your father announced that Bridget St. John was the writer coming today."

"Sorry about that. I'm sorry for so much. Maybe I should just turn the lamp off and let you go to sleep."

"Now, what kind of a sleepover would that be?"

"I'm afraid it's not going to be a fun one, Mom. I've got

something I need to tell you."

"I knew that the second I saw you coming through the gate. A mother's intuition. And besides, a daughter doesn't usually leave home and not even call if everything is rosy. Whatever it is, you can tell me."

"I was so angry when I left, but I wasn't angry at you. I was angry with myself. I messed everything up. Everything was my fault."

"Now, it might feel that way, but you know that's not true. Sophie's accident was nobody's fault."

"We had a big fight the night before."

"You two fought all the time. I know it must be hard thinking that the last night you had together you spent fighting, but having a fight didn't cause Sophie's accident."

"She was not herself that morning. I should have made her talk to me, but instead I let her channel her anger into a foolish challenge to ski the hardest slope. I was still upset and went right along with her. *Bring it on, bitch* was the last thing I said to her before it happened."

"Oh, sweetie. I am so sorry that's how you remember it, but even taking her challenge did not cause the accident. Accidents just happen. I have to believe that. I can't put my energy into blaming anyone. And you shouldn't either."

"Mom. There is more I need to tell you. I need to tell you what the fight was about."

"You don't have to, Olivia. It's not going to change anything."

"I know that. But I can't live with my secret any longer."

Olivia picked up the unicorn, hugging it to her chest as she continued.

"I believe Sophie has forgiven me, so now I need you to, and then eventually I can forgive myself."

"I'm listening."

"You and Dad thought Sophie had a false pregnancy. She told you that, but that was not true. Sophie was about fourteen weeks along when she miscarried. She was devastated. She made me promise not to tell you. She said it would be easier if you just thought she hadn't been pregnant at all. She knew you guys weren't happy about it and didn't really like Mark much. So she recovered without letting on what she had just gone through. She told me over and over again how she couldn't have gotten through it without me."

"Oh, Olivia. I had no idea. I knew she was upset about the breakup, but I wish she'd told me about losing the baby."

"I have to keep going, and the rest is harder. Sophie was still pretty fragile about the miscarriage and then the breakup when we decided to go on the ski trip. I was hoping the week away would be the pick-me-up she needed. I was hoping she might meet someone to help her get over Mark. The evening had started out fine, and everyone was having a great time. We'd all had a fair amount to drink and Hilary let something slip that escalated into the fight we had when we got back to our room. Hilary told Sophie that Mark had cheated on her, but what she hadn't said was he'd cheated with me. I slept with my sister's boyfriend."

"Oh my God, Olivia. How did she take that?"

"Not great, as you can imagine, but that wasn't the worst part. I think she would have been upset with me for a while, but it was the next confession that really hurt her. This is the part that's been killing me."

"Well, you might as well keep going. The telling can't be any worse than living with whatever it is."

"At first I thought I was in love with Mark, and he told me he was in love with me. We didn't know how we were going to break it to Sophie, but we knew we had to. Then she told him she was pregnant. And as if that wasn't enough to complicate things, a month later my strip turned pink. Mark had managed to knock up both of the Wright twins."

"Oh, Olivia, did you have a miscarriage too?"

"No. I was such a coward I decided it would be easier to stop seeing Mark and terminate the pregnancy. I hadn't meant for everything to happen simultaneously. I'd made my appointment before Sophie lost the baby, and I went ahead with the abortion in secret, not wanting to add to Sophie's pain. Possibly my intentions were good, although she didn't see it that way. She was so angry at me for ending my baby's life when she would have done anything to still be carrying hers.

"That's what we fought about that night. I will never forgive myself for putting Sophie in such a state. She shouldn't have been on that ski hill that morning in the frame of mind she was in. I should have made her stay back, but instead I avoided her until we got to the top of the hill, knowing how angry and disappointed she was with me.

"When I saw the paramedics rushing up the hill for her, I knew I was being punished. I was the heartless beast she accused me of being, and because of that I would lose the person I loved most in the world. But in the days and months afterward, I knew my punishment would not be so straightforward as losing her; I would be given the torture of watching her and the rest of my family suffer for what I'd done."

Sylvia wrapped her sobbing daughter in her arms until exhaustion pulled them both into a deep sleep.

Chapter Twenty One

Sylvia woke up while the room was still dark and slid quietly out of bed. She pulled the blinds down and tiptoed out of the room. She would leave Olivia to sleep as long as she could. Olivia's angry outbursts in the months after Sophie left the hospital had seemed so exaggerated and selfish, and by times she'd lost patience with her daughter. Afterward Sylvia would feel guilty for losing her patience. It was clear Olivia was heartbroken and worried about her sister, and being unable to process her grief was lashing out at those who loved her the most.

She should have known there was more to Olivia's behaviour. She shouldn't have given up so easily. But it had almost been a relief when Olivia stormed out of the house that day, accusing her mother of not caring about her. She had been exhausted. Those first few months of learning to deal with the new Sophie had been excruciating. Not having to deal with Olivia had been a relief.

Thank God Olivia had found her way back and allowed herself to be vulnerable enough to reach out to her family. Would Olivia have ever gone to the Rexdale house and unburdened herself, or had Kent's retreat brochure brought her back? Kent's retreat, but it had been her discovery of this property that started it all and ended up being the perfect place for Olivia to come to when she was ready.

Kent and Tyler were the first two down for breakfast.

"What are you cooking up this morning, Dot?" Tyler asked.

"Just bacon and eggs, toast, and fried potatoes. Nothing fancy."

"Dot, everything you cook is great," Tyler said. "Can I get you a coffee, Kent?"

"Thanks, Tyler. I heard you mowed the lawn while I was away. I appreciate that."

"No problem. I enjoy yard work."

"Me, not so much, but luckily there's not a lot to do right now. The lawn and a few maintenance things. Next year I might hire someone to do a bit more landscaping, but this year the focus was on getting ready to open."

"Doesn't need a lot of landscaping. The location is beautiful in itself."

"I may need to hire a caretaker to look after things. I'm considering moving back to Toronto and running the retreat from there. I'll need someone in the winter, anyway, since I'm sure this beautiful location gets a fair dumping of snow."

"You might want to think about getting a ride-on mower with a snow-blower attachment. The government probably plows the road right up to the gate, so a snow blower would probably be all a person would need to keep the driveway clear."

"That sounds like a good idea. Do you know anything about lawn tractors and what kind I should look at?"

"I worked for a landscaping snow removal company a few years ago. All their rigs were Kubota."

"Would you mind coming with me when I go to buy one? I wouldn't have a clue what to look for."

"Sure. Just let me know when you're going."

"We'll have to go before you leave on the tenth. I'm not sure how long I'm staying after that. I hope to work things out so I can be back in Toronto by the middle of the month."

"You're heading back to Toronto?" Dot asked.

"Thinking about it. This place pretty much runs itself. You've certainly taken away any worry I had about feeding people. Marjorie is doing a great job cleaning and Sylvia has helped a lot with the mentoring aspect. I just need to look after promotion and finances, and I can do that in Toronto. A few loose ends to tie up, but we'll see."

"Mom tells me there might be someone in Toronto you want to get back to," Olivia said, sitting down beside her father at the table.

"Did she?" Kent stammered.

"Dad, I'm not a child anymore. People have affairs. It's kind of refreshing to find out my father isn't perfect."

"I'm far from perfect, Liv."

"Join the club, Dad."

Sylvia lingered in front of her cottage, wishing she could just open the door and go inside and be home. The walk this morning felt so different. She had headed along the road and walked further than usual. Her thoughts were fixed on how different things would be if both girls had had full-term pregnancies, giving birth months apart with or without Mark. They wouldn't have gone on the ski trip. They would be living very different lives today. Would she and Kent have strengthened their relationship as grandparents?

Sylvia sat on the steps of the cottage. A good cry was in order. She seldom let the what ifs catch up to her, but they were flooding her brain this morning and she would just give in to them for a few minutes. She would cry and feel sorry for herself and for her girls. She would cry, thinking of the time coming when she would not have Nan. She would mourn a marriage that hadn't been all bad. She would just sit and cry.

"So, this is the cottage?" Olivia said, sitting down beside her mother.

"How did you know I was here?"

"Nan said you had gone for a walk in this direction. Are you okay?"

"I'm fine. Yes, this is my cottage. It's perfect, don't you think? My own little place nice and close to Nan, Sophie, and Irma. A part of the retreat but separate. It feels exactly what I need right now."

"Being here feels exactly like what I need too, Mom. I've been thinking."

"That always worried me when you were a kid. You were the best one for coming up with outlandish ideas."

"I don't think it's outlandish. You know Dad is thinking of going back to Toronto. He didn't exactly tell me about Darcy, but he didn't deny it either. Well, I thought I could take over running the retreat. He might need to keep the financial part of it; as you know, I'm not the best with money, but I could do the booking, coordinating, and general managing. I was thinking we could set up a roster of authors to fill guest spots. The guest authors could do the mentoring and conduct workshops. I have a few other ideas too. The retreat could give me a small salary and maybe I would take a few courses and get back on track."

"You *have* been thinking."

"What do you think?"

"First of all, I'd be thrilled if you stayed, and so would Nan and Sophie. I want to spend most of my time writing, so I wasn't keen on having to be more involved in the retreat if your father went back to Toronto. I wouldn't mind contributing a bit, though, and I think having guest authors is a really good idea. I think your father would be all for your involvement too. And he is good with money."

"Did you guys sell the house?"

"Yes. I'm sorry. I should have let you know."

"I could have called. It seems weird that I'll never be in that house again. It's the only home I ever knew."

"You wouldn't believe how much it sold for. Your father had the idea we were going to upgrade and put the money into a bigger house, but I found the lodge and that changed everything."

"Bet that wasn't easy. Changing Kent Wright's mind about something is no simple task."

"I was determined to bring Nan back to New Brunswick. Seemed that's where I needed to be too."

"Well, now it appears it's where I need to be as well."

"That sounds great to me. Go ahead and run it by your father."

Veronica looked up, waiting for Grace's reaction to what she had just read to her.

"Oh my goodness, dear, that is powerful. It can't be easy writing this. How are you doing?"

"I am better than I've been in a long time, a very long time. In fact, I can't remember ever being this good. I am getting worried about leaving, though."

"I know what you're saying. Being here has been such a blessing. I know how hard it was for you to come, but you've faced so much and come such a long way toward healing. And we've made such close friends here."

"I keep thinking of going back to my lonely apartment and my tedious job. I plan to keep writing, but it won't be easy."

"I will go back to a big, sprawling house. Maybe it's sold

and I will have reached the top of the list for an apartment in the seniors' home. It's a lovely seniors' home, but I dread the loneliness too."

"Yeah, nine more days and we leave and go our separate ways."

"Whatever you do, Veronica, you need to keep writing. You can't let anything get in your way now that you've finally started."

"You too, Grace. We are writers and we need to put that first."

"What would you think about two, eccentric authors living together in a big, old mansion on a lake? Why don't you move to Port Hope, into my house? I could take it off the market and stay put if I had you there for company. My son will think I've lost my mind, but I don't really care what he thinks."

"Oh my God, Grace. I don't even know what to say. I don't have any income except a small monthly cheque. I wouldn't be able to contribute much."

"I'm not worried about money. I'm an old lady living a comfortable life in a house big enough for three families. I can't think of anything better than having a friend live there with me. I think it's a perfect plan for both of us."

"Well, it's worth considering. We could do up a contract of some kind. I would sign something saying I don't expect any compensation. I don't want your son thinking I'm moving in so I can inherit your estate."

"Don't be ridiculous. Wallace has been well looked after

and will continue to be. I am of sound mind and can still make my own decisions. Let's not worry about who I'm leaving my estate to. Let's just think about living our best lives right now."

"You are such an angel, Grace. I feel so lucky that our paths crossed."

"As do I, my dear girl. As do I."

<hr />

"You found her," Evelyn said as Sylvia and Olivia walked through the door. "Sylvie, you look a fright."

Sylvia didn't speak but walked through the kitchen toward Nan's room. Evelyn rose and followed her.

"Can you lie with me for a minute?" Sylvia asked.

"Of course I can. You've been crying."

Sylvia ran her fingertips along the raised ridges of the faded quilt covering her grandmother's bed.

"We've lain on this quilt so many times, Nan. Me crying and you comforting. Stunned as the quilt and maybe even the comforter, Irma says."

"This old quilt has had some tears drop on it, that's for sure. How about telling me what's got you crying today?"

"I have no reason to be feeling like this. I'm so glad Olivia is here. I'm excited about moving into the cottage. I'm good, so how come I feel so sad?"

"The thing about feelings is they come whether we want them to or not."

"I went to the Reversing Falls Bridge once. I parked at the restaurant and walked across the bridge. I stood looking down at the roiling falls so far below. I imagined pulling myself up onto the railing and standing there on the precipice. Cars slowed down, drivers probably wondering if I was a jumper. I stared down at the water and thought about Mom actually climbing up and hurtling down to her death. Why can some face a precipice and pull back and others throw themselves over?"

"Your mother was not well. Drugs were clouding her judgement."

"I remember standing in the foyer of the church while someone I didn't even know was singing 'Ava Maria.' You were standing beside me, waiting to walk me down the aisle. The pews were filled with strangers. I caught a glimpse of myself reflected in the window, wearing the wedding dress I'd picked out in a hurry, hoping it would hide my pregnancy. In that moment I felt like I did that day on the bridge, staring down at the water below. I had a choice, and I'm still not sure I made the right one."

"Oh, Sylvie. I was part of the choice you made. I was convinced Kent would provide the security and stability for you that I had always wanted so badly for your mother."

"I know it's terrible of me to be so hung up on this after all these years. I need to let it go. I need to let a whole lot of things go."

"Letting go of things isn't a onetime deal, it's a continual exercise. Your mother died forty-eight years ago, and I still find myself going to the pain and regret of it. Life is a continual back-and-forth of the emotions and challenges that take us to the edge of the precipice, as you call it. Each time we just have to work at stepping back again and carrying on. The people we love help us to do that."

Irma came to the doorway "Olivia and I kind of made the mistake of mentioning slushies and Sophie's a bit wound up. How about you two get up and we'll all take a trip to the Irving?"

"Sounds like a great plan," Sylvia said.

⁓⁓

Kent pulled the cover off the hot tub and adjusted the controls. He stepped in and sat down, waiting for his daughter to come out and join him. It had been a busy day, and they'd barely had a chance to talk. Supper had been a bustle of conversation, and afterward, when Olivia approached him asking to talk privately, he'd suggested the hot tub. Everyone else seemed to be heading to the beach. Tyler had prepared another bonfire, which apparently was now a nightly ritual.

Three more writers would arrive in a few days. He'd finalized all the details this afternoon and their reply emails were filled with enthusiasm and anticipation. Dr. Daniels was flying in from Saskatchewan. Nora Taylor and Wendy Wilson were driving here together from northern New Brunswick. He had assured the three of them that there was a vibrant group of writers here and they could look forward to some meaningful interactions.

The bond among the current participants was evident, but he supposed he really couldn't take the credit. He was pleased that the inaugural retreat had been successful, overall. He was optimistic, considering the registrations that were already booked over the next few months. The Wright Retreat as a business venture was in the black so far.

"How's the temperature, Dad?" Olivia said.

"Wonderful. Come on in."

"Look at that night sky. You don't see that in downtown Toronto."

"No, I suppose not. What did you get up to today?"

"I went to see Mom's cottage. We all went to the Irving for slushies. Mom and I went for a swim. The day flew by, actually."

"So, Richard told me you quit a few weeks ago."

"I was done the middle of August, and I let my apartment go at the end of the month because I knew I was coming here."

"Do you have a plan after the month is up?"

"I wanted to talk to you about that. I talked it over with Mom today and she thinks it's a good idea."

"She thinks what's a good idea?"

"I'm thinking if you want to go back to Toronto, maybe I could stay and run the retreat. You could manage the financial part of it, but I could do the bookings, the programming, and the coordinating of it from here. I have a few ideas, like maybe having guest authors and running day-long writing workshops as well as the live-in options already in place. I also want to take some online courses and could do that from here."

"Wow, you've given this some thought. So your mother thought it was a good idea?"

"Yes. She wants to get back to writing full-time and doesn't want to have to be too involved with the retreat. I think it would be good for Sophie and Nan to have me here, too."

"Your sister would love having you around, and Evelyn would too. All the family together again. Except for me, but I guess I messed that up."

"Mom seems really happy, Dad, the happiest I've seen her for a long time. Maybe things happen for a reason. You deserve to be happy too. We all do."

"Yeah, we do. Well, let's figure out the logistics of you staying and managing things. You'll need a salary, of course. We can swing that. I'll calculate all the costs and projections. Give me a proposal regarding guest authors and any other ideas you have so I can figure all that in. This might just be the answer for all of us. I am a big-city boy, you know. I never really saw myself hunkering down here for the winter. You might be feeling the same after you stay awhile."

"I'll take my chances. Right now I can't think of anywhere I'd rather be. Are you going down to the bonfire?"

"No, I'm going to call it a night. But you go ahead."

"Love you, Dad."

"I love you too, Livvie girl. I think I'll go over and have a look in on your sister before I go up to bed."

Chapter Twenty-Two

Sylvia happened to be coming back from her walk when Dennis Walker pulled up to the lodge.

"Hi, Sylvia. Nice morning. I've got the key for you if you'd like it. The owner thought you might want it a few days early in case you wanted to start moving a few things in before Friday."

"That would be great. I've been walking by, wishing I could go in. I assume the furniture that's there is staying."

"Yes. He asked me to remove some of the personal items, some photographs and such. He wondered if I'd found the sign his grandparents used to hang out front. He wanted you to have it if I found it and asked me to ask you if you would mind hanging it, and calling the cottage 'Luna Sea' like his grandparents did."

"Did you find the sign?"

"No. I'll let him know I didn't find it."

"Please tell him I will make sure to hang a sign back on the post that says *Luna Sea*. I think it's a perfect name, even though there is nothing crazy about me moving into that cottage. It might be the sanest thing I've ever done."

Sylvia took the key, then turned and walked into the lodge

kitchen. "The realtor just dropped off the key to me."

"Well then, I expect you want to get right over there and have a walk in by yourself," Irma replied.

"I would. I've been wanting to just stand inside and let it sink in that that sweet little cottage is mine. Do you mind if I leave again?"

"Of course not. Sophie's just getting around, and I'll help her get dressed and have breakfast."

"I am so glad you're here."

"I loves it too. Now be gone with ya. Go sit in that little cottage with yourself."

Sylvia walked to the cottage. She turned the key and opened the wooden door, recalling trying the knob on that snowy January day. Besides pictures missing off the walls and a few items removed, it looked as she remembered it the day Dennis Walker had showed her through. But this time it felt entirely different. Looking around, she quickly decided on a few changes she'd make in this front room.

Moving into the largest bedroom, she noticed the view from the big window. This room would be her office. What a delight it would be during all seasons to sit at her desk while gazing out at the water. Right now the furniture, a lovely antique bed with matching dresser and wardrobe, filled the room. She would keep the wardrobe and put it out in the front room.

The single bed and smaller dresser in the other bedroom would suit her needs just fine. She didn't need room for company, as the lodge would be available for visitors and already housed the people who meant the most to her. She could set this cottage up completely for herself. There was something so freeing about that. Everything she kept and everything new she added would be intentional. She looked forward to the process.

Sylvia heard the door open and walked back out into the front room.

"Olivia came over," Irma said. "She's cooking waffles for her and Sophie. Thought I'd pop over and have a peek. Hopes ya don't mind me being nosey."

"Not at all. You're my first visitor. Isn't it precious? Just exactly what I need. First time I'm lived alone in my entire life."

"My mudder used to say, 'If you make friends with yourself, you'll never be alone.'"

"So you don't think I'm being selfish?"

"Selfish? Now listen here, girl. You raised two children, stayed married to a man for thirty years, looked after your grandmother, cared for Sophie alone these last years, and put all of that before yourself. You went along and went along and now you're finally doing something just for you. About fuckin' time is how I look at it."

"Well, turns out I can do that because you did the same."

"I guess that's true. Aren't we a pair, now?"

Olivia took the keys from her father, assuring him she'd have no trouble driving the fifteen-passenger van into Moncton.

"It's not a bus, Dad, and I'll have to drive it when I have pickups to do at the airport."

"How many are going shopping, anyway?"

"Everyone but you and Tyler. So you can take Mom's vehicle to go look at lawn tractors. Even Dot said she'd come. We'll all be gone at lunchtime, so we just have to get back in time for her to get supper ready."

"So it's a shopping spree?"

"Yeah. Mom got the key this morning so she can start moving things into the cottage. She needs some furniture and house wares. She needs to stock her cupboards. We're going to Costco, Canadian Tire, and some furniture stores. And Irma and Dot want to do some shopping for the housewarming."

"All right, but be careful. It's got a backup camera, but check your mirrors too. And try to find pull-through parking spaces in case you can't judge how long the van is."

"Yes, Dad. Stop worrying."

~⁓⁓~

"Dad finally consented to me taking the van. All aboard, and let's get some shopping done."

Irma and Sophie climbed into the van, going to the very back. Sophie, clutching her armload of stuffed animals, seemed excited about the trip. Melanie, Grace, and Veronica got into the next row of seats. Dot, Evelyn, and Janice situated themselves, and Sylvia got into the passenger seat.

"Where to first, Mom? I have no idea where I'm going."

"Dot, maybe you should have sat up here to give Olivia directions."

"Oh, I can navigate from back here. Pretty straightforward to get to the highway. We can go to Costco first and then decide. You want to buy some furniture, right?"

"Yes. I don't need a whole lot. I want a desk, a couple of bookshelves, new couch, and a couple of comfy chairs. The bed in the small bedroom will be fine for me. I have a few things to sell or give away."

"Marjorie said she could give the cottage a good cleaning tomorrow if you'd like her to. She might buy whatever you don't want, as she's trying to furnish her mother-in-law's house to get it ready to rent."

"Yes, it would be a favour to me for her to just take what she wants as she cleans. I plan on filling my space only with what I need and what brings me joy."

"Have you been reading Marie Kondo, Mom?"

"No. I'm just really looking forward to filling my little cottage with beautiful things and only things that mean something to me."

"Well, we're here to help you find some beautiful things," Irma called from the back.

"Would you like to have the sunset painting for your cottage?" Melanie asked.

"I would love to buy it from you and hang it in my office."

"I'm happy to give it you."

"She gave me the clothesline one," Veronica said.

"Time to start selling your paintings, Melanie," Janice said. "Your work is amazing."

"Thank you," Melanie said.

"We all need to take our work seriously and believe in its worth," Grace said.

⁓⁓

Kent pulled the Rav out of the parking lot of Bayview Truck and Equipment.

"Well, I think we negotiated a pretty good deal, Tyler. Thanks for your help. I had no idea what to look for."

"No problem. What were the chances of stumbling on just the rig you need? And they just got it in yesterday. Used, but in great condition and a good price."

"You'll still be here to try it out when it gets delivered. And you can show me what I need to know."

"Are you still thinking about hiring a caretaker?"

"Yes."

"I'd be interested in the job. I talked it over with Abby. We figure if she keeps her job and I had the part-time caretaker job, we could probably make a go of it, giving both of us time to write. We'd have to find a place around here to rent, though."

"That would save me having to look for someone. I was thinking twenty hours a week at twenty dollars an hour. You could always stay in the lodge until you found a place. For a few weeks, anyway. Olivia has taken a room and I thought I'd keep one for when I come so I can't be tying up any more rooms, but I only have three more writers coming in September, and two of them are sharing a room. I do have two weeks in November when I'll need all ten rooms, but we'll figure that out later. I must say, I won't mind handing over the juggling of all that to Olivia."

—❦—

"You didn't need to stay back with me," Evelyn said.

"I don't mind at all," Melanie said. "That was enough shopping for me."

"Enough for me too, but I'm an old woman. That was a nice lunch, wasn't it?"

"Yeah, it was great. It was so nice of you all to invite me along. I'm not very social."

"Nothing wrong with keeping to yourself, dear."

"I wasn't always this way, but now I find it really hard to talk to people. I guess that's what happens when..."

"It is a lovely September day. You know you don't have to talk to me. If I sit here long enough I'm liable to doze off."

"I don't mind talking at all. It's kind of nice, actually. Dawson made sure I had fewer and fewer friends, and by the end of it I had no one to talk to."

"Who was Dawson, dear?"

"My boyfriend. He was almost my husband, but thank goodness I got away before I made that mistake."

"Well, that is good. You should be very proud of that. Not every woman gets away from the man harming her. My daughter was not so lucky. She died forty-eight years ago tomorrow, an anniversary date that never gets easier."

"Oh, I'm so sorry, Evelyn. Did her partner kill her?"

"Not technically, but as far as I'm concerned he did. He got her on heroin, and she took her own life."

"I am so sorry. Was she your only child?"

"Yes. Thank God for Sylvia. She came to us when she was almost five, and she kept my husband and I from letting our grief overcome us. Oh, how he loved his Sylvie girl. He would have adored the twins."

"When did you lose your husband?"

"A long time ago, my dear. Let's talk about something else. Have you got lots of art supplies back at the lodge? You've been painting up a storm."

"I haven't got any canvases left, but I've got my sketch pad, so I can work on sketches of what I might paint next."

"Isn't that an arts-and-crafts shop across the parking lot?"

"Yes, it is."

"Then why don't you lead this old lady across there and I'll buy you some canvases."

"You don't have to do that."

"I know I don't, but if I didn't want to, I wouldn't say so.

How about I buy them and you can paint me something before you go?"

"I'd love that. Should we go in and tell the others where we're going or leave a note?"

"If they come out before we get back, they'll just have to wait. I don't figure they'll leave without us."

⌒⌒⌒⌒

Sophie was happily weaving the shopping cart up and down the aisles under Irma's close supervision. Ahead of them Olivia and Sylvia had already filled their cart with throw cushions, some bedding, towels, and some wall decor.

"I love the beachy things," Sylvia said. "Seems so fitting. And I love the splash of colour this bedspread will give to my little bedroom."

"Dot is finding you all kinds of kitchen things," Veronica called from the next aisle. "She's like a kid in a candy store."

"She said you can veto anything you don't want," Grace added.

"And there might be a few things in Irma's cart you're not allowed to look at," Janice said. "They have a housewarming theme going on."

"It has been so much fun having you all with me to shop," Sylvia said. "I know the salesgirl at Leon's was thrilled you all encouraged me to buy as much as I did."

"You only live once, my dear," Grace said. "And your little cottage should be everything you want it to be."

"You're right. Could you put that pole lamp and those two table lamps in your cart? Ours is running out of space. Oh, and that one would be perfect for my desk."

Chapter Twenty-Three

"I'll play the part of Benson," Tyler said as everyone was finishing breakfast. "Let's have a workshop this afternoon. It's been a while since we've had any readings. Looks like it might rain all day anyway. How about we meet back here at two?"

"Thanks, Tyler," Kent said. "I guess I kind of dropped the ball on planning lately. Benson and Gavin kept me on track. I'll get the fireplace going and rearrange the furniture to make a circle for the afternoon session."

"No problem. I think the beauty of this place is the organic way the mentoring and supporting has happened."

"That might be, but I can't always depend on that. Olivia came up with a plan that I think will work perfectly. She's going to stay and manage the retreat. I'll manage the financial part from Toronto, but she'll look after everything else."

"Oh, that's great, Olivia," Veronica said. "You must be thrilled, Sylvia."

"We're all thrilled," Sylvia replied.

"I'll put a signup sheet on the table," Tyler said. "Let's hear from anyone who wants to read."

"I have a piece to read," Olivia said.

"I'll make a few snacks," Dot said.

"It's going to be some hard leaving this place," Janice said.

"That's for sure," Grace added.

Olivia sat at the table in her room and pulled up a page on her laptop. Last night after coming back to her room from the bonfire, she'd sat down to write her confession, beginning with a definition of plagiarism. Looking over at the pile of papers on the bench, she recalled the email she'd received back from Uptown Press a few days ago. Olivia sensed the accusations of fraud and immorality and threats of legal action were masking Molly Jordan's true feelings of embarrassment and humiliation at being duped into thinking she had discovered a promising young author when what she had accepted was a copy of an already published work; work that had been written by a Giller-longlisted author. No doubt Molly Jordan's confidence had been undermined, but dissolving the contract would probably be the end of it.

It would not be easy to read this essay this afternoon, but Olivia had decided to confess in this way in front of the group, not just to her mother. She had already shared the confession that needed to be just for her mother, had the weight of that secret lifted and felt Mom's love and forgiveness. So now admitting the stupidity of what she had done needed a public confession and a final action to unburden herself.

Melanie reread the poem "Loose Dresses" she'd just finished. She hoped Veronica did not take offense to her words, which mirrored some of what Veronica had told her. It was so weird how the vision of dresses strung on the long clothesline had come to her without any knowledge of what this building's function was in the late sixties and early seventies.

Melanie herself had been born to a teenaged mother, but times had changed by then. Her mother had been given a monthly income from Social Services and her first months of motherhood had been in a small south end apartment in Saint John. Melanie was a few months old before her grandmother broke down and accepted her daughter's shame and reached out to help. By the time Melanie was two they were living with her grandmother, and by the time she was six, "Mommy" was long gone. Grammy and Bob had raised her even after Tammy grew up, got married, and started her real family.

Could she read this poem to the group this afternoon and keep her distance from the undercurrent of hurt and abandonment the lines of this poem held for her? Melanie stood to read the poem aloud, rehearsing the delivery she knew she was capable of giving. She was well practised in disguising her insecurity and masking her pain.

⤟⤠

"The writing in this room is so impressive," Sylvia said. "I must say I will be proud to have my name connected to any one of you as published authors."

"This whole experience has been great," Tyler said. "And I'm not just talking about finding the love of my life."

"I couldn't ask for more than what I received by coming back here," Veronica said.

"Wonderful all round for me," Grace added. "Oh, and by the way, Veronica has accepted my invitation to move to Port Hope and live with me. It is a win-win. I get companionship and encouragement with my writing and she gets to write full-time."

"That is great news," Janice said. "I submitted my manuscript today."

"Congratulations," Veronica and Grace chorused.

"Your poem was very moving, Melanie," Janice said.

"Thank you. First one I've ever shared with anyone. Finishing paintings and poems. This place is magical."

"I think it's magical how you sensed the history of this place," Veronica said. "It means a lot to me."

"Olivia, didn't you say earlier you had something to read?" Tyler asked.

"Yeah, I do have something to read. It's a bit of a downer, but I may as well get it over with."

Olivia picked up her backpack from off the floor beside her chair. She unzipped it and pulled out a pile of papers, setting them on the coffee table. Then she pulled out a hardcover book showing everyone the cover.

"This is Mom's third book," Olivia said, holding it up to show the cover, then the photograph on the back cover.

"Wow, that was taken a while ago," Sylvia said. "That's the same photo Kent used in the brochure. A more recent one might scare people away."

"Don't be silly. You still look great," Grace said.

Olivia reached into the backpack and pulled out her laptop. She opened it and began reading.

Plagiarism

To take and use as one's own, the thoughts and writings of another

For a whole year I faithfully and obsessively wrote every day. I would open this book and meticulously type every word, every sentence, and every conversation, changing only character and place names. Before starting I would turn to the back cover and stare at the picture of my mother. In doing that I would tell myself the story I needed so badly to believe. I told myself she had let me down. She was a fake, a phony, always more concerned about her readers than her own flesh and blood. I told myself that her writing had stolen my childhood, that in spending her life writing she had robbed Sophie and me of the mother we deserved.

Obsessive, psychotic, whacko, you might be thinking. Why would anyone take all the time and effort needed to completely copy a book while making small, deliberate changes? I considered every word I was stealing as payment for something that had been stolen from me. I was determined to complete the exercise of writing it and then go through the submission process until a publisher accepted it. My goal was to follow through until I held a book in my hands with my photograph on the back cover. I wanted my mother to find it in a bookstore or on a library shelf and see the name Bridget St. John on the spine and finally see me, my worth, my value, my existence.

I spent two years in this unhealthy mindset and know now it was to shield myself from really feeling anything else. Believe it or not, I was successful in finding a publisher. A small Toronto press accepted my manuscript, had me sign a contract, and gave me a small advance. An editor was engaged to begin work with a release date projected for Spring 2020. Unbelievable, right? A person cannot copy someone else's book and get it published. Plagiarism is wrong. Copyright laws prevent such things from happening.

While sitting in the foyer waiting to meet with the small press owner, I noticed a brochure on the coffee table in front of me. The name Wright Retreat got my attention. I picked it up to look at and saw the exact picture I'd looked at each night when I sat down to write. I saw a picture of this lodge and the Northumberland Strait. I read all the retreat details and options.

I went into that meeting and actually signed a contract for the release of my book. My book was a huge lie, but I accepted the small advance cheque and shook the publisher's hand. As I left, I picked the brochure up off the coffee table and stuck it in my backpack.

The brochure was my wakeup call, my moral compass, my north star. When I got home I ripped up the contract and the cheque. I began the process of registering for the Wright Retreat, knowing my coming here was coming home and coming back to reality. I was ready to take a long, hard look at my act of plagiarism and see it for what it had been. In doing that, I had to force myself to really look at my mother's face and remember the truth.

The truth was my mother was everything a mother should be.

The woman whose face I'd demonized was always present in a loving and caring way. Her smile accompanied every accomplishment I knew, whether large or small. That face was in every crowd at all my soccer games, piano recitals, and skiing competitions. That face was right beside me when I woke up after having my tonsils out. That face was contorted with anguish as my mother tried to comfort me at Sophie's hospital bedside. And more important than anything, that face showed forgiveness when I came here to start again.

The day I arrived, I told Janice that I always wanted to be my mother. That is so true, but the unhealthy obsession I had with copying her work and fooling someone into believing I was as good as she was is not the way I truly want to be her. I want to be her in the way that she has loved us, cared for us, and put us before her own needs. I want to be the woman my mother is. I don't want to be an exact copy, but I want to be created and molded because of who she strived to be when raising me and who she is today.

Mom, I want you to take this manuscript, this pile of paper that was produced around a lie, and burn it at tonight's bonfire. I am done with the lie and only have time and energy for the truth. I will keep searching for that truth. I want to write, but I want to write my own words not yours. Plagiarism is wrong on so many levels. It is the easy way out of finding your own words and trusting your own understanding.

Olivia stood frozen while calculating her escape, tears in her eyes, trying to avoid looking at anyone especially her mother. In her peripheral vision she saw her mother coming toward her.

Sylvia hugged her daughter. "I am so proud of my girl. And the new manager of the Wright Retreat just delivered her first workshop presentation. Plagiarism is an important topic for any author."

Sylvia picked up the pile of papers and handed them to Tyler. "Should be pretty easy to get the fire started tonight."

Dot walked into the circle carrying a large platter. "Here are the snacks I promised."

"Let's open some wine and celebrate our new manager and raise a glass to all the writing that's been done in this place," Kent said.

"This special, rejuvenated, magical place," Veronica said. "We've all contributed to filling this building with an energy, an honesty, a caring and loving spirit, and I believe by doing that we've cleared out the darkness, the misery, and the suffering these walls once contained. That is a gift to me and to every girl who suffered under this roof."

⁓

The rain starting up again convinced everyone but Sylvia and Janice to leave the bonfire and head up to the lodge.

"It's a nice, warm rain, and I don't expect I'll melt," Janice said.

"I won't either. I'm in a bit of a trance watching Olivia's rewritten version of my work become sparks, the sentences black ash swirling around in the wind, and the chapters smouldering under damp wood on this beautiful shore in the province where I was born. Profound or too much wine?" Sylvia asked.

"Just the right amount of wine for you, and the right amount for me. Funny how folks offer alcoholics a drink, thinking a glass or two won't hurt. Took me a while to realize the right amount of alcohol for me is none at all."

"I never drink this much, and I'll probably feel like hell in the morning, but tonight I'm just enjoying myself. I feel so much pressure lifted with Olivia taking over the retreat, Irma helping out with Sophie and Kent planning on going back to Toronto."

"Can you believe Olivia copied the whole book word for word and actually found a publisher?" Janice asked. "You've got to give her kudos for effort."

"Olivia's determination has always been her strong point. Once she sets her mind to something, she sticks to it like a dog with a bone. It makes me sad that she spent three years being so angry at me."

"Sometimes anger is all you've got. Casey spent a long time putting all her energy into being angry at me. If I was the villain, she didn't have to look any closer at herself or at the real source of her pain. Putting everything you have into blaming the people who hurt you leaves you hollow and does nothing to lift the burden of pain. I know this from spending years obsessed with condemning the Catholic Church, the residential school system, the perpetrators of my misery. But healing comes from realizing the damage you do to yourself by letting blame and anger rule you. They say forgiveness is more for the forgiver than the forgiven."

"Olivia had to start by forgiving herself."

"That's often where it needs to start. None of us are perfect, after all."

"I am going to miss you, Jan."

"Well, we're not going to move in together like Grace and Veronica, but I think our friendship will continue. Seems to me that would be good for both of us."

"That's for sure. When I think back to how apprehensive I was about having ten authors descend on my private paradise, I have to chuckle. Little did I know how monumental some of the relationships would turn out to be."

"I agree with what Veronica said earlier: this is a pretty special place. And I think writers bring a certain amount of vulnerability and honesty with them, which allows for some meaningful interactions. Isn't that what we strive for through our writing?"

"It's what we should strive for. I'm not sure my earlier work did. I've been thinking as I've watched these pages burn that the book Olivia picked was the one I'm the least proud of. I wrote it at a time I was just going through the motions. I was an empty shell, so afraid to feel anything. I wrote that book in a haze of denial and pain. Olivia did the same while rewriting it. But I'm not going to spend any time lamenting what that book lacks. I'm just going to look ahead and put my authentic self into my current work."

"I'm really getting wet now, and I'm thinking you're ready for a good night's sleep. Tomorrow is another day. Let's say goodnight to this one."

Chapter Twenty-Four

Dr. George Daniels had once been a name held in high regard. His reputation was exemplary. His surgical prowess was known far and wide, and his salary reflected that. How was it that now his most pressing job was emptying the cat's litter box? George scooped out the hard lumps of shit and flushed them. He dumped the used granules into a kitchen catcher, relined the box, and shook fresh litter, distributing it evenly. Why he even kept the damn cat was beyond him. It had been Rose's cat, and at first it seemed out of the question to get rid of her. But Rose had been dead five years, and still this cat ruled the roost.

Stella purred and rubbed her matted fur against his trousers. Mrs. Livingston from next door had agreed to come feed and water the cat and empty the litter box while he was away for the two weeks. He'd considered the one-month retreat, but that felt a bit excessive. But registering for this retreat was his way of committing to finally getting serious about writing the memoir he'd started at Rose's urging.

He could hear Rose's voice echoing in his head. "George, you've lived a very interesting life. You pulled yourself up by your bootstraps and made something of yourself. You've got more stories to tell than the *Reader's Digest*, and if you don't tell them, who will?"

He'd bought the computer and set it up in the spare room ten years ago and started writing, but months later, Rose's diagnosis sidelined that. Every once in a while in the last five years, he would think about getting back to it. A few months ago he had joined a writer's group and started thinking seriously about getting back to his memoir. *If not now, then when?* was the mantra of the group.

Emily brought a brochure for the Wright Retreat to a meeting a few weeks ago. George had jotted down the website address and had a look at the retreat details on line. After considering the options, he'd decided to register for the two-week retreat. He'd gone out and bought himself a laptop and made all the arrangements to go away. Mrs. Livingston had been the last detail to firm up. Tomorrow he would fly to Moncton, New Brunswick. Right now was the *when*, and he was determined to make the two weeks count. *Doctor in the House* was finally going to get written. Rose would be so proud of him.

⁓

Wendy Wilson backed her car into Nora's driveway. Backing it in with no traffic in sight was a better idea than trying to back out onto the road in tomorrow's early morning traffic. She had mapped out the route and the drive from Perth Andover to Petit Cap would take about four hours. That was why she had decided to come to Nora's and stay the night and leave from there in the morning.

"We're not writers," Nora had said when Wendy presented the idea of going to the Wright Retreat to her a few weeks ago.

"It doesn't matter. All levels of writers welcome, it says. You don't need to have written anything or be published. My God, you and I can write as well as most, I expect, if we put our minds to it. Better than that one who wrote those Fifty Shades of Whatever books. Terrible writing, Marilyn tells me. Anyway, it's not the writing I'm interested in. Three meals a day and lovely accommodations, it says. We never had that the last time we stayed there. We've always talked about going back someday and putting the horror of that place to rest.

"When Marilyn showed me the piece in the paper about the Wright Retreat, I knew the place right away. It's been all fixed up and renovated, but I knew it as soon as I saw it. You don't forget a place that took so much from you. That place is burned in my memory, and that's why I think going back there is something I need to do. Something we both need to do."

Nora said, "Ten days seems long enough."

"When's the last time either one of us got away for two weeks to a place where all our meals were prepared and we didn't have to lift a finger to clean or care for anyone? Ten days might be long enough to work through our feelings, cleanse ourselves, and bury our hatred and disgust for the bastards who ran that place, but it seems to me two weeks of relaxation and rest would be a gift we can give ourselves in the process.

Going there won't bring our baby boys back or take away the pain of living all these years since they took them from us, but maybe two weeks can bring us some peace."

In the end Wendy and Nora had sent in their registration money and told Kent Wright they would share a room for two weeks. A much nicer room, they assumed, than the room they'd shared with four other girls forty-seven years ago.

~~~

Sylvia stepped back and looked at the colourful duvet and throw cushions on the single bed. Marjorie had started with the bedrooms and moved on to cleaning the kitchen, so Sylvia was busily setting up her bedroom. The furniture she'd bought yesterday was being delivered later today, and she was anxious to set up her office. Marjorie's husband, Walter, had already loaded all the furniture she was getting rid of, and Marjorie was boxing up the other items.

Yesterday on the way back from shopping, they'd dropped off all the bags. Dot's kitchen purchases had been extensive, but Sylvia hadn't put anything away yet. She would wait for Marjorie to clean all the cupboards and drawers out. She'd gotten all the staples from Costco and would put those away later too. She didn't plan on doing a lot of cooking here, but it would be nice to have her cupboards stocked just in case.

Nan's cupboards had always been bursting. Papa used to tease her, saying if for some reason they couldn't get to the mainland, she'd have enough provisions to last for ten years.

What a contrast Nan's bounty was to the empty cupboards and bouts of hunger Sylvia could remember from her early years. Thank goodness her girls had never had to experience the want and uncertainty she had before coming to Nan and Papa. And Nan had always been a part of her girls' culinary experiences. Nan had done the majority of the cooking.

Maybe this little kitchen would be the place Sylvia came into her own in the cooking department, although why would she eat alone when she could enjoy Dot's cooking or have her meals with Irma, Nan, and Sophie? Maybe her routine would be eating breakfast here and alternating her lunch and supper between the lodge and apartment. She would figure it out, but for today she would just enjoy putting everything in order and getting ready for tomorrow, when she would move into her new home.

~~♦~~

"So, I hear you are the new caretaker, Tyler," Dot said.

"Yeah, I think so. I told Kent I was interested in the job. The only thing in the way right now is finding a place for Abby and me to live. It needs to be near, since we don't have a car, and it has to have dependable internet, because Abby will be working from home when she gets here."

"Marjorie has a house to rent. It's her mother-in-law's house, and it will be all furnished. Her thoughts are to rent it seasonally, but I'm sure she'd be happy to rent it to you and Abby. It's right next door to Marjorie and Walter, and I think their internet is good. She's cleaning Sylvia's cottage right now if you want to walk over and ask her."

"I might just do that. To think of staying to work in this place that has given me so much already seems too good to be true."

"Life gives back what you give it, Tyler. You came with an open heart and welcomed the blessings it had for you. This place used to strip good things and punish the people under its roof. Dishing out blessings here has been long overdue."

⁓

Veronica walked farther into the woods. A few minutes ago, becoming overwhelmed, she'd set her journal and pen down and left her room. At first she thought she'd find Grace or Janice and let either woman calm her and distract her from the memory she had been writing about. But once downstairs she realized she didn't want anyone to interrupt the processing today's writing had started.

Veronica came to the moss-covered statue and slumped to the ground. It had stood so tall on a slab of stone just a few feet from the lodge. The day she arrived she thought the statue was grotesque and frightening but soon learned that some of the other girls placed notes or small gifts on the base of the statue, believing the matriarch towering above them had the power to grant wishes and make dreams come true.

Veronica had gone out to the statue three nights after Elizabeth was born. The lodge was quiet, and no one stirred as she moved through the hall, down the stairs, and out to the dew-covered grass. Under the dark, star-studded sky, the statue cast a dark shadow. Veronica stopped her shaking and reached up to touch the cold stone hands as if the statue would return the clasp and give her the comfort she so desired.

Weeks before, Veronica had stolen a pair of pink knitted booties from a donated basket of used infant wear, tucking them between her breasts and later hiding them in her room. She'd known her baby was a girl. She'd felt it since the first stirring and the frightening realization she was having a baby. In her shame and fear, she clung to the thought of holding a baby girl and loving her daughter as her mother had loved her. Mother had freely hugged and kissed, teased and praised, laughed and showed affection. Even from her ward, separated by a glass barrier, her mother would blow kisses and her face always showed how badly she missed her little girl.

Veronica would be a good mother. She wanted to make a life for her daughter and never let anyone hurt her. But Sister Dorcas had snatched her from her arms and left her powerless. Maybe the Holy Mother could intervene and grant Veronica her deepest desire. She knelt on the wet grass and set the booties on the pedestal. She clasped her hands and spoke her desperate prayer.

The next morning the booties were gone, and Veronica took that to be a sign that her prayer had been heard. She rushed to where Patricia was hanging the laundry, bursting with the excitement of her faith and belief in the statue's power.

"I think there is a fresh grave," Patricia said. "Sister Dorcas just went into the woods carrying a bundle, and Thomas followed behind with a shovel."

~~~

Tyler was just about to knock when Sylvia opened the front door.

"Hi, Tyler. What's up?"

"Don't mean to bother you, but I was looking for Marjorie."

"She's in the kitchen. Come on in."

"Getting moved in, are you?"

"Yes. I'm getting some things set up. Leon's is supposed to be coming. They should be here soon. Heard you and Kent bought a ride-on yesterday. And you're taking the caretaker job?"

"No secrets around here. Yeah, I hope to. Dot said Marjorie has a house to rent."

"I do," Marjorie said coming out of the kitchen. "It's not a fancy house, but it's well built and easy to heat and I've cleaned it top to bottom. My mother-in-law wasn't the best housekeeper, even in her prime."

"Abby and I would like to rent it. I suppose I should ask how much and stuff like that. And how's the internet?"

"We were going to rent it by the week to tourists, but no reason why we couldn't rent it to you and Abby. It would be

nice actually to have neighbours year-round. How does five
hundred dollars a month sound, and you'll pay your own util-
ities. There is a wood furnace and Walter filled his mother's
wood shed last fall, and she got away before winter so there's
lots of wood. As far as the internet, ours is good. Just last year
we got high speed when they put a new tower in. I don't know
that much about it, but Walter says it is a lot better than it
was."

"Dot says it's furnished?"

"Yes, we got rid of the really nasty stuff, but the rest isn't
bad. And Sylvia gave us a real nice bedroom set and the armchairs that were in this room."

"The bedroom set is beautiful, but I don't need it," Sylvia
said. "The couple who owned this cottage were married for
sixty-three years. I hope the set can bring you and Abby that
kind of longevity."

"Hope so too. Sure going to give it a try. Oh, here's the
Leon's truck. I'll go see if they need any help."

Veronica sat back down at the table in her room and
picked up her pen. Rushing into the woods, she'd heard Sister
Dorcas screaming for her to stop. She'd kept going and sunk
to the ground, pawing at the fresh dirt. She had kicked and
cursed at Sister Dorcas as she pulled her up from the ground.
Two other nuns came to Sister Dorcas's aid, but even the three
of them could barely manage the kicking, screaming girl who

was a fraction of the size of any of them. Father Tucker intervened and grabbed her shoulders, shaking her violently before slapping her face.

"Hush," he had barked. "The devil has you in his grips. Stop your foolishness and be silent."

"You were the devil," Veronica spoke aloud in the quiet room. "And I will not be silent."

⁓⁓⁓

"Mom, everything looks great," Olivia said. "You didn't waste any time. You've even got your office set up. I'm impressed."

"Marjorie cleaned and took everything I didn't want. Tyler was here when Leon's came and he stayed to help me put everything in place. Janice came by a bit later and we arranged my office. I just have a few boxes of books and things to bring over from the apartment, to unpack tomorrow."

"Are you coming to the lodge for supper?"

"Yeah, I'm almost done here. One more thing to do, and I'm glad you're here to do it with me."

Sylvia walked across the room and picked up an oval sign that was propped against the wall.

"Come out and hang this with me."

Luna Sea

"Did you have it made, Mom?"

"No, I stole it, actually, on the January day I came to look at the lodge property. I parked in front of this cottage and the sign was hanging from the chains. I took it and put it in the trunk of the rental car, packed it in my suitcase, and took it back to Toronto."

"I didn't know you had a touch of kleptomania."

"There was just something about the sign. Before I even considered buying this cottage I felt drawn to it. The name of this little cottage spoke to me about the crazy idea I had that I belonged here. I remember thinking it had been left dangling off the post for that reason. Crazy? Maybe, but nothing about it seemed crazy to me. It just seemed right, right from the very beginning."

"Welcome to your Luna Sea, Mom."

Chapter TwentyFive

"Road trips are different than they used to be," Nora said, sliding back into the passenger seat. "I need as many bathroom breaks these days as the kids used to take, especially when we were toilet training them. Jim used to swear every time Melissa would shout 'pee pee!' and half the time she wouldn't even go when we stopped."

"Now it's grandkids being toilet trained, although I swear Logan will still be in diapers when he starts kindergarten if Jackie doesn't get her act together," Wendy said. "He goes on the potty for me, but she slaps a diaper on him. What does Jim think about our trip?"

"He didn't say too much. He knows it's not a subject I like to talk about. What about your family?"

"The kids don't meddle in my life since the divorce. Jackie basically only comes around when she needs me to babysit, and God forbid I should give her any advice. I didn't actually tell any of them where I was going. They don't know anything about that place. Terry knew I had a baby before he met me, but I never saw any sense in telling the kids."

"Are you nervous about being there?"

"I don't know if nervous is the right word exactly. I knew

right away I needed to go when I saw the picture. It won't feel the same as it did when I was fourteen and scared shitless. I've been remembering the day I got there. You were the first girl I saw or heard I guess. I think you were hollering at Sister Dorcas about something."

"Oh probably. She always had a pick on for me, but I gave it right back. I probably hadn't hung the laundry out proper-ly. She'd make girls take everything off if one item was out of place. I used to give her lip about it every time. I never saw the difference if a pair of underwear was beside a dishtowel."

"Do you remember CeCe? She was the only nice one there."

"God love her. I've often thought of her over the years when I had to feed four kids with not much money. She tried her best to take the little bit they gave her and make good meals for us."

"I remember she used to send the two of us to Mr. Beauchamp's store when she needed something. She used to give us each a dime to buy candy. I'm sure it was her own money. I see an Irving up ahead. I'm going to stop there so we can get some snacks. I expect the meals will be good, but it won't hurt to have a stash in our room. God knows we never had that luxury back in the day. Remember the room search-es?"

"God, yes. Once I had a bag of jaw breakers hidden at the back of my drawer and got grounded to my room for the rest of the day with no lunch or supper and no brown sugar on my porridge the next day."

⌒⌒⌒

Irma and Dot carried the bags into the cottage.

"It looks sweet in here," Dot said. "Didn't take long for Marjorie to clear out what Sylvia didn't want and Sylvia to set everything up. It looks so fresh and welcoming."

"Look at her office," Irma said. "She hung the sunset painting Melanie did. It's perfect on this wall. Seems fitting to have a picture of the lodge in her new office. I'm so happy for her."

"Let's put these streamers up and put out the paper cups and plates. Evelyn suggested the nautical theme because Sylvia's grandfather was a fisherman."

"I love the inflatable lobster. She's going to be so surprised," Irma said.

"Olivia had the good idea of getting her to go to the airport with her to pick up the writer. Did you know Kent plans on moving back to Toronto soon?"

"And Tyler is taking the caretaker job. And he and Abby are going to rent Marjorie's mother-in-law's house. So much happening around here."

"Looks ready for a party," Dot said, stepping back and looking at the decorations.

Irma opened the front door. "Let's tie the Welcome Home balloon to the post at the end of the drive so Sylvia can see it when they come by. Luna Sea, what a sweet name for this little place."

❦

"Where are you ladies headed today?" asked the cashier.

"The retreat down the road," Wendy answered.

"Oh, that writing retreat. Nice. Are you both writers?"

"Neither of us, actually," Nora said. "It's more like a pilgrimage for us. We both stayed there years ago, 1972 actually."

"Oh. You probably knew my aunt Cecelia. She used to cook there."

"CeCe was your aunt? Yes, we knew her. Is she still living?"

"She is, but she has dementia and has gone into a nursing home in Moncton. My cousin cared for her as long as she could."

"Your aunt was sweet. We were just saying how good she was to us. It would have been nice to see her."

"I'll tell my cousin you were asking about Cecelia. How long are you staying at the retreat?"

"Two weeks."

"Well, have a good stay. Maybe you'll be back in sometime."

❦

George Daniels shifted his long legs, trying to get comfortable. The last flight he'd taken had been with Rose, and in her weakened state he'd practically had to carry her on and off the plane. She'd been determined to visit her hometown of Saint John, New Brunswick, one more time. The only living relative, a cousin on her mother's side, had picked them up from the airport and driven them into the city. Before settling into the hotel, Rose had asked Priscilla to drive by her childhood home on the north end of Saint John. The building was dilapidated, windows boarded up, and what had been intricate gingerbread trim was hanging from the eaves. Rose had wept at the sight.

"Mother would be mortified. Father kept the yard immaculate, the lilac and rose bushes pruned and healthy. This was once the nicest house on the street."

During the visit George had met with a real estate company and purchased the Adelaide Street house. He'd hired a contractor to renovate and convert the large house into three apartments. Upon completion, he had hired a rentals man to look after the property and manage the building.

Rose had been thrilled with the gesture, and the undertaking had proven to be quite lucrative. George had purchased the homes on either side and had them renovated too, increasing the value of Rose's childhood home and the amount of rent he could charge for the apartments in each building.

Lately George had begun thinking that perhaps it was time to sell all three buildings. *You can't take it with you* kept reverberating in his mind every time he met with his accountant. With no one to leave his property to, he was considering liquidating some of his assets and giving the money to charity. A hospital wing or clinic bearing his name might be a fitting legacy.

And surely to God if he could get his damn memoir written he could invest the money to self-publish it. And why wasn't he flying first class? Old, frugal habits were hard to break, apparently.

～⁀ᔟ⁀～

Kent got off the phone from talking to Darcy and scrolled through the Air Canada site trying to find a flight that would work for Monday. Staying until then would give him time to prepare Olivia to take over, and he'd be here for Sylvia's house-warming. He felt restless and anxious. He was glad Olivia had offered to go pick up Dr. Daniels. He wasn't on top of his game this afternoon. For some reason he kept going back to that terrible day in April 1978.

That day, Kent set the Sam the Record Man bag down on the concrete step and reached to open the flap of the metal mailbox. Being able to present his mother with a letter from Manulife stating they would pay his father's death benefit would raise his mother's spirits. The crewcut he was sporting was in hopes of doing the same thing.

"You look more like a sheepdog than my son," she'd said last night before bursting into tears and leaving the table without taking a bite of the TV dinner Kent had prepared.

He'd felt so guilty lying this morning, saying Mr. Hayward had given him extra hours and that he had to be at work at nine, but the trip downtown had been worth it. First he'd gone to the barbershop and let Mr. Vitantonio cut his long hair.

"A smart boy who wants to look like a boy. My own grand-son has a ponytail, for God's sake."

Kent had told himself the haircut deserved a trip to Sam the Record Man, and the three albums were purchased with money he should have given to his mother. He'd given her his whole paycheque last week.

Kent pulled out the two envelopes, both of which were bills and not the correspondence he'd been hoping for. The damned insurance company took the premium money from Richard Wright for all the years he'd paid into the policy but were now disputing his cause of death. Being hit by a bus apparently was considered suicide when an eyewitness said she heard the man's last words before stepping off the curb into the path of the oncoming bus.

He couldn't even keep his fucking mouth shut in his final cowardly act, Kent thought as he opened the front door and called to his mother.

Getting no response, Kent figured his mother was sleeping and went to his bedroom. He removed the cellophane wrapper and placed the Eric Clapton album on the turntable. The volume might be on the loud side, but if it roused his mother and caused her to come ask him to turn it down, that would be more of an effort than she'd made in weeks.

Kent tried to shut everything out but the guitar riff and repetition of the first track. "Cocaine," not an option but a musical diversion. No time or money for substance abuse when you were the primary income earner and the most stable member of the household, regardless of the fact you're seventeen, still in high school, and fitting in as many hours of a part-time job as possible. Who could blame him for taking the morning off and doing something he wanted to do for a change?

A few lines into the second track Kent was batting at the tears streaming down his cheeks. What seventeen-year-old boy instantly thinks of his mother when Eric Clapton sings "You Look Wonderful Tonight"? But all Kent could see was how his mother used to look when she actually gave a damn about how she looked. His mother was a woman who never left the house without lipstick. Her weekly hair appointment was more important to her than oxygen, she pressed every piece of clothing she wore and accessorized impeccably.

The contrast to the woman who now barely left her bedroom, seldom brushed her hair, and wore her threadbare pink chenille bathrobe like a uniform was a stark reminder of the collateral damage his father's decision to end his miserable, pathetic life had caused. He could have dealt with losing his father if his mother hadn't been dragged along with him as if she'd been hit by the same bus.

Fuck, Kent thought. He wasn't letting this happen without a fight.

<hr />

"Did you know Dad's mother?" Olivia asked.

"No. She died when he was seventeen. I didn't meet him until he was thirty-one. He seldom talks about her. Seldom talks about anything, but I'm not going to start listing his faults. I'm not going to be one of those divorced mothers who badmouths my ex to his children."

"And you're okay with the divorce?"

"I'm more than okay with it. Your father is a good man. He always provided and looked after us all, but the marriage is over. I have no problem with him and Darcy and whatever that will be."

"I'm not calling her Mom."

"Did Dad give you the Wright Retreat sign?" Sylvia asked as Olivia pulled into the airport parking lot.

"Oh yes. He gave me a spiel about displaying it prominently so Dr. Daniels can see it. It's hilarious how controlling Dad can be."

"He has made control an art form, but I gave up getting him to try to see the reason for that."

⁓⁓

"I thought staring at the picture enough times would make arriving here easier," Wendy Wilson said, pulling into the yard and parking in front of the large log building. "I can barely breathe. I look up at that door and even though my practical brain tells me it's a different door, my emotional brain expects Devil Dorcas to come walking out."

"I know," Nora said. "I started shaking when you turned onto the road. Before we got to the last cottage I wanted to beg you to stop the car and let me out. What the hell were we thinking, coming back here?"

"Deep breath in, deep breath out," Wendy said, more to herself than to Nora. "We can do this. There is nobody here who can hurt us."

"Nobody could ever hurt us more than those bastards did," Nora said. "Let's just do this and get it over with."

Dot came out on the veranda. She had seen the car drive up and figured it was the two women who were expected to arrive this afternoon."

"Hello. I'm Dot, the cook. No one else seems to be around to greet you."

Wendy got out of the car, stepped onto the wide steps and extended her hand to the woman. "Wendy Wilson and Nora Taylor. We're a bit weary from the long drive. We would appreciate going right to our room to rest a bit."

"Supper is at six. Mr. Wright, Olivia, and Sylvia will be here then and make all the introductions. It's a lovely place and there are some real nice people here."

"Well, that's a switch," Nora said as she followed Dot into the building.

~~~

Kent walked into the kitchen before heading down the hall to see if his mother was in her room. There was no evidence that she had had any lunch; his cereal bowl the only dish in the sink. Dishes in the sink or anything out of place was not the way Florence Wright kept house. She was as proud of her home as she was of her appearance and her wardrobe. In all the chaos his father created, his mother kept a smile on her face and an immaculate demeanour and home. To the world outside, the Wright family at 11 Needham Street in Rexdale was the perfect family.

Not finding his mother in her room, and with the bathroom door wide open, he proceeded down to the basement. The rec room was another one of his mother's proud achievements. They'd been first on the street to finish a room in the basement. She'd chosen an orange shag carpet and had until recently raked and fluffed it daily. She had placed a comfortable davenport and two reclining leather chairs facing the RCA television stereo combination and kept its glossy walnut finish dusted and waxed. A large sunburst clock hung on the wall above it.

Mom was not in the rec room. Kent could hear the washing machine motor behind the closed door. Mom was very proud of her Kenmore washer-dryer set, and despite the fact they'd been placed in the unfinished section of the basement, she had created an organized laundry area with shelves, a folding table, and an ironing station. Kent felt encouraged by the sound he heard and the thought that his mother had mustered enough energy to put in a load of laundry.

He saw the step stool first and later wondered why he'd focused on the fact that it had been tight up against the washer, as if the metal stool couldn't possibly scratch the enamel finish. And the dent in the cover of the washing machine was another sight his sleepless nights would take him to. The stool and the dent took front and centre, because his mind would not allow him to go back to the sight of his mother's lifeless body hanging from the noose she'd created from a belt and the sash of her pink chenille bathrobe fastened around the heavy wooden beam above the washer and dryer she'd been so proud of.

Such effort, such planning, such deliberate execution orchestrated by a woman who had barely gotten out of bed for the last month.

"I got my hair cut, Mom," Kent gasped.

<hr />

Dot placed the platter of roast beef down in front of Dr. Daniels. Introductions had been made and dishes of vegetables were being passed around the table. Sylvia and Evelyn had come over for the introductory supper. Irma had come over for a plate for her and Sophie and gone back to the apartment. Sylvia had filled her plate before she realized that Kent was not seated at the table.

"Has anyone seen Kent?" Sylvia asked.

"I saw him from the big window upstairs," Tyler said. "He was walking along the beach."

"I'll run out and call him for supper," Sylvia said. "I'll be right back."

Low tide exposed the sandbars amid large pools of shallow water. Sylvia kicked off her sandals and waded barefoot to catch up to where Kent was walking a ways out, seemingly oblivious to her advancing on him.

"Supper's ready, Kent. Are you okay?"

"Not sure. I've had a rough afternoon," Kent replied, picking up his pace.

"What's wrong?"

Kent stopped. Tears streamed down his cheeks. "I shouldn't have left that day. I went all the way downtown to go to Sam's so I could buy three albums, two I never even put on the turntable. Eric Clapton's *Slowhand* was the first one I destroyed. Vinyl is not as easy to break as you might think. I set fire to the album jackets in the burning barrel but broke the albums into small pieces and threw them in the dumpster at work. She wouldn't have done it if I'd stayed home."

Sylvia wrapped her arms around Kent as he let the sobs come.

"It wasn't your fault, Kent. You know if it hadn't been that day it probably would have been another. You were a kid doing the best you could. It wasn't your fault."

"See, there's a reason I don't let myself think too much. Fuck, this place has a way of wrenching out emotions, whether a person wants it to or not. Time for me to go back to Toronto."

"I know it's hard to go to painful places, but it won't kill you. It might even be a good thing once in a while."

"Maybe you're right, but I'm not strong like you, Sylvia. I keep a tight lid on for a reason. I come from a line of chicken shits. Being strong is not my inheritance. I can't take the chance I might follow in my parents' footsteps."

Sylvia kissed Kent's cheek and pulled him closer. "I think you are plenty strong, Kent Wright. You will be fine even if you let emotion sneak in now and again. Now come have some supper and meet the three new writers. This retreat was your idea, after all."

Kent walked out of the water, tucked in his dishevelled shirt, and unfolded his rolled-up pant legs. "And a fine idea, if I do say so myself. It's going to keep you in the manner you've become accustomed to, Mrs. Wright."

"Yes, thank you for that, Mr. Wright. Oh, and by the way, I go by Drummond these days."

"We're back where we started, Sylvia Drummond."

"Not exactly, but it's all good, Kent. Now finish pulling your sorry arse together. My food's getting cold."

～ჯ～

"I built the bonfire in front of your cottage tonight," Tyler said. "You're sleeping there tonight, right?"

"I know you guys have something up your sleeves," Sylvia said. "Olivia wouldn't stop or let me go back over to the cottage when we got home from the airport."

"She's moving into her new home tonight," Janice said, turning to Wendy and Nora.

"And we might have a little party planned," Dot said.

"They were just building those cottages the year we were here," Wendy said.

"I used to walk by them as they took shape and pretend Wendy and I would each live in one when we grew up," Nora added.

"What year were you here?" Veronica asked. "I had my baby here in 1969."

"We were the class of 1972," Wendy chuckled. "Not alumnae that celebrate reunions. I assume you didn't leave here with your baby either."

"No, my baby died."

"Wendy and I gave birth the same day," Nora said. "We both had boys."

"Twins, the other girls called them," Wendy said. "Both had heads full of dark, thick hair and looked so much the same, except one so tiny and the other looking three months old the day he was born. Our baby bookends, we called them."

Veronica stood to take her plate to the dishwasher, tears filling her eyes. She recognized the undercurrent of pain in the women's words. Whether the baby boys were adopted, possibly carried out in the arms of the same woman who took the babies when she'd been here, or buried near Elizabeth, she knew the pain lingered, and coming here had been for them as difficult as it had been for her.

"It's very nice to meet you, Wendy and Nora," Veronica said, approaching the table again. "This is a different place than the place you remember. I hope you find the peace you're looking for."

◦◦◦◦◦

Irma met Sylvia on the veranda. "Come on, girl. Evelyn, Sophie, and Olivia are already at the cottage. Sophie has been hollering "Surprise!" all afternoon, and we couldn't contain her any longer. Marjorie said she'd come take her home in a bit so Evelyn and I could stay longer."

"You are a saint, Irma Church."

"What's this Church shit? I'll go by Doyle, thank you."

"Okay, let's get this housewarming thing over with."

"Housewarming? Who says there's a housewarming?" Tyler said, opening the sliding door.

"Come on, all of you, Sylvia is expecting a housewarming," Dot said as she walked to the door, a large pot and wooden spoon in her hands. "In my day we called it a shivaree and made lots of noise."

"Weren't shivarees given for a bride and groom?" Veronica asked.

"We're having a *divorce* shivaree," Dot said.

"Can the ex-husband attend?" Kent asked stepping out on the veranda.

"Absolutely," Janice said. "But you might get roasted."

"What kind of a bonfire is it?" Dr. Daniels asked.

"Come on, everyone," Dot called as she started banging on the pot.

"When we get there, let Sylvia go in first," Irma instructed. "Sophie is so excited to jump out and surprise her mother."

"You're coming over, right?" Veronica asked Wendy and Nora.

"Absolutely," Wendy said.

⤝⤜

"Sophie is having a wonderful time," Kent said, sitting on the couch beside Evelyn.

Sophie was still hollering "Surprise!" intermittently and throwing the inflatable lobster around the crowded room. Each time someone threw it back to her, she would giggle and look for her next target.

"She is indeed. Marjorie might have a job calming her down and getting her to bed tonight. I think I'll head over soon. I'm feeling a bit weary."

"I'll walk you over when you're ready."

"I'd like to say that's not necessary, Kent, but I'm a bit shaky on my feet these days, and the last thing I need is to stumble in the dark and break a hip. I will just find Sylvie and say goodnight and we can go."

Evelyn disappeared for a few minutes, then returned.

"Did you find her?"

"Yeah, she was out on the back deck. It's a sweet little cottage, isn't it?"

"Yes it is. I'm very happy for Sylvie."

"I've been waiting all summer to give you a talking to. At first I had it in my mind that this retreat business was too much for Sylvie on top of having to look after Sophie and me. I was going to tell you I thought you should just let this place be your retirement home and start spending more time with your wife. But what did I know?"

"I am sorry about the marriage, Evelyn. I never intended to hurt Sylvia."

"I know that. And she never wanted to hurt you. I realized a while ago that I might have interfered too much over the years. I should have stayed put and let you two start your marriage without me muddying the water."

"I think if you'd stayed put, Sylvia would have gone back to White Head too. Sometimes I think she just married me to make you happy."

"Oh my, Kent. Lately I realize more than ever that trying to relive the past is a stupid waste of time. You know, the morning Paddy left for the last time, we heard the marine forecast and I almost asked him to stay home while I was packing his lunch. I spent a lot of time over the years regretting that. But he was a fisherman, and I had learned early on to keep my worrying under control. I never got caught up in the risk of his job; I couldn't let myself. I let him go every morning, and every night I said a thankful prayer when I heard him come through the door."

"I almost booked a trip south for a vacation the year Sophie had her accident. I was going to surprise everyone with a family trip to Mexico, but it was tax season and I decided I couldn't afford to take the time off. God, I wish I'd booked that trip."

"It's like I said, no point to it at all. We do the best we can with what we know at the time, and that's all we can ever do. You'll go back to Toronto and things with Darcy might work out and they might not. Sylvia, the girls, and I will stay here and life will happen. I will die and life will go on. All we can really do is try to be the best we can be and treat people with kindness and love while we're here. You have always treated me that way, Kent, and I am thankful. You were not perfect, none of us were. We made mistakes but we were and still are a family."

"Thank you, Evelyn. And don't do that dying too soon."

"We'll see. Love you."

"Love you too."

Chapter Twenty-Six

"You announced that breakfast wouldn't be until nine o'clock as Marjorie was helping you into the car last night," Tyler said.

"I do not drink," Dot said, taking the cup of coffee Tyler had just poured her.

"No worries, Dot. You were a riot last night. Life of the party."

"Oh my God, I can only imagine. Do I have any apologies to make this morning?"

"Oh, I don't think so. I think Dr. Daniels enjoyed how many times you called him a *handsome Marcus Whelby*, whoever that is."

"Oh my goodness. Bacon, bagels, and boiled eggs is all I can muster this morning."

"And why is that?" asked Janice with a sly smirk on her face.

"I cannot hold my liquor, apparently," Dot replied. "There'll be no drinking for this old girl at your housewarming, Tyler."

"Hangovers are a tough taskmaster," Janice said. "Just ask an old girl who knows."

"Hope you'll dispense with this doctor nonsense and just call me George," Dr. Daniels said, coming into the room.

"Or Marcus at the very least," Grace added.

"That was quite the party," Wendy said. "Loved the sing-song around the fire. Nora's still sleeping. She had one cooler too many last night. You folks sure know how to make a couple of ladies feel welcome."

"I told you this place was different from the last time you were here," Veronica said.

"Not run by the Catholics, for one thing," Janice said.

"A car just pulled into the yard," Melanie said, coming in from the veranda. "Two women. Are we expecting more writers?"

"No, I'm pretty sure we're not," Kent said, looking toward Olivia.

"It looks like the lady who works at the Irving," Olivia said.

"It is Brenda," Dot said. "And that's her cousin Connie."

"Is Connie's mother Cecelia?" Wendy asked.

"Yes," Dot answered.

Wendy went out the door to meet the women who were coming up the steps.

"You look like your mother," Wendy said.

"Are you Wendy or Nora?" Connie asked. "I told Mom two women who stayed here in the seventies were asking about her and she said your two names right away. Some days she doesn't even know me."

"Oh my goodness. God love her. She was the best thing about this place. I'm Wendy."

"Is Nora here?" Connie asked.

"She's still upstairs."

"I got Brenda to bring me. I don't know if you're interested, but I've got something to show you both and lots to tell you. My mother told me lots of stories about this place and about you two. I'd always heard the names Wendy and Nora when she talked about working here. My mother got the place shut down, you know. She worked here for ten years, but it was what was done to you two that finally made her put a stop to what was happening here."

"I'm going to go get Nora," Wendy said. "I'll be right back. It has not been easy coming back here, and we would appreciate anything you could tell us. We thought the world of Cecelia."

"Come right in, ladies," Dot said from the open door. "I'm a little late getting breakfast this morning, and you're more than welcome to join us. Tyler, get these ladies some coffee."

~⁂~

Sylvia opened her eyes, taking in the surroundings of her small room. The colourful duvet was on the floor, and the clothes she'd been wearing were flung over the yellow straight-back chair in the corner. Olivia had put her to bed after practically dragging her away from the dying fire. Dot and she had been belting out "Take Me Home, Country Roads." Everyone else had left.

The night had been so much fun. When she walked through the door to Sophie's excited "Surprise!" and Nan and

Olivia's smiling faces, her heart had filled with joy. The little cottage quickly filled with everyone from the lodge and several neighbours.

Irma and Dot had decorated in a nautical theme, and the inflatable lobster that flew through the room until Marjorie finally convinced Sophie to go home was a clear sign that Papa was attending the celebration too. Seeing the moonlight shining down on Kent and Nan as they walked across the yard toward the lodge had filled her with emotion. It had certainly been a night to savour, to write about and remember forever.

Sylvia considered the luxury of rolling over and going back to sleep but decided instead to get up, have a quick shower, and head over to the lodge for the late breakfast Dot had announced would happen as Marjorie loaded her in the back seat of her car. Who knew Dot was such a party girl?

"I brought some of Mom's diaries," Connie said after Nora came to the table. "Mom has always kept a diary, faithfully. She still tries to, but her writing is pretty much illegible now. She used to have the five-year kind; you know, the ones with the page for each date divided into five sections. Each little section was filled with information about the weather, the meal she prepared, the shopping she did, or some community news like a birth or death.

"The diary she started in 1972 was like that, but Mom wrote full pages on most of the dates. It is this diary that tells the most about what was happening here and what finally made her go to the authorities. Your names are in this one a lot. I have a few pages marked, but you are free to read the whole thing. I can leave it with you."

A girl named Wendy arrived today. It broke my heart to see how afraid she is. Nora took her under her wing right away. God love that feisty girl. Another huge screaming match between her and Sister Dorcas today.

"Wow," Wendy said. "I don't even know what to say."

"To think I was the feisty one back then, and now I'm such a wimp," Nora said.

"Did she write every day?" Wendy asked.

"Yes."

"Can I see what she wrote on September 4?" Wendy asked.

"That was the day our babies were born," Nora added.

Wendy took the green leather diary from Connie and leafed through to find the date. The room was silent for the few seconds it took Wendy to read the entry to herself. Tears filled her eyes and she batted them away, then took a deep breath before reading it aloud.

Wendy and Nora's labour pains started within minutes of each other, even though Wendy's due date is three weeks away. Sister Dorcas was so annoyed and seemed personally offended at the inconvenience, as if the girls had intentionally decided to give birth on the same day as the Bishop's visit. She told me to take them to the attic room and lock the door.

"They locked you in a room?" gasped Grace.

"At first we were quite happy to be by ourselves," Nora said. "Neither one of us wanted the parade of nuns who usually crowded into the room while a girl gave birth, reciting the rosary while praying for the sinner's forgiveness."

Wendy kept reading.

It was hours before I could check on the girls. No one else had gone up, and by the time I got there they were both in heavy labour. I tried my best to comfort them before going down to tell Sister Dorcas their time seemed close and someone needed to attend to them. "They got themselves in this predicament," she said. "Let's see how well they do getting out of it."

"Oh my God," Veronica said. "Do you know how many times I heard that? I can hear her voice spitting that at every girl. What a lie. Not one of us got ourselves in the state we came to them in. We were kids, and most of us had been abused, and some stupid enough to believe whatever boy had sweet talked them. None of us had any clue what we were in for."

Wendy began reading again.

I could hear their screams through the open window as I stood preparing the supper meal. Finally I went to Father Tucker and said, "If someone doesn't go to those girls right now I am calling an ambulance."

"By the time they came to us my baby's head had crowned," Wendy said. "When I looked over at Nora, all I could see was blood, and she was so weak I thought she was dying."

Two baby boys were born before midnight. Poor Nora was so torn from the big baby she delivered. Wendy's baby was tiny but strong. What brave girls. God love their souls and damn the souls of the cold-hearted women in this place. I cannot believe the God I serve would sanction such inhumanity.

"Mom had always been critical of the way the nuns treated the girls, but what happened that day was the beginning of the end. She was already considering calling the authorities to report the treatment, but what happened a few days later was the final straw."

"I don't think I can read what she wrote that day," Wendy said.

"I think we are both afraid to hear what exactly happened," Nora said. "The morning the police arrived and social workers came to get us all, we knew the shit had hit the fan, but driving away that morning I know I blocked a lot out."

"Why don't you just read the rest on your own?" Connie said.

"Can you tell her thank you from us?" Wendy asked.

"I certainly will. Like I said, she doesn't know a lot of what's going on these days, but she remembers the past clearly. She was always proud of shutting this place down. Proud, but ashamed she hadn't done it earlier. She was given a hard time by some people. Mother was a devoted Catholic, but with the way she was treated afterward, she stopped going to Mass. It was a heartbreak for her."

"Oh my God," Nora said after she and Wendy got back to their room. "I really don't know if I can handle this."

"I know, but it was nice of CeCe's daughter to come and give us this. And how cool that CeCe still remembers us."

"Can you even remember what room they put us in?"

"She said attic, but I think it was a room out back, there were outside stairs up to it," Wendy answered. "Probably where Sylvia's apartment is now. It was a big room used for storage mainly, but there were two beds in there. Remember how cold and damp it felt at first?"

"I remember how terrified I was when the pains got so bad and no one came. You kept telling me we were going to be all right, but I was sure I was dying."

"It was criminal, leaving two kids alone to give birth. I think they hoped we would die, or at least they didn't care if we did."

"Thank goodness it was CeCe who put us up there, or they may not have come to help us or our babies," Nora said.

"I used to imagine that no one came and that somehow we cut each other's umbilical cords, broke the door down, and escaped with our babies."

"They didn't let me hold him at all," Nora said. "Sister Dorcas wrapped him in a blanket and took him out right away. It was Tabitha who told me what he looked like and that both our babies had curly black hair. She called them twins."

"Oh my God, I forgot about Tabitha. She was the mentally challenged girl they let feed and care for the babies."

"I really don't know if I want to read anything else," Nora said passing the diary to Wendy.

"We knew this wasn't going to be easy, but we came here to find some peace, to maybe uncover some truth. This little book is more than we hoped for."

"Okay, read some more. Start with September 5."

Poor Nora lost a lot of blood and is very weak. I took her broth several times today. Sister Maria finally changed her bloody bedding and washed her. The poor girl should probably have been sent to the hospital. I pray the damage done delivering that huge baby will not deter her from having more children in the future.

"Thank God it didn't," Nora said.

September 6. Just two babies here right now, and those two little boys are the talk of the place. Twins, they're calling them. Even Sister Dorcas seems taken with them. Poked my head in to see them this afternoon and fell in love. They are so adorable and seem so in sync with each other. The tiny one starts to cry and the big one joins in. Tabitha says they do it every time. How precious is that?

September 7. I was surprised to hear Sister Dorcas has already arranged for the adoption of one of the twins. I hate to think of separating those two precious babies and was hoping they would allow them to stay longer. Those poor girls are not even allowed to see their babies, let alone hold them and feed them. Both are suffering with the agony of their milk coming in and I took them hot compresses several times today. I did not tell them Miss Cleary was coming tomorrow. God love them, they know how it works here, but it's so hard. It is painful to see it every time. There have been so many heartbroken girls over the years and so much sadness. And the tragedy of what happened to Patricia, of course. I do wonder if this is the best way to care for unwed girls. Babies being adopted by good families is probably making the best of a bad situation, but so many weak babies have died here. Maybe hospital births would give those tiny souls a better chance. At least this time the tiny one seems strong enough to survive.

September 8. I can barely put pen to paper tonight. I am in such a state of rage and fury. I am exhausted from the hours I have just spent convincing someone to take my accusations serious-ly. Father Tucker got to the detachment before me and initially it seemed his warning about my mental state had been believed. But somehow my perseverance paid off and a charge was laid. Authorities will be conducting an investigation, which will start with a raid in the morning, and all the girls being taken into custo-dy by Social Services. I have blown the lid off and have no regrets. I was so shocked when it was the tiny baby Sister Dorcas passed to Miss Cleary.

"Oh my God," Nora and Wendy said simultaneously.

"My baby was adopted on this very date," Wendy cried.

"Keep reading," Nora whispered.

"I was overwhelmed with the emotion of seeing that tiny, frag-ile baby being separated from his twin after so heartlessly being removed from his mother. I felt the overpowering urge to go see the other baby. The shock on Sister Maria's face when I burst into the room made her guilt and remorse so obvious. She released her hold

on the pillow, which was completely covering the baby. I rushed to the crib and pulled the pillow away and saw the lifeless body of that precious boy, his eyes open, vacant and glassy. "He was the seed of Satan," Sister Maria said, all the colour draining from her face. She slumped to the floor as I snatched up the baby's body and fled from the room. I was met at the foot of the stairs by Father Tucker and Sister Dorcas and they both wrenched the little body from my arms. I knew as I ran out the door that before I even got to the Port Elgin detachment that precious child would be buried in the woods and everything I would accuse them of would be denied with the full force of the Catholic church behind them. But I knew too I would never sleep another night without declaring all the evil I knew that place had perpetrated. God save my soul and receive that small child and keep him safe in your arms.

"And on this date, *my* child died," Nora cried.

⤙⚭⤚

Veronica had gone back up to her room after breakfast and attempted to concentrate enough to write, but the earlier interactions had left her jittery and anxious. She could still hear the words *You got yourself in this predicament* and was nearly choking with rage. How many girls had been told that the baby they carried was a sin they had committed? And how many babies had been allowed to die because the church considered their conception evil and depraved? What her father had done was evil, but Elizabeth should not have been not condemned to death for his sin.

Veronica paced the room, thinking of the anguish Wendy and Nora were likely feeling, faced with reading the truth of the days around the birth and death or adoption of their babies. She felt the need to reach out to comfort them but wasn't sure it was her place. But who else here knew first-hand the pain this place had caused?

Veronica knocked lightly on the door.

~~~

Sylvia pulled into a parking spot in front of the emergency department; Olivia jumped out and opened the back door to help her grandmother out.

"I don't know why you're making all this fuss, Sylvie. I'm just overtired, I think."

"Nan. Dr. Daniels thought we should bring you to the outpatient and make sure everything is all right."

"You didn't have to bother him."

"Nan, you fainted."

"I don't think I fainted. I just had a weak spell. And I don't need that wheelchair, Olivia.

After breakfast, Sylvia had automatically gone right up the stairs to the apartment after leaving the lodge. She had the screen door open before she remembered she didn't live there anymore. Just ready to joke about that mistake, she looked over at Irma and sensed the seriousness of what she'd just walked in on.

"I just caught her in time," Irma said. "Evelyn, can you walk into the living room to lie down?"

"Well, of course I can walk."

"I'm going to run over and get Dr. Daniels," Sylvia said.

"I don't need a doctor."

⤙⤚

Veronica led Wendy and Nora through the stand of birch trees.

"Do you remember the statue that used to stand out front?" Veronica said.

"Oh my God, I forgot about that. I never even noticed it was gone," Nora said.

"Well, it's right here," Veronica said pointing to the moss-covered marble hump on the ground. "It's partially buried. Its pedestal is a few feet away, still intact."

"The pedestal; the girls used to leave things there, with prayers, I think, although I never did," Wendy said.

"I did," Nora said, her voice shaking with emotion. "Remember Saturday nights during the summer, the nuns would invite the young people from the area. Father Tucker would play the guitar and the nuns would sing and clap, letting on this place was a welcoming summer haven. They would let the girls who weren't too obviously pregnant attend. We weren't allowed to go because our bellies were massive. They gave us our Revels inside."

"I always snuck out with my Revel," Nora continued. "I

never ate it but pulled the wrapper off and laid it on the pedestal. My grandmother loved vanilla ice cream, so after setting the Revel down I would pray for her forgiveness, beg her to come and get me and let me go back home. The next morning I would see the wooden stick, which I took to be a sign that my prayer was not heard. But the next week I would try again."

"What did you think you needed forgiveness from?" Veronica asked.

"I was so excited the day the package came. Grannie had ordered two new bras from the Eaton's catalogue for me. She said I was going to have breasts like my Aunt Myrtle and we needed to get them contained. Up until then I'd been wearing two tight undershirts under my clothes, trying to hide my growing breasts. I spent hours looking at the pretty undergarments on the glossy pages. I felt so grown up and womanly thinking of the two lacy brassieres the package held and rushed to my room to try them on.

"I was just reaching around to fasten the pink silky one when my Uncle Denny burst into the room. Uncle Denny was a grown man, but simple, and he was always funny and kind to me, but in the next few moments I was terrified of him. He was a big man and strong and I was sure he would crush me when he threw me down and got on top of me. With each thrust I thought I would die."

"Your uncle raped you." Veronica asked. "You had nothing to be forgiven for."

"My grandmother blamed me. She said I tempted Denny by flaunting my breasts. She said it wasn't his fault, he was just a man, and what he did would not be spoken of again. That became a problem when a few months later we realized the consequences of that one act.

"My grandmother said that I must have seduced Denny more than once, as it was impossible to get pregnant the first time. She was so convincing I started questioning my own memory."

"Oh my God, Nora. You never told me any of that," Wendy said.

"It was a long time before I could let go of the shame and guilt I felt. The saddest thing was I loved my Uncle Denny and missed the way things had been before. And I missed my grandmother. I somehow convinced myself I had ruined everything by coveting the frilly bras I'd seen on the pages of the Eaton's catalogue."

"And the church just reinforced your guilt," Veronica said. "Why pile such shame upon a young girl for an act she was powerless against? And then to smother an innocent child branded as the devil's seed. My baby was conceived by incest as well, so she received the same condemnation. They starved her to death, believing each hour she weakened was proof of God's judgement."

"This story must be told," Wendy said.

～⁓ᔓ⁓～

"It's just for a few days, Nan," Sylvia said. "They're going to do all the tests Dr. Keating ordered and check everything out.

Right now this is the best place for you. We'll be back tomorrow."

Sylvia got into the passenger side of the Rav. It had been so hard to leave Nan looking so frail and helpless, and by the time she'd gotten on the elevator she'd started crying. Olivia pretty much led her through the lobby and out to the parking lot and into the vehicle.

"I could have driven," Sylvia said.

"It's okay, Mom. I'll drive. It's okay to be upset, too."

"What will we ever do without her?" Sylvia said, starting to cry again.

"We don't have to think about that yet. She'll be back home before we know it."

"Maybe, but we are going to have to face the inevitable."

"I know, but we'll get through whatever happens, together."

"I am so glad you're here."

"Me too."

Chapter Twenty-Seven

Somehow the breakfast conversation had found its way to a discussion about the buried statue in the woods.

"I think it's just fine that someone hauled it into the woods and attempted to bury it," Wendy said. "I hated the damn thing. I'd already had enough of the Catholic church by the time my foster mother dropped me off here. At age ten, when I'd been put into the care of Mrs. Bastarache, I was dragged to mass once a week with the eight other wards she had at the time and was completely overwhelmed by the beauty and ceremony of St. Patrick's. Before that I only went to church one week of the year for Daily Vacation Bible School at the Baptist church, and the message they camouflaged with crafts, snacks, and catchy songs was frightening. Every year I'd get saved, hoping I could escape hellfire and condemnation. Little did I know the Catholics' fancy Latin words and prayers held just as much judgement."

"My vote would be to leave it buried," Janice said. "This place has a dark and sad history, and I think it's great that people like you, Nora, and Veronica can come here and face that past, but it seems fitting to me that the elements erode that statue and dirt, moss, and weeds cover it."

"Some of us took comfort in it being there," Nora said. "For me she was a strong, loving mother looking over us and receiving our petitions. A lot of us prayed to her, left tokens and treasures, hoping for her to answer our prayers."

"How did that work for you?" Janice asked. "I briefly thought the Madonna on the mantel behind the closed door of my abuser would hear my pleas and save me, but I gave that thought up real quick."

"I placed baby booties on the pedestal, praying that my baby would live," Veronica said. "Sister Dorcas told me she died right away, but I could hear her faint cry, and Tabitha talked about a baby girl four days after Elizabeth was born. I snuck out at night and laid them on the concrete pedestal. I thought if the pink booties were gone in the morning it would mean she was still alive."

"How naive and gullible we were," Nora said. "Each one of us meekly went along with what was done to us. I used to think I was so brave when I would fight back about stupid things, but I never fought for my own child."

"You were weak after such a traumatic birth experience, and we were powerless and outnumbered," Wendy said.

"We were kids," Veronica said. "Adults, especially nuns and priests, were the authority. We had been taught to be respectful and not question that authority."

"It was a whole authoritative system," Janice added. "The church was sanctioned by the government, and children, whether white or Mi'kmaq, had no voice, no rights and no advocates."

"Maybe the statue should be put back in place to call attention to that injustice," Dot said.

"And maybe years from now more people will come to find some closure from their own traumatic experiences here. The statue would be a beacon for that," Veronica said.

"I wonder what it would take to put her back out front," Grace said. "The pedestal is there, right?"

"Yeah, it's pretty much intact," Veronica said. "The statue itself would need to be cleaned, maybe some of the features restored, although leaving her in her present state might be more authentic and meaningful."

"I was born in 1941 at the Ideal Maternity Home in East Chester, Nova Scotia," George said. "You've heard of butter-box babies? Well, I was one of the lucky ones adopted, not buried in a wooden box. Sold, actually, and you would think people who invested money in a child would treat him as their own, but even though I have no idea what my lineage is, it never measured up to the Daniels family's expectations. William and Lila Young and the evil perpetrated under that roof were finally exposed. I take comfort in knowing the shame of that place far exceeds any shame my young mother had to bear. I think exposing this place for what it was is just as important. Maybe erecting the statue would play a part in that."

~~~

"So your dad is leaving this afternoon," Tyler said, sitting down beside Olivia on the veranda.

"Yeah, I'm taking him to the airport after lunch. I guess he thinks between the two of us we can keep this place running."

"Marjorie says I can move into the house tomorrow. I'm excited to get it ready for Abby to come."

"Any idea when she's coming?" Olivia asked.

"Not until October."

"Well, that's exciting."

"What's exciting?" Veronica asked stepping out onto the veranda.

"Abby will be back in October," Olivia said.

"October is a big month for lots of us," Veronica said. "I've called and given my notice at work and on my apartment's lease. I plan on being in Port Hope by Thanksgiving."

"Wow, that's nice," Olivia said. "And Mom's going into the Animal Rescue League this afternoon to pick out a dog."

"Oh, maybe I'll go with her," Tyler said. "Marjorie said we can have pets, and I thought I'd surprise Abby with a dog."

"You don't think you should wait and let her pick one out with you?" Olivia said.

"I thought I'd just see what's there. She will love any kind of dog."

"It's hard to believe our retreat is over tomorrow," Veronica said. "And what a month it's been."

"Who knew when we met at the bus station what it had in store for us?" Tyler said.

"I know, right? I was so nervous about coming back here and so cautious about letting anyone know my connection to this place, and so much has happened. Meeting Wendy and Nora has been so important to my own healing as well. Wendy is fired up to dig deep into the history of this place and expose the secrets it holds. She says she's not a writer, but I think she'll surprise herself once she starts researching and writing things down.

Sylvia and Tyler walked into the big room. Kennels lined both walls and the cacophony of dogs barking was loud but not unpleasant. Each caged dog seemed to be saying "Look at me," "What about me?" "I'm cute," "Take me home."

Tyler stopped in front of the cage to look at a chocolate brown lab mix. The information sheet said her name was Hershey, a five-year-old spayed female. Her tail was wagging frantically and her barks changed to a gentle howl. The attendant opened the cage door, and Hershey bounded toward Tyler as he knelt to welcome her.

"Love at first sight," Sylvia said, walking farther along the line of cages. She stopped as she came to the last cage in line. Her eyes fixed on a large sheepdog cowering in the corner.

"He's still a bit spooked. Buddy's only been here two days, and when the others kick up a fuss, he withdraws. He is good with other dogs but isn't the aggressor. Buddy's nine years old, a mature neutered male, but still healthy and active. He came from a good home, but the owner is dying with stage-four cancer and is unable to care for him. He was heartbroken to bring him here and will be so relieved if he finds a good home so quickly. Buddy will be a great companion for the right person."

"Can we take him outside?" Sylvia asked.

"Yes. I'll put him on a leash and walk him by these crazies. Here's a leash for Hershey," she said passing it to Tyler. "You can bring her out too."

Sylvia walked Buddy across the yard.

"He knows all the commands and is very obedient. You can take his leash off and he'll stay."

"Sit," Sylvia commanded, and Buddy immediately sat right up against her leg, looking to her for his next command.

"Good boy, Buddy. Come," Sylvia said, walking across the grass.

Buddy walked beside Sylvia, his tail wagging wildly in anticipation. "Stay," Sylvia said, patting Buddy's shaggy head.

"How fast was that?" Tyler said later, getting into Sylvia's vehicle. "Finding the right dog was so much quicker than filling out the paperwork."

"I know, right? I just wanted to let Buddy jump in the Rav and come home with me. And they took to each other right away. I think Hershey and Buddy are going to be good friends."

"If we get approved, and I mean if *I* get approved. God, as I filled out the application I questioned whether I should be a dog owner. Describe yourself, how many hours will your pet be alone, what problems are you willing to work on? God, maybe I should have filled out a similar application before I got married. Darlene should have filled one out too. If she'd checked off the box *I'm not willing to work on any problems*, we could have saved a lot of time and trouble. And her truthful answer to the question *Under what circumstances would you return the animal?* would have been good to know."

"I'm sure you'll get approved, Tyler."

"Hope so. But I wonder if I should have waited until Abby got here to fill it out with me. Would some of the things listed be possible reasons for returning Hershey? What about a new baby? We haven't even discussed having kids. What if Henry visits and the dog bites him? Oh my God, maybe a dog is a bad idea."

"Relax, Tyler. You'll be approved, you'll bring Hershey home and give her a good life. Abby will be thrilled to have a real dog again. Everything is going to be good. Let yourself believe in the life you deserve to have. You and Abby both deserve a happy life, and you're doing all the right things to achieve that."

"Thank you for saying that."

⁓⌇⁓

After hugging her father goodbye, Olivia stood back, watching him get into the security line before heading to the arrivals gate. The board said the flight from Toronto was on time and should land in about twenty minutes. Olivia would grab a coffee then sit down and wait for Abby to arrive. It felt so good to be a part of the surprise. Abby had emailed Kent Wright three days ago asking to be picked up at the airport, and it just happened his flight to Toronto and her arrival were the same day, at around the same time.

Keeping the secret had been a bit difficult this morning when Tyler started talking about moving into the house tomorrow and Abby not moving here until the first of October. But Olivia hadn't told anyone, not even when her mother said she and Tyler were going to look for dogs this afternoon. She almost blurted out the secret, telling her mother she would be bringing Abby back with her from the airport.

⁓ᔆ⁓

"You're sure you don't mind that I stopped at the hospital before going home?" Sylvia asked Tyler as they stepped into the elevator.

"Are you kidding? I'm happy to come see Evelyn. It's not like I'm leaving tomorrow like the rest of the one-monthers. I won't be at the retreat, but I'll be at the lodge and still writing, which is the best thing about the way things have worked out. Any idea when Evelyn can come back home?"

"No. She had all the tests the doctor ordered, so hopefully they will discharge her soon. Maybe the nurses can tell me something."

Evelyn was sitting up in the chair sipping a cup of tea when Sylvia and Tyler walked in to her room.

"Well, what brings you two in here on such a nice day?"

"I suppose if you'd known we were coming you'd have baked a cake, Nan."

"Not baking much these days, but I can offer you a cup of tea if nothing else. Sylvia, you know where the kitchen is."

"We've been in looking at dogs, Evelyn," Tyler said.

"Dogs?"

"Yes, Nan. Tyler moves into Marjorie's house tomorrow and wants a dog before Abby gets here."

"And you're finally getting the dog you always begged for. They're not in the car, are they?"

"No, Nan. We had to fill out applications, and now we wait to get approved. Hopefully we'll get them by the weekend. My dog's name is Buddy. He's a great big friendly sheepdog. Tyler is getting a chocolate lab named Hershey."

"Well, isn't that great. I hope I get to meet them."

"Of course you'll get to meet them," Sylvia said.

"Have they said when they're letting you out of here, Evelyn?" Tyler asked.

"Sylvia, pop in and ask the nurse at the nurses' station when you go to make tea. They don't tell an old lady anything, but maybe they can tell you."

Sylvia returned to the room carrying two cups of tea. "You're getting discharged in the morning, Nan. If I'm here by nine o'clock I can see the doctor and then take you home."

"Well, praise the Lord for that," Nan said. "I was worried I was going to die surrounded by these drab depressing walls with the stink of Lysol in my nostrils, not the sweet smell of saltwater and fresh air at that paradise you bought to be my last home."

⤙⤙⤚⤚

A text message notification came on the Bluetooth just as Sylvia pulled up to the lodge. She stopped the vehicle and pushed play to hear the text from Kent saying he'd arrived in Toronto. With her attention on the screen she didn't see what prompted the exclamation of "Oh my God," Tyler's startled reaction to seeing Abby step out the door.

Tyler was out of the vehicle in a flash, running up the steps and scooping Abby up in his arms.

"Oh my God, Abby," Tyler kept repeating. Everyone filed out the door to see the reunion. Olivia smiled broadly with the satisfaction of pulling off the surprise.

"What are you doing here? When did you get here? How did you get here? Did you know about this, Olivia?"

"Yes. I was bursting to tell you this morning, but Abby wanted it to be a surprise. I picked her up when I dropped Dad off."

"Are you surprised?" Abby said.

"Surprised? Yes, I'm surprised. I couldn't believe my eyes when I saw you standing there. Oh my God. What a great surprise."

⤙⤙⤚⤚

"It smells like Christmas in here," Veronica said, walking into the kitchen.

"Thanksgiving, actually," Dot replied. "I decided this morning I'd make a turkey dinner after hearing talk about October and Thanksgiving. Seems fitting with so much to be thankful for, and that was before I knew Abby was coming."

"Who but you could pull off a turkey dinner at short notice?" Grace added.

"I had a turkey in my freezer, and I got Marjorie to pick me up some sweet potatoes and a squash. I even managed to make a couple of pumpkin pies, but I had to use canned pumpkin."

"Oh my goodness, what a travesty," George said from across the room.

"So, a farewell dinner disguised as a Thanksgiving feast," Veronica said. "Among all the wonderful memories I take away from this place this time, the meals and companionship are at the top of the list."

"Where are the lovebirds?" Grace asked.

"They've gone over to see the house. Marjorie and Walter are coming for supper too. We are going to have one big send-off, Thanksgiving party tonight."

"Too bad Evelyn won't be here," Grace said.

"She's coming home tomorrow," Veronica said. "Sylvia said she hopes to get her home before we leave so we can say good-bye. It is going to be so hard leaving. I certainly never felt that way the last time I left this place."

"It has been quite the month all round, hasn't it?" Dot replied. "I am going to miss you all."

"You'll still have me," George said. "And Melanie, Nora, and Wendy."

"Oh, the cooking won't stop," Dot said. "It never does."

"I think you like it that way," Grace said.

Chapter Twenty-Eight

The sun was just rising when Sylvia pulled herself out of bed and walked groggily into the kitchen. She filled the coffee pot with water and poured it into the reservoir. These quiet moments in the dim light of her little cottage were her favourite of the day. She had risen early every morning since moving in and treasured the quiet solitude.

Her priority today was to get Nan back home, then the goodbyes, which she was not looking forward to. Jan had become such a dear friend and confidant, and she had gotten close to both Veronica and Grace. Olivia would drive Grace to the airport this afternoon and drop Jan off at the bus station. Sylvia had offered to drive Veronica home to Quispamsis.

With coffee cup in hand, Sylvia sat down on the couch and looked around the room. Last night she had opened the storage box at the back of the cottage and lifted out the set of snowshoes she'd placed there on that snowy January day. Bringing them inside, she propped them up against the wardrobe in the front room, deciding to make them part of the decor until she would actually use them to trudge through the snow around the property this winter. Perhaps some might think having snowshoes among beach-themed decor was odd, but it seemed perfect to her.

⁓⤳⁓

Abby rolled over, snuggling into Tyler's arms. She was eager to begin the day. Dot had offered them the use of her car so they could drive into Moncton to shop for the things they needed for the house. It was amazing what Marjorie had provided, but they needed groceries, some bedding and towels. They were also going to stop at the SPCA so Abby could meet Hershey.

"Good morning, beautiful," Tyler whispered.

"Wake up, sleepyhead. We have a big day ahead of us."

"What? We can't stay like this all day?"

"No, we can't, Casanova."

"I'm taking a rain check. Once we're settled into our own house we are going to have a long, leisurely, stay-in-bed-making-love kind of day."

"Sounds like a plan. Now get up."

⁓⤳⁓

"I think it's ludicrous thinking pills or anything that doctor can do are going to prevent the inevitable. We all die. Our time comes, and that's all there is to it."

"I know, but taking a prescription and following a few instructions might just keep you with us a bit longer."

396

"I know, and I'm sorry for being so cranky. I just want to get back home. The whole time I spent in that hospital bed I kept thinking of how wonderful the last few weeks have been. First you brought me to that beautiful place, where I could step outside and smell my past. Every time I gazed at the sky and water, I was filled with memories of the wonderful years I had living on White Head with your grandfather, your mother, and you. I was so blessed to have the life I had. Then those lovely people came. Irma was a breath of joy and an angel to our sweet Sophie. Dot has been a wonderful friend, and I know she'll keep you fed and nurtured. Veronica and Grace have been a blessing, and Janice got you writing again, which was my prayer for you. Kent will keep things running from afar, and I know you will want for nothing. And our precious Olivia came back to us, happier than I've seen her in such a long time."

"Nan, you sound like you're taking inventory before you go. I am not ready for you to go."

"Yes you are. You are as ready as you'll ever be. We are never ready to lose the ones we love. I was certainly not prepared to lose your mother. I was not ready for Paddy to go, but what he left behind kept me going forward. That is all we can ever hope for. You will go forward."

"The retreat did give us a lot, didn't it? I was so angry at Kent when he turned my quiet paradise into a writing retreat. But look how it turned out, Nan. Look at the friends and family we have been given because of the very thing I was so angry with him about."

"It won't be easy saying goodbye to Veronica, Grace, and Janice, but goodbyes don't mean they are gone. The people we allow in our hearts stay there. And Abby surprised Tyler. How romantic is that? I am so happy you have them in your life too. I wish I could see what that brings. My hope is years of happiness, a houseful of children, and old age for those two kids. God love them both. Wish I could meet Buddy. Not sure why I never got you a dog."

"Nan, now you're just rambling. Sure that nurse didn't slip you something with your breakfast?"

"Can't an old lady talk anymore? Get me home. Irma's a good listener."

⚬

Dot stood on the veranda, tears streaming down her cheeks as she watched the van drive away, followed by Sylvia and Veronica in the Rav. She had held it together earlier as she stood at the counter making turkey sandwiches while Veronica, Grace, and Janice carried their suitcases through the great room and out the door. Melanie had gone to Moncton with Abby and Tyler, wanting to buy a frame for the painting she had completed for Evelyn's homecoming gift. George was upstairs writing, and Wendy and Nora had gone to Turnbull's to visit Cecilia.

She was alone now and could let the waterworks come. *Get your crying over,* she thought, *then get back to work.* She was making a feast for Abby and Tyler's housewarming supper tonight and wanted the majority of cooking done before they got back so the menu would be a surprise.

She'd been so happy to take this job but had had no idea how life-changing it would be. It was so much more than a job. The friendships she had made in this last month had given her more joy than she ever could have predicted. It was so hard to see Veronica, Grace, and Janice leave, but she knew they would return.

And having Irma, Abby, and Tyler stay was wonderful. Sylvia and Evelyn felt like family to her, and Olivia and Sophie like grandchildren. And all the grief and guilt that had weighed her down for fifty years had lifted. What a wonderful gift taking this job had been. This lodge had indeed been refurbished, rejuvenated, and reborn, and Dorothy Fleming had played a part in that. She wiped her tears and went back to the kitchen.

The drive back from Quispamsis felt to Sylvia like time she was being given to catch her breath. Just past Hampton she put a Jim Cuddy CD in the player and let the first two songs quiet her thoughts. Driving had always been a de-stresser for her, even when it had been in the slow-moving congestion of the 401. She was clipping right along on this highway, though, and was already past the Salisbury Big Stop.

Sometimes in the early days of Sophie's recovery, Sylvia would put Sophie in the car and go for long drives. The passing landscape seemed to quiet Sophie's distress, and she often fell asleep. She had done the same thing as an infant, while Olivia reacted in the opposite way whenever she was in the car.

Sylvia would get back just in time to take Irma, Nan, and Sophie to Tyler and Abby's housewarming supper. She hoped the outing would not be too much for Nan but was sure her grandmother wouldn't consent to staying home. She would take Nan back home after supper and would be quite happy to call it an early night herself. There had been so much to process today.

The day seemed like such a dividing line, the first one-month retreat over. In some ways it seemed so much longer than a month, while at the same time it had flown by. So much had happened. So many stories were shared, so many tears, life decisions made, and her marriage, which had been over for a long time, had ended officially. Irma had come into their lives, freeing her up and taking the massive weight of caring for Sophie off her shoulders. Olivia had returned, which lifted a weight as well.

She had her own little home and could write full-time, choosing the amount of interaction she would have with future retreat participants. She was better and stronger than she had been in a very long time. Maybe Nan was right about her being more prepared than before for the inevitable loss ahead. Ready did not mean willing, though. She would put thoughts of Nan dying out of her mind. Papa used to say "Do not borrow tomorrow's troubles today."

Sylvia turned the volume up and belted out the lyrics along with Jim Cuddy. The sign ahead stated three kilometres to her exit. She was almost back home.

~~~⌇~~~

"It's our lighthouse," Nan exclaimed as she tore the last piece of wrapping paper from the painting. "How did you know what our lighthouse looked like?"

"It's called Google, Nan," Sylvia said. "It's beautiful, Melanie. What a lovely gift."

"I suppose she didn't even tell you she bought me art supplies the day we went into Moncton," Melanie said. "I promised her a painting. I'm just glad I got it done in time for her homecoming."

"That was very thoughtful of you," Sylvia said.

"It is just lovely," Evelyn said. "My Paddy sailed past that lighthouse every time he left harbour and sailed back toward it every time he came home to me. What a wonderful gift you've given me, Melanie. Thank you."

"Let's hang it right up," Irma said. "Where do you want to hang it, Evelyn?"

"Well, I think I want it in my room. Waking up and going to sleep looking up at that lighthouse will be a comfort and a reminder to me that I'll be joining my beloved Paddy when it comes my time to sail away home."

"You are killing me with all this going home talk," Sylvia said. " Once Irma hangs the painting, let's get going to Abby and Tyler's and see what Dot has been cooking up all day. Tonight is a night to celebrate."

❧

Cecilia Foster picked up the glass and took a sip of the fizzy ginger ale. The girl had been in a few minutes ago, setting a drink and cookie on her table and she'd immediately tossed the cookie into the garbage can. A cookie wrapped in cellophane. It looked like cardboard and was probably drier than a sandstorm in a desert. How hard would it be for them to make a decent cookie? If she could find her recipe box, she'd dig out some cookie recipes and give them to that girl when she came back in.

Cecelia turned her head to see two women coming into the room. One came right over, sitting in the chair by the window, and the other one stood at the end of the bed.

"Hello, CeCe," Wendy said.

"I used to make a good oatmeal cookie. My recipe made a big batch. Chewy and buttery. They were chewy and buttery."

"They sure were," Nora said. "Your molasses jam jams were yummy too."

"You've had my molasses jam jams? That was my mother's recipe."

"We sure have, CeCe," Wendy said. "You were some good cook."

"I'd like to show the cook here a thing or two. Do I know you?"

"We're Wendy and Nora."

"You had those sweet twin boys. Do you have the precious babies with you? I love rocking a new baby. You were crying. I am so sorry. Women will travail in childbirth because Eve ate the apple. I threw my cookie away. Don't tell the girl I threw my cookie away. Sister Dorcas will holler. Do I know you?"

"It's okay, CeCe. We won't tell her you threw the cookie away. We brought you a muffin, a delicious muffin our cook made."

"I made this muffin? Are these blueberries? Did I pick these blueberries on Cooper's Bluff?"

"I think so. Take a bite," Wendy said.

"I make good muffins. Cinnamon and brown sugar on the top make them tasty."

"Yes, they are tasty. You always cooked us good food, CeCe. Thank you."

"You are welcome, Wendy and Nora. Could you help me find my recipe box? I am so tired. I don't know if I can get supper ready. I think Father Tucker is mad at me."

"No one is mad at you, CeCe. You did the right thing," Wendy said, moving to hug the woman's frail shoulders. "We love you, CeCe."

"I love you too, dear. Are you the nurse?"

"No. Do you need the nurse?" Nora asked.

"The nurse will look after the babies. Twins, sweet little twins."

The *Sylvie D* was rocking violently. As she clutched the railing tightly, water sprayed up, soaking her bell-bottom jeans. She called to Papa, but her voice was swallowed in the wind. Looking into the wheelhouse, she could see the back of his yellow slicker, his sou'wester pulled down, hiding his profile. She called out again, afraid to loosen her grip for fear the waves would wash her over the side. Thunder cracked and lightening lit up the dark sky.

"Just pull that rope up, Sylvie," Papa said, the sky now a vivid blue, the water calm.

"I can't," Sylvie cried. "I'm not strong enough."

"Of course you are, Sylvie girl. You are my strong, brave girl."

The fog seemed to roll in, followed by a veil of sleet.

"It's getting dark, Papa. How are we going to find our way home?"

"We look for the light, Sylvie girl. No matter how dark the sky gets, the light will guide us in. First we look to the lighthouse; the rotating lamp casts its light over the dark water and we just need to head toward it. Then when we near the shore we'll search the horizon for the porch light. That small bulb will cast a light so clear we will know our way. We will always know our way. That's why we leave it on, Sylvie girl. We always leave it on so those we love will see it shining no matter what and they will find their way."

Sylvia woke with a start. Flashing lights were bouncing off the walls of the front room and into her small bedroom.

Flashing lights and sirens. She pulled back the covers and put her bare feet on the floor. As she walked toward the front window, the flashing lights became more distant the siren still echoing. A loud rapping sound turned her attention to the front door. Sylvia stumbled across the room and opened the door.

"It's Nan," Olivia cried, falling into her mother's arms.

Epilogue

The morning light streamed into Veronica's third story bedroom. She opened the doors of the spacious closet and reached for her suitcase. The old tapestry bag sat on the top shelf, and moving it brought a flicker of memory. She could still not make herself throw the old thing out. She lifted the black vinyl suitcase off the shelf and remembered dragging that suitcase, heavy with empty journals, up the bus stairs when she travelled to the Wright Retreat four years ago.

Olivia had asked her to come as August's guest author and read from her newly published *Fifty Yellow Roses*. The Wright Retreat had experienced two years of restrictions and travel bans caused by the pandemic and was just beginning to recover. Veronica and Grace had spent the Covid years quite content isolated in their lovely lakeside home. Wallace had happily stepped up to deliver groceries and supplies, relieved to have Veronica in the house with his mother. And forced exile in this beautiful home with Grace had certainly helped Veronica concentrate on writing and publishing the novel she was now packing copies of into her open suitcase.

As part of bringing the lodge back to life, Olivia had invited the writers from the inaugural retreat to come on the first weekend of Veronica's mentorship. Gavin and Jonathan had declined, but all the others were coming. Grace was looking forward to staying the month with Abby and Tyler, anxious to assume her role as great-grandmother. Veronica was excited to see everyone but didn't want the anticipation to overshadow her obligation as guest author.

Veronica finished packing before heading down the hall to her office to put the finishing touches on the writing workshops she'd spent the last few weeks preparing. She chuckled thinking of Benson commandeering workshops, steering them all to a place where he could sing his own praises.

Olivia had sent pictures updating them on the changes and improvements at the lodge. Tyler had added several gardens and built a lovely gazebo near the path to the wooded area, now a sacred burial ground with several plaques and crosses. Dr. Daniels had paid to refurbish and erect the half-buried statue in the same place it had stood years ago. Wendy's work had exposed the dark history of the lodge when it was a Catholic home for unwed mothers, bringing several women back to exorcise their demons. But for Veronica the lodge no longer held the deep secrets, the fear and foreboding. She knew when she returned tomorrow, she would walk the wooded path to where her precious baby girl was buried fifty-four years ago and breathe peaceful, not anguished breaths.

Was it the writing that had released her, or simply telling her story to another human being? Did it matter if one person or one million read her book? Will her story help unlock a buried story for someone else? Veronica did not know the answers to questions she was posing in her first presentation, but felt confident the questions would make a good starting place for a writing workshop; a workshop Veronica Savage was giving fellow writers at the Wright Retreat.

Acknowledgments

Acknowledgments For The Wright Retreat

Thanks to Terrilee Bulger and Acorn Press. Thanks to Penelope Jackson who again worked her editing magic with wisdom, sensitivity and grace. Thank you to Cassandra Aragonez and Kenny Vail for the cover and interior design. Thank you to authors Gerard Collins and Lesley Crewe.

Sincere thanks to Dr. Imelda Perley (Opolahsomuwehs), University of New Brunswick for her wise advice, caring input and support.

To Janie Simpson and Gerard Collins who plan, organize and carry out writing retreats in wonderfully, creative settings. I have been lucky enough to participate in Italy, Scotland and St. Andrew's and highly recommend the Go and Write Retreats to any writer whether aspiring or established.

To Odette Barr and YoAnne Beausejour Beauchamp who welcomed me to their beautiful home and property on the Northumberland Straight which became the setting for the Wright Retreat. I feel as if I spent a year there while I crafted this story and will instantly return whenever I open the pages of this book.

As always thanks to Burton, Meg, Cody, Emma, Paige, Chapin, Brianne, Anthony, Skyler, Bella, Caleb and Jenna.